REALMS

THE FIRST YEAR OF
CLARKESWORLD MAGAZINE

OTHER WORKS EDITED BY MAMATAS AND WALLACE

NICK MAMATAS
Phantom 0
The Urban Bizarre

SEAN WALLACE
Bandersnatch, with Paul Tremblay
Best New Fantasy 1
Best New Fantasy 2
Fantasy, with Paul Tremblay
Fantasy Magazine
Horror: The Best of the Year, 2007 Edition, with John Betancourt
Horror: The Best of the Year, 2008 Edition, with John Betancourt
Phantom, with Paul Tremblay
Weird Tales: The 21st-Century, with Stephen H. Segal

REALMS

THE FIRST YEAR OF
CLARKESWORLD MAGAZINE

———

Edited by Nick Mamatas and Sean Wallace

REALMS: THE FIRST YEAR OF CLARKESWORLD MAGAZINE

———

Wyrm Publishing
www.wyrmpublishing.com

For more information, contact Wyrm.

ISBN: 978-0-8095-7248-9 (paperback)
ISBN: 978-0-8095-7258-8 (hardcover)

Visit us at:

www.clarkesworldmagazine.com

TABLE OF CONTENTS

TABLE OF CONTENTS

———

TURN THE PAGE, PRESS RETURN

Nick Mamatas

There are two major theories when it comes to editing the online literary journal.

The first theory is the simplest: treat it just like a paper journal, even if it is nearly impossible to balance a laptop (much less an eighty-pound eMac like the one I have on my desk) on your lap while on the commode. Secret studies have shown that the washroom is where 90% of the world's literary journals are read.

The second theory is in the decided minority: take full advantage of the new medium by presenting new types of fiction: hypertexts, microfiction to be sent to cell phones and other gadgets, memoirs in lengthy blog form, etc.

Well, if you want both an online magazine, such as the one I edit, and a book to be made of your stories, such as this book, neither theory works very well. Reading large amounts of text remains difficult on screen, and many people find the reading of long fiction on screen especially problematic. And of course, one cannot easily transport a hypertext onto the printed page. <CLICK HERE FOR VIDEO DEMONSTRATING DIFFICULTY OF USING HYPERLINKS IN PRINTED MATTER.>

For *Clarkesworld Magazine*, my editorial choices were guided by both the online medium and the ultimate goal of paper reprint. This means that my primary goal was to cultivate the audience of a popular magazine and not the audience of a literary journal. That latter audience is, of course, made up nearly exclusively of emerging writers who read just enough of a journal to know whether they should or should not submit their own fiction to it. An audience that small and ingrown would also obviate the need for this handy volume.

Hi there, reader-who-isn't-also-a-writer, it's a pleasure to meet you.

Popular magazines are popular largely thanks to the fact that they are cheap enough to get rid of. Magazines determine their ad rates not based on the number of copies they sell, but on some multiple of that number. You may buy a magazine, and then your spouse may read it, or at least flip through it and thus catch some of the advertisements. Then after you're both done with the latest issue, someone else may snag it off your coffee table or go sorting through your recycling. Even if you're one of those people who read a magazine once and then rush off to seal it in Mylar and place it gently on a shelf with the rest of your periodical collection—you know, even if you're a big ol' kook!—your habits are counterbalanced by the number of magazines in medical waiting rooms.

Online magazines, however, have no "pass along." So when reading for *Clarkesworld*, I made it a point to select only those stories that would send readers off to their email client or their blogs to send the story to all their friends, creating an active pass along. "Look at this weird story!" I wanted them to say. "You have to read it." There was no room for the "good ol' fashioned yarn" in *Clarkesworld*, or for one more comfortable variation on the stories we have all read before. Every month had to be a parade, the next Wrestlemania, an unexpected volley of bottle rockets, or some really interesting if nigh unidentifiable roadkill.

Also, because it gets tedious to read long stories online, all the stories had to be short. I set a 4000-word limit somewhat arbitrarily, but I think it worked. The end result is that *Clarkesworld* stories combine the shock of a bear trap on your ankle with the handy convenience of a sandwich. You may not want to read this book cover to cover all at once. It might spoil your supper.

To gain some attention in the overcrowded online milieu, I also took another unusual tack. Unlike virtually every other editor of short fiction, I never use form letters for rejections. I promised myself that I, or my twin brother Seth whom I keep hidden from the world so that he might better play me for half of our waking hours, would read at least the beginning of every short story and explain why the story, if rejected, failed to please. For this, some people have called me a sadist and an egomaniac. Others, generally those who have actually read some of the stuff that comes into magazines and journals on a daily basis, have called me a masochist.

I prefer to think of it as taking the long view. Despite the claims of those interminable how-to manuals on the subject, writing and submitting one's work requires no special bravery. All one need be is a smidge tougher than a bowl of milquetoast, and you can hack it. As it happens though, in the Western world the idea of writing and publishing is considered somewhat effete, even feminized, which means that lots and lots of hothouse flowers waste their time and money on writer's conferences and MFA programs and the aforementioned interminable manuals.

Well, there are two things you can do with a flower: fertilize it, or nip it in the bud. My comments did the fertilizing. Seth, he was the bud-nipper. Really. The end result was a great anthology, thanks to a year of making it clear to writers what we didn't want. *Anthology* is an ancient Greek word referring to the gathering and artful arrangement of flowers. Hope you like our first bouquet.

Go on, take a whiff of *this*!

A LIGHT IN TROY

_____

Sarah Monette

She went down to the beach in the early mornings, to walk among the cruel black rocks and stare out at the waves. Every morning she teased herself with wondering if this would be the day she left her grief behind her on the rocky beach and walked out into the sea to rejoin her husband, her sisters, her child. And every morning she turned away and climbed the steep and narrow stairs back to the fortress. She did not know if she was hero or coward, but she did not walk out into the cold gray waves to die.

She turned away, the tenth morning or the hundredth, and saw the child: a naked, filthy, spider-like creature, more animal than child. It recoiled from her, snarling like a dog. She took a step back in instinctive terror; it saw its chance and fled, a desperate headlong scrabble more on four legs than on two. As it lunged past her, she had a clear, fleeting glimpse of its genitals: a boy. He might have been the same age as her dead son would have been; it was hard to tell.

Shaken, she climbed the stairs slowly, pausing often to look back. But there was no sign of the child.

Since she was literate, she had been put to work in the fortress's library. It was undemanding work, and she did not hate it; it gave her something to do to fill the weary hours of daylight. When she had been brought to the fortress, she had expected to be ill-treated—a prisoner, a slave—but in truth she was mostly ignored. The fortress's masters had younger, prettier girls to take to bed; the women, cool and distant and beautiful as she had once been herself, were not interested in a ragged woman with haunted half-crazed eyes. The librarian, a middle-aged man already gone blind over his codices and scrolls, valued her for her voice. But he was the only person she had to talk to, and she blurted as she came into the library, "I saw a child."

"Beg pardon?"

"On the beach this morning. I saw a child."

"Oh," said the librarian. "I thought we'd killed them all."

"Them?" she said, rather faintly.

"You didn't imagine your people were the first to be conquered, did you? Or that we could have built this fortress, which has been here for thousands of years?"

She hadn't ever thought about it. "You really *are* like locusts," she said and then winced. Merely because he did not treat her like a slave, did not mean she wasn't one.

But the librarian just smiled, a slight, bitter quirk of the lips. "Your people named us well. We conquered this country, oh, six or seven years ago. I could still see. The defenders of this fortress resisted us long after the rest of the country had surrendered. They killed a great many soldiers, and angered the generals. You are lucky your people did not do the same."

"Yes," she said with bitterness of her own. "Lucky." Lucky to have her husband butchered like a hog. Lucky to have her only child killed before her eyes. Lucky to be mocked, degraded, raped.

"Lucky to be alive," the librarian said, as if he could hear her thoughts. "Except for this child you say you saw, not one inhabitant of this fortress survived. And they did not die quickly." He turned away from her, as if he did not want her to be able to see his face.

She said with quick horror, "You won't tell anyone? It's only a child. A . . . more like a wild animal. Not a threat. Please."

He said, still turned toward the window as if he could look out at the sea, "I am not the man I was then. And no one else will care. We are not a people who have much interest in the past, even our own."

"And yet you are a librarian."

"The world is different in darkness," he said and then, harshly, briskly, asked her to get out the catalogue and start work.

Some days later, whether three or thirty, she asked shyly, "Does the library have any information on wild children?"

"We can look," said the librarian. "There should at least be an entry or two in the encyclopedias."

There were, and she read avidly—aloud, because the librarian asked her to—about children raised by wolves, children raised by bears. And when she was done, he said, "Did you find what you were looking for?"

"No. Not really. I think he lives with the dog pack in the caves under the fortress, so it makes sense that he growls like a dog and runs like a dog. But it doesn't tell me anything about . . . "

"How to save him?"

"How to love him."

She hadn't meant to say it. The librarian listened too well.

"Do you think he wishes for your love?"

"No. But he keeps coming back. And . . . and I must love someone."

"Must you?"

"What else do I have?"

"I don't know," he said, and they did not speak again that day.

She did not attempt to touch the child. He never came within ten feet of her anyway, the distance between them as impassible as the cold gray sea.

But he was always there, when she came down the stairs in the morning, and when she started coming down in the evenings as well, he came pattering out from wherever he spent his time to crouch on a rock and watch her, head cocked to one side, pale eyes bright, interested. Sometimes, one or two of the dogs he lived with would come as well: long-legged, heavy-chested dogs that she imagined had been hunting dogs before the fortress fell to the locusts. Her husband had had dogs like that.

The encyclopedias had told her that he would not know how to speak, and in any event she did not know what language the people of this country had spoken before their world ended, as hers had, in fire and death. The child was an apt mimic, though, and much quicker-minded than she had expected. They worked out a crude sign-language before many weeks had passed, simple things like *food*, for she brought him what she could, and *no*, which he used when he thought she might venture too close, and *I have to go now*—and it was ridiculous of her to imagine that he seemed saddened when she made that sign, and even more ridiculous of her to be pleased.

She worried that her visits might draw the fortress's attention to him—for whatever the librarian said, she was not convinced the locusts would not kill the child simply because they could—but she asked him regularly if other people came down to the beach, and he always answered, no. She wasn't sure if he understood what she was asking, and the question was really more of an apotropaic ritual; it gave her comfort, even though she suspected it was meaningless.

Until the day when he answered, *yes.*

The shock made her head swim, and she sat down, hard and not gracefully, on a lump of protruding rock. She had no way of asking him who had come, or what they had done, and in a hard, clear flash of bitterness, she thought how stupid of her it was to pretend this child could in any way replace her dead son.

But he was all she had, and he was watching her closely. His face never showed any emotion, except when he snarled with fear or anger, so she did not know what he felt—if anything at all. She asked, *All right?*

Yes, the child signed, but he was still watching her as if he wanted her to show him what he ought to do.

She signed, *All right,* more emphatically than she felt it, but he seemed to be satisfied, for he turned away and began playing a game of catch-me with the two dogs who had accompanied him that morning.

She sat and watched, trying to convince herself that this was not an auspice of doom, that other people in the fortress could come down to the beach without any purpose more sinister than taking a walk.

Except that they didn't. The locusts were not a sea-faring people except in the necessity of finding new countries to conquer. They were not interested in the water and the wind and the harsh smell of salt. In all the time she had been in the fortress, she had never found any evidence that anyone except herself used the stairs to the beach. She was trying hard not to remember the day her husband had said, casually, *A messenger came from the lighthouse today. Says there's strangers landing on the long beach.* Little things. Little things led up to disaster. She was afraid, and she climbed the stairs back to the fortress like a woman moving through a nightmare.

Her louring anxiety distracted her so much that she asked the librarian, forgetting that he was the last person in the fortress likely to know, "Who else goes down to the beach?"

The silence was just long enough for her to curse herself as an idiot before he said, "That was . . . I."

"You?"

"Yes."

"Why? What on earth possessed you?"

His head was turned toward the window again. He said, "You spend so much time there."

At first she did not even understand what he was saying, could make no sense of it. She said, hastily, to fill the gap, "You're lucky you didn't break your neck."

"I won't do it again, if you don't want."

She couldn't help laughing. "You forget which of us is the slave and which the master."

"What makes you think I can forget that? Any more than I can forget that I will never see your face?"

"I . . . I don't . . . "

"I am sorry," he said, his voice weary although his posture was as poker-straight as ever. "I won't bother you about it again. I didn't mean to tell you."

She said, astonished, "I don't mind," and then they both, in unspoken, embarrassed agreement, plunged hastily into the minutiae of their work.

But that evening, as she sat on her rock beside the sea, she heard slow, careful footsteps descending the stairs behind her.

Come! said the child from his rock eight feet away.

Friend, she said, a word they'd had some trouble with, but she thought he understood, even if she suspected that what he meant by it was pack-member. And called out, "There's room on my rock for two."

Friend, the child repeated, his hands moving slowly.

No hurt, she said, and wondered if she meant that the librarian would not hurt the child, or that the child should not hurt the librarian.

Yes, he said, and then eagerly, *Rock!*

"What are you doing, this evening?" the librarian's voice said behind her.

"Teaching him to skip stones." She flung another one, strong snap of the wrist. Five skips and it sank. The child bounced in a way she thought meant happiness; he threw a stone, but he hadn't gotten the wrist movement right, and it simply dropped into the water. *Again!* he said, imperious as the child of kings.

She threw another stone. Four skips. The librarian sat down beside her, carefully, slowly.

She said, "What is the sea like, in darkness?"

"Much more vast than I remember it being, when I had my sight. It would do the generals good to be blind."

"Blindness won't teach them anything—they have never wanted to see in the first place."

"You think that's what makes the difference?"

"We learn by wanting," she said. "We learn by grieving."

Shyly, the librarian's hand found hers.

The child threw a stone.

It skipped seven times before it sank.

304, ADOLPH HITLER STRASSE

Lavie Tidhar

When they came for Hershele Ostropol it was not at night but in the middle of the afternoon, and they came quiet and with no warning, with just a polite knock on the door. He had taken it to be the postman, carrying a late delivery of one of his special magazines; but the two who stood in the doorway wore no uniforms, and only their eyes betrayed who, and what, they were.

They called him by his real name, which was Hanzi, but they knew who he really was and he knew then that it was over; the knowledge washed him in lethargy, and a sense of futility made him open his hands as if in a shrug, his fat fingers opening limply, sweat dampening his palms.

They had interrupted him writing, it was another one of his stories. The computer was left switched on in his small study (Granddad's old room), and his special books and magazines lay in plain view on the desk.

He knew then that it was over; and he went with them without a fight and let them steer him into the dark Mercedes that waited for him, as he knew it would, outside.

How it began, how Hanzi Himmler first came to assume the identity of Hershele Ostropol, he could hardly articulate. But it can be pinpointed to two events that both happened close together: he was given the new computer, and he caught his grandfather with a prostitute.

The computer was a Bulgarian Pravetz. Along with the modem the computer came with a small communications program and a list of telephone numbers for several Bulletin Board Systems in and around Berlin. The first time Hanzi connected to a BBS was late on the night of his birthday, when his parents were sleeping and he had the telephone line to himself. He dialed the first number on the list, and found himself confronted with a colorful welcome screen.

On the BBS, Hanzi discovered that night, he could download small programs, and text files and even code, and he could post messages on the BBS which other people could then read. He chose his first identity that night, his first login name. He wanted Nighthawk, but ended up being Nighthawk1 as the first name was already taken.

Hanzi didn't care. He read the public posts, and he downloaded a text file that contained a hundred and eleven dirty jokes and, more importantly, he also downloaded a file containing the telephone numbers of many other BBSs.

For him, it was a discovery. He felt like Ernst Schafer must have felt on his expedition to Tibet to prove the origin of the Aryan race, as if he too were an explorer in a new and mysterious land. He had found a door to a new world, and everything was suddenly possible.

Everything . . . Granddad, Hauptabschnittsleiter Himmler, lived with his son and daughter-in-law in the solitary room on the ground floor by the garden. He was once a distinguished Head Section Leader, but had retired many years back and now spent most of his time in his room, unseen by his family. He was not a well man, and Hanzi knew Herr and Frau Himmler worried about him.

Hanzi returned home early one day from school, with a sore throat and a headache that buzzed little flies on the inside of his skull. His parents were away, and Granddad should have been asleep in his room. But he wasn't.

As Hanzi came through the door he heard strange sounds coming from his grandfather's room towards the back. He listened carefully, the words and the sounds making him feel strange, though he couldn't then define what it was he felt, exactly. It took him a while to realize they were the sounds of sex.

He edged his way down the corridor. His head still hurt and an uncomfortable erection was building in the pants of his khaki uniform. The door to Granddad's room was ajar, and light spilled out from it onto the darkened corridor. The voices were louder, and more persistent. Granddad, and a woman. She was shouting something, and as he came closer he could hear the words, so clear that they cut through his mind like sharp crystal, and remained there forever. They had the tang of well-rehearsed, stock lines, though he only understood that later.

"You disgust me! You sick, perverted old man! You're nothing but a dirty Jew!"

Through the open door Hanzi saw Hauptabschnittsleiter Himmler crouching naked on the bed, his thin, wrinkled buttocks raised in the air. Above him stood a middle-aged woman dressed in the old uniforms of an S.S. officer, holding a riding crop in her hand. As she spoke she hit the old man hard against his rear, making him scream.

"What are you? I said, what are you, animal?"

"I'm a Jew!" the old man cried. "I'm a dirty Jew!"

"And what do we do to dirty, disgusting Jews?" the woman asked. Hanzi caught sight of her sagging white breasts below the open leather coat. She had bright red nipples that looked squished over the pale twin mounds of her chest. It made him feel both scared and excited.

"Punish them!" the old man said. He was breathing rapidly, and his voice was muffled now, his speech unclear. Hanzi saw his grandfather's face turn against the white fluffy pillow it was resting on. The old man looked back at the aged S.S. officer. A little drool rested at the left corner of his mouth. "Punish me, mistress . . ." he said. "Spank me. Hurt me!"

The woman, whose face had so far remained calm, almost bored while the old man's face was turned away, had now assumed a new expression: she smiled slowly, licking her red lips as she exposed yellowing teeth. "You should have gone to the gas chambers," she said. "You disgust me." The riding crop went up, came down again with a sharp whack.

"Yes," the old man said. "Yes. Yes!"

Something sticky and warm spread in Hanzi's undergarments, and he shuddered and bit his fist until it hurt.

He stood there for a long moment, mortified. Inside the room the noise slowly abated. He looked inside—and saw that the woman was looking directly at him now—and she was smiling.

She reached her hand out—he always remembered the long pale fingers, the bright red varnish on the nails—and gently shut the door.

"That'd be fifty Reichsmarks again, Herr Himler," he heard her say through the closed door.

"Thank you, Helga, yes," Hanzi heard his grandfather say. His voice had regained its old authority; he sounded nothing like the pathetic creature that begged to be spanked. "I shall expect you again the same time next week." Hanzi retreated at the sounds of movement from inside. A moment later he could hear the door open, and the clicking of heels against the floor.

"Make sure . . . " he heard the old man say, and the woman laughed, and said, "I know, I know, I'll go through the back door."

Hanzi waited in the kitchen, afraid to move, afraid to make a sound, until he heard the back door open and close. His grandfather had not come out of his room.

Finally, he went up to his room, and switched on the computer.

At the library Hanzi found pictures of Jews in a large, leather-bound book on one of the top shelves. They were of grotesque-looking creatures, alien and frightening. He stared at them, repulsed, fascinated—he couldn't have described the feelings he felt. Not then. He also stared down the librarian's top, trying to see her breasts when he thought she wouldn't notice him.

On another visit, the librarian showed him an old documentary film, Fritz Hippler's *The Eternal Jew*, and its images of hordes upon hordes of rats drowning in sewers filled Hanzi with frightened fascination.

"There is not much information." The librarian sighed, and she removed her glasses and wiped them with the hem of her sweater. "It's better that way."

"Yes, Miss," Hanzi said. Yet something drew him to find out more, a dark fascination that grew inside him like an obsidian rose and made him spend himself alone in bed at night. Sometimes he thought of the pictures, and sometimes of the librarian, removing her glasses and lifting up her sweater, revealing soft pale skin underneath.

That day, after watching the film, he logged in to several of the local BBSs and posted a brief message on each, asking about those strange, forgotten beings, the Jews.

Nothing happened the first day, or the one after. In fact, a full week passed before he had a reply.

A private message. It contained a telephone number, and a login name and a password.

He sat in his room. His parents were asleep. He dialed the number, and connected to the the Judenhacker BBS.

The judenhackers called it Slash. It stood for the "/" sign in Jewish/Nazi stories. They gathered to re-imagine the relationship with that vanished, mysterious race, writing stories with titles such as "the Stalag of Death," telling stories of concentration camps, of stalags, where sadistic Aryan female guards were captured by their former slaves the Jews, recreating powerful sexual fantasies from third-hand memories of a time that was gone and would not come again.

All quiet, Hanzi thought. The house was secure. He was alone.

On his head he wore a homemade yarmulke, and pinned to his cheeks were long pretend side curls, and as he masturbated he nodded his head to a prayer he didn't know.

I'm seventeen, he thought as he covered himself up, a vague lack of satisfaction irritating at him. The stories were no longer enough. I should . . .

He chose a pen name for himself that night, a handle: Hershele Ostropol, after a forgotten Jewish legend of a storyteller. Already, he knew what he wanted to do, what his purpose was, and that night he sat in front of the keyboard and wrote his first story, and published it in the morning.

It was called *The Last Jew and the Virgins of the Rhein*.

The Last Jew and the Virgins of the Rhein, Part I
By Hershele Ostropol

The Jewish youth lies in wait for hours on end . . . spying on the unsuspicious German girl he plans to seduce . . . He wants to contaminate her blood and remove her from the bosom of her own people.—Adolf Hitler, Mein Kampf

He drove carefully over the blasted roads and into Paris, avoiding with ease the few checkpoints the army had thrown up half-heartedly outside the city. The war had ended, after all. They had won. There were no more Jews.

He parked the Volkswagen in the darkened Latin Quarter, on the left side of the Seine from Notre Dame. He stepped out of the car into the cool air, inhaling the scent of sewage and roasting chestnuts on the breeze. For a moment he remembered a time before the war, when he visited Paris with Miriam and the baby . . . He forced the memory away and began marching into the maze of alleyways and shuttered shops that was the Quartier Latin.

There. It was an ancient stone building, its windows carefully blank. He stood in the shadows and watched.

There was a sentry on duty outside the heavy oak door. A solitary working streetlamp cast a hazy glow over the entrance, and he watched, carefully observing, as the striking young girl stood up and stamped her feet on the ground. She was blonde, a pure-blooded Aryan. Her golden hair was cut short at the shoulders, spilling over pale, delicate cheek-bones. She wore a tailored black coat that opened momentarily when she moved, revealing dark leather, the flash of a white thigh. He looked closer, observing, memorizing: long silk stockings stretched over those long, beautiful legs—and a black sleek handgun was strapped to one thigh.

Virgins of the Rhein. He felt a shiver of apprehension run down his back. He had to remind himself the girl was a cold-blooded assassin; attractive—and deadly.

The door opened, spilling more light onto the pavement, and he heard the momentary sound of laughter and piano music from inside. A second girl was framed in the doorway, and his eyes traveled over her long, muscular body that was clad only in a body-hugging black dress, extenuating her firm, large breasts and flat stomach.

The girl marched down the steps and stood facing the guard. She snapped a sharp salute that was followed by the other guard.

"All quiet, Helga?"

"All quiet Ma'am!"

The tall blonde nodded. Her lips were bright red, and when she smiled they revealed between them rows of white teeth. "Go back inside, Helga. I'll take over for a while. You're needed in the basement to help with the prisoners."

"Ma'am!" The guard, Helga, snapped another salute, and smiled at her superior. Her tongue ran over her lips slowly, as if she was already contemplating her job inside the thick walls of the building. The two women stood close to each other, their faces almost touching. "Go," the tall blonde murmured. "The prisoners . . . need you. Leave them alive."

"For a while longer," Helga whispered. The two women's lips touched lightly, almost hungry.

"Go," the leggy blonde said. She laid long, delicate fingers on Helga's shoulders and stripped her slowly of her long coat. The hidden watcher felt himself getting aroused almost against his will as Helga's perfect form was revealed. The tall blonde covered herself with the coat. "Go," she said again, and this time it was a command.

Helga obeyed. She walked up the steps and disappeared inside the mansion, closing the door behind her. The hidden watcher looked at the woman that remained.

It was time to act.

He stepped out of the shadows and walked briskly towards the blonde woman . . .

TO BE CONTINUED.

Hershele sat in the basement of the Technische Universität Berlin, the converted computer lab. He was working, but it wasn't on homework, though he had to hand in an assignment in the morning. The assignment was about a new kind of viral electronic mail that the papers were calling Goebbels Mail, a kind of mass advertising of products. Hanzi didn't care. He was writing.

The lab was empty, warm. Outside the snow fell, and through the window he could dimly see his beat-up Volkswagen being covered in white. It was silent, comforting, safe.

He stood and looked around, but could see no one. He slipped the yarmulke from his pocket and put it on his head. He sat in front of the keyboard and felt a tingle in his fingers, and down below.

His story had been well accepted, he thought, and it made him smile. It was the feedback that almost drove him now, more than the other kind of gratification.

There was a lively debate about his story on the BBS, ranging from the congratulatory "keep going, it's really good," to the nitpickers (it was an old English word. It came from slavery, when there were still African people to enslave) who argued over the minute details of the story, on whether the clothes were right for the period, to Hershele's choice of car for his character.

But there was interest, and several more discreet messages who assured him his story was affecting them in the same way slash stories have always affected him. "Too softcore," was another comment, and so, now, Hershele allowed himself greater liberty as he began to write the shorter, second part of what he was already planning would become an ongoing series.

Tucked away in the basement, Hershele forgot his audience and wrote only for himself, a metal Star of David pressing painfully into his palm as excitement made him close his fingers in an involuntary fist.

The Last Jew and the Virgins of the Rhein, Part II
By Hershele Ostropol

"Stop!" the blonde woman said, pointing the carbine in his chest. Her cat eyes examined him leisurely, almost hungrily.

The Last Jew raised his hands calmly to shoulder height. In his left hand he was clutching a brown wallet: the paperwork inside it had cost him a small fortune several months ago from an old forger in Nice.

"Standartenfuehrer Walther Viter, S.S," he said.

His eyes followed the blonde's heaving chest, followed exposed contours of her breasts up to her face, to the eyes widening in surprise, to the red tongue moistening her full lips. Surprise? Anticipation? A touch of fear?

He lowered his hands and watched the blonde raise the carbine. "Colonel, I did not know . . . "

He saw the subversive light in her eyes and didn't hesitate. There was only one way to act from the start and he didn't hesitate, he reached out and grabbed the blonde, pulling her closer to him, his hands resting on her breasts, his erection pressed again her soft back side. "Do not underestimate me, Fraulein," he said softly as she squirmed against his body, "I am here to inspect, and to judge. The hand of the S.S.—" and here he shoved his hand between the blonde's legs, feeling her hidden mound grow moist against his finger—"reaches a long, long way."

He released her and watched her sway. "Lead on," he said, and motioned for her to proceed him up the stairs to the mansion. Almost as an afterthought he picked up the carbine and pointed it between the blonde's eyes. "Don't make me repeat myself," he said. He watched in silence as she wriggled up the stairs, her smooth ass moving sensuously against the leather.

He followed her into the headquarters of the Virgins of the Rhein, and closed the door softly against the darkness outside.
TO BE CONTINUED.

"Yes, of course I was pleased with the Last Jew's fake German identity—the colonel's name I made from adding together the names of Fredrick Viter and Walther Rauff, both rather obscure historical figures. The contents were harder, the sense of something major happening almost—or so I like to think—palpable," Hanzi said. He was sitting in a coffee shop on Göring Strasse with his friend.

His friend was also a colleague. They worked for Deutsche Bank together. His name was Hermann.

"I also enjoyed your *Nazi Biker Sluts—Why Won't You Come Out Tonight?*" Hermann now said. "Quite risqué, I thought."

"I hope so," Hanzi said. They were quite alone. No one was listening.

"And I thought *Nazi Super Sex Toys Last All Summer Long* was almost poetic," Hermann said. He was something of a fan, and he began to look shiny with perspiration. "Too bad the Last Jew had to come to an end."

"I couldn't keep it up," Hanzi said. The last installment of The Last Jew and the Virgins of the Rhein was published just as he got the job. His parents had died soon after, in a train crash when they went to visit relatives in Vienna, and Hanzi stayed to live alone in the family home.

"I also liked your monograph on *The Fetishizing and Eroticizing of the Jew,*" Hermann said. "Thought provoking." He coughed and looked at his feet. "So what are you working on now?"

Hanzi smiled. It was a strange, almost ethereal smile. "I'll show you," he said. "Meet me next week, at the house."

They drank the rest of their coffee in silence and admired the girls who passed them by.

The house was at number 304, Adolf Hitler Strasse. It was a comfortable white-fenced house in a quiet suburb of Berlin, with neatly-trimmed lawn at the front. But when Hermann arrived there, Hanzi was gone.

His last story was found on his desk, uncompleted. Hermann found the house undisturbed, the door open, Hanzi's ancient Pravetz still turned on, the word-processing program still running, the story incomplete on the screen. Hanzi's special books and magazines lay in plain sight over the desk: it was as if Hanzi, perhaps getting up to answer a knock on the door, had then simply disappeared.

The story was called Hershele Ostropol in the Stalag of Death, and it began like so:

Hershele Ostropol in the Stalag of Death

When they came for him it was not at night but in the middle of the afternoon, and the two women came quiet and with no warning, with just a polite knock on the door. He had taken it to be the postman, carrying a late delivery of one of his special magazines; but the two who stood in the doorway wore no uniforms, and only their eyes betrayed who, and what, they were.

Hanzi knew then that it was over; the knowledge washed him in lethargy, and a sense of futility made him open his hands as if in a shrug, his slim fingers opening limply, sweat dampening his palms.

They had interrupted him writing, it was another one of his stories. The computer was left switched on in his small study, and his special books and magazines lay in plain view on the desk.

He knew then that it was over; and he went with them without a fight and let them steer him into the dark Mercedes that waited for him, as he knew it would, outside.

The two female S.S colonels sat opposite him in the car, leather skirts riding up their pale thighs. Their lips were colorless, without lipstick, and their blonde hair gathered like dew on their shoulders.

"What will you do with me?" he whispered, unconsciously licking his lips. The woman on his left had brought out a horse whip and was stroking it, almost tenderly.

"What will we do with you?" she asked. A gold swastika plunged from her neck into her bosom, hung on a thin necklace. She looked out of the window. "We will teach you what it really means," she said, "to be treated like a Jew."

The car purred as it went into motion; and soon it was gone from Adolf Hitler Strasse, heading towards . . .

TO BE CONTINUED.

THE MOBY CLITORIS OF HIS BELOVED

Ian Watson and Roberto Quaglia

Yukio was only a salaryman, not a company boss, but for years he'd yearned to taste whale clitoris sashimi. Regular whalemeat sashimi was quite expensive, but Yukio would need to work for a hundred years to afford whale clitoris sashimi, the most expensive status symbol in Japan.

Much of Yukio's knowledge of the world came from manga comic books or from anime movies which he watched on his phone while commuting for three hours every day. He treasured the image of a beautiful young ama diving woman standing on the bow of a whaling boat clad in a semi-transparent white costume and holding sparklingly aloft the special clitoridectomy knife. An icon far more wonderful than that of Kate Winslet at the front of the *Titanic*! Americans might have their *Moby Dick*, but Yukio's countrymen (or at least the richest of them) had their Moby Clitoris Sashimi.

The beautiful young ama woman would take a deep breath, dive, swim underneath a woman-whale, grasp her 8-centimeter clitoris, then with one razor-sharp slash cut off the clitoris and swim away very fast. On the deck of the whaler the crew would wait for the ama to climb back aboard, her costume now see-through due to wetness.

And then the whalers would harpoon and kill the whale, because it would be too cruel to leave a female whale alive after amputation of her clitoris. In this respect the Japanese differed very much from certain Islamic and African countries which cut off the clitorises of human girls, so that men should not feel inadequate about their own capacity for orgasms.

Whenever the Japanese were criticised for hunting whales, it was the harvesting of clitorises which empowered them to continue. And of course Japan observed a strict clitoris quota, so that enough female whales would continue to copulate pleasurably and repopulate. Thus, while it was true that whale clitoridectomy directly pleasured only the richest individuals, every Japanese citizen who enjoyed eating whales also benefitted.

This Yukio knew. Yet he still yearned to taste whale clitoris sashimi for himself! Most men have licked a woman's clitoris, although probably they haven't eaten one; but the organ of ecstasy of a female whale sliced thinly was said to possess a taste beyond words.

When Yukio's vacation came—the usual very hot and humid fortnight in August—he didn't surrender his holiday back to the Nippon Real-Doll Corporation, as he had done in previous years, in the hope of more rapid promotion through the copyright department. Instead, he took a train from Tokyo (and then a bus) the hundred kilometers to Shirahama City where ama diving women lived. He would seduce an ama to love him. They would marry. She would get a job on a whaling boat. For him she would smuggle clitoris sashimi . . .

To his consternation Yukio soon discovered that the ama women of Shirahama, who dive for red seaweed, sea snails and abalone, looked nothing like the icon in his mind. For one thing, they weren't slim but were muscular from exercise—and chubby, to cope with cold water. For another, their faces were darkly tanned, not a lovely creamy-white. For a third, their voices were loud and raucous, perhaps due to damage from water pressure; and their speech was quite vulgar. For a fourth, they didn't wear semi-transparent white garments, but orange sweatshirts, thermal tights, and neoprene diving hoods. And for a fifth, their average age seemed to be over sixty. Even if one of those fat vulgar grannies wanted a lover and husband, how could Yukio excite himself enough to woo her?

Disconsolate, he went to get drunk. Presently he found himself outside **The Authentic Ama-Geisha Inn**. The name seemed promising.

Inside, he was amazed to find waiting several beautiful, slim young hostesses dressed in the correct long, white semi-transparent costumes, and also wearing white high heels. Perched jauntily on their foreheads were diving masks. One hostess wore her very long hair in an oily black rope which would excite a bondage fetishist or a flagellant considerably.

Soon this hostess, whose name was Keiko, was leading Yukio into a private room—which contained a low table, plastic cushions, and a small, blue-tiled pool set in the floor of tatami matting, which was plastic too; plastic would dry more quickly than straw matting. He knelt. Keiko knelt and poured some Johnnie Walker Black Label. She giggled and said sweetly, "You may splash me whenever you wish!"

Thus revealing more of her breast or thigh or belly . . .

"But you're the ama of my visions!" Yukio exclaimed. "Why aren't you diving in the sea? You would look so beautiful."

Already he was a bit in love with Keiko, even though the plan had been for an ama to fall in love with him.

"I'm an ama-geisha," Keiko explained. "Only *you* can wet me, not the sea."

"I've seen amas just like you with the whaling fleet! Only," and he recollected his apparently foolish plan, "not with such wonderful hair as yours. They dive for whale clitorises," he added.

Keiko giggled again. "A real ama does that."

"*A fat old granny?*"

Keiko's job was to please him, and Yukio seemed to prefer intellectual stimulation rather than getting drunk and splashing her, so the astonishing truth emerged—a truth known to most inhabitants of Shirahama, but which the media patriotically chose not to publicise.

Each whaling ship carried a real ama and also a false ama (or rather an authentic iconic ama). The real ama, old and fat, foul-mouthed and lurid, would harvest the clitoris while the false ama—who looked more real—would wait in the water beside the ship. The false authentic ama would then take the clitoris from the real inauthentic ama and would climb a steep gangplank back on board deck, her garment delightfully see-through. Meanwhile the old fat ama would sneak on to the ship from the rear, using the ramp up which dead whales were winched.

This substitution made whale-hunting seem graceful and elegant and sexually exciting in the eyes of the world—slightly akin to marine bull-fighting—and justified the high price to gourmets of clitoris sashimi.

Yukio stared at Keiko. "Wouldn't you rather be on a whaling ship, than here? With your wonderful rope of hair you'd set a new style for cartoon books and films. I can license your image for you." Yukio's work did indeed consist in copyright matters concerning Real Dolls modelled upon porn stars. "I'm a specialist. You'd earn a big fee." And Yukio would be the lovely Keiko's agent and manager, and because of this, he would become her Beloved! And at last he would eat whale clitoris sashimi.

Keiko was wide-eyed.

"Agreed?"

Before Keiko could change her mind, Yukio picked up his glass of Johnny Walker Black Label and threw the contents over her, wetting and revealing a delightful breast.

"Kampai!" he exclaimed, to toast her—but in his mind he was shouting 'Banzai!' for victory.

The whaling industry normally recruited deep-sea ama from communities such as Shirahama, but Yukio needed Keiko with him in Tokyo to register her image. Keiko could stay in his little apartment in a highrise in the suburbs.

So Keiko exchanged her authentic ama costume and high heels for jeans and a blouse, and piled her rope of hair upon her head, hiding it with a scarf, because nobody must steal her image on a phone en route! Already Yukio felt paranoid and jealous.

On the train Yukio looked at the news on his own phone, and a headline caught his eye: THROW THE WHALE AWAY!

A meeting in South Korea of the International Whaling Commission had ended in confusion. As usual the dispute was about whether to save whales or eat them. The Japanese delegate had suddenly declared that whale clitoris sashimi was a cultural treasure unique to Japan. If foreigners forced the Japanese to stop eating whalemeat, the Japanese would continue to harvest whale clitorises—but to please world public opinion they would throw the rest of the whale away. They would accomplish this grand gesture by compassionately exploding all clitoridectomised whales using torpedos packed with plastic explosive, since nuclear torpedos were unacceptable.

"That will make clitorises even more valuable and prestigious," Yukio said to Keiko.

"I have a clitoris too," she replied.

"But not a whale clitoris." Or at least not yet, he thought.

Maybe the Japanese delegate's statement was intended to bewilder the World Wildlife Fund, which had been picketing the meeting. Under the United Nations' Declaration of Cultural Rights, it was forbidden to attack or slander any country's unique cultural icons, such as the Golden Arches of MacDonald's or the Eiffel Tower. Now that Japan had registered whale clitoris sashimi as a cultural treasure, that gourmet experience was protected from criticism—and if there were no clitorises to be sliced, obviously the experience would become extinct. To preserve the cultural experience, the Japanese must continue to hunt whales.

Yukio's apartment was a four-mat one, which was better than living and sleeping in a room only the size of three tatami mats; but still it was rather crowded by two people, unless those two people were intimate. So Yukio found himself examining Keiko's clitoris, causing her to sigh with plea-sure. Then he went to sleep and dreamed that every century a magical woman-whale would appear offshore, to provide sashimi from her clitoris for the Empress of the time. On the brow of this whale: a white mark exactly like a chrysanthemum flower. During the subsequent hundred years, the whale's clitoris would regenerate.

Yukio awoke in the morning, thinking immediately about the possibilities of *cloning* clitoris. Keiko had already risen and was now kneeling, dressed in her authentic iconic ama costume which real ama no longer wore. Truly she had the graces of a geisha. Obviously a woman's clitoris couldn't possibly taste as wonderful as a whale's, yet what if cloned human clitoris could be marketed profitably enough so that the genius who thought of this became rich enough to afford to eat whale clitoris?

Since Yukio had no idea how to clone anything, an alternative occurred to him. These days, because pigs and people are very alike, pigs provided transplant organs for human beings. Maybe a million people had inside them pig hearts or lungs or livers or kidneys. When the pigs were sacri-ficed to provide transplants, the rest of the pig, including the clitoris in the case of female pigs, would probably go into pet food.

What if Yukio were to buy the sex organs of pigs, to provide a source of clitorises? These could be packaged in tiny jars as human clitorises, and sold over the internet! Upon the label, a photo of a genuine human clitoris, with a certificate of authenticity which would be correct since the picture at least was genuine. *Delicious clitorises, cloned from this very clitoris you see!* Realistically, Keiko might *not* obtain a job on a whaling ship—yet she could still help Yukio to achieve his goal.

Truly, his trip to the seaside had inspired him, probably because the clean air contained more oxygen in it than in the city.

Yukio took his phone, and soon he was photographing Keiko's clitoris while she assisted him. He wasn't quite sure if her clitoris was the usual size but it was certainly very noticeable. Using Photoshop, he could get rid of the surrounding flaps of flesh familiar to users of porn magazines, leaving only the clitoris itself in the picture. His computer could print many labels. In a truly iconic sense he would indeed be cloning Keiko's clitoris, or at least its image. In his excitement he almost forgot to go to work.

On the commuter train, he used his phone to search for Pig Organ Farms and for Food Bottlers. Genius is to perceive connections where none were seen before.

When he returned home that night, Keiko was already lying asleep on the futon, still dressed as an ama and wearing her diving mask for even greater authenticity. Her long rope of hair seemed like an oxygen tube. The TV set was showing young men eating as many worms as they could as quickly as possible. It was the popular weekly show *Brown Spaghetti Race*, sponsored by the Dai-Nippon Cheese Company. The more Parmesan the contestants poured on the wiggling worms, the less difficult it was to pick them up using smoothly lacquered chopsticks.

Would consumers be more excited by "genuine canned cloned human clitoris sashimi" or "genuine ama clitoris sashimi (cloned)"? Maybe the label should show Keiko smiling as she held her photoshopped clitoris to her own lips with *chopsticks*? Would the suggestion of auto-cannibalism excite buyers? Was his ideal market gourmets who couldn't afford whale clitoris, or sexual fetishists? Or both?

Yukio sat on the edge of the futon beside Keiko and regarded her tenderly. He lifted her rope of hair, closed his lips upon the end of it, and blew into the hair as though to supply her with more oxygen, such as she had been accustomed to at the seaside. Maybe, subconsciously at least, that was the reason why she had put on the diving mask.

"Keiko-san," he told her politely, although she was asleep, "there is a change of plan."

It took Yukio some hard work and organisation and most of his savings to set up the Genuine Cloned Ama Clitoris Sashimi Company, or GCACSC for short. The sexual organs of organ-donor pigs must be rushed by courier, refrigerated and ultra-fresh, to the Greater Tokyo Bottling Company, where a dedicated employee dissected out the clitorises for bottling. Irrelevant vaginas and labia and also penises and balls were cooked and minced and canned to become Luxury Pig-Protein sent as food aid to starving Communist North Korea, with the full co-operation of the government's Japan-Aid programme, which subsidised the project and praised Yukio's initiative and sense of social responsibility, while respecting his wish to remain anonymous. The donor farm believed that the complete sexual organs were being processed, which in the case of male pigs was true; and Yukio had no wish to enlighten them.

He enlightened the gourmet public about the availability of cloned ama clitoris sashimi by means of a clever spam program, which he bought in the Akihabara electronics district. A spam program was appropriate since the word spam originally meant 'spiced American meat.'

Every night after Yukio came home from the Nippon Real-Doll Corporation, he printed labels for the jars and boxes and address labels and dealt with an increasing number of internet orders and payments. He had rented a garage for delivery of the little unlabelled jars of clitorises, which were received there during the day by Keiko, dressed ordinarily. She would then change into her ama costume, stick the labels on to the jars, skillfully fold the beautiful little cardboard boxes which Yukio produced on his printer, fit a jar into each, and stick on an address label.

Keiko was very busy; and so was Yukio. What with Yukio's regular work at the Real-Doll Corporation and his after-hours work at home, he became a bit like a Zen monk who had trained himself in No-Sleep, or not much— now he slept standing up in the commuter train instead of looking at manga and anime on his phone; consequently he never watched the News in either manga or anime format. All he knew was that orders were pouring into his home PC. The spam had done its job sufficiently well that consumers were spontaneously spreading the word of the new and affordable (although not cheap) gourmet delight. Keiko told him that by now magazines were writing stories about, and TV channels were talking—she had done some phone interviews. Apparently Yukio was being hailed as the new Mr Mikimoto, but Yukio had no spare time to pay much attention.

Mikimoto-san was the man who invented cultured pearls by putting irritating grains of sand inside oysters, at Pearl Island. To suggest that his cultured pearls were as good as naturally occuring pearls, he had employed amas to dive into the sea around Pearl Island for tourists to admire, and in fact, according to Keiko, Mikimoto-san had invented or revised the see-through costumes of the amas. The ama water-ballet actresses would bring up real oysters, which might or might not contain real pearls, for the tourists to eat authentically in the Pearl Island Restaurant.

One evening an astonishing thing happened. Yukio had woken up automatically as usual in time to get off the commuter train, and was walking away from the station homeward when he saw Keiko coming towards along the street dressed in schoolgirl uniform!

"Why have you become a schoolgirl?" he cried out, but Keiko walked past, ignoring him.

Then along the street came another schoolgirl Keiko, then another, then a couple together.

They were real schoolgirls wearing false faces—latex masks of the real Keiko!

"Excuse me," Yukio said to a false Keiko, "but where did you get that mask?"

The schoolgirl paused, but remained silent.

Of course, she couldn't speak while wearing that mask because Yukio wasn't speaking to her but to the mask. Should he reach out and peel the mask from her true face? That might constitute assault, or even a new perversion, of unmasking schoolgirls.

"Please tell me," he begged.

She bowed slightly, then beckoned—gestured him back towards the station.

Like a tourist guide for the deaf she led him inside the station to a vending machine. It was one of those that sold the used panties of virgins, which old men would buy and sniff. But now it also sold something else in little bags: those masks of Keiko.

Quickly Yukio bought one. The packaging showed the upper body and face of Keiko, just as on the labels of the jars of clitorises. Keiko held to her lips with chopsticks a clitoris, although now she was using her left hand rather than her right—evidently she had been photoshopped. A speech bubble above her head read: *Eat my virgin clitoris.*

That was the cheeky message conveyed by the mask. Identities concealed, schoolgirls could tease men naughtily without a blush, without even saying a word or making a gesture. What innocent, or wicked, erotic power they would feel! Clitoris power. Maybe the packaging of other masks had different speech in the bubbles. Or maybe not. Or maybe yes.

Quickly Yukio googled non-manga non-anime News on his phone.

He saw a picture, taken through a window, of a classroom in which all the girls were wearing identical Keiko masks to the consternation of the teacher. He saw a picture of a playground where a dozen Keikos of different heights were strolling. A craze had hit the whole of Japan, probably spreading among schoolgirls everywhere by txt!

Because of trousers, he noticed some boys too, who were also wearing Keiko masks. Ah, the boys were doing that so as to save face!

He asked the Keiko who still lingered by the machine, "Keiko, did you *do* this without consulting me? To prove that you're clever too?" What a perfect ecological loop, that the same machines which sold the used virgin underwear of schoolgirls should provide the same schoolgirls with these masks . . .

But of course she wasn't the real Keiko, and besides she had no intention of speaking.

How could Keiko have organised the rapid manufacture of all the masks and their supply to vending machines? Yukio ripped open the packaging and unfolded the latex mask. On the back of the chin, to his horror he saw: ™ *Nippon Real-Doll Corp.*

Had he fallen asleep at work without realizing and talked in his sleep? Had he been too clever for himself? Had part of him exploited himself schizophrenically out of company loyalty? Or had the company security-psychologist decided that Yukio was behaving oddly, and investigated his computer?

Oh foolish Yukio, to have copyrighted the label with Keiko's image in his own name at work, borrowing the company's copyright software—that was how they had found out!

But then the company perceived a unique business opportunity: the Real-Doll Corporation could turn real schoolgirls everywhere into clitoris-power dolls of his Keiko! A million texting schoolgirls could spread a craze within a few days, or maybe a few hours. And Yukio couldn't complain or sue, nor could Keiko. For one thing, Yukio had committed industrial theft. But, even more worryingly, the Real-Doll Corporation's psychologist-detective may have also found out the true source of Genuine Cloned Ama Clitoris Sashimi.

Yukio bowed to the false Keiko, then hurried home.

"Who are you?" he said to Keiko in the four-mat room. Quickly he explained what he had discovered—Keiko had been too busy labeling in the rented garage that day to watch any news. And he added: "You must wear a mask from now on, or else I won't know you!"

"Do you mean wear my diving mask?"

"More like a mask of Kate Winslet, I think . . . No, wait!"

The big oval of latex cut from the Keiko mask fitted the diving mask perfectly. Superglue secured it. Her false eyes, false nose, and false mouth squeezed flatly against the inside of the glass, as if she had dived to a depth of such pressure that her features had become two-dimensional. Her photoshopped clitoris forever would touch her flat lips.

Since the false genuine face which she wore a few centimeters in front of her real face was in fact her true face, this negated that falsity and bestowed a mysterious and mystical authenticity upon her actual face, even though that was now invisible, as mystical things often are.

A Zen-like state came over Yukio. He knelt before Keiko, like Pinocchio praying to the Blue Fairy to make him real. By not-seeing what he was seeing, Yukio began to worship her countenance.

Unseeing too, a blind goddess, Keiko heard his mantra of worship.

"My Beloved, My Beloved, My Beloved . . . "

Whale clitoris sashimi was only an illusion, from which Yukio was now freed by enlightenment. Probably its sublime taste was also an illusion caused by exorbitant price. He would eat Keiko's clitoris instead.

LYDIA'S BODY

————

Vylar Kaftan

The girl did everything for him. She polished his boots with bear grease and swept the floor with a willow broom. She washed the sheets, both sets, once a week. She dried them on a clothesline near their house—the one-room log cabin she guessed he'd built himself. Sometimes the Wisconsin breeze blew more dirt into the sheets as they fluttered, the linen stained with human fluids she couldn't scrub out.

He went hunting most days, the man she believed to be Lydia's father. Sometimes he'd stroke her hair and say, "I'll be back by nightfall, my Lydia, with fresh meat." The girl smiled at him, grateful for his presence at night when the panthers screamed. He trudged off through the forest, shotgun slung to his back, and she closed the door behind him. The door had no lock. No one was around for miles except the Chippewa, who ignored them.

The girl leaned against the door each morning, in the single room that had become her new home—her prison. She repeated to herself, in case she forgot: My name is Amanda Barnes. I'm twenty-six years old. I was born in 1980. I don't belong here. But then she looked at her body, the unfamiliar skinny arms, her work-raw hands, and wondered how much longer she'd stay.

Mix cornmeal with water, and bake into johnnycakes. Thrust the dash into the churn with regular strokes.

This body knew its required tasks. The body's hands mixed the cornmeal, stoked the stove, braided the onion tops together and hung them in the attic. Amanda found these chores instinctive—a way of listening to her core, where some ancestral spirit guided her. No words were spoken—she simply knew, the way she knew her heartbeat.

Of course she'd told the man who she was—two years ago, when she woke up here. He'd blamed the fever and given her medicinal whiskey that she vomited back up. She couldn't blame him—her story was unbelievable. How should she tell him she'd fallen asleep and awoken in another time, with no idea how she'd gotten here? She was only a little surprised to discover that the body had magic in it. Dishes cleaned faster than expected. The dirt floor swept itself at the barest touch. Magic must have brought her—but she couldn't reverse it.

Her old life was fading away. She remembered drinking cinnamon lattes, driving to work, skimming the Internet personals—these were the habits of a film character somewhere, in a theater she had been in once. They happened in darkness, and when the movie ended she was here, blinking in the sunlight of 1838.

Mend shirts with tiny stitches, overlapping each other so they look like white paint. The tighter your stitches, the less likely they'll rip. I'm careful when mending his shirts.

He'd come home at night, with a dead deer or even a bear. Amanda marveled at how he slung the corpse around, the meaty weight under full control. She sometimes watched him working shirtless, as he smoked meat in a hickory fire or planted potato seeds. When he split firewood, the log cracked on the axe's downstroke—almost before he touched it, like the wood opened itself for him. He worked to provide for her—not *her*, but Lydia, whose body she was in.

Amanda had thought about leaving, but there was nowhere to go. The nearest town was forty miles away, and she didn't know what direction. Wisconsin was frontier territory—just fur traders, Indians, and settlers who wanted to avoid other people. She'd asked where town was, but he didn't say. "Why would you go there, Lydia?" he'd ask. "It's too far, and there's nothing to see. Someday I'll take you, when you're older."

Someday. Amanda clung to that idea, as she scrubbed their undergarments. She didn't know what magic had summoned her, nor who Lydia was. If something connected her to this body, she couldn't see it. She'd stopped praying to find her way home. Even her mantra—My name is Amanda Barnes—felt useless. Just unrelated syllables—a spell with its life drained away. With each day, the idea of leaving became harder to remember. Despite her mantra, there was *him*, and he was the only reason she saw that drew her to this time.

It was impossible not to love him. That was the problem. Perhaps if she'd grown up here—if she remembered him swinging her in his arms, or leaning down to ruffle her hair—perhaps then, she could accept him as a father. But Amanda was twenty-six, and this man not much older—thirty-three, or a bit more. He was attractive, kind, and hardworking. He brought in fresh-killed meat, and hoed the potatoes with his strong arms, and once he shot a wolf that was nosing around the cabin door.

On Sunday nights, they sang hymns together. Their voices blended, tenor and soprano, and Amanda knew she could never tell him how she felt. He thought he was her father. Maybe, in a sense, he was—but he was all she had. At night as she listened to him sleep across the room, she thought about how they harmonized on the high notes, and how cold it was to sleep alone.

I like how gravy simmers. A bubble pauses, swelling on the surface. It grows so large it might escape and float away. But the bubble bursts, because it must. It returns to the pot, to be served for his dinner.

He came home one night, flushed with November's chill. "Poor huntin' out there."

Amanda served his meal, buttering his potatoes. The attic was full of onions and smoked meat. Soon the blizzards would begin, and she—again—would be stuck inside the cabin for six months. Last year she'd gone nearly mad with boredom. Still—sometimes he'd go looking for fresh meat, and she'd worry. What if he didn't come back? What if a wolf attacked him? What would she do on her own?

"What happens to me?" she asked aloud.

"Hmmm?"

"What happens to me," she said, changing her train of thought, "in a few years? I'm nearly grown. What then?"

He chewed on his venison. "I dunno," he said. He spoke with difficulty, as if he'd been considering it. "Frank might want you. He's the man I trade with in town."

"Am I property, to be given away?" she asked bitterly.

"Lydia! I wouldn't do that." He stabbed his fork into the fried onions. "I wouldn't give you to any man you didn't want."

"Well, I have to think about my future." Future—the word recalled something, about the butterscotch candies she kept in her desk . . . She shook her head. My name is Amanda Barnes . . .

He stirred the onions around his plate. "Want me to find someone for you? I could send you back East to work as a servant. I don't got any living relatives. It's just us, Lydia. You 'n me. At least out here, it's *just* us. We can live any way we want. No one will bother us."

"Who would cook for you if I left?"

He set his fork down. The fire in the hearth crackled. "I don't need much. I'd get on all right."

"Alone?"

He stood up. An upset person had nowhere to storm to, except the attic loft. Even there no one could hide, not long—everything was visible from below. He moved to the fire, next to the glassless shuttered windows. "I'd get a wife, I suppose."

"Why haven't you?"

"I don't want one."

Amanda took a guess. "Because of my mother?"

He jumped like she'd shot him. He turned to face her. "Yes."

Amanda closed her eyes. "Do I look like her?"

His response was hoarse, and a long time coming. "Yes. Yes, you do, Lydia."

He likes his meat fried with potatoes. The potatoes are in the attic. He never goes up there—that place is my own. Listen. A blizzard is coming.

Amanda was in the attic, getting a string of onions for supper. All meals were the same each week—potatoes and onions, and whatever meat he brought home. He never came up here—somehow, she knew. She had memories that felt like someone else's. He was hunting again. Amanda worried about him, alone in the woods. But he took his shotgun, and he kept it well-oiled.

She kept thinking of the way he'd spoken the name Lydia. She'd heard that note—the longing for his absent wife—his loneliness, alone with his daughter in the wilderness. But he'd chosen this life for them—to live undisturbed by others. Free.

Her kerosene lamp gave little light in the attic. It was early March. The windows were shuttered for the season. Overhead the wind blew across the roof. A blizzard, she knew—no, it wasn't *her* knowing that. The deep instinct told her. She hated the blizzards, hated the way they buried the house and trapped her inside. If he were home when it started, he'd stay—but otherwise, he dug shelter where he could, and she was alone.

She tugged on an onion string. All winter, she'd thought about him—as they slept in their beds, and as they sang together. She saw how he looked at her. He was thinking it too, and probably hating himself. A father and daughter—no, that couldn't be. But she wasn't his daughter. She was Amanda Barnes, whether he believed her or not.

The string broke. Onions tumbled to the floor. One rolled behind the cornmeal barrel. Amanda hunted it down and scooped it up like a runaway softball. She used to play softball—when was that? In her past, which was now her future. She felt shaky as the wind howled. The blizzard was coming. He would take shelter somewhere, and she was alone.

Amanda cradled the rough onion in her hand. Every crop was hard-fought. Each onion grew from his sweat, as he worked to feed them both. Tears ran down her face. Winter was driving her mad—hands scratching inside her, a voice trying to shout, a feeling colder than snowdrifts. Something hateful rose inside her like a ghost, until she thought she would burst.

She threw the onion against the wall. It's March that does this to me, she thought, only March. She wanted to vanish into the snow with this magic body. A wish—but wishes were powdery snow melting in sunlight, gone before a season ended. If she could wish herself into happier times—but she knew no spells, and the body only seemed to do household magic. The things it knew, perhaps, from when Lydia was here.

But now it was Amanda's body. She was stuck in this house, this time. This life was hers—to suffer through, or to find happiness. She picked up the onion. "My name is Amanda Barnes," she said aloud. That man was not her father, and she could do as she pleased. No one would stop her.

The wrong wish is a dangerous spell, cold like ice. It traps the careless. It freezes you under the surface and never melts. I made a mistake. I need my body back.

Downstairs, the door crashed open. Amanda dropped the onion. Lydia's father stumbled in with a swirl of snow, his arm clutched across his coat. His hand pressed bloody snow against his shoulder.

"Lydia," he called, "I've shot myself."

The girl scrambled down the attic ladder. He staggered to his chair and shrugged his coat off. He tore his shirt away, ripping the stitches like paper. The wound was more blood than injury. She grabbed strips of cloth and put water on the stove. He would live—but her body was cold, like the blizzard had swept inside the house.

"An accident," he said. "My own fault—careless. So distracted—aahh!"

He sucked in his breath as she cleaned his wound with water. "No. Bring whiskey."

She fetched the bottle from the shelf. He poured it over his shoulder, hissing when the alcohol burned the wound. The brown liquid mixed with blood and ran down his arm. He took a swig of whiskey. He swirled the liquor in the bottle, and drank three more times.

She took the whiskey. Her hands shook. The wind rattled the shutters. Behind his back she took a drink herself. The liquid burned her throat and warmed her, like she hadn't felt for months. She drank again, to drive away March, and loneliness, and the dark hatefulness inside her.

"More," he muttered, and she handed it back. He drank deeply, leaving the bottle half-full. He set it down. "I'm fine. Help me wrap the wound."

The girl obeyed, and the magic worked—her hands knew where to put the cloth, where to tighten or leave loose. The whiskey burned inside her like a kerosene lamp flame—banishing darkness, past, and future. There was only this moment, touching his skin, easing his pain. His breathing slowed, and his muscles relaxed. When she finished, she pulled her chair over and leaned on his good shoulder. She might have lost him, she realized, and she would have been alone—with the blizzard, and the cabin, and a lifetime stretching ahead of her.

"I don't know what I'd do without you," he said. He took her hand and squeezed it. Her heart raced. She leaned over to kiss his cheek. He turned his head to say something—and she brushed against his mouth.

I can do what I want, Amanda thought fiercely. She kissed his lips, her tongue exploring their closed line. He moaned once, then opened to her. Their tongues fought inside him, tasting of whiskey.

Amanda stroked his hair. The room floated around her. "Shh," she said, moving her mouth away. "It's all right." The instinct inside her screamed *no, you can't*—and she silenced it. This was her life now.

He grabbed her waist and pulled her onto his lap. He plowed into her mouth like a starving man. Amanda's breath quickened. His hardness pressed through his workpants against her leg. She wondered if this body could hex him. Her hand slid up his thigh, brushing against—

He shoved her away. She tumbled to the floor, bruising her hip. He reeled against the chair and clutched his forehead. "Oh, God, oh Mary, Jesus—" he muttered.

Amanda crawled away. The room spun. His voice rang over the crackling fire: "We can *never* do that again, do you hear me? Never." He yanked the door open. Blizzard winds swirled in. He swore and slammed the door, not looking at her. "Go to the attic. Stay away. Go away."

"I'm not your daughter!"

"Stop it!"

"My name is Amanda Barnes—"

"*Stop it!*"

She couldn't. The words poured out like blood, staining the space between them. "Don't you see how I've changed? I'm not her anymore. I love you. Look at me—you know I'm not her!"

He whirled around, and she read doubt in his eyes. For a moment, she dared believe. Then his expression hardened, like he'd built a barrier against her—against himself. "It's not possible."

"I swear it's true. You *know* it's true."

"We can never be that way. No matter what we want." He pulled the Bible off the shelf and went to his bed. He faced the wall and opened the book. He didn't turn the pages.

Never. She could never have what she wanted, never leave, never hope. Deep inside her, something clawed to get out. It was that instinct, that voice—the one she'd trusted until now. Amanda glanced at the attic ladder, but it was too hard to climb. She stumbled to her bed and collapsed, drunk and exhausted. Her stomach heaved, but she kept its contents down. Even when she closed her eyes, she was spinning out of control. She couldn't fight anymore. The darkness would bury her—like this damned cabin under ten feet of snow.

No, you can't—I won't let you—

She was fighting for her life, the girl: only one body for both of them, two minds in the same magic flesh—one born there, and one summoned against her will. It should have been an exchange—Lydia's wish come true. The spell should have let her escape her hated life. It had been the wrong wish. The wrong wish could kill.

Lydia's spell failed, and she had paid for it. Trapped under Amanda's presence, she'd waited, cold as burial, imprisoned inside her own flesh. Somewhere in the future was a soulless body—Amanda's body, the one Lydia wanted. She knew now: her magic couldn't take her there. But it could still free her from this self-made prison.

She waited until Amanda was weak. The fight was brief—the body's magic ran deep like a well, and Lydia knew how to tap it. Amanda did not, and was defenseless. Lydia rose from the icy place inside and summoned power from her own blood. She started with her fingertips, the muscles clenching at her command, and worked her way into the body's organs. She wrapped Amanda in tendons and bile before pushing her into darkness. Lydia buried her in the body, grieving. Her guilt was a stain she would never scrub out. But she felt her life returning, once she controlled her body again.

Lydia woke in her familiar bed. It was night. Her head felt fuzzy, like she'd woken from a bad dream. Her tongue was cotton-dry. She looked toward her father's empty bed. A candle stub cast its light across the patchwork quilt. Next to it stood the empty whiskey bottle, reflecting the flame into a shining stripe.

She sat up, wondering where he might be. Then she knew—by instinct, like breathing. She knew where he was, the way she knew what he wanted.

A shadow crossed in front of the flickering candle. A breath touched her face, smelling of liquor. His hands pressed her shoulders against the bed. "No," Lydia whispered, sick with whiskey and buried desire. Her stomach lurched as her fingers curled toward him. "No, we can't—we can't—"

He said, "Oh God." The candle went out.

URCHINS, WHILE SWIMMING

Catherynne M. Valente

> On the third day the ardent hermit
> Was sitting by the shore, in love,
> Awaiting the enticing mermaid,
> As shade was lying on the grove.
> Dark ceded to the sun's emergence;
> By then the monk had disappeared,
> No one knew where, and only urchins,
> While swimming, saw a hoary beard.
> —Aleksandr Pushkin
> Rusalka, 1819

I: Snail Into Shell

Rybka, you have to wake up.

At night she always called me *rybka*. At night, when she shook me awake in my thin bed and the dirt-smeared window was a sieve for the light of the bone-picked stars, she whispered and stroked my temples and said: *rybka, rybka*, wake up, you have to wake up. I would rub my eyes and with heavy limbs hunch to the edge of the greyed mattress, hang my head over the side. She would be waiting with a big copper kettle, a porcelain basin, the best and most beautiful of the few things we owned. She would be waiting, and while I looked up at the stars through a scrim of window-mud and window-ice, she would wet my hair.

She was my mother, she was kind, the water was always warm. The kettle poured its steaming stream over my scalp, that old water like sleep spreading over my long black hair. Her hands were so sure, and she wet every strand—she did not wash it, understand, only pulled and combed the slightly yellow water from our creaking faucet through my tangles.

48

URCHINS, WHILE SLEEPING

Rybka, I'm sorry, poor darling. I'm so sorry. Go back to sleep. And she would coil my slippery hair on the pillow like loose rope on the deck of a ship, and she would sing to me until I was asleep again, and her voice was like stones falling into a deep lake:

> *Bayu, bayushki bayu*
> *Ne lozhisya na krayu*
> *Pridet serenkiy volchok*
> *Y ukusit za bochek*

In the morning, she called me always by my name, Kseniya, and her eyes would be worry-wrinkled—and her hair would be wet, too. While she scraped a pale, translucent sliver of precious butter over rough, hard-crusted bread, I would draw a bath, filling the high-sided tub to its bright brim. We ate our breakfast slick-haired in the nearly warm water, curled into each other's bodies, snail into shell, while the bath sloshed over onto the kitchen floor, which was also the living room floor and the bathroom floor and my mother's bedroom floor—she gave me the little closet which served as a second room.

In the evening, if we had meat, she would fry it slowly and we would savor the smell together, to make the meal last. If we did not, she would tell me a story about a princess who had a bowl which was never empty of sweet, roasted chickens while I slurped a thin soup of cabbage and pulpy pumpkin and saved bathwater. Sometimes, when my mother spoke low and gentle over the green soup, it tasted like birds with browned, sizzling skin. All day, she sponged my head, the trickle ticklish as sweat. The back of my dress clung slimy to my skin.

Before bed, she would pass my head under the faucet, the cold water splashing on my scalp like a slap. And then the waking, always the waking, and hour or two past midnight.

Rybka, I'm sorry, you have to wake up.

My childhood was a world of wetness, and I loved the smell of my mother's ever-dripping hair.

One night, she did not come to wet my hair. I woke up myself, my body wound like a clock by years of kettles and basins. The stars were salt-crystals floating in the window's mire. I crept out of my room and across the freezing floor like the surface of a winter lake. My mother lay in her bed, her back turned to the night.

Her hair was dry.

It was yellowy-brown, the color of old nut-husks—I was shocked. I had never seen it un-darkened by water. I touched it and she did not move. I turned her face to me and it did not move against my hand, or murmur to me to go back to sleep, or call me rybka—water dribbled out of her mouth and onto the blankets. Her eyes were dark and shallow.

Mama, you have to wake up.

I soaked up the water with the edge of the bedsheet. I pulled her to me; more water fell from her.

Mamochka, I'm sorry, you have to wake up.

Her head sagged against my arm. I didn't cry, but drew a bath in the dark, feeling the water for a ghost of warmth in the stream. It was hard—I was always so thin and small, then!—but I pulled my mother from her bed and got her into the tub, though the water splashed and my arms ached and she did not move, she did not move as I dragged her across the cold floor, she did not move as I pushed her over the lip of the bath. She floated there, and I pulled the water through her hair until it was black again, but her eyes did not swim up out of themselves. I peeled off my nightgown, soaked with her mouth-water, and climbed in after her, curling into her body as we always did, snail into shell. Her skin was clammy and thick against my cheek.

Rybka, wake up. It's time to wet my hair.

There was no sound but the tinkling ripple of water and the stars dripping through the window-sieve. I closed my mother's eyes and tucked my head up under her chin. I pulled her arms around me like blankets. And I sang to her, while the bath beaded on her skin, slowly blooming blue.

Bayu, bayushki bayu
Ne lozhisya na krayu
Pridet serenkiy volchok
Y ukusit za bochek

II: The Ardent Hermit

I met Artyom at university, where I combed my hair into a tight braid so that it would hold its moisture through anatomy lectures, pharmacopeial lectures, stitching and bone-setting demonstrations. At lunch I would wait until all the others had gone, and put my head under the spotless bathroom sink. Pristine, colorless water rushed over my brow like a comforting hand.

There were no details worth recounting: I tutored him in tumors and growths, one of the many ways I kept myself in copper kettles and cabbage soup. This is not important. How do we begin to remember? One day he was not there, the next day his laugh was a constant crow on my shoulder. One day I did not love a man named Artyom, the next day I loved him, and between the two days there is nothing but air.

Artyom ate the same thing every day: smoked fish, black bread, blueberries folded in a pale green handkerchief. He wore the spectacles of a man twice his age, and his hair was yellowy-brown. He had a thin little beard, a large nose and kept his tie very neatly. He once shared his lunch with me: I found the blueberries sour, too soft.

"When I was a girl," I said slowly, "there were no blueberries where we lived, and we would not have been able to buy them if there were. Instead I ate pumpkin, to keep parasites from chewing my belly into a honeycomb after the war. I ate pumpkin until I could not stand the sight of it, the dusty wet smell of it. I think I am too old, now, to love blueberries, and too old to see pumpkins and not think of worms."

Artyom blinked at me. His book lay open to a cross-section of the thyroid, the green wind off of the Neva rifling through the pages and the damp tail of my braid. He took back his blueberries.

When there was snow on the dome of St. Isaac's and the hooves of the Bronze Horseman were shoed in ice, he lay beside me on his own thin mattress and clumsily poured out the water of his tin kettle over my hair, catching the runoff in an old iron pot.

"You have to wake me in the night, Artyom. It is important. Do you promise to remember?"

"Of course, Ksyusha, but why? This is silly, and you will get my bed all wet."

I propped myself up on one elbow, the river-waves of my hair tumbling over one bare breast, a trickle winding its way from skin to linen. "If I can trust you to do this thing for me, then I can love you. Is that not reason enough?"

"If you can trust me to do this thing, then you can trust me to know why it must be done. Does that not seem obvious?"

He was so sweet then, with his thin chest and his clean fingernails. His woolen socks and his over-sugared tea. The sharp inward curve of his hip. I told him—why should I not? Steam rose from my scalp and he stroked my calves while I told him about my mother, how she was called Vodzimira, and how when she was young she lived in a little village in the Urals before the war and loved a seminary student with thick eyebrows named Yefrem, how she crushed thirteen yellow oxlips with her body when he laid her down under the larch trees.

Mira, Mira, he said to her then, I will never forget how the light looks on your stomach in this moment, the light through the larch leaves and the birch branches. It looks like water, as though you are a little brook into which I am always falling, always falling.

And my mother put her arms around his neck and whispered his name over and over into the collar of his shirt: *Yefrem, Yefrem.* She watched a moth land on his black woolen coat and rub its slender brown legs together, and she winced as her body opened for the first time. She watched the moth until the pain went away, and I suppose she thought then that she would be happy enough in a house built of Yefrem and his wool and his shirts, and his larches and his light.

But when she came to his school and put her hands over her belly, when she told him under a gray sky and droning bronze bells that she was already three months along, and would he see about a priest so that her child might have a name, he just smiled thinly and told her that he did not want a house built of Vodzimira and her water and her stomach, that he wanted only a house of God and some few angels with feet of glass, and that she was not to come to his school any longer. He did not want to be suspected of interfering with local girls.

My mother was alone, and her despair walked alongside her like a little black-haired girl with gleaming shoes. She could not tell her father or her own mother, she could not tell her brothers. She could think of no one she could tell who would love her still when the telling was done. So she went into the forest again, into the larches and the birches and the moths and the light, and in a little lake which reflected bare branches, she drowned herself without another word to anyone.

I swallowed and continued hoarsely. "When my mother opened her eyes again, it was very dark, and there were stars in the sky like drops of rain, and she saw them from under the water of the little lake. She was in the lake and the lake was in her and her fingers spread out under the water until there was nothing but the water and her, spanning shore to shore, and she moved in it, in herself, like a little tide. She had me there, under the slow ripples, in the dark, and the silver fish were her midwives."

I twisted the ends of my hair. A little water seeped out onto my knuckles.

Artyom looked at me very seriously. "You're talking about *rusalka*."

I shrugged, not meeting his gaze. "She didn't expect it. She certainly didn't think her child would go into the lake with her. When I was born, I swam as happily as a little turtle, and breathed the water, and as if by instinct beckoned wandering men with tiny, impish fingers. But she didn't want that for me. She didn't even want it for herself—she pressed her instinct down in her viciously, like a stone crushing a bird's skull. She brought me to the city, and she worked in laundries, her hands deep in soapy water every day, so that I would have something other than a lonely lake and skeletons." I picked at the threads of the mattress, refusing to look up, to see his disbelief. "But we had to stay wet, you know. It is hard in the city, there are so many things to dry you out. Especially at night, with the cold wind blowing across your scalp, through the holes in the walls. And even in the summer, the pillow drinks up your hair."

Artyom looked at me with pale green eyes, the color of lichen in the high mountains, and I broke from his gaze. He scratched his head and laughed a little. I did not laugh.

"My mother died when I was very young, you know. I have thought about it many times, since. And I think that, after awhile, she was just so tired, so tired, and a person, even a rusalka, can only wake herself up so many times before she only wants to sleep, sleep a little while longer, before she is just so tired that one day she forgets to wake up and her hair dries out and her little girl finds her with brown hair instead of black, and no amount of water will wake her up anymore."

My hands were pale and shaking as dead grass. I tried to pull away from him and draw my knees up to my chest—of course he did not believe me, how could I have thought he might? But Artyom took me in his arms and shushed me and stroked my head and told me to hush, of course he would remember to wake me, his poor love, he would wet my hair if I wanted him to, it was nothing, hush, now.

"Call me *rybka*, when you wake me," I whispered.

"You are not a rusalka, Kseniya Yefremovna."

"Nevertheless."

The frost was thick as fur on the windows when he kissed me awake in the hour-heavy dark, a steaming basin in his hands.

III: By the Shore, in Love

It took exactly seventeen nights, with Artyom constant with his kettle and basin as a nun at prayer over her pale candles, before I slept easily in his arms, deeper than waves.

On the eighteenth night my breath was quick as a darting mayfly on his cheek, and he reached for me as men will do—he reached for me and I was there, dark, new-soaked hair sticking to my breasts, rivulets of water trickling over my stomach. I smiled in the dark, and his face was so kind above me, kind and soft and needful. He closed his eyes—I could see at their edges gentle creases which would one day be a grandfather's wrinkles. When our lips parted he was shaking, his lip shuddering as though he had just touched a Madonna carved from ice, and I think of all the things I remember about Artyom, it is that little shaking that I recall most clearly, most often.

I was a virgin. Under the shadows of St. Isaac's and a moon-spattered light like blueberries strewn on the grass I moved over him with more valor than I felt—but one of us had to be brave. He guided me, but his motions were so small and afraid, as though, after all this time, he could not quite understand or believe in what was happening. I felt as though I was an old door, stuck into my frame, and some sun-beaten shoulder jarring me open, smashing against the dusty wood. It hurt, the widening of my bones, the rearrangement of my body, ascending and descending anatomies, sliding aside and aligning into a new thing. Of course it hurt. But there was no blood and I kissed his eyebrows instead of crying. My hair hung around his face like storm-drenched curtains, casting long shadows on his cheekbones.

"Ksyusha," he said to me, tender and gentle, without mockery, "Ksyusha, I will never forget how the light looks on your stomach in this moment, the light through your hair and the frozen windows. It looks like water, as though you are a little brook into which I am always falling, always falling."

The bars of the window cut my chest into quarters. He arched his back. I clamped his waist between my thighs. These things are not important—no one act of love is different much in its parts from any other, really. What is important is this: I did not know. I bent over him, meaning to kiss, only meaning to kiss—and I did not know what would happen, I swear it.

The lake came out of me, shuddering and splashing—my mouth opened like a sluice-gate, and a flood of water came shrieking from me, more water than I had ever known, strung with weeds and the skeletons of fish and little stones like sandy jewels.

It tasted like blood.

I choked, my body seized, thrashing rapture-violent, and it gushed harder, streaming from my lips, my hair, my fingertips, my eyes, my eyes, my eyes wept a deluge onto the thin little body of Artyom. The windows caught the jets and drops froze there, hard knots of ice. I screamed and all that came from my throat was more water, more and more and more.

His legs jerked awkwardly and I clutched at him, trying to clear the water and the green stems from his mouth, but already he convulsed under me, spluttering and spitting, reaching out for me from under the growing pool that was our bed, the bubbles of his breath popping in the blue—the bed was a basin and the water steamed and I wet his hair in it, but I did not mean to, I could not close my mouth against it, I could not stop it, I could not move away from him and it came and came and his bones beneath me racked themselves in the mire, the whites of his eyes rolled, and I am sorry, Artyom, I did not know, my mother did not tell me, she told me only to live as best I could, she did not say we drag the lake with us, even into the city, drag it behind us, a drowning shadow shot with green.

I would like to remember that he called out to me, that he called out in faith that I could deliver him, and if I try, I can almost manage it, his voice in my ear like an echo:

"Ksyusha!"

But I do not think he did, I think he only gurgled and gasped and coughed and died. I think the strangling weeds just passed over his teeth.

He never tried to push me off of him, he never tried to sit up. His face became still. His lips did not shake. His skin was pale and purpled. The water rippled over his thin little beard as it slowly, slowly as spring thaw, seeped into the mattress and disappeared. The snow murmured against the glass.

IV: Shell Into Snail

Rybka, you have to wake up.

She rubs her eyes with little pink fingers and turns away from me, towards the wall.

Rybka, I'm sorry, you have to wake up.

She yawns, stretches her legs, and wriggles sleepily towards the edge of the bed. I am waiting, kneeling on the floor with our copper kettle and a glass bowl. I am her mother, I understand the shock of waking, the water is always warm. She stares up through the window-glass at the stars like salt on the skin of a black fish as I pour it over her scalp, clear and clean. I comb it through every strand—her hair is so soft, like leaves. Afterwards, we lie together in the dark, my body curving around hers like a shell onto its snail, our wet hair curling slowly around each other. I sing her back to sleep, and my voice echoes off of the walls and windows, where there is frost and bare branches scraping:

Bayu, bayushki bayu
Ne lozhisya na krayu
Pridet serenkiy volchok
Y ukusit za bochek

Her hair is yellowy-brown under the wet, but damp enough to seem always black, like mine. Her eyes are so green it hurts, sometimes, to look at them, like looking at the sun. She swims very well for her age, and asks always to be taken to the mountains for the holidays. She is too little for coffee, but sneaks sips when I am not looking—she says it tastes like wet earth.

There is money for coffee, and kettles, and birds with browned, sizzling skin. We can see a bright silver scrap of the Neva through our windows, and the gold lights of the Liteyny Bridge. A woman who can set a bone is never hungry. I wash my hands more than anyone on my ward—twelve times a day I thrust my skin under water and breathe relief.

I taught her before she could read how to braid her hair very tightly. In the morning I will call her Sofiya and put a little red cup full of blueberries floating in cream in front of her, and she will tell me that after the kettle, she dreamed again of the man with the thin little beard and the big nose who sits on the side of a lake and shares his lunch with her. He has larch leaves in his lap, she will say, and he tells her she is pretty, and he calls her rybka, too. His beard prickles her cheek when he holds her. I will pull my coffee away from her creeping fingers and smile as well as I am able. She will eat her blueberries slowly, savoring them, removing the purple skin with her tongue before chewing the greenish fruit. I will draw us a bath.

But now, under the stars pricking the window-frost like sewing needles, I hold her against me, her wet eyelashes sticking together, her little breath quick and even. I decide I will take her to the mountains. I decide I will not.

Rybka, poor darling, I'm sorry, go back to sleep.

I wind her hair around my fingers; little drops like tears squeeze out, roll over my knuckles.

We are as happy as we may be, as happy as winters with ice on the stairs and coats which seem to always need patching and wet hair that freezes against our shoulders and the memory of still eyelids under water may leave us.

I am not tired yet.

THE OTHER AMAZON

——

Jenny Davidson

I like a bricks-and-mortar bookstore as much as the next person—don't even ask me how much I spent last week at Porter Square Books—but I've got an Amazon habit like you wouldn't believe. It's true that I've held out against the lure of one-click ordering. I even practice a stringent routine of self-editing: I fling things into the shopping cart, leave them there for a week or two and then go back and dump as many as I can ("save for later" the happy compromise between purchase and deletion) before taking the fatal step of typing in my password and navigating my way to further credit-card debt. At the end I almost always choose super-saver shipping. It makes me feel economical, and also my apartment is already so full of books that the extra waiting-time doesn't make much difference; two-day shipping gives my Protestant soul the burn of indulgence, while the overnight charges ruin all my pleasure in a package whose prompt arrival becomes the stomach-turning reproach to my own shameful extravagance.

There are exceptions, of course, books I want so badly that I'll pay any amount of money to get them in my hands as soon as I can. These painful precipitants of expensive longing include books released in the United Kingdom before they appear in the United States (if, that is, they are published here at all). International shipping charges are extortionate, but I simply *had* to have Kazuo Ishiguro's latest novel the instant it came out in England. Other Amazon UK sprees have included the intelligent and vaguely Joan Aikenesque romances of Victoria Clayton, who when she was a teenager in the early 1970s published two delightful children's books (*The Winter of Enchantment* and *The House Called Hadlows*) under her maiden name Victoria Walker, and new novels by Diana Wynne Jones and Eva Ibbotson, books which at once enchant and torment me by seeming always to be released months sooner on the other side of the Atlantic. It is both sinister and convenient, the way that as an American customer you don't even have to re-enter any of your information (passwords, payment details, shipping addresses) on the British site.

Online shopping finds its psychic home in the hours after midnight when you can't sleep and you're bouncing off the walls just desperate for something good to read. Not that you're not surrounded by books already, but it's like looking in the fridge when you're hungry late at night: you could perfectly well eat that strawberry yogurt (it's not even past its sell-by date!) or the grilled chicken breast left over from dinner but somehow all you can think about is the local sushi place which closed hours ago. Of course there is a certain masochistic fulfillment to sitting there at the computer and placing an Amazon order with money you don't have, it's a lot like smoking too many cigarettes or using a blunt pair of scissors to cut your bangs too short in the bathroom mirror, they are all activities whose allure swells with every hour past midnight.

So one night in early January (this is 2006 I'm talking about) I put a bunch of stuff in the shopping cart and paid for it all and then more or less forgot about it until the box showed up a week later. I retrieved it from the hallway, tucked it under my arm and let myself into the apartment. I dropped my bag on the floor, then slit the tape along the seam of the box with my keys and dealt with the annoying inflated plastic packing thingy (what is the name for those useless pouches?). Inside I found new translations of two major canonical Russian novels (presumably ordered in the grip of an attraction not nearly strong enough to survive the presence of their actual Oprah-sanctioned heft) and a just-released hardcover novel that seemed in contrast to be vibrating audibly with desirability.

After making the sound Homer Simpson makes when he sees a donut, I picked the book up in my left hand and started reading the first lines of the opening as I stumbled in the direction of the bathroom. I awkwardly used my right hand to unbutton my jeans and pull down my underpants to pee; I didn't want to put the book down even for a second.

Now, if you don't really care about books, you might want to skip the next part. What you've already read is mainly in aid of setting the scene of my compulsions, and so as long as you're obsessed with *something* (Nigella Lawson's chocolate-cake recipes, for instance, or baseball or knitting or whatever—the details are immaterial) you can probably identify with me. But the book I had in my hand that night in January was genuinely drool-worthy in a way that's difficult for me to get across to the non-avid-novel-reader. It was Michael Chabon's *The Yiddish Policemen's Union*, one of the most anticipated releases of 2006; I knew it was going to be magically good and it completely lived up to my expectations. I turned off my phone and lay down on my stomach on the bed and read like a maniac all the way through to the end. The only thing I wanted after that was to turn the clock back six hours and have the whole thing to read all over again.

A confession: for years I turned up my nose at Michael Chabon without having read him. Something about the eagerness, the love even, with which his fans spoke of his writing just annoyed me. (Mostly—I am perfectly willing to admit this, I am not a good person—out of irritation and envy at not being a critically-acclaimed and also best-selling novelist myself.) I did not see the movie adaptation of *Wonder Boys* , nor did I read the book; I did not care to read the irritatingly titled *Mysteries of Pittsburgh* and when I checked *The Amazing Adventures of Kavalier & Clay* out of the library I found the dust-jacket distinctly off-putting and returned it without having even cracked it open when it was recalled for another patron's use. And though I once accidentally claimed to have read Chabon's short-story collection *Werewolves in their Youth* during one of those drunken late-night bar conversations where you can hardly hear the other person speak over the jukebox, I realized the next day that the book I had read was actually Victor Pelevin's *A Werewolf Problem in Central Russia*.

But the one kind of book I love above all other things is young-adult fantasy and when Michael Chabon published a book called *Summerland* that could have been hand-crafted by highly skilled psychic artisans in exact response to my dream-book specifications, I picked it off the shelf at the store and paid for it and went home and read it at once. And it was a work of genius, a brilliant and beautifully written fiction for readers of all ages that I found more interesting and more pleasing and more complex and altogether more delightful than almost any other book I have ever read.

Summerland showed a close acquaintance with the D'Aulaires' *Norse Gods and Giants* , a book I renewed from the library every single week of third grade because I couldn't bear the idea of not having it in my possession. I loved everything about that book: the strange words, funny as well as ominous (Niflheim!); the rainbow bridge to Asgard (what can I say, I was an eight-year-old with a pair of X chromosomes and it is not surprising that I liked rainbows); the wolf Fenris (I spent many hours trying to figure out how and why Fenris also made an appearance in the Chronicles of Narnia, it was a fact no less mind-bending than the way that the characters in Madeleine L'Engle's books about the Austin family had somehow actually read her *Wrinkle in Time* series). In my favorite story, Thor bets he can drink more than any man in the hall of the Jotun Utgardsloki, but when he takes a deep draught (I loved the word "draught") from the drinking-horn he is surprised to find it almost as full as before; it turns out that the tip of the drinking-horn reaches down all the way into the sea. Thor has caused the oceans to ebb with his thirst. (The D'Aulaires' book has recently been re-released in the children's collection of the New York Review of Books, with a very good preface by Chabon himself.)

In short, I loved *Summerland* , I got all of Chabon's other books and read them and loved them also and he found a place on my list of most-favorite writers, people whose novels I buy in hardcover the instant they come out without carping about the cost. Thus *The Yiddish Policemen's Union* , just as entrancing as Chabon's earlier books and enticingly set in an alternate-history version of 1940s Alaska settled by Jewish refugees (in the world of the novel, there is no such place as Israel).

It wasn't until I was eating a late dinner (English-muffin pizza, something I learned to make as a small child in Montessori school and still fall back on when I'm low on groceries—if you keep them in the fridge, English muffins stay edible if not exactly fresh for an amazingly long time) that a certain uneasiness came over me.

Hadn't I read somewhere recently that the publication of Chabon's new novel had been delayed? He had announced on his website that the book had been rushed into the publishers' hands without sufficient time for editing, and though it meant canceling tour dates and pushing back the publication date from spring 2006 to winter 2007 he had decided to take more time for the good of the book. Which made tons of sense.

Yet this novel bore none of the signs of having been rushed into production. (If you want to know what some of those are, read Zadie Smith's *On Beauty*.) It was perfect in every respect.

I pushed away my plate—the food had somehow become cold and lumpy in my stomach, I didn't think I'd be able to swallow the rest of the second muffin half—and went to the computer to see what was up.

What was up was that the book I had just read did not exist.

It was still on the Amazon website with an April 2006 publication date, but this was January, not April, and even the April date had clearly been superseded, Chabon's author site made that very clear.

I had just read an imaginary book.

Was I hallucinating?

The book looked perfectly ordinary from the outside. It had blurbs from Philip Roth and Thomas Keneally and Michael Moorcock and a slightly over-the-top author photo covering the whole back cover. I opened to the title page and flipped it over.

Copyright © 2007.

It was only January 2006. You might get a book in December that had the next year's date on it, especially if you'd wangled an advance copy from the publicist. But no publisher would print books with the copyright dated a full year in advance.

The next day I went to the best independent bookstore in the area, where I was told that the novel's publication date had definitely been pushed back to 2007 and encouraged to purchase one of Chabon's existing novels in paperback.

For a day or two I felt pretty strange. But I soon decided to keep it to myself. If I was losing my mind, this was after all an exceptionally pleasant way to do so. And what I found over the next few months was that if I sat down at the computer in the right state of bleary-eyed mental receptivity, opening my mind up to what I most wanted to read in the world and sticking a book in the cart without looking too closely, I was sure to get something good.

In this way I obtained Jonathan Lethem's massive and totally heart-breaking novel about Stanley Kubrick and Neil Gaiman's hilarious and yet also outrageously moving tale about the Wild Boy of Aveyron (the cover had blurbs from J. M. Coetzee and Margaret Atwood and a sticker proclaiming it the winner of the Booker Prize for 2009) and Robin McKinley's sequel to the vampire novel *Sunshine*. (It wasn't a sequel, actually, more like a prequel about the heroine Rae's father set twenty-some years before *Sunshine* begins, bearing a roughly comparable relation to that book as *The Hero and the Crown* does to *The Blue Sword*, but it was absolutely delightful and I wasn't going to complain about it, was I?)

After a little while I realized it could work for dead authors as well as living ones. I got the last novel in Rebecca West's tetralogy, the series that begins with *The Fountain Overflows* (my favorite novel of all time) and continues through two—now three, I guess you'd have to say—posthumously published volumes. I got Byron's *Memoirs* , and they were even funnier and more amazing than his letters. I got a complete set of the works of Jane Austen in twenty-three volumes.

I am reclusive at the best of times, and also somewhat secretive, and though I couldn't explain it (well, if you've ever read a fairy tale, you can imagine what was going through my head) I had a feeling that the strange gift I had been given, my access to this other Amazon, could be taken away just as easily as it had been visited upon me. That exposing it to the cold light of reason—or to friends' skepticism and mockery—could do no good. Wary at first that the books I received from the other Amazon might be as addictive as the Turkish delight Edmund gets from the White Witch, moreover, I soon consoled myself with the thought that books from regular Amazon or from the library continued to captivate me as well. In other words, I was already addicted to reading.

Then my friend Leif came to town for a conference. (I had known him for some months before I realized his name was not Leaf, his fair hair should have tipped me off to his Scandinavian ancestry but he had misleadingly been brought up by hippies in a geodesic dome in the Pacific Northwest so it was a very natural mistake.) Leif had a hotel room for the first two nights of his trip, but he worked for a worthy non-profit that kept costs down wherever possible, in this case by expecting him to find his own lodging for the Saturday-night layover that would make his flight affordable.

As a compulsive reader and writer and all-round workaholic I generally avoid having visitors, but sometimes you can't say no. I inflated the Aerobed and put the sheets on with a familiar mixture of anticipation and bitterness, I liked Leif and I had stayed at his apartment in San Francisco for almost a week two summers ago but it nonetheless makes me slightly crazy to have visitors. The place gets all cluttered up (I am too lazy to deflate and reinflate the bed, for instance, so it gets propped up against the wall during the day, sheets and all) and it seriously cuts into my reading and writing time.

"What *is* this?" he said late Saturday night, plucking a book from the shelf and beginning to look through it. We had eaten Thai food and drunk a lot of beer and now we were finishing the last part of a bottle of Scotch that one of my students had given me the semester before. I had smoked three of his cigarettes and was not very happy about this tobacco recidivism.

I saw the volume in his hand and flinched. It was one of the Austen novels—I can't remember now which one—*Alice and Adela* , maybe, or possibly *Self-Possession* (my favorite, I think, out of the ones I hadn't read before).

He looked at me.

"What's going on?" he asked. "Should I know what this is?"

I had forgotten that Leif was a Janeite. In general he only read worthy books about the destruction of the environment and socialist politics and various kinds of injustice, but he had a passion for Austen's novels, indeed he read them all again every year and had a huge collection of Austen movie adaptations on DVD.

If I had remembered, I would have hidden the books in the back of a closet where he would never have seen them. It was too late for that now. Also I was drunk. Also it was a long time now of not having told anybody about this incredibly cool thing that was happening to me. It's like having an affair with a married man. At first it's exciting keeping it to yourself. Then it becomes burdensome. Finally you're basically dying for a chance to unload your story, and you just have to hope the floodgates open when you're in the company of someone trustworthy.

I explained it all to Leif in more or less the same way I've just explained it here, only more drunkenly. I was rather rambling and discursive and he several times had to bring me back to the point. We drank more whisky. Meanwhile he was getting more and more excited.

"Don't you see, though?" he said, getting up and starting to pace around the apartment.

I could see he was excited, but I couldn't see what about.

"You'll be able to do all sorts of things with this!"

"Like what?" I asked.

"You've got a *responsibility* ," he said. "You've got the ability to change history, in a roundabout way at least. You could order a book called, say, 'What Brought Bush Down.' Or 'Saving the Polar Ice-Caps.' Or 'The Triumph of Alternate Energy in the United States.' And the world would come into alignment with it, wouldn't it?"

I stopped and thought about this. I wasn't sure he was right—the idea that Neil Gaiman would win the Booker Prize in 2009 seemed more wish-fulfilling than likely, though of course the right committee might see why it was such a good idea—but on the other hand I could sort of see where Leif was coming from.

There was one obvious problem, though.

"I don't think you understand," I said. I was really pretty drunk at this point, so I wasn't at all ashamed. "I mean, I don't have the vaguest idea how this works, but one thing I know is that I have to really *want* the book."

"But how could you not want to read a book called 'The End of Republican Hegemony in the United States,' especially if it might have some predictive power?" Leif asked (you could see he meant every word of it, too).

I hated to pop the bubble, but it had to be done.

"Leif," I said.

"What?"

"What kinds of book do I like reading?"

He glanced along the shelves next to him. It wasn't really his kind of question. "Uh, novels?" he said.

"Novels. A lot of novels. Some literary biographies, and some popular science books. But almost entirely novels."

"But you could still get excited about the reversal of global warming, couldn't you?"

I was forced to confess that there was absolutely no chance of me mustering the level of excitement necessary to summon a book about the reversal of global warming from the other Amazon. (I didn't even want to read the ones they had at regular Amazon, for God's sake.)

When he finally got it, his face fell. Really, literally: the muscles got all droopy and sad.

"But there must be something you could get," he said, "something that would make a difference in the world."

"Like what?"

He cast about for a minute. Then he said the name of a well-known advocate of sociobiology, someone I have often described as the hatchet-man of evolutionary psychology (I could hardly stand to say his name, I disliked his opinions so much), someone I talk about obsessively (that's obsessive hatred, not obsessive love) to anyone who will listen.

"What about him?" I asked.

"Well, what if you got hold of his memoir and it was called something like 'How I Learned to Hate Evolutionary Psychology and Decided Women are Just As Good As Men and Subsequently Channeled My Energies into Explaining Why Nurture Often Trumps Nature, Thereby Persuading the Government to Put Vast Sums Into Public Education'. . . ."

"That's a pretty awful book title," I said, but I felt a twinge of curiosity. I also felt drunk, tired and nicotine-poisoned. I got up and poured the last of the whisky into my glass, topping it up with cold water from the tap. I didn't offer any to Leif.

"Well, you're the writer, you come up with something better. Don't lie to me, though; I know you want to read that book."

And we went into the other room and I sat down at the computer and Leif annoyingly hung over my shoulder giving me instructions I didn't need and five days later I received a package that when I opened it turned out to include the hatchet-man's recantation in the form of a memoir titled *Here I Stand* (an allusion, I thought, to a famous passage in the writings of Martin Luther). And I spent the evening reading it and it was pretty great and I put it down with a smile on my face (I completely agreed with everything he was saying, I especially liked the way he abased himself in his lavish repentance for that former identity as high-profile apologist for genetic determinism) and I went into the other room to check my e-mail.

One of my students had sent me a link to a news story. I clicked through to CNN.com and learned there that the hatchet-man had been hospitalized earlier that evening.

I told myself it was nothing to do with me.

But I couldn't sleep. I kept checking the news, and around 8:40 the next morning the AP said that the hatchet-man was dead of a cerebral aneurysm.

Had I done a violence to this man?

Over the next few days I became increasingly certain that my reading his words—or at least the words I had somehow caused to be printed with his name affixed to them—had actually killed the man. His brain must have rebelled, it seemed to me, at the incompatibility of his real-world beliefs and the ideas espoused in the book that had come into my possession.

When Leif asked me about it, I laughed off the story of the other Amazon and said pious words about the hatchet-man of late lamented memory (and I felt relatively untroubled doing it, a few years earlier *Time* had printed the hatchet-man's lavish and completely disingenuous eulogy for a man he was known to have considered the avatar of fuzzy thinking and wrong-headedness and so it was both [a] only fair and [b] common politeness). It was easy to persuade my friend that it had all been an elaborate hoax. In any case, Leif didn't really want his idea of Austen devastated by a larger canon. He didn't care about novels otherwise. Probably he was so drunk that night, it all seemed like a dream.

If you're expecting a Faustian twist at this point, a fit of repentance on my part or something like that, forget about it. The only difference now is that I pay off my credit card in full every month. This is possible because of a large infusion of cash that came my way when I was commissioned to write a book—this is no joke, the agent approached me a week or two later, we sent out my proposal a month afterwards and following a successful three-way auction I signed the contracts in September—critiquing the hatchet-man's writings and the whole school of evolutionary psychology.

The book's coming along well. I've been very careful so far not to plagiarize from the memoir, it doesn't seem fair, but I am certainly finding it an extremely helpful resource. $112.78 at the other Amazon is the exact same thing as $112.78 at the regular one, I have learned, except that I now own, among other things, a brand-new Penguin edition of *The Mystery of Edwin Drood*, Dickens' fourth-to-last novel and one of my favorites. People who call it a minor work have never read the amazing ending.

The conclusion turns out to be more or less totally sublime, Dickens does the whole divided self thing even better than Robert Louis Stevenson

(Jasper killed Drood while the opium fit was upon him, but lacking any memory of it became convinced of Neville's guilt—somehow Jasper's being in the grip of these uncontrollable desires and compulsions makes him perversely more sympathetic than any of the good guys). The real satisfaction, though, lies in seeing what happens with the minor characters. I have always been half in love with Mr. Sapsea and his wife's tombstone, with stone-working Durdles (he has "Tombatism" instead of rheumatism!) and his stone-throwing Deputy, and those stones and tombs lead directly to Jasper's exposure in the cathedral burial-ground. By the way, although there's something absurdly compelling about Dickens' awful heroines (I feel the psychological pull of that sort of heroinedom), surely in the end it's safer—more *permanent*—to play a minor role than a major one, to be the person whose modest action at the periphery of the drama tweaks a strand elsewhere so as to give the sense of an ending?

ORM THE BEAUTIFUL

Elizabeth Bear

Orm the Beautiful sang in his sleep, to his brothers and sisters, as the sea sings to itself. He would never die. But neither could he live much longer.

Dreaming on jewels, hearing their ancestor-song, he did not think that he would mind. The men were coming; Orm the Beautiful knew it with the wisdom of his bones. He thought he would not fight them. He thought he would close the mountain and let them scratch outside.

He would die there in the mother-cave, and so stay with the Chord. There was no one after him to take his place as warden, and Orm the Beautiful was old.

Because he was the last warden of the mother-cave, his hoard was enormous, chromatic in hue and harmony. There was jade and lapis—the bequests of Orm the Exquisite and Orm the Luminous, respectively—and chrysoprase and turquoise and the semiprecious feldspars. There were three cracked sections of an amethyst pipe as massive as a fallen tree, and Orm the Beautiful was careful never to breathe fire upon them; the stones would jaundice to smoke color in the heat.

He lay closest by the jagged heap of beryls—green as emerald, green as poison, green as grass—that were the mortal remains of his sister, Orm the Radiant. And just beyond her was the legacy of her mate, Orm the Magnificent, charcoal-and-silver labradorite overshot with an absinthe shimmer. The Magnificent's song, in death, was high and sweet, utterly at odds with the aged slithering hulk he had become before he changed.

Orm the Beautiful stretched his long neck among the glorious rubble of his kin and dozed to their songs. Soon he would be with them, returned to their harmony, their many-threaded round. Only his radiance illuminated them now. Only his eye remembered their sheen. And he too would lose the power to shine with more than reflected light before long, and all in the mother-cave would be dark and full of music.

He was pale, palest of his kin, blue-white as skimmed milk and just as translucent. The flash that ran across his scales when he crawled into the light, however, was spectral: green-electric and blue-actinic, and a vermilion so sharp it could burn an afterimage in a human eye.

It had been a long time since he climbed into the light. Perhaps he'd seal the cave now, to be ready.

Yes.

When he was done, he lay down among his treasures, his beloveds, under the mountain, and his thoughts were dragonish.

But when the men came they came not single spies but in battalions, with dragons of their own. Iron dragons, yellow metal monsters that creaked and hissed as they gnawed the rocks. And they brought, with the dragons, channeled fire.

There was a thump, a tremble, and sifting dust followed. Cold winter air trickling down the shaft woke Orm the Beautiful from his chorale slumber.

He blinked lambent eyes, raising his head from the petrified, singing flank of Orm the Perspicacious. He heard the crunch of stone like the splintering of masticated bones and cocked his head, his ears and tendrils straining forward.

And all the Chord sang astonishment and alarm.

It had happened to others. Slain, captured, taken. Broken apart and carried off, their memories and their dreams lost forever, their songs stripped to exiled fragments to adorn a wrist, a throat, a crown. But it had always been that men could be turned back with stone.

And now they were here at the mother-cave, and undaunted to find it sealed.

This would not do. This threatened them all.

Orm the Beautiful burst from the mountain wreathed in white-yellow flames. The yellow steel dragon was not too much larger than he. It blocked the tunnel mouth; its toothed hand raked and lifted shattered stone. Orm the Beautiful struck it with his claws extended, his wings snapping wide as he cleared the destroyed entrance to the mother-cave.

The cold cut through scale to bone. When fire did not jet from flaring nostrils, his breath swirled mist and froze to rime. Snow lay blackened on the mountainside, rutted and filthy. His wings, far whiter, caught chill carmine sparks from the sun. Fragile steel squealed and rent under his claws.

There was a man in the cage inside the mechanical dragon. He made terrible unharmonious noises as he burned. Orm the Beautiful seized him and ate him quickly, out of pity, head jerking like a stork snatching down a frog.

His throat distended, squeezed, smoothed, contracted. There was no time to eat the contraption, and metal could not suffer in the flames. Orm the Beautiful tore it in half, claw and claw, and soared between the discarded pieces.

Other men screamed and ran. Their machines were potent, but no iron could sting him. Neither their bullets nor the hammer-headed drill on the second steel dragon gave him pause. He stalked them, pounced, gorged on the snap-shaken dead.

He pursued the living as they fled, and what he reached he slew.

When he slithered down the ruined tunnel to the others, they were singing, gathered, worried. He settled among their entwined song, added his notes to the chords, offered harmony. Orm the Beautiful was old; what he brought to the song was rich and layered, subtle and soft.

They will come again, sang Orm the Radiant.

They have found the mother-cave, and they have machines to unearth us, like a badger from its sett, sang Orm the Terrible from his column of black and lavender jade.

We are not safe here anymore , sang Orm the Luminous. We will be scattered and lost. The song will end, will end.

His verse almost silenced them all. Their harmony guttered like a fire when the wind slicks across it, and for a moment Orm the Beautiful felt the quiet like a wire around his throat. It was broken by the discord of voices, a rising dissonance like a tuning orchestra, the Chord all frightened and in argument.

But Orm the Courtly raised her voice, and all listened. She was old in life and old in death, and wise beyond both in her singing. Let the warden decide.

Another agreed, another, voice after voice scaling into harmony.

And Orm the Beautiful sat back on his haunches, his tail flicked across his toes, his belly aching, and tried to pretend he had any idea at all how to protect the Chord from being unearthed and carted to the four corners of the world.

"I'll think about it when I've digested," he said, and lay down on his side with a sigh.

Around him the Chord sang agreement. They had not forgotten in death the essentialities of life.

With the men and their machines came memory. Orm the Beautiful, belly distended with iron and flesh, nevertheless slept with one eye open. His opalescence lit the mother-cave in hollow violets and crawling greens. The Chord sang around him, thinking while he dreamed. The dead did not rest, or dream.

They only sang and remembered.

The Chord was in harmony when he awoke. They had listened to his song while he slept, and while he stretched—sleek again, and the best part of a yard longer—he heard theirs as well, and learned from them what they had learned from his dinner.

More men would follow. The miners Orm the Beautiful had dined on knew they would not go unavenged. There would be more men, men like ants, with their weapons and their implements. And Orm the Beautiful was strong.

But he was old, and he was only one. And someone, surely, would soon recall that though steel had no power to harm Orm the Beautiful's race, knapped flint or obsidian could slice him opal hide from opal bone.

The mother-cave was full of the corpses of dragons, a chain of song and memory stretching aeons. The Chord was rich in voices.

Orm the Beautiful had no way to move them all.

Orm the Numinous, who was eldest, was chosen to speak the evil news they all knew already. You must give us away, Orm the Beautiful.

Dragons are not specifically disallowed in the airspace over Washington, D.C., but it must be said that Orm the Beautiful's presence there was heartily discouraged. Nevertheless, he persevered, holding his flame and the lash of his wings, and succeeded in landing on the National Mall without destroying any of the attacking aircraft.

He touched down lightly in a clear space before the National Museum of Natural History, a helicopter hovering over his head and blowing his tendrils this way and that. There were men all over the grass and pavements. They scattered, screaming, nigh-irresistible prey. Orm the Beautiful's tail-tip twitched with frustrated instinct, and he was obliged to stand on three legs and elaborately clean his off-side fore talons for several moments before he regained enough self-possession to settle his wings and ignore the scurrying morsels.

It was unlikely that he would set a conducive tone with the museum's staff by eating a few as a prelude to conversation.

He stood quietly, inspecting his talons foot by foot and, incidentally, admiring the flashes of color that struck off his milk-pale hide in the glaring sun. When he had been still five minutes, he looked up to find a ring of men surrounding him, males and a few females, with bright metal in their hands and flashing on the chests of uniforms that were a black-blue dark as sodalite.

"Hello," Orm the Beautiful said, in the language of his dinner, raising his voice to be heard over the clatter of the helicopter. "My name is Orm the Beautiful. I should like to speak to the curator, please."

The helicopter withdrew to circle, and the curator eventually produced was a female man. Orm the Beautiful wondered if that was due to some half-remembered legend about his folk's preferences. Sopranos, in particular, had been popular among his kin in the days when they associated more freely with men.

She minced from the white-columned entry, down broad shallow steps between exhibits of petrified wood, and paused beyond the barricade of yellow tape and wooden sawhorses the blue-uniformed men had strung around Orm the Beautiful.

He had greatly enjoyed watching them evacuate the Mall.

The curator wore a dull suit and shoes that clicked, and her hair was twisted back on her neck. Little stones glinted in her earlobes: diamonds, cold and common and without song.

"I'm Katherine Samson," she said, and hesitantly extended her tiny soft hand, half-retracted it, then doggedly thrust it forward again. "You wished to speak to me?"

"I am Orm the Beautiful," Orm the Beautiful replied, and laid a cautious talon-tip against her palm. "I am here to beg your aid."

She squinted up and he realized that the sun was behind him. If its own brilliance didn't blind her pale man's eyes, surely the light shattering on his scales would do the deed. He spread his wings to shade her, and the ring of blue-clad men flinched back as one—as if they were a Chord, though Orm the Beautiful knew they were not.

The curator, however, stood her ground.

His blue-white wings were translucent, and there was a hole in the leather of the left one, an ancient scar. It cast a ragged bright patch on the curator's shoe, but the shade covered her face, and she lowered her eye-shading hand.

"Thank you," she said. And then, contemplating him, she pushed the sawhorses apart. One of the blue men reached for her, but before he caught her arm, the curator was through the gap and standing in Orm the Beautiful's shadow, her head craned back, her hair pulling free around her temples in soft wisps that reminded Orm the Beautiful of Orm the Radiant's tawny tendrils. "You need my help? Uh, sir?"

Carefully, he lowered himself to his elbows, keeping the wings high. The curator was close enough to touch him now, and when he tilted his head to see her plainly, he found her staring up at him with the tip of her tongue protruding. He flicked his tongue in answer, tasting her scent.

She was frightened. But far more curious.

"Let me explain," he said. And told her about the mother-cave, and the precious bones of his Chord, and the men who had come to steal them. He told her that they were dead, but they remembered, and if they were torn apart, carted off, their song and their memories would be shattered.

"It would be the end of my culture," he said, and then he told her he was dying.

As he was speaking, his head had dipped lower, until he was almost murmuring in her ear. At some point, she'd laid one hand on his skull behind the horns and leaned close, and she seemed startled now to realize that she was touching him. She drew her hand back slowly, and stood staring at the tips of her fingers. "What is that singing?"

She heard it, then, the wreath of music that hung on him, thin and thready though it was in the absence of his Chord. That was well. "It is I."

"Do all—all your people—does that always happen?"

"I have no people," he said. "But yes. Even in death we sing. It is why the Chord must be kept together."

"So when you said it's only you . . . ."

"I am the last," said Orm the Beautiful.

She looked down, and he gave her time to think.

"It would be very expensive," she said, cautiously, rubbing the fingertips together as if they'd lost sensation. "We would have to move quickly, if poachers have already found your . . . mother-cave. And you're talking about a huge engineering problem, to move them without taking them apart. I don't know where the money would come from."

"If the expense were not at issue, would the museum accept the bequest?"

"Without a question." She touched his eye-ridge again, quickly, furtively. "Dragons," she said, and shook her head and breathed a laugh. "Dragons."

"Money is no object," he said. "Does your institution employ a solicitor?"

The document was two days in drafting. Orm the Beautiful spent the time fretting and fussed, though he kept his aspect as nearly serene as possible. Katherine—the curator—did not leave his side. Indeed, she brought him within the building—the tall doors and vast lobby could have accommodated a far larger dragon—and had a cot fetched so she could remain near. He could not stay in the lobby itself, because it was a point of man-pride that the museum was open every day, and free to all comers. But they cleared a small exhibit hall, and he stayed there in fair comfort, although silent and alone.

Outside, reporters and soldiers made camp, but within the halls of the Museum of Natural History, it was bright and still, except for the lonely shadow of Orm the Beautiful's song.

Already, he mourned his Chord. But if his sacrifice meant their salvation, it was a very small thing to give.

When the contracts were written, when the papers were signed, Katherine sat down on the edge of her cot and said, "The personal bequest," she began. "The one the Museum is meant to sell, to fund the retrieval of your Chord."

"Yes," Orm the Beautiful said.

"May I know what it is now, and where we may find it?"

"It is here before you," said Orm the Beautiful, and tore his heart from his breast with his claws.

He fell with a crash like a breaking bell, an avalanche of skim-milk-white opal threaded with azure and absinthe and vermilion flash. Chunks rolled against Katherine's legs, bruised her feet and ankles, broke some of her toes in her clicking shoes.

She was too stunned to feel pain. Through his solitary singing, Orm the Beautiful heard her refrain: "Oh, no, oh, no, oh, no."

Those who came to investigate the crash found Katherine Samson on her knees, hands raking the rubble. Salt water streaked opal powder white as bone dust down her cheeks. She kissed the broken rocks, and the blood on her fingertips was no brighter than the shocked veins of carnelian flash that shot through them.

Orm the Beautiful was broken up and sold, as he had arranged. The paperwork was quite unforgiving; dragons, it seems, may serve as their own attorneys with great dexterity.

The stones went for outrageous prices. When you wore them on your skin, you could hear the dragonsong. Institutions and the insanely wealthy fought over the relics. No price could ever be too high.

Katherine Samson was bequeathed a few chips for her own. She had them polished and drilled and threaded on a chain she wore about her throat, where her blood could warm them as they pressed upon her pulse. The mother-cave was located with the aid of Orm the Beautiful's maps and directions. Poachers were in the process of excavating it when the team from the Smithsonian arrived.

But the Museum had brought the National Guard. And the poachers were dealt with, though perhaps not with such finality as Orm the Beautiful might have wished.

Each and each, his Chord were brought back to the Museum.

Katherine, stumping on her walking cast, spent long hours in the exhibit hall. She hovered and guarded and warded, and stroked and petted and adjusted Orm the Beautiful's hoard like a nesting falcon turning her eggs. His song sustained her, his warm bones worn against her skin, his voice half-heard in her ear.

He was broken and scattered. He was not a part of his Chord. He was lost to them, as other dragons had been lost before, and as those others his song would eventually fail, and flicker, and go unremembered.

After a few months, she stopped weeping.

She also stopped eating, sleeping, dreaming.

Going home.

They came as stragglers, footsore and rain-draggled, noses peeled by the sun. They came alone, in party dresses, in business suits, in outrageously costly T-shirts and jeans. They came draped in opals and platinum, opals and gold. They came with the song of Orm the Beautiful warm against their skin.

They came to see the dragons, to hear their threaded music. When the Museum closed at night, they waited patiently by the steps until morning. They did not freeze. They did not starve.

Eventually, through the sheer wearing force of attrition, the passage of decades, the Museum accepted them. And there they worked, and lived, for all time.

And Orm the Beautiful?

He had been shattered. He died alone.

The Chord could not reclaim him. He was lost in the mortal warders, the warders who had been men.

But as he sang in their ears, so they recalled him, like a seashell remembers the sea.

AUTOMATIC

Erica L. Satifka

He rents his optic nerve to vacationers from Ganymede for forty skins a night. She finds him in the corner of the bar he goes to every night after work and stays in until it's time to go to work again, sucking on an electrical wire that stretches from the flaking wall.

"That's not going to kill you any more," she says.

He ignores her, grinding sheathed copper between brown-stained molars.

"My name is Linda Sue. I want to make babies with you."

"That rhymes," he says.

"Will you do it or not?"

"Or not."

Linda Sue stamps her foot. "Come on."

"I'll take you out first. Then we'll see." He takes her by the hand and leads her out of the bar, out into the heart of downtown New York City.

New York City, population three hundred and twenty.

He guides her to a restaurant he knows where the food is stacked in piles on hygienic white counters and the electricity works. She has two eyes and two hands and one set of lips, which means she is pretty. They each take a few slabs of food—the food here is free—and sit on the ground. He tells her about his life and her eyes open wide as headlights.

"I've never known anyone who had a job before."

"It's not a job. It's a career." He works at a factory, pouring liquid plastic into molds shaped like four-tined forks. "I have a quota to fill."

"Why don't you just ask the Ganys for plastic forks? Why does someone need so many plastic forks anyway" She tears off a corner of her foodslab; it comes off onto her fingers like cotton candy. Or insulation.

"They're not for me, they're for people."

"I don't have to work. I don't like to. I just ask the Ganys for everything. They like to give us stuff."

"Well, I don't ask them." He doesn't think about the creatures dancing spider-like on his nerve. "I'm self-sufficient."

"Are we going to fuck or what?"

"Later, later. If you're good."

In Central Park they walk past a rusted-over carousel. She's drunk from the amber-colored alcohol-infused drinkslab she's consumed, and he's propping her up, forcing her to walk straight.

"I think I'm in love with you," she slurs.

"You don't know what that word means."

They pass a pair of Ganys wrapped in the form of two wall-eyed Jamaican teenagers, humans whose bodies were either sacrificed to or commandeered by the intelligent energy beams. The girls giggle and point as they pass. He flips them off.

"That wasn't very nice."

"They patronize us. Don't you see how they patronize us? There's too many of them in this city. I want to get away from here, out into the country. Will you come with me?"

"Nobody lives in the country."

"Exactly." But he knows it is pointless; nobody lives in the country because there is no way to live in the country. The farms are all poisoned and the shadow of the plague still lingers. The Ganys, knowing this, constructed an invisible olfactory wall, to keep humans and germs from mingling.

He will never leave New York City. Always a hotel, never a tourist.

The story of the plague goes like this:

Once you could be certain that you would not spontaneously grow legs from your shoulder blades and arms from your buttocks. You could be reasonably sure that ears would not sprout on your cheeks overnight. Then the plague happened, and you couldn't take that for granted anymore.

Until the Ganys came.

They get back to the bar and she takes off her clothes. Her ribs stick out like a xylophone. The foodslabs keep them alive, but they aren't the right kind of nourishment. But you couldn't expect intelligent energy beams to understand food.

Linda Sue's body is fuzzy and indistinct, a peach-colored blur. His vision is cloudy from the tourists in his head. He crawls back to his corner.

"Aren't you going to fuck me now? Aren't you going to give me my babies?"

"No, I'm still not ready."

"Oh, screw you! You're crazy. Why don't you get the Ganys to fix that for you? They fixed it for me."

Now all you want to do is mate, he thinks. Not make love, you can't love anymore. Mate with the last members of your species so you can bring us back from the brink of extinction. That's all it is.

"I can't."

She shakes her head. "I'm leaving. I can find some other male to give me my babies. I don't need you." She slams the lockless door behind her. He hunkers down in the corner.

He awakes to unclouded vision. The vacationers checked out of his optic nerve as he slept. He rubs his empty eyes and stumbles to the corner market, where he throws down a few skins and picks up some foodslabs.

"You don't have to pay for those," the Gany monitoring the electricity says.

"Yes, I do."

It would be so easy, he thinks sometimes, to go down to the place where the Ganys congregate, the place where you can go rent your body for a day or a lifetime to their volunteers, and just turn yourself over. Shut off your brain for as long as you wanted, and you'd get a nice pile of goodies when your assignment was over. But he'd never done that. Renting his eyes was as far as he'd go. And even that was done not out of love for the aliens or the desire for material objects but the knowledge that, if he did not do it, he would be marked a traitor and slated for commandeering.

The Ganys have taken a special interest in humans. They had cordoned them off in cities with invisible olfactory walls, so that the remaining humans would be able to find one another more easily. And of course, they had brought The Cure. All of it was done for our—no, he thinks, their—own good.

He takes a dramatic bow, as if addressing a live audience. And in a way, he is.

He's leaving the city today. He crams a stack of foodslabs into a looted knapsack and heads north on foot. He walks until the sun is directly overhead and then stops by a river to eat.

The river is contaminated; he can smell the plague in it, festering. But there are drinkslabs in his pack, too. He tears off a few chunks of the tasteless foam and presses on.

A half hour later he is halted by a smell halfway between burning plastic and dog shit. I've reached it, he thinks. The wall between New York City and the rest of the world. He holds his breath and trudges through the wall, but it is no use. He can't hold his breath forever. His chest deflates and the putrescent odor fills his nose and lungs, as if the dog shit is being shoveled into his mouth by the handful. He gags, and vomits up a piece of semi-digested foodslab. Choking, he runs out of the wall, and takes a whiff of pure air.

He didn't even make it past the fifty yard line.

Plunging back in, he finds the smell has changed. Now it's the scent of burning tires. He moves to the right and hits a wall of solid rotting flowers. Moving forward, there is a stench like fish guts being baked in the sun. He stumbles backwards, and falls into the strong arms of a stranger.

"Hello there, little guy," a park ranger says. He looks into the ranger's crossed and clouded eyes. A Gany.

"I couldn't get past the wall," he says. His eyes are running with tears and there is vomit on his chin.

"You shouldn't be out here all alone." The ranger gestures at his vehicle. "C'mon, let me give you a ride back home."

He doesn't want to take charity from a Gany, but he doesn't like the prospect of walking three and a half hours either, especially since he still can't breathe in all the way and his stomach feels swollen and fluttery. He gets in the vehicle.

"You have a mate back at home?" Of course, that's the first thing the ranger would say.

"No."

"Human beings should be fruitful and multiply. It says so in your holy book." The Gany speaks with the friendly, homey Upper New York accent that was the ranger's voice when he was in control of the body, but he can sense the cold analytical tone of the intelligent energy beam guiding it.

He grunts and turns back to the window. Less than twenty minutes later the four-wheel-drive all-terrain vehicle pulls up in front of his bar. That fucking Gany read his mind.

"You be safe now, partner."

He slams the door.

In the apartment building across the street two humans are mating. For a moment, he wonders what it would be like to forget everything, become a creature of instinct, every moment of your life unscripted and so automatic.

Then he goes back into the bar.

CHEWING UP THE INNOCENT

———

Jay Lake

Ariadne's a beautiful kid, you know what I mean? The kind of child that people stop and look at when we walk down the street, her little hand in mine. The Daddy hand, the cross-the-street hand, the I'm-worried hand that drops away the moment there's a swing to be swung on or kids with jump ropes or chalk. Little fingers, not so little any more, but still they clutch at me with an echo of that infant monkey grip, don't-drop-me-from-this-tree-Daddy firm until she runs shrieking into her future.

And I don't mean beautiful-pretty, either. Though God knows she's cute enough. I mean charisma to turn your head and a thousand-watt personality that can hold a room full of people. It's not the RSO's on the county watch list I worry about. It's what will become of her. All that raw go-go in one little head and one little heart. And only six years old.

I've painted this kid half a hundred times, photographed her so much I've gone through two digital cameras. Elaine doesn't get it. "Quit screwing around with that stuff," she tells me.

"Look, the way the light falls on her face."

"So turn on the lamp."

"That's not what I mean, hon—"

"Come on. Pay attention." Then we're off in some half-hearted argument about the cats or her friend Lynette's divorce or who might have swiped the stone chicken out of the back garden and what the hell we could do about it anyway.

Until I'm down in the basement, developing black and white or sketching on sheets of foolscap taped to the walls. Ariadne, Ariadne, Ariadne. If I capture my daughter just right, maybe it will be okay to let her go.

I never did get the point of art jams, not for years. My buddy Russell finally pushed me into one, about a year after my first montage ran in Oregon Alive! "Get out there, Jim. Take some fucking board and a sack of markers and go down to Speed Racer's. It's cool, man, I mean, just fucking cool."

He's a hippie forty years out of time, Russell, with long hair and a taste for women's underwear—with or without the women still attached—and a sense of purpose when it comes to my life. His own, that's a different issue, but Russell ain't married with the most beautiful kid in the world looking him in the eye every day.

Russell's been kicking my tail since we were both in our twenties. I still remember sitting in a Denny's out on I-5 somewhere, on our way to some party down in Salem I'd probably forgotten about before I got home that night. "Look, man, you've got a hand a lot of artists would kill for. I've seen you whip off napkin sketches of the waitress that got our tab lost. Work."

I laughed over the ruins of my Grand Slam. "You're so full of shit, long-hair. Work, my ass. You wouldn't know the meaning of the word if I fed you the dictionary."

He got real serious for a moment. "I ain't got your hand, either, Jim."

"Fuck my hand. I got projects due." Marketing, bane of everyone's existence. Someone's got to write the scripts for those damned calls you get just when you're sitting down to dinner. That was—and is—me. "Hello, Mr. Smith, I'm calling about your long distance service."

If only we could wire our phones to your oven timers, John Q. Public, we'd have it fucking made.

So there went the party, and there went some years, and I won and lost a few girlfriends drawing good sketches of them. Some of those sketches a little too good. Elaine got interested after seeing me scribble on someone's kitchen cabinets with a charcoal briquette one boring Labor Day cookout.

She was pretty, petite, cuter than anyone I'd seen in a while. "So," this woman says to goofy me, "you draw anything besides roses?"

"Sometimes."

Smiles traded back and forth, and the long slide into marriage began. Who needs an art jam when you've got love at home?

Years come and years go, but children are forever.

"Daddy," she says to me one day. "I'm thinking about trees."

"Photosynthesis, baby. Big green air machines."

"You're weird, Daddy."

Or this one: "Daddy, how do I know what I see is real? I know the light hits my eyes and goes into my brain, but is that sidewalk really there? What about that dog?"

What the fuck do I look like, Socrates to her Plato? (See, a liberal arts education is good for something besides writing call scripts and training sales people.) Or maybe Aristotle to her Alexander. This kid's going to conquer the world some day. Who the hell wouldn't love her beyond reasonable measure?

My heart aches every time I see her. I don't ever want her to have what I had. Or didn't have.

Or whatever.

God damn it, I'm an artist, screw the words.

Times like this, I go off and draw dark things with claws and teeth and distant eyes and mommy breasts. Then, sometimes, I roll them up, take them out in the yard when Elaine's not around, and set them on fire.

But sometimes, sometimes, I sell them.

West Coast Design Review , last August issue. Fourteen hundred bucks for a illustration of my dreams of childhood. Lewis and Clark realized in a Geigeresque biomechanical mode, Sacajawea as a maternal ovoid.

Most people have to pay for their God damned therapy. I get paid to perform my own.

Paging Doctor Freud to the studio, there's an aesthetic emergency in progress.

Russell: "Draw more. Get out. Mix with the boyz and grrls."

Me: "I'm too old for this shit, got a kid to raise. Plus I got to run the early shift tomorrow since Shirl's out at her aunt's funeral."

Russell: "Jim, you're going to be middle-aged toast soon. You've got a gift. Fucking use it."

Elaine: "Family comes first."

Then I'm back in the basement drawing evil mommy eating her boy over and over again like some tragic Greek hero, and hiding the pictures from my wife until I can burn them.

Or send them out.

"Daddy, daddy, daddy, daddy, daddy, daddy, daddy, daddy, dad—"

"What!?"

"Look what I can do." And she spins a one-handed cartwheel across the basement tile.

For the love of God, I'd have to go to the hospital if I tried that. Hell, I couldn't do that when I was six. Walking in straight lines wasn't exactly a specialty of mine. Screw cartwheels.

"That's terrific, sweetie."

"Will you teach me to walk on my hands?"

"Uh . . ."

And she's off. The phone rings, upstairs calling. It's easier than shouting through the floorboards and scaring the cats. "Pay attention to her."

"I'm on deadline." A piece for Columbia River Review, Woody Guthrie dying on the cross with his guitar in the hands of a Roman soldier. Not big money, but a nice commission. Could be seen by the right people in Seattle, San Francisco. Could get some prints out of it. I'd been thinking about getting into prints. Russell's influence.

The exasperated sigh. The angry, ticking silence on the open line. The kid hurling herself against the basement door like some angry monomaniacal special ed student instead of the girl genius that she is.

"I'm busy . . ."

And then I was alone, shit-heel number one for a couple of days around our house.

So we were down at Speed Racer's. Everybody there who wasn't a drop-in is either too young, cool and good-looking for me, or they were long-established, settled into the scene. I felt like a cross between the new kid on the block and a dirty old man. I mean, I'm sorry, but twenty-some-things in black minis are just too hot for me.

Where the fuck have the years gone?

At least I managed to get off a few million phone calls along the way. I could have started this stuff in my twenties and saved myself a lot of trouble.

I would have left right then, but Russell had his fingers pressed hard into my elbow. He was wearing this sequined cocktail dress, which he actually looks pretty good in on account of his narrow ass and long legs, until you see the beard up front.

"You're sitting over here, Jim," he says, like I'm the tard.

Then somebody's shouting out themes and there's a fight between two Realists—I think, I never understood what they were screaming except that they both spoke shittier French than I do, merci beaucoup—and somebody was peeling off the biggest damned roll of butcher paper I've ever seen and the easels were out.

So I went deep. It was like surfing, finding that energy, riding that wave. Mommy's in the basement, chewing up the innocent, look out boy, she's gonna get you. Markers squeaking, memories squealing, spiders crawling out of their memory holes. After a while—a couple of hours maybe?—I look up from a place where my scalp's been tingling and my sweat's been pouring and I was shaking like I ain't done since I got over a bad case of being fifteen, and there were about eight people standing in a semicircle behind my chair.

Russell was just smiling, beer in his hand. The rest of them were . . . well . . .

I looked down at my drawing board and jumped out of my chair.

"Jesus," I said, "that thing would scare a priest."

Some sweet young thing in a black mini hugged me and whispered something in my ear I didn't catch. It was French, and I'm pretty sure so was her tongue. Then there was beer and someone taped my evil-Mommy into the middle of a kaleidoscope of politicians and helicopters and camels and we had a grand old party that went on way past my curfew.

On the way home, I wondered what the fuck had just happened to me.

Granddaddy was an old man when I met him. I think he was born old. He had that tough Texas soul that didn't give much of a shit for anything but Jesus, plowing the hard red dirt, and saving four percent down at the Piggly-Wiggly by arguing the night manager into the ground.

He loved me, I know that. I know that like I know the wind loves the Cascade forests. And his love brought lightning from heaven and seven kinds of hell if I lied about who ate the last Hydrox, and the metal end of the belt for being too noisy after seven o'clock. God is watching you, boy. God loves you, but He's got his eye on you.

Family comes first, boy. God took care of His boy, and I'm gonna take care of you the same way.

Family first.

"Daddy, Paulie showed me his penis." And she dissolved into giggles.

A moment of panic. Elaine and I had talked about this a lot—we communicated pretty good, except when it really counted. Mommy's in the basement, but Daddy's in charge upstairs. "Hey, kid, you know that's not talk we want to hear. His penis is private to him, and your vagina is private to you."

"Penis, penis, penis." Another one-handed cartwheel.

"Sweetie."

"Penis?"

Ignore, ignore, ignore. "Sweetie, if he does anything like that again, you need to tell me or Mommy right away."

"Silly Daddy, all the boys do it."

So I went and drew some more.

"You're spending too much time in the basement, Jim."

I shrugged. "Sorry." There was a picture nagging me, a bull mammoth striding down Grand Avenue, stomping the busses and cars into the pavement. But the vehicles would all be brass, or maybe copper, shiny in some weird way that I couldn't quite figure out yet.

"Is this important? You know I'm really proud of you, but you need to spend more time with us."

"Okay."

The next day, an hour of Lynette's divorce and what the first grade mothers were up to and when I tried to talk about the problems of rendering metallics, a blank stare.

We never talk about my work. My love. My fire.

That and we haven't had sex at all in eleven months. Not half a dozen times in two years or more.

But down at Speed Racer's, the girls like me. And they care about art.

"Family, boy," my grandfather says, stomping his way down Grand Avenue. He's tall as the Hawthorne Bridge's draw towers, and he's got that bulldog face I haven't seen above ground since 1973. I can see Dad in him, too, the two of them wrapped together in one giant male ancestor.

I must be dreaming, but I can't find my fingers for the proverbial pinch.

Where the hell was my family when I needed them? Where the hell were the holding hands, keeping me out of the street and free from worry, those long-ago years when the monsters in the basement had gotten real in the life of some kid with my name and face?

"Family, boy," my grandfather says again, and the sky shakes with his voice. His teeth are the hoods of Cadillacs, and the turbines of Bonneville Dam spin in his eyes.

When did Granddaddy become a force of nature, I wonder, as the winds blow me into dark, waiting mouths far below the pavement.

I won the Meadows Prize. The pre-eminent competition for early-career illustrators. Judged out of Omaha, Nebraska of all places. Russell had badgered me to enter it. Elaine had cheered me on. Ariadne just thought it was funny.

"We'll be expressing you the prize money," said a snippy-polite woman on the telephone. "I do hope you can make it out here to Omaha for the ceremonies."

"Yes, ma'am." Omaha, center of the nation's call center industry. What with my career in telemarketing, I'd been to Omaha a hundred times. Why couldn't they hold the damned awards in Hollywood or something?

"I'm so proud of you," Elaine had said.

"Daddy won an award surprise," Ariadne had said.

Smiling, we flew off to our eventual ruin.

Art jams. Shows. An early gallery date at a place just outside downtown Seattle. Did you have enough? Did you do enough? Russell, finally dropping away from pushing me because my momentum had gotten ahead of my inertia. Who needs fucking telemarketing anyway? Other than my mortgage holder, I mean.

And the commissions started coming in. People wanted to look at my pictures of the darkness.

I stopped burning my illustrations.

I started photographing, drawing, painting Ariadne more and more.

Elaine started complaining about the trips, the distraction, the ride.

But I kept getting the sweats and the tingles and that place inside me where light blazed up and cast a shadow on my drawing table until something burned into being. And sometimes that burned thing was good.

Every once in a while, it was damned good.

Who the fuck ever knew I could do this?

Eleven years of marriage and I had to go fall off a cliff over someone else. What the hell was wrong with me? Thirty years in his grave and Granddaddy is shouting even now.

I'd gone off to San Francisco for a big show on the strength of my Meadows win. My chance to be seen along with some of the great names in the illustration field. People whose work I'd been admiring since I was a kid.

Some of whom knew my name these days.

It was glorious. Tuxedos and two-hundred-dollar bottles of champagne and the art press from New York and L.A. and even Tokyo. I mean, SoHo this ain't, but there's layers and layers inside every world.

Who needs telemarketing?

The fire was hot inside me. The world loved me. And she came walking by.

I won't tell you who she is. An artist, like me. The rest of it's nobody's business but hers and mine. And we didn't get up to any business between us, not serious business at any rate. I know better.

Barely, at least on my end of the affair.

But I walked out with a flute of bubbly in my hand through a cascade of photo flashes into the Mission District night and wondered how the hell my heart had felt free to roam when my head knew far, far better.

It was a long drive back to Oregon. Lots of head time.

The fire burned in my head, in her eyes, in my hands trembling on the wheel as the miles clicked by and my thoughts spun.

I called Russell from the car somewhere up around Weed. The hour was very, very small. "I'm hosed, buddy."

He yawned. "Take a number, man. Aren't you up a little late?"

I'd thrown the champagne flute out the window a hundred miles ago, but my tongue was still loose. "I'm never going to sleep again. I don't want to dream."

"What happened? You get arrested or something?"

"I got success disease, Russell."

"Some people have all the luck. Go to sleep, man."

"Not at eighty miles an hour."

"Pull over. Call me tomorrow."

I got a room up at the state line, crashed out, didn't sleep ten minutes the whole night. Four hours later, avoiding Elaine, I called Russell again.

"I'm going to block your number, man, keep this shit up."

"Yeah, yeah." How many nights had we drunk away his gender issues? "Look, what's wrong with me?"

"For one, you make too fucking many phone calls."

"Seriously. Russell, dude, I got the fire. The fire's got me."

Russell knew from the fire. We'd talked about it enough. "Yeah . . . ?"

"I either got to dive all the way in or quit this stuff."

"Uh . . . yeah?"

"There's a girl, Russell."

"You didn't . . . did you?"

I hated the way his voice rose. Almost hopeful. "No," I snapped. "But I could have. And that scares me shitless."

"Um, man, look, this ain't exactly a surprise."

"It is to me."

"Not to some of us. You're going somewhere, man. This is your way of finally noticing it."

I hung up on him and got back out on the highway. Five more hours of blacktop should do me good.

Item: I live in a house where I can sit in none of the chairs. They are dainty and lovely and not for me.

Item: I live in a beautiful house.

Item: Elaine won't look at my work, or talk about it.

Item: I am well-loved.

Item: I am a fly trapped in tree sap, no longer happy to live in amber.

Item: I am well-loved.

Item: My life is on fire.

Item: I am well-loved.

Item: I can see those flames in her eyes.

Item: I have a child. But I married my mother.

Item: Family, boy. Family first, or you'll feel the metal end of my belt.

"So, how was your trip, Daddy?" Ariadne has her serious, I'm-talking-like-a-grown-up voice.

"Busy, sweetie."

The phone rings. Upstairs calling. There is strain in Elaine's voice, irritation barely concealed at my wandering ways. The art jams, the conferences, the shows. San Francisco. "Could you come up here, please, and talk to me."

The Mommy demons with their glittering teeth follow me everywhere now. I carry my basement in my head all the time, and my scalp prickles.

Speed Racer's was pretty quiet on Tuesday morning. I'd skipped out on a loyalty program meeting and two quarterly account reviews.

Like any of that stuff mattered.

Waiting for Russell, I suddenly realized I'd been happy being a marketing monkey all these years. Happy until I'd set fire to my life with art.

"Hey," he said. My buddy was wearing a pink Hello, Kitty! top with cupped sleeves and one bra strap showing. This over Bermuda shorts and a pair of Docs so clunky he could have gone stevedoring in them. In Omaha that outfit would have gotten him beaten, then arrested. In Portland no one noticed.

"Hey." I couldn't get much more than that out.

"How's the art fire?"

"Burning." I'd been doodling a chrome-steel breast on my napkin. The nipple had razor spikes barely sticking above the bumps. I pushed it over to him.

"You need a date, man."

"I'm leaving," I said.

"I just got here."

"No, no. I mean, I'm leaving Elaine."

"Oh."

There was a latte-punctuated silence that lasted quite a bit longer than our normal pauses. Finally he filled it. "Art or family, huh?"

"Art or family. There is middle ground, I guess. Nothing but compromises." I pushed my face into my hands, as if there were wisdom to be found at the junction between my knuckles and my cheekbones. Talking through my palms, I said, "Anything else will be endless negotiation. I've had years of practice stalling what I want and need."

"You've grown apart." I could hear the rustle of his shrug. "It happens."

My eyes stung. Thank God for concealing fingers. "Ariadne. It's Ariadne."

"You're not running out on your kid, man. You're running into the fire. She'll love you for it."

Someday.

Love yesterday, love tomorrow, love someday. But fire today.

"Come here, boy." Granddaddy always smelled of tobacco and sweat, and whatever that old man lotion is they sell down at the drugstore.

I sat on his lap. It was like climbing a polyester cliff face. Hands bigger than my head closed around my thin wrists.

"Family," he hissed hot in my ear, this man who'd been married to the same woman for going on fifty years and never called her by her first name. "Family always comes first."

You never knew the fire, Granddaddy. Or if you did, you walked away from it. And sir, with all respect to your seniority in the armies of the dead, I can't tell you which of those things might be the more sad.

There's never any reason to leave your family behind. When Mom and Dad did it to me and left me with him, I came to swear that I'd never do the same to any child of mine.

Especially that beautiful kid with her hand tucked between my fingers.

Now Daddy's in the basement, chewing up the innocent.

ATTAR OF ROSES

Sharon Mock

The shadow of my father's citadel falls over me and still I tremble. Still I look perpetually over my shoulder as though you follow me, you who are banished from this land forever. In my fever I think that it is you who dries the leaves on the trees, blows away the petals of the rose. But no, it is only autumn, nothing more.

My father will be heartbroken. And you, you cannot lend me words to explain what I have done.

They say that when I was born, blossoms spread on the rose bushes outside my mother's birthing chamber. They say that where I step, blood-red petals spring from the earth. The first, my father tells me, is a legend. The second has been known to happen on occasion, though only by my design.

I was born deep in the northern mountains, far from the great confederacies, where my father nurtured his magic without interference. His was the power of earth, roots of stone and springs of water. My gifts, on the other hand, were merely decorative—grace and beauty and youth forever born anew in spring. Sorcerers traveled from the tradelands to court me, Rosalaia, Blossom of the North. I would have none of them. My father sent them all away. Far better for me to grant my grace at my father's side, take my consorts from the young men of the city, make our land a well-defended paradise.

For centuries I believed that this was the life for which I was intended.

My father hated the west. Great sorcerers ruled great nations through conquest and slavery, not the treaties and alliances that governed our more civilized lands. He never spoke of the reasons for his enmity, so I assumed the lords had offended him in some way.

We could not afford to abolish all intercourse with the western nations. When caravans and emissaries arrived at our citadel, I was banished to my chambers, forbidden to set eyes on the barbarians. But I knew the secret passages of my father's citadel at least as well as he did, and when I tired of my ignorance I slipped out to catch sight of one of these westerners for myself.

I needed no lantern to navigate the darkness. I had played here often enough as a child, and used the passages when I wished to go down to the city, though my father would not have cared if I had left by the front door. As though by instinct I found myself at the ledge that overlooked the audience chamber.

The spyhole was camouflaged within the whorls of my father's throne, so I had a perfect view of the westerner. He had not the courtesy to clean himself before the audience. He wore traveling clothes dull with dirt, and his yellow-white hair clung to his narrow head. He spoke of grain monopolies in a tedious drone, and my father responded with far more courtesy than the man deserved.

Then, as my father consulted with his minister, the westerner's gaze came to rest on the throne. It was as though our eyes met, though reason said he could not see me. Still my heart rushed and pounded, my knees gave way, and I had to wait until my strength returned before I could retreat to my chambers again.

I should have known, even then. The citadel obeys my father's will. He could have kept me in my rooms, the very stones locking me away. Yet only now do I realize he cared not what I saw, as long as I remained unseen. All he wanted was to keep me hidden from you.

That winter a solitary emissary came to our citadel bearing a seeing-stone. When my father gazed into it, he saw a path of fresh green grass cutting through the snow, a constellation of southern armies set upon it.

You knew of my existence, the girl who made the roses bloom. Even in the civilized east, the Avenarch had many allies. You asked for my hand in marriage, and made certain my father could not refuse.

My father came to me with the terms you had set. His eyes were red, his face worn and polished as river stone. He had aged a hundred years since I had greeted him that morning. He lay the scroll in my lap and shook his head. "You don't have to do this, my daughter," he told me in a voice stung with grief.

I read over the scroll, the promises of extravagant dowry, and did not understand.

"You could flee. Across the ocean, where his agents . . . ."

"Why should I flee?"

"Look to the west, beyond the mountains. See the powers that lie in that accursed realm. Then you'll understand."

I did as my father bade. Shut my eyes, let my perception travel westward along root and bough, out of my father's holdings, through snowbound passes and wild forest. The sweet scent of loam and sap took on a cloying edge, the promise of rot. *Rosalaia.* The wind whispered my name like petals on silk. *Come to me. Let me look at you.*

Fear overcame my arrogance then, and I opened my eyes. The smell of dead roses clung to the back of my throat.

"It is a travesty," my father said. "I would not give you to him for all the world."

"Then why don't you send him away like the others?"

With trembling hands my father passed the seeing-stone to me. I saw, then, and knew what would happen if he refused you. Your eastern agents would kill him, claim our holdings and our powers for their own. Then— and here was a message intended not for my father but for me, and only having heard your whispered voice could I perceive it—then your agents would hunt me down and bring me back to you, to serve not as betrothed but as slave.

I looked up from the stone, into my father's face. "I will go to him." I kept my voice steady, full of solemnity and sorrow. Yet my heart leapt with exultation. Here was what I had been born for, here was the life that awaited me, rich and decadent, flowers twining in the bones of a corpse.

He shut his eyes, pressing back tears, valiant as stone. He handed me a golden locket, and out of respect I did not open it, as much as I desired to see your face. He turned from me, stopped at the doorway, hands grabbing the lintel. "He has outlived dozens of wives, my daughter," he said. "Do not think you'll be the exception."

On the day I was to leave my father's citadel, word came that you were dead. Another sorceress had slain your body, sundered your spirit, set herself up as queen in your place. My father wept for joy at the news. I did not weep, not in my father's presence, lest he perceive the nature of my tears.

I knew I should have been glad for my reprieve, for your love would have consumed and destroyed me. You never promised me anything different. But you had chosen me, plucked me from my father's vine, whispered to me secretly through those long nights. I slept with your locket under your pillow to dream of your fair face. With you gone, my purpose was gone as well.

Decades passed. The sorceress who had murdered you in turn let her own life be forfeit, gave the land over to men without magic. The new regime banished all sorcery, replaced true power with common machines. Many refused to deal with such barbarians, but my father had no such scruples. He was happy to trade with the west, now that my betrothed posed no threat.

The breach of my engagement changed me. I was no longer the first blush of spring but the decadence of midsummer, bees among the roses, fruit ripe on the vine. My step was heavy, and the scent of crushed petals lingered as I passed.

One midsummer there came another man from the west. He was nothing like you, a trader and a trader's son, not a thimbleful of power in him. Yet he was handsome enough, bright and cheerful. My every movement fascinated him. He was in love with magic, drunk on it, as only those born outside its grasp can be.

I let Parlan woo me, encouraged him with fair words and smiles, let my heart warm with the thought of his presence. He knew nothing of my true age or nature. Never did I speak of you to him. Enough that he knew I had been once betrothed, widowed before I wed. I could not tell him that my betrothed had died in his grandfather's day, that his homeland made a holiday of your annihilation.

When the time came for him to return to his homeland, he asked me to come away with him. I agreed, let him spirit me away in the night. I told myself I was lonely, too lonely to spare a thought for my father. My heart had been sworn to the west, I had to see for myself the fate I had escaped. I must have known I lied to myself, even then, but the truth was too shameful to admit.

Parlan promised me his hand in marriage. I knew the offer was empty, even if he did not. His family had power and standing; he'd not be allowed to marry a woman from the sorcerous East. But I said nothing, for I wished my lover to see me as less than what I was.

As soon as we approached within ten leagues of my lover's homeland I understood why he had fallen for me so. The air stunk of smoke and oil, and the sun's rays struggled weakly through the cloudless sky. Trees dropped leaves and branches, crops grew pale and lanky as though starved of energy. Animal carcasses littered the ditches, feeding unfamiliar and misshapen vermin. Of course, I thought. You had drawn your strength from the currents of nature, just like me. Your murder had turned this land against itself.

I did not know. I was still innocent. I had no way to see the truth.

At night I wept despite myself, wept at the thought of being trapped in this blighted land. I told Parlan it was homesickness. Close enough to the truth. I had lived too long in my father's artificial paradise. I'd grow accustomed to this place in time.

I never did meet the man who was supposed to become my father-in-law. Parlan set me up in an apartment in a fashionable district of the city and went to share the good news. He returned, predictably, in tears, one cheek red. "He won't hear of it. He says he'll disown me! Oh, Rosalaia, my only love, I will do right by you, I swear it, I'll find work, I'll—"

I placed my hand on his cheek to silence him, to guide his handsome face toward mine. "Hush," I said. "You will not lose me. You need not think of my honor. Don't you see, I gave it all up when I followed you?"

He wept and cursed, but in the end his courage did not match his intentions. His father set up a hasty marriage to a woman below his station, one who could not afford to dishonor even a loveless marriage of convenience. In exchange for this public show of respectability Parlan was allowed to keep me as his mistress. I cared nothing for my reputation, nor for the gifts my lover brought to assuage his guilt. It was a small price to pay for being here, in this hateful city that would have—should have—been our shared domain.

It was the cusp of autumn when the stranger came to my door. A woman as tall as a man, dressed in a plain gray suit, dark hair unfashionably short. Even for a westerner she kept close self-possession, so that I could not read the simplest thing about her. But I was not easy to intimidate, and I greeted her with an innocuous smile.

"You are Rosalaia?" the woman asked, her harsh intonation robbing my name of all poetry.

"I am. Have we been acquainted? For I fear—"

"We have not."

Surely she was an agent of my lover's father, come to send me home. I stood aside and let the woman enter. She stepped only far enough to allow the door to close, then looked me over with eyes of a blue so pale they might as well have had no color at all.

"Why are you here?" she asked me.

I cast my eyes downward. "I realize I have been too foolish and too forward," I murmured, my accent thicker than I usually allowed it. "Forgive me. I have been in love. Surely you must understand this."

I'd meant it as a stupid aside, the words of a coquette. Yet the woman stared, cold and sharp, as though I'd touched truth. It made no sense; this was not somebody to be made the fool by love.

"This isn't a place for you, princess. You should go home."

Princess? What had Parlan said about me? Didn't he understand the danger? "You mistake me—" I began.

"No. I do not." As she spoke she let her self-control loosen so that I might see what lay beneath. Energy, subdued, controlled. Iron and fire and human will, each in precisely measured components. The woman before me was a sorceress in her own right. And her skill and power put my own to shame.

I gave up playing at innocence. "I don't understand."

"There is a reason," she said, "why sorcery has been abolished in this land. You might believe it is to protect the powerless from those who would exploit them. But perhaps it is to protect the sorcerers from themselves. Go home, Rosalaia. You've seen what the Avenarch did to this land. There's nothing for you here."

I looked at her curiously. Did she know of my history? The sorceress who had overthrown the Avenarch was dead, executed under the new laws of this nation. But sorcerers are notoriously difficult to kill.

"And if I choose to stay?"

She shut her eyes, and when she opened them again, she no longer met my gaze. "Then I suppose I'll clean up after you when you're done."

The years in that blighted land passed long as centuries. I saw my lover more and more seldom, and out of respect for him I took no other man. He had given me what I wanted, and I had only myself to blame if I was dissatisfied with the results. The words of the western sorceress lingered in my mind. I could not say why her visit had aroused such fear. Yet I dared not indulge myself even with flowers in winter, lest I draw suspicion.

After several years my lover came to me, his eyes red with the tears that came so naturally to him. "My wife is with child," he told me.

I turned away. I knew he lied. He'd tired of the forbidden and exotic, that was all. To be thrown aside for a common woman stung my pride. But the poison of the land had taken hold of my veins, and I could not stir myself to anger.

"Go to her," I said. "She needs you now."

"Rosalaia," he gasped. "I'm so sorry—"

I had no doubt. Pity tempted me to turn and comfort him. He'd never been strong of will, even at his best. He'd be better off without me.

I was grateful to him, I realized, grateful even for the lie. He had set me free. My thoughts grew clear again, and I knew what I had come to this land to do.

Would you not think they would make the site of your downfall a monument, the spot where your blood soaked the soil a place of pilgrimage? They have not. Instead they have locked it away, set guards around the perimeter to keep your legacy inviolate.

I passed through like shadow, leaving behind nothing but the breath of roses. It is a crater now, where once stood your citadel. Somewhere there would have been your throne, and mine beside you. Somewhere there would have been your bedchamber, where we would have been made as one.

No animals moved across the barren ground. No night-hunting bird crossed the moon overhead. Yet the air was thick with the scent of grass and blossom, welcoming me.

I fell to my knees. The hardpan cracked and turned to loam under my hands. My fingers were roots prying through the soil, hungry for what little power you might have left for me. I breathed in deeply of the blood and rot that feeds the battlefield, coaxes brambles from the bones of the dead.

Finally you've come. I was starting to lose hope.

The plain grew gray and faded, and before me stood a being of light. It showed me the face I had seen in the locket, but it was only an image it wore, as I might put on an embroidered gown for company. This creature had never been human.

My father was so looking forward to meeting you. Rosalaia, mountain rose of the north. How precious you must be, to be kept so carefully hidden away from him. A foul wind stirred the hair at the nape of my neck like a caress.

There were things about sorcery I knew only from their absence. Books my father refused to read, lessons he refused to teach, tales he refused to share. I had no words for the being that stood before me, naked and glorious, skin bright as congealed starlight.

"What are you?" I breathed, tasting perfume at the roof of my mouth.

I am the Avenarch's only son. The only one that matters. He reached out to me, brought me to my feet. *Do you want to see?*

I did not. But the spirit left me no choice in the matter. It bent forward as though to kiss me, infusing me with its presence, and I saw what you had done. I heard the screams of children and tasted the tears of their mothers. Blood suffused my vision like a veil. How had I gone so long without knowing the power that lies in sacrifice? My father had kept that knowledge hidden from me. But you, you understood it better than anybody. Had you lived, you would have taught it to me. Fed our own children to your golden god, your most enduring creation, as you had for hundreds of years.

I would have learned. I would have been strong, endured what your other brides could not. I was worthy.

Shall we avenge him, mother, bride? I cannot do it on my own, he is torn from me, tossed across the sea, the sea separates us, shall not let us be again as one. But you are born to this, innocence and cruelty, petal and thorn.

It would have been different if you had asked. I could deny you nothing, I know that now. But this being before me was not human, and I had not fallen far enough to follow him.

The spirit's power entered me against my will. Branches ran like blood through my veins, thorns tore out of my flesh. Too late I understood the gray woman's warning. They had outlawed all sorcery in this land to keep this spirit asleep within the earth. And in my thwarted desire I had brought it back awake again.

A voice called my name, over and over, very far away. I did not recognize it. An endless waste of foul pleasure stretched between it and me.

The sky brightened, harsh and pitiless, like a break in the clouds of winter. I recognized, now, the voice of my lover—my true, human lover, not the beast that had tried to consume me. Still the spirit's presence smothered me. Black roses bloomed in my eyes, and I could not see.

"Help her," Parlan screamed, to whom or what I could not tell.

"I have." The other voice was cold and inhuman to my broken ears.

"Look at her, you can't—do something!"

The sound of flesh against flesh. A slap. " You did this. You brought her here, you—how could you have been so stupid?"

"I loved her. How was I supposed to know?"

In the silence wires grew like crystallized iron. The gray sorceress. She had judged me from the first, and I had met her every expectation.

"Why didn't you stop her?" Parlan asked, with more will than I had ever heard from him.

I felt the woman's anger in the silence. "It wasn't worth the scandal. I doubt she'd have survived if you hadn't gone after her."

Parlan took me in his arms. Roots tore from the ground, and I cried out in pain.

"Get her out of here," the sorceress said. "Take her back to her father. That's all that's left for her now." And with those words she banished me from your citadel forever.

———

I cannot return to my father. I cannot let him see my corruption. This much mercy I still have, though it tears at me to perceive it.

Grass dies where I walk. Still with each step roses bloom, petals red as the blood that thorns tear from hooves and feet.

My lover stays by my side and refuses to leave. In my strongest moments I tell him to return to his wife, but he will hear none of it. Once faithless, in my infirmity he finds an excuse for valor and for loyalty. I will break his heart, I will drink all that is good from him, and still he chooses to stay.

Near the border of my father's holdings we stop to rest. "I can't," I murmur. I rest my head against Parlan's chest, and he strokes my hair as though I am still beautiful. Does he not smell the stench of death that clings to me? Or am I still sweet to him, like roses on a funeral bed?

"What is it, love?" he asks me.

"I can't go back to my father. I don't want him to see me this way." I shiver. I am always shivering now.

"Where do you want to go? Anywhere, I'll take you, we'll find a way, just tell me."

"You should go home."

"I won't leave you, Rosalaia."

I know where I want to go. One gift that demon spirit has granted me. He's told me where to look.

My voice is sweet, pleading, and poor Parlan has no way to know my intent. "Away," I whimper. "Away from all of this, away—across the sea, as far as I can get."

"Of course," my lover says. Of course. He could say nothing but. I have no right to ask this of him. But then, I suppose it is his fault for choosing to stay.

I have always been like this, charming, manipulative, deceitful. Petal and thorn. I have always been the perfect consort for you.

CLOCKMAKER'S REQUIEM

Barth Anderson

Krina nudged her clock, and it crept up her long neck, closer to her ear, tiny claws tickling. "Left. Left again," it whispered. "Forward."

Behind Krina walked the confidante, a spider-limbed girl with lip rings to seal her mouth. She kept close to Krina, whose inventions always found the right way, no matter how the ziggurat changed, and the skirts of their cloaks stirred swirls of the maroon dust that seemed to gasp from the mortar and paving stones.

"The salon is located up there this afternoon," the clock whispered to Krina. "Up the Ascent."

Today the Avenue of Ascent was a vast flight of stairs beneath a sky of ceiling windows, and a regiment of urbanishment troops inclined upon the steps in a cove of sunlight, their stiff shirt collars sprung open like traps. Up and down the great flight, fruit sellers stacked their wares for climbers to buy, making the Avenue of Ascent a cascade of color. Blood-red loaves. Foreign lemons. Ripe, adorno pears. Pomelos.

Krina stopped and stared at the big orbs of yellow-green pomelos, considering. Instinctively, she touched the small, spiny back of her other clock, a lookout wrapped about her right thumb and the sibling to the one lit upon her neck. The lookout whispered the futures into her ear, when she raised her hand to her shoulder:

"People will all see the same time together, the apprentice will say to you, Krina. A tool, that apprentice will call the thing he's created. Stop him. Don't let him."

The confidante watched Krina staring at the stack of spongy pomelos, light fingertips resting on her lips as if the tight line of locking rings might not be enough to prevent her from cautioning her mistress from buying one.

The fruit-monger caressed the round brow of a pomelo, flicking dust from its green rind. "Fancying a sweet-tart, duchess?" he said from behind his bandana, which was wet and dusty at the mouth. To him, it was simply fruit. He had no idea what the pomelo meant in Krina's caste or he might not have said, "Only half a crona."

Shadows from a dove flock zigzagged up the Ascent, the moment passed, and Krina shook her head. Then she lifted the hem of her cloak and walked up the steps.

The apprentice will be safe, yes? said the confidante in handslang.

"We clockmakers are the engines of the ziggurat," said Krina, turning and climbing the stairs. "I'd save everyone if I did it now with his clocks unmade. Besides, why do you care?"

The confidante took Krina's left hand and pressed handsigns against Krina's palm in a series of pats, the equivalent of whispering to a hand-slanger. *Assassinating based on whispers from lookouts? Tragic.*

"You needn't scold." Krina snatched her hand back. "I didn't buy any."

Krina led the way, lookout hissing and slithering along her shoulder, and in their deep pockets, the confidante's hands said, *You are an ungrateful, rebellious confidante.*

With heavy, hand-hewn beams of brandy-colored wood overhead, buttery lantern light pooled on the floor, and the room smelled of wood fire, yam griddlecakes, and the scent of spilled wine turning to vinegar. The apprentice's workshop was a lovely corner of the salon, near what had once been Krina's own shop. The large coterie in attendance for the young man's debut drifted from the tables of clocks to the tables holding bottles of wine and back. There was an eagerness to become a throng. Krina accepted a drink from her confidante and they walked to the tables where his clocks were displayed.

"I *told* you. There they are. The beginning of the end," whispered the lookout with a nip at her ear, as Krina looked down the row of dally maple clocks.

The apprentice was a square-faced and sincere looking youth in old work boots who immediately stopped talking to his colleague and faced Krina when he saw her from the corner of his eye. Nearby, in the wide-open space of his workshop, drunker guests were flailing hilariously through an impromptu reel.

Krina, with the care of a gardener removing aphids from a favorite rose bush, brushed a fine file of the ubiquitous red dust from a nautilus curve in the clock's scrollwork. The clock lifted one paw to her gratefully, and she smiled down into its face, which, oddly, was merely a round disc with hashmarks and numbers as if to represent actual features that would be added later. "What kind of clock are you?" she said, lifting it. The clock's feet kicked and tail lashed as she turned it upside down. "Are you finished?"

The apprentice glanced at her wine-stained teeth. "It's just a protoytpe. But you've never seen a clock like this." He sounded chary, as if he expected a reprimand or contradiction.

The blank, featureless face shined at Krina like a little moon, and she thought of the ominous warning her lookout had whispered to her regarding this clock. "No, never. Tell me about it."

Many high-heels clopped on the tiles, and a wine-soaked nonet struck up a song that was either a reel or a staggering waltz. "It's not like the clocks you made, Krina," he said over a burst of laughter from the dancers. "You can tell time by this clock."

The room was warm with so many bodies, which she hoped would hide the rise of angry color to her cheeks. "Rather presumptuous. Me telling the clock time?"

"It's meant for people to use. I have to figure out a way to make many of them, for many, many people." The apprentice stammered when he saw her wince at his words, but soldiered on with his explanation. "Think of it as a tool."

The lookout on her shoulder murmured and growled.

"A tool?" It looked wrong to her, the apprentice's faceless clock, like a fish walking upright in grass and sun. "A tool to do what?"

"To," he hesitated, as if searching for words that wouldn't offend her, "to measure time as a people, to bring people together. So people will all see the same time. Right now everyone makes clocks to create whatever time they want. But this—it's—it tells a time that everyone can agree on."

"That's the idea," said a passing livery officer with a firm, manly nod to the apprentice. "Quantify it. Time shouldn't be subjective. We should have one time. I've always thought that." With two glasses of wine held high, he meant to keep walking but stopped. "How does that clock work?"

"We know when and where we are with this clock. Always. But I'm still combing out snarls," he said, shaking his head at the clock. "It needs little hands. Maybe chimes to tell us a common time."

"Now your clock is telling *us* time?" Katrina chided. "I thought we were telling it time."

"Well, *I'll* look forward to seeing your clock when it's finished, and so will my company," the livery officer said. "This mad place needs all the help we can get."

From the cowl of Krina's cloak, the little lookout hissed, "See? What did I tell you?"

"We don't need it," Krina said to the officer's back, as he took his wine away. "Farmers have roosters, and bread bakers know the rhythm of a rise in their stiff wrist bones. No one wants these clocks of yours, because everyone here prizes the license to do as we will. This? This is not our way."

"Not yet," the apprentice said, grinning from Krina to her confidante.

Putting her hands in her pockets, the confidante lowered her gaze, sipping wine through a straw, as if the apprentice's grin were a gift she couldn't accept here.

Ah, there it is, Krina thought watching the young man.

His clock shifted its feet, jostling the other clocks on the table, who hissed and spat at the eyeless thing. Why would anyone, she wondered, tolerate being told that one's time was the same as everyone else's—no worse, no different, no more painful, no more beautiful, fortuitous, or grand? In a place where time has reshaped the very architecture, what effect would such a clock have? One of the other clocks took a swipe at the blind clock, which recoiled, unable to defend itself. "We have a responsibility to keep time, yes, but we must keep it well. Vibrant and strong. It's just cruel," she said, "creating something with a face and no eyes."

She lifted her gaze from the crippled clock to see if her words had reached him, and the apprentice nodded slowly to her, perhaps already building another clock in his mind. "Send me your next," she said, "as soon as you've built it."

"Oh, I plan to," the apprentice said, and for the first time, there was a note of challenge, even threat in his voice.

Krina donned her cloak, and, as she pulled up her hood, she whispered to her confidante, "Go back and buy three pomelos from the fruit-monger, please."

The confidante shut her eyes as tightly as her mouth and, when Krina turned her back, handslanged, *Oh, I plan to.*

Dusk threw shadows across the chamber but Krina didn't light any lamps or candles. She liked the violet calm of early evening, so she stood in the center of her black brocade rug and felt the darkness deepen while her brother's friends fell into an ode for strings and percussion. She didn't want the wags here tonight, but she could retreat to her apartments if they grew tiresome.

"What's wrong, Krina?" her brother, Lemet, asked after bobbing his head to the music for some time. "You're being particularly ominous tonight."

Cellos and drums rolled and tolled. "I'm afraid of what that new apprentice at the salon will do with his clock," Krina said.

Lemet was a clockmaker, too, had the same broad, strong hands as Krina. He patted his knees in time to the drums and said, "What do you mean? What's to fear?"

"His clocks will kill our clocks, the ziggurat," Krina said.

"You're paranoid."

"My lookout told me," she said. "I'm very serious. My confidante is stacking three pomelos in the apprentice's doorway, as we speak."

Lemet turned the corners of his mouth down as if to say that was a judicious move on his sister's part.

"Oh?" A cellist smirked in appreciation, fingers fretting near his pierced ear. "Is someone about to come down with offcough? The blackspot. Do you use a poisonist, Krina?"

"We pay our dues and use the Method, like everyone in this room," her brother said in calm reprimand, not appreciating the insinuation that Krina was hiring mercenaries. To Krina, he said sotto voce, "Why the Method? You have clocks that could undo the apprentice, right? Use them. Eclipse him."

"Too many people actually want his damn clock. You should have seen the crowd around his salon table."

Lemet showed his sister that he was annoyed with her seriousness by turning his attention back to the musicians.

"It's like the ziggurat has a death wish," she said to his profile.

"Such fascism," said a violinist. "Who would want a clock that *unifies* time?"

Keeping the measure with just a tad more emphasis until the violinist looked at him, the drummer said, "Oh, yes, who would want a unified time?"

Now the musicians were annoying him, which seemed to annoy Lemet further. "Music, yes. But not all of life. That's so beyond boring, and it's beneath us—it's below our—it's—"

"Yes, there are no words," said Krina, appreciating her brother's stammer. She stood and looked down at a wide esplanade near the lagoon below. Drifts of maroon dust were splayed across the cobblestone concourse, and young boys in great cloaks and kerchiefs over their faces were attempting to sweep the fine powder into pails. Futile work. The very mortar of the ziggurat gasped silt into the air. "This dust."

A bassoon moaned across the cellos and bass drum.

In birdskin slippers, Krina's feet slid across the floor into her own apartments, away from her brother and his revelers. They would go all night, and she wasn't in the mood to join them. As she shut the door on the boom of a throaty cello, the first clock she had ever built, with intricate, interlocking pinewood scales leaned kindly against her ankle. Seizing the clock by its fat, solid coils, she looked into its eyes of agate.

Immediately, a strange emotion came over Krina and she brought the clock close, embracing it. Though she stood in the center of a darkening room, she was overcome with an emotion she'd never felt before, a feeling that rays of setting sunlight descending through pipe smoke would one day elicit. She'd built this clock to impart the sense of a time yet to be. She could smell sweet tobacco, years of resin in a beloved pipe that would trigger the lonely sadness. She could actually see the sight of warm, orange light sloping through layers of smoke. Why a pipe, or this time of day, and what as yet unmet lover would she identify with this light?

She let the clock slide out of her arms onto the rug and watched it sidewind beneath a wooden secretary as two smaller, very sturdy clocks galloped into the room, their little hooves thumping the floor, but they were more interested in nipping at one another, and so chased away into the bedroom, kicking a rug across the floor as they ran. Following them, rapt, briefly interested in their cavorting, timeless sense of time, Krina started from an applause of wooden wings. She stepped forward, suddenly, stamping her foot hard to keep her balance, as a heavy, graven thing dropped upon her shoulder. Its digging talons grabbed her and grabbed again, as it settled in place next to her right ear. She turned and looked into the clock's pure-gold eyes. "Give me your time, love," she whispered to it.

Swaths of purple light on the divan and armoire blanched to silver-blue as moonlight replaced dusk, and the murmur of squadrons on the steps became the chatter of bats and swallows.

Krina went to her balcony and looked out at the Ascent. Everyone in the ziggurat enjoyed the feeling of their times growing strange and familiar and strange again, rewinding their clocks and hauling the sun back into the sky, or reverting the ziggurat back into old neighborhoods long ago rearranged by the advance of many, many other times, and remaking of church towers and wide green spaces into clusters of childhood homes so that the lonely song of a piano could play up the alley like wind, as once it did.

From here she could see whole neighborhoods tinged maroon, and the light seemed rusty from dust. *The ziggurat is already dying,* she thought, watching streets sidewind like her pinewood clock. *It won't be able to defend itself from this new kind of time.* For through her clock's eyes, she could also see the world as the apprentice would make it, staring blankly back at her from the streets of the refashioned ziggurat, streets preordained and measured like those hashmarks on the betrayer's clocks once and for all time.

The clock gave a birdlike turn of its head and, on oak talons, sidestepped away from her cheek: Unclench, clench; unclench, clench. Looking back, it said, "We clocks will become rulers."

"Rulers?" cooed Krina at her clock.

"Not just devices of measurement, but despots. The future is in order now."

"No, the future is in doubt, I've made sure of that," Krina said in cold return. "The Method and I will sing a requiem in blackpost shortly."

She looked out on the vista of the ziggurat's urbanishment, as if from away and above—a rare sight and one that only this clock afforded her. A continent raised and floating with a ziggurat built upon its widest salt flat, this landmass's stratified bedrock stood upon thin air, rivers spilling into gulfs of nothing. "You'll have your confidante mark the apprentice?" the clock said. "A stack of pomelos for the Method to find its sacrifice?"

"Snuff the bonfire while it's still just a lit match," Krina answered.

"You can't assassinate every young innovator. And you can't urbanish the ziggurat from reality forever," her clock said. "It's dying, disintegrating."

"I know." From here she could see the ziggurat's soaring aqueducts vanishing into the gasping, rust-colored cloud that enshrouded the city. The urbanishment was a clockmaker's dream—literally—and clockmakers like Krina believed they would dream the ziggurat and its continent aloft, unmake, and remake it forever. She said as in a breathless prayer, "But there's no other way but our way."

"Apparently," said the clock before soaring off, "there's at least one other."

In the street below two fish sellers hailed each other, and Krina backed away from the balcony in a shuffling step, as if beginning a quiet parlor-dance, but then purple shadows engulfed her into a black, unfeeling fugue, swallowing her away into a strange room, into a bed, laying her down beneath velvet duvets. The room's darkness was so black she couldn't see walls but believed this might well be her own bedroom. Time was a surprising lover—this wasn't unusual, to find one's self whisked away in the passionate embrace of another's time. She closed her eyes and waited for clarity, listening to the sound of rapid dripping in the dark, a sound like water wanting to be a stream.

"How do you know?" said a disembodied whisper.

Krina lay still, steeped in her fear. She opened her eyes slowly, as if her eyelids parting would make too much noise. But her eyes were useless, and her gaze slid across the impenetrable dark.

Then there was another sound, a sound like skin sliding on skin. A patting, caressing noise. Someone else was in the room, too.

"Yes, but there's no way to know if she has it, yet," said the whisperer.

Has it? Krina wondered. *What do I have that they want? They mean to steal something from me?*

Pat. Pat. Press. Pat.

Perhaps these thieves didn't even know she was here, but, in the dark stillness, Krina wondered if she could get to one of her clocks. If she could call the walkaway or her farfar, she could pull up the stitches of this time, but she couldn't raise her hand to call for her clocks. Her arms felt foreign, heavy. What was wrong? Even her mind, she realized, was a swaying, lumbering thing, unable to pounce and seize on simple facts. Who was in this room? Was this even her room? What could they want to steal? More pressing and patting, like a pair of soft hands clapping very quietly in the darkness, and through it, over it, suffusing the room, was that mechanical, trickling sound.

"Look at that. A dart?" The voice was male. Young.

A dart? The Method has been here, she thought. But for whom? Who was this? Krina felt so warm, dizzyingly warm, and her throat was dry as sand. Had she met this young man at a party? She tried to recall the voice, but like her gaze flitting across the dark, her mind couldn't connect thoughts. Krina almost felt she should know that caressing skin-on-skin, hand-on-hand noise, too, but her lugubrious mind pondered over it in stupid wonder. She'd been at a party earlier. Two of them.

Press. Pat. Caress. Pat.

"She has it," the young man said, no longer whispering, "The whole ziggurat will know soon."

Feet shuffled in the dark, retreating into a space, a chamber beyond, then someone came close to Krina. She stiffened in terror, sightless eyes skimming across the black before her. She couldn't even raise a hand to defend herself, as she sensed the nearness of someone, felt the heat of a body, and smelling the very faintest smell of fruit. Of citrus.

Scent of a pomelo delicate, yet distinct, stacked somewhere in this room, Krina guessed.

Someone marked *me*? Krina thought. But I thought I'd marked someone else. Who was that that I had marked?

A hand scooped under her elbow, lifting it slightly. Another hand pressed itself into her palm, making warm shapes there, a series of symbols made with thin fingers. Handslang.

Your clocks died surprisingly fast. In sympathy. Sorry. Your brother is gone now. Sorry. I brought the pomelos in from your doorstep.

Her confidante retreated from the bedside and dissolved into the somewhere beyond this space that was filled with fear, fever, and her heavy indolent thoughts. Sleep came and went in slow blinks of consciousness, and the circling of this hatching plot was maddening, like a lantern-and-shadow show that had been scrambled and shuffled into nonsense. Finally, deep, orange light broke the darkness, and Krina could see her own arms now, the intricate constellations of fine, black bursts in her skin, and she was so weak that she could barely think what this disease was called. Black. Black something. Someone was here with her, in this strange room, sitting in a chair. A man. His work boots creaked in the quiet, and the rocking chair answered offbeat. She could see his silhouette against a window of bright, rancid light filtering through dust outside, and light knifed through curls of pipe smoke overhead. Her beloved clocks were gone? Blackspot. That was it. Lemet, too? The salon? Where was she? Where was her home? Was this even the ziggurat? Perhaps she had been stolen and secreted away as part of an insurrection, and the urbanishment was at an end. She could smell sweet tobacco in a leather pouch nearby and felt grateful for the lonely smell of it. Feeling oddly nostalgic for pipe smoke (hadn't she only ever smelled this tobacco while holding the fat coils of her clock, peering into this very future?), Krina turned to look for the man's pipe on the nightstand, but saw instead the faceless clock squatting there, staring at her in dumb sightlessness and tap, tap, tap, tapping out its hateful, perfect measures.

SOMETHING IN THE MERMAID WAY

─────

Carrie Laben

As fall crept on and the storms got worse, the supply of monkeys ran low.

At first, we actually prospered, because we were able to use the monkeys that the other shops could not. The best monkeys for making into mermaids, by most standards, were the suckling young—their skins were pliant and they were of a size that matched well with many common fish. But my mother, in her youth, had developed a process that let her shrink the larger monkey skins—even the full-grown monkeys who often died in defense of their young and whose rough pelts the hunters would part with for small coins—down to an appropriate size, without drying them out too much to work with.

Thus we had survived ten years ago when the monkeys had been exterminated from Isla Scimmia, turning the name into a cruel joke that outlanders used to taunt the inhabitants for our dark coloring and the heavy hair on our arms. More than half of the families who made mermaids then had since left the island altogether, some for Rome, some for the New World or parts still more exotic. One notable family, a husband and wife and five daughters ranging from a twenty-five-year-old spinster to a toddling child, had all drunk arsenic.

Mother was disgusted. She'd held the family in high regard before; along with her own, they'd been among the few original mermaid-making families to survive when the mermaids themselves went away, to weather the early storm of competition from Fiji, to cope with the way the fish seemed to shrink every year and the fickleness of the sailors who were always looking for some new novelty. The eldest daughter had been her particular friend.

But these days, according to Mother, everyone was a degenerate. She announced it loudly as she ducked into the workshop, shaking the rain out of her loose dark hair. "Degenerates! Think they can sell me stinking half-rotten monkeys for twice, three times the usual price. They'd try to sell a shell to an oyster and ask for pearls in payment."

She held two packages—by the smell of them I could tell that she'd managed to find a few acceptable monkeys. She almost always did, even when Annagrazia and I came home empty-handed. I took one of the packets, wrapped in coarse oiled cloth, and untied the ends to reveal one of the small grey North African monkeys.

"You got the good kind," Annagrazia said, unwrapping the other bundle and laying it on the table beside her knives.

"Too big," Mother said, and fished out a packet of glass eyes from the pocket of her cloak. "It will take days to shrink them properly." The shrinking process was Mother's pride and our salvation, and she hated it—it was long, tedious, it produced smells that gave her headaches. To hear her talk she'd as soon never do it again. But she laughed at the women who came to try to buy the secret from her.

Annagrazia picked up her knife and tried the blade carefully against the inside of a coarse-haired leg. The lower half of the monkey would be discarded, of course, but there was no need to cut it to ribbons—the fur could still be used to line boots or collars. "I like these grey ones though. They look the most like real mermaids."

"Like those white-eyed idiots at the docks would know a real mermaid from a hole in the fence."

"I don't care if they know. I know." She slid the knife along the inside of the leg, skirted the groin, and split the belly. I thought for a moment that she had cut too deep and the rotting intestines would spill, but the knife glided along and left the muscles in place. "Which reminds me. Did you get brown eyes?"

"Blue eyes. The sailors like blue."

"There never was a mermaid with blue eyes," Annagrazia said, as she had so many times before.

"There never was a mermaid that was actually half monkey and half salmon either."

When Annagrazia finished skinning the monkey, I took the body away to clean and bone and see if any meat could be salvaged.

Just before the storms finally broke, I noticed that Annagrazia was looking pale and sick. The quality of her work was falling off a bit too—

not enough that I could see it, but enough that she cursed and wept at her tools before Mother patted her hand and told her it was good enough, it would still sell.

Annagrazia threw her needle across the workshop and ran to the kitchen.

Three days later, Mother sent me to the apothecary for pennyroyal.

"You've left it too late," she was scolding when I got back.

"I haven't. I had an idea. I can make a mermaid that looks real, Mama, when you see . . . "

"And your plan required fucking some sailor boy from the docks?"

"A man from one of the island families would have been better, but it makes no nevermind. Our blood is thick. Anyway, my stupid sailor boy was able to give me some brown glass eyes."

"You and those eyes!" I thought for a moment that Mother might slap her. But Mother never slapped Annagrazia. She shook her head and snatched the pennyroyal from me and went for the kettle.

The baby slipped out in a mess of bloody unnamable fluid, and never drew a breath before it was out of the world. Tradition called those babies the happy ones.

"Let me hold it," Annagrazia said, and I placed it in her arms. "There, look. The hair is so fine on the arms, and the eyes are brown."

Mother smiled. "You're right. Our blood is strong. No sailor boy in that."

Annagrazia reached for the knife she'd kept by the bedside in readiness.

When the mermaid was finished, it was indeed perfect.

"The spitting image of my grandmother," Mother said triumphantly. "This is the finest mermaid that has ever come out of any shop on this island since our ancestors died out. The price we can put on this—we could fool a ship's doctor with it."

"We can't sell it," Annagrazia said. "It's too perfect. This is the best thing I will ever do. I will keep it."

Then Mother did raise her hand to slap her, but Annagrazia was holding her skinning knife and they stood staring at each other for a long time.

"I will keep this one," Annagrazia said with a smile, "but I can make more."

THE THIRD BEAR

Jeff VanderMeer

It made its home in the deep forest near the village of Grommin, and all anyone ever saw of it, before the end, would be hard eyes and the dark barrel of its muzzle. The smell of piss and blood and shit and bubbles of saliva and half-eaten food. The villagers called it the Third Bear because they had killed two bears already that year. But, near the end, no one really thought of it as a bear, even though the name had stuck, changed by repetition and fear and slurring through blood-filled mouths to *Theeber*. Sometimes it even sounded like "seether" or "seabird."

The Third Bear came to the forest in mid-summer, and soon most anyone who used the forest trail, day or night, disappeared, carried off to the creature's lair. By the time even large convoys had traveled through, they would discover two or three of their number missing. A straggling horseman, his mount cantering along, just bloodstains and bits of skin sticking to the saddle. A cobbler gone but for a shredded, bloodied hat. A few of the richest villagers hired mercenaries as guards, but when even the strongest men died, silent and alone, the convoys dried up.

The village elder, a man named Horley, held a meeting to decide what to do. It was the end of summer by then. The meeting house had a chill to it, a stench of thick earth with a trace of blood and sweat curling through it. All five hundred villagers came to the meeting, from the few remaining merchants to the poorest beggar. Grommin had always been hard scrabble and tough winters, but it was also two hundred years old. It had survived the wars of barons and of kings, been razed twice, only to return.

"I can't bring my goods to market," one farmer said, rising in shadow from beneath the thatch. "I can't be sure I want to send my daughter to the pen to milk the goats."

Horley laughed, said, "It's worse than that. We can't bring in food from the other side. Not for sure. Not without losing men."

Horley had a sudden vision from months ahead, of winter, of ice gravelly with frozen blood. It made him shudder.

"What about those of us who live outside the village?" another farmer asked. "We need the pasture for grazing, but we have no protection."

Horley understood the problem; he had been one of those farmers, once. The village had a wall of thick logs surrounding it, to a height of ten feet. No real defense against an army, but more than enough to keep the wolves out. Beyond that perimeter lived the farmers and the hunters and the outcasts who could not work among others.

"You may have to pretend it is a time of war and live in the village and go out with a guard," Horley said. "We have plenty of able-bodied men, still."

"Is it the witch woman doing this?" Clem the blacksmith asked.

"No," Horley said. "I don't think it's the witch woman."

What Clem and some of the others thought of as a "witch woman," Horley thought of as a crazy person who knew some herbal remedies and lived in the woods because the villagers had driven her there, blaming her for an outbreak of sickness the year before.

"Why did it come?" a woman asked. "Why us?"

No one could answer, least of all Horley. As Horley stared at all of those hopeful, scared, troubled faces, he realized that not all of them yet knew they were stuck in a nightmare.

Clem was the village's strongest man, and after the meeting he volunteered to fight the beast. He had arms like most people's thighs. His skin was tough from years of being exposed to flame. With his full black beard he almost looked like a bear himself.

"I'll go, and I'll go willingly," he told Horley. "I've not met the beast I couldn't best. I'll squeeze the 'a' out of him." And he laughed, for he had a passable sense of humor, although most chose to ignore it.

Horley looked into Clem's eyes and could not see even a speck of fear there. This worried Horley.

"Be careful, Clem," Horley said. And, in a whisper, as he hugged the man: "Instruct your son in anything he might need to know, before you leave. Make sure your wife has what she needs, too."

———

Fitted in chain mail, leathers, and a metal helmet, carrying an old sword some knight had once left in Grommin by mistake, Clem set forth in search of the Third Bear. The entire village came out to see him go. Clem was laughing and raising his sword and this lifted the spirits of those who saw him. Soon, everyone was celebrating as if the Third Bear had already been killed or defeated.

"Fools," Horley's wife Rebecca said as they watched the celebration with their two young sons.

Rebecca was younger than Horley by ten years and had come from a village far beyond the forest. Horley's first wife had died from a sickness that left red marks all over her body.

"Perhaps, but it's the happiest anyone's been for a month," Horley said. "Let them have these moments."

"All I can think of is that he's taking one of our best horses out into danger," Rebecca said.

"Would you rather he took a nag?" Horley said, but absent-mindedly. His thoughts were elsewhere.

The vision of winter would not leave him. Each time, it came back to Horley with greater strength, until he had trouble seeing the summer all around him.

Clem left the path almost immediately, wandered through the underbrush to the heart of the forest, where the trees grew so black and thick that the only glimmer of light came from the reflection of water on leaves. The smell in that place carried a hint of offal.

Clem had spent so much time beating things into shape that he had not developed a sense of fear, for he had never been beaten. But the smell in his nostrils did make him uneasy.

He wandered for some time in the deep growth, where the soft loam of moss muffled the sound of his passage. It became difficult to judge direction and distance. The unease became a knot in his chest as he clutched his sword ever tighter. He had killed many bears in his time, this was true, but he had never had to hunt a man-eater.

Eventually, in his circling, meandering trek, Clem came upon a hill with a cave inside. From within the cave, a green flame flickered. It beckoned like a lithe but crooked finger.

A lesser man might have turned back, but not Clem. He didn't have the sense to turn back.

Inside the cave, he found the Third Bear. Behind the Third Bear, arranged around the walls of the cave, it had displayed the heads of its victims. The heads had been painstakingly painted and mounted on stands. They were all in various stages of rot.

Many bodies lay stacked neatly in the back of the cave. All of them had been defiled in some way. Some of them had been mutilated. The wavery green light came from a candle the Third Bear had placed behind the bodies, to display its handiwork. The smell of blood was so thick that Clem had to put a hand over his mouth.

As Clem took it all in, the methodical nature of it, the fact that the Third Bear had not eaten any of its victims, he found something inside of him tearing and then breaking.

"I . . . " he said, and looked into the terrible eyes of the Third Bear. "I . . . ."

Almost sadly, with a kind of ritual grace, the Third Bear pried Clem's sword from his fist, placed the weapon on a ledge, and then came back to stare at Clem once more.

Clem stood there, frozen, as the Third Bear disemboweled him.

The next day, Clem was found at the edge of the village, blood soaked and shit-spattered, legs gnawed away, but alive enough for awhile to, in shuddering lurches, tell those who found him what he had seen, just not coherent enough to tell them *where*.

Later, Horley would wish that he hadn't told them anything.

There was nothing left but fear in Clem's eyes by the time Horley questioned him. Horley didn't remember any of Clem's answers, had to be retold them later. He was trying to reconcile himself to looking *down* to stare into Clem's eyes.

"I'm cold, Horley," Clem said. "I can't feel anything. Is winter coming?"

"Should we bring his wife and son?" the farmer who had found Clem asked Horley at one point.

Horley just stared at him, aghast.

———

They buried Clem in the old graveyard, but the next week the Third Bear dug him up and stole his head. Apparently, the Third Bear had no use for heroes, except, possibly, as a pattern of heads.

Horley tried to keep the grave robbery and what Clem had said a secret, but it leaked out anyway. By the time most villagers of Grommin learned about it, the details had become more monstrous than anything in real life. Some said Clem had been kept alive for a week in the bear's lair, while it ate away at him. Others said Clem had had his spine ripped out of his body while he was still breathing. A few even said Clem had been buried alive by mistake and the Third Bear had heard him writhing in the dirt and come for him.

But one thing Horley knew that trumped every tall tale spreading through Grommin: the Third Bear hadn't had to keep Clem alive. *Theeber* hadn't had to place Clem, still breathing, at the edge of the village.

So *Seether* wasn't just a bear.

In the next week, four more people were killed, one on the outskirts of the village. Several villagers had risked leaving, and some of them had even made it through. But fear kept most of them in Grommin, locked into a kind of desperate fatalism or optimism that made their eyes hollow as they stared into some unknowable distance. Horley did his best to keep morale up, but even he experienced a sense of sinking.

"Is there more I can do?" he asked his wife in bed at night.

"Nothing," she said. "You are doing everything you can do."

"Should we just leave?"

"Where would we go? What would we do?"

Few who left ever returned with stories of success, it was true. There was war and plague and a thousand more dangers out there beyond the forest. They'd as likely become slaves or servants or simply die, one by one, out in the wider world.

Eventually, though, Horley sent a messenger to that wider world, to a far-distant baron to whom they paid fealty and a yearly amount of goods.

The messenger never came back. Nor did the baron send any men.

Horley spent many nights awake, wondering if the messenger had gotten through and the baron just didn't care, or if Seether had killed the messenger.

"Maybe winter will bring good news," Rebecca said.

Over time, Grommin sent four or five of its strongest and most clever men and women to fight the Third Bear. Horley objected to this waste, but the villagers insisted that something must be done before winter, and those who went were unable to grasp the terrible velocity of the situation. For Horley, it seemed merely a form of taking one's own life, but his objections were overruled by the majority.

They never learned what happened to these people, but Horley saw them in his nightmares.

One, before the end, said to the Third Bear, "If you could see the children in the village, you would stop."

Another said, before fear clotted her windpipe, "We will give you all the food you need."

A third, even as he watched his intestines slide out of his body, said, "Surely there is something we can do to appease you?"

In Horley's dreams, the Third Bear said nothing. Its conversation was through its work, and Seether said what it wanted to say very eloquently in that regard.

By now, fall had descended on Grommin. The wind had become unpredictable and the leaves of trees had begun to yellow. A far-off burning smell laced the air. The farmers had begun to prepare for winter, laying in hay and slaughtering and smoking hogs and goats. Horley became more involved in these preparations than usual, driven by his vision of the coming winter. People noted the haste, the urgency, so unnatural in Horley, and to his dismay it sometimes made them panic rather than work harder.

With his wife's help, Horley convinced the farmers to contribute to a communal smoke house in the village. Ham, sausage, dried vegetables, onions, potatoes—they stored it all in Grommin now. Most of the outlying farmers realized that their future depended on the survival of the village.

122

Sometimes, when they opened the gates to let in another farmer and his mule-drawn cart of supplies, Horley would walk out a ways and stare into the forest. It seemed more unknowable than ever, gaunt and dark, as if diminished by the change of seasons.

Somewhere out there the Third Bear waited for them.

One day, the crisp cold of coming winter a lingering promise, Horley and several of the men from Grommin went looking for a farmer who had not come to the village for a month. The farmer's name was John and he had a wife, five children, and three men who worked for him. John's holdings were the largest outside the village, but he had been suffering because he could not bring his extra goods to market.

The farm was a half-hour's walk from Grommin. The whole way, Horley could feel a hurt in his chest, a kind of stab of premonition. Those with him held pitchforks and hammers and old spears, much of it as rust-colored as the leaves now strewn across the path.

They could smell the disaster before they saw it. It coated the air like oil.

On the outskirts of John's farm, they found three mule-pulled carts laden with food and supplies. Horley had never seen so much blood. It had pooled and thickened to cover a spreading area several feet in every direction. The mules had had their throats torn out and then they had been disemboweled. Their organs had been torn out and thrown onto the ground, as if Seether had been searching for something. Their eyes had been plucked from their sockets almost as an afterthought.

John—they thought it was John—sat in the front of the lead cart. The wheels of the cart were greased with blood. The head was missing, as was much of the meat from the body cavity. The hands still held the reins. The same was true for the other two carts. Three dead men holding reins to dead mules. Two dead men in the back of the carts. All five missing their heads. All five eviscerated.

One of Horley's protectors vomited into the grass. Another began to weep. "Jesus save us," a third man said, and kept saying it for many hours.

Horley found himself curiously unmoved. His hand and heart were steady.

He noted the brutal humor that had moved the Third Bear to carefully replace the reins in the men's hands. He noted the wild, savage abandon that had preceded that action. He noted, grimly, that most of the supplies in the carts had been ruined by the wealth of blood that covered them. But, for the most part, the idea of winter had so captured him that whatever came to him moment-by-moment could not compare to the crystalline nightmare of that interior vision.

Horley wondered if his was a form of madness as well.

"This is not the worst," he said to his men. "Not by far."

At the farm itself, they found the rest of the men and what was left of John's wife, but that is not what Horley had meant.

At this point, Horley felt he should go himself to find the Third Bear. It wasn't bravery that made him put on the leather jerkin and the metal shin guards. It wasn't from any sense of hope that he picked up the spear and put Clem's helmet on his head.

His wife found him there, ready to walk out the door of their home.

"You wouldn't come back," she told him.

"Better," he said. "Still."

"You're more important to us alive. Stronger men than you have tried to kill it."

"I must do something," Horley said. "Winter will be here soon and things will get worse."

"Then do something," Rebecca said, taking the spear from his hand. "But do something *else*."

The villagers of Grommin met the next day. There was less talking this time. As Horley looked out over them, he thought some of them seemed resigned, almost as if the Third Bear were a plague or some other force that could not be controlled or stopped by the hand of Man. In the days that followed, there would be a frenzy of action: traps set, torches lit, poisoned meat left in the forest, but none of it came to anything.

One old woman kept muttering about fate and the will of God.

"John was a good man," Horley told them. "He did not deserve his death. But I was there—I saw his wounds. He died from an animal attack. It may be a clever animal. It may be very clever. But it is still an animal.

We should not fear it the way we fear it." Horley said this, even though he did not believe it.

"You should consult with the witch in the woods," Clem's son said.

Clem's son was a huge man of twenty years, and his word held weight, given the bravery of his father. Several people began to nod in agreement.

"Yes," said one. "Go to the witch. She might know what to do."

The witch in the woods is just a poor, addled woman, Horley thought, but could not say it.

"Just two months ago," Horley reminded them, "you were saying she might have made this happen."

"And if so, what of it? If she caused it, she can undo it. If not, perhaps she can help us."

This from one of the farmers displaced from outside the walls. Word of John's fate had spread quickly, and less than a handful of the bravest or most foolhardy had kept to their farms.

Rancor spread amongst the gathered villagers. Some wanted to take a party of men out to the witch, wherever she might live, and kill her. Others thought this folly—what if the Third Bear found them first?

Finally, Horley raised his hands to silence them.

"Enough! If you want me to go to the witch in the woods, I will go to her."

The relief on their faces, as he looked out at them—the relief that it was he who would take the risk and not them—it was like a balm that cleansed their worries, if only for the moment. Some fools were even smiling.

Later, Horley lay in bed with his wife. He held her tight, taking comfort in the warmth of her body.

"What can I do? What can I do, Rebecca? I'm scared."

"I know. I know you are. Do you think I'm not scared as well? But neither of us can show it or they will panic, and once they panic, Grommin is lost."

"But what do I do?"

"Go see the witch woman, my love. If you go to her, it will make them calmer. And you can tell them whatever you like about what she says."

"If the Third Bear doesn't kill me before I can find her."

If she isn't already dead.

In the deep woods, in a silence so profound that the ringing in his ears had become the roar of a river, Horley looked for the witch woman. He knew that she had been exiled to the southern part of the forest, and so he had started there and worked his way toward the center. What he was looking for, he did not know. A cottage? A tent? What he would do when he found her, Horley didn't know either. His spear, his incomplete armor—these things would not protect him if she truly was a witch.

He tried to keep the vision of the terrible winter in his head as he walked, because concentrating on that more distant fear removed the current fear.

"If not for me, the Third Bear might not be here," Horley had said to Rebecca before he left. It was Horley who had stopped them from burning the witch, had insisted only on exile.

"That's nonsense," Rebecca had replied. "Remember that she's just an old woman, living in the woods. Remember that she can do you no real harm."

It had been as if she'd read his thoughts. But now, breathing in the thick air of the forest, Horley felt less sure about the witch woman. It was true there had been sickness in the village until they had cast her out.

Horley tried to focus on the spring of loam beneath his boots, the clean, dark smell of bark and earth and air. After a time, he crossed a dirt-choked stream. As if this served as a dividing line, the forest became yet darker. The sounds of wrens and finches died away. Above, he could see the distant dark shapes of hawks in the treetops, and patches of light shining down that almost looked more like bog or marsh water, so disoriented had he become.

It was in this deep forest, that he found a door.

Horley had stopped to catch his breath after cresting a slight incline. Hands on his thighs, he looked up and there it stood: a door. In the middle of the forest. It was made of old oak and overgrown with moss and mushrooms, and yet it seemed to flicker like glass. A kind of light or brightness hurtled through the ground, through the dead leaves and worms and beetles, around the door. It was a subtle thing, and Horley half thought he was imagining it at first.

He straightened up, grip tightening on his spear.

The door stood by itself. Nothing human-made surrounded it, not even the slightest ruin of a wall.

Horley walked closer. The knob was made of brass or some other yellowing metal. He walked around the door. It stood firmly wedged into the ground. The back of the door was the same as the front.

Horley knew that if this was the entrance to the old woman's home, then she was indeed a witch. His hand remained steady, but his heart quickened and he thought furiously of winter, of icicles and bitter cold and snow falling slowly forever.

For several minutes, he circled the door, deciding what to do. For a minute more, he stood in front of the door, pondering.

A door always needs opening, he thought, finally.

He grasped the knob, and pushed—and the door opened.

Some events have their own sense of time and their own logic. Horley knew this just from the change of seasons every year. He knew this from the growing of the crops and the birthing of children. He knew it from the forest itself, and the cycles it went through that often seemed incomprehensible and yet had their own pattern, their own calendar. From the first thawed trickle of stream water in the spring to the last hopping frog in the fall, the world held a thousand mysteries. No man could hope to know the truth of them all.

When the door opened and he stood in a room very much like the room one might find in a woodman's cottage, with a fireplace and a rug and a shelf and pots and pans on the wood walls, and a rocking chair—when this happened, Horley decided in the time it took him to blink twice that he had no need for the *why* of it or the *how* of it, even. And this was, he realized later, the only reason he kept his wits about him.

The witch woman sat in the rocking chair. She looked older than Horley remembered, as if much more than a year had passed since he had last seen her. Seeming made of ash and soot, her black dress lay flat against her sagging skin. She was blind, eye sockets bare, but her wrinkled face strained to look at him anyway.

There was a buzzing sound.

"I remember you," she said. Her voice was croak and whisper both.

Her arms were mottled with age spots, her hands so thin and cruel-looking that they could have been talons. She gripped the arms of the rocking chair as if holding onto the world.

There was a buzzing sound. It came, Horley finally realized, from a halo of black hornets that circled the old woman's head, their wings beating so fast they could hardly be seen.

"Are you Hasghat, who used to live in Grommin?" Horley asked.

"I remember you," the witch woman said again.

"I am the elder of the village of Grommin."

The woman spat to the side. "Those that threw poor Hasghat out."

"They would have done much worse if I'd let them."

"They'd have burned me if they could. And all I knew then were a few charms, a few herbs. Just because I wasn't one of them. Just because I'd seen a bit of the world."

Hasghat was staring right at him and Horley knew that, eyes or no eyes, she could see him.

"It was wrong," Horley said.

"It was wrong," she said. "I had nothing to do with the sickness. Sickness comes from animals, from people's clothes. It clings to them and spreads through them."

"And yet you are a witch?"

Hasghat laughed, although it ended with coughing. "Because I have a hidden room? Because my door stands by itself?"

Horley grew impatient.

"Would you help us if you could? Would you help us if we let you return to the village?"

Hasghat straightened up in the chair and the halo of hornets disintegrated, then reformed. The wood in the fireplace popped and crackled. Horley felt a chill in the air.

"Help you? Return to the village?" She spoke as if chewing, her tongue a fat gray grub.

"A creature is attacking and killing us."

Hasghat laughed. When she laughed, Horley could see a strange double image in her face, a younger woman beneath the older.

"Is that so? What kind of creature?"

"We call it the Third Bear. I do not believe it is really a bear."

Hasghat doubled over in mirth. "Not really a bear? A bear that is not a bear?"

"We cannot seem to kill it. We thought that you might know how to defeat it."

"It stays to the forest," the witch woman said. "It stays to the forest and it is a bear but not a bear. It kills your people when they use the forest paths. It kills your people in the farms. It even sneaks into your grave-yards and takes the heads of your dead. You are full of fear and panic. You cannot kill it, but it keeps murdering you in the most terrible of ways."

And that was winter, coming from her dry, stained lips.

"Do you know of it then?" Horley asked, his heart fast now from hope not fear.

"Ah yes, I know it," Hasghat said, nodding. "I know the Third Bear, *Theeber, Seether*. After all I brought it here."

The spear moved in Horley's hand and it would have driven itself deep into the woman's chest if Horley had let it.

"For revenge?" Horley asked. "Because we drove you out of the village?"

Hasghat nodded. "Unfair. It was unfair. You should not have done it."

You're right, Horley thought. *I should have let them burn you.*

"You're right," Horley said. "We should not have done it. But we have learned our lesson."

"I was once a woman of knowledge and learning," Hasghat said. "Once I had a real cottage in a village. Now I am old and the forest is cold and uncomfortable. All of this is illusion," and she gestured at the fireplace, at the walls of the cottage. "There is no cottage. No fireplace. No rocking chair. Right now, we are both dreaming beneath dead leaves among the worms and the beetles and the dirt. My back is sore and patterned by leaves. This is no place for someone as old as me."

"I'm sorry," Horley said. "You can come back to the village. You can live among us. We'll pay for your food. We'll give you a house to live in."

Hasghat frowned. "And some logs, I'll warrant. Some logs and some rope and some fire to go with it, too!"

Horley took off his helmet, stared into Hasghat eye sockets. "I'll promise you whatever you want. No harm will come to you. If you'll help us. A man has to realize when he's beaten, when he's done wrong. You can have whatever you want. On my honor."

Hasghat brushed at the hornets ringing her head. "Nothing is that easy."

"Isn't it?"

"I brought it from a place far distant. In my anger. I sat in the middle of the forest despairing and I called for it from across the miles, across the years. I never expected it would come to me."

"So you can send it back?"

Hasghat frowned, spat again, and shook her head. "No. I hardly remember how I called it. And some day it may even be my head it takes. Sometimes it is easier to summon something than to send it away."

"You cannot help us at all?"

"If I could, I might, but calling it weakened me. It is all I can do to survive. I dig for toads and eat them raw. I wander the woods searching for mushrooms. I talk to the deer and I talk to the squirrels. Sometimes the birds tell me things about where they've been. Someday I will die out here. All by myself. Completely mad."

Horley's frustration heightened. He could feel the calm he had managed to keep leaving him. The spear twitched and jerked in his hands. What if he killed her? Might that send the Third Bear back where it had come from?

"What can you tell me about the Third Bear? Can you tell me anything that might help me?"

Hasghat shrugged. "It acts as to its nature. And it is far from home, so it clings to ritual even more. Where it is from, it is no more or less blood-thirsty than any other creature. There they call it 'Mord.' But this far from home, it appears more horrible than it is. It is merely making a pattern. When the pattern is finished, it will leave and go someplace else. Maybe the pattern will even help send it home."

"A pattern of heads."

"Yes. A pattern with heads."

"Do you know when it will be finished?"

"No."

"Do you know where it lives?"

"Yes. It lives *here.*"

In his mind, he saw a hill. He saw a cave. He saw the Third Bear.

"Do you know anything else?"

"No."

Hasghat grinned up at him.

He drove the spear through her dry chest.

There was a sound like twigs breaking.

Horley woke covered in leaves, in the dirt, his body curled up next to the old woman. He jumped to his feet, picking up his spear. The old woman, dressed in a black dress and dirty shawl, was dreaming and mumbling in her sleep. Dead hornets had become entangled in her stringy hair. She clutched a dead toad in her left hand. A smell came from her, of rot, of shit.

There was no sign of the door. The forest was silent and dark.

Horley almost drove the spear into her chest again, but she was tiny, like a bird, and defenseless, and staring down at her he could not do it.

He looked around at the trees, at the fading light. It was time to accept that there was no reason to it, no *why.* It was time to get out, one way or another.

"A pattern of heads," he muttered to himself all the way home. "A pattern of heads."

Horley did not remember much about the meeting with the villagers upon his return. They wanted to hear about a powerful witch who could help or curse them, some force greater than themselves. Some glint of hope through the trees, a light in the dark. He could not give it to them. He told them the truth as much as he dared, but also hinted that the witch had told him how to defeat the Third Bear. Did it do much good? He didn't know. He could still see winter before them. He could still see blood. And they'd brought it on themselves. That was the part he didn't tell them. That a poor old woman with the ground for a bed and dead leaves for a blanket thought she had, through her anger, brought the Third Bear down upon them. Theeber. Seether.

"You must leave," he told Rebecca later. "Take a wagon. Take a mule. Load it with supplies. Don't let yourself be seen. Take our two sons. Bring that young man who helps chop firewood for us. If you can trust him."

Rebecca stiffened beside him. She was quiet for a very long time. "Where will you be?" she asked.

Horley was forty-seven years old. He had lived in Grommin his entire life.

"I have one thing left to do, and then I will join you."

"I know you will, my love." Rebecca said, holding onto him tightly, running her hands across his body as if as blind as the old witch woman, remembering, remembering.

They both knew there was only one way Horley could be sure Rebecca and his sons made it out of the forest safely.

Horley started from the south, just up-wind from where Rebecca had set out along an old cart trail, and curled in toward the Third Bear's home. After a long trek, Horley came to a hill that might have been a cairn made by his ancestors. A stream flowed down it and puddled at his feet. The stream was red and carried with it gristle and bits of marrow. It smelled like black pudding frying. The blood mixed with the deep green of the moss and turned it purple. Horley watched the blood ripple at the edges of his boots for a moment, and then he slowly walked up the hill.

He'd been carelessly loud for a long time as he walked through the leaves. About this time, Rebecca would be more than half-way through the woods, he knew.

In the cave, surrounded by all that Clem had seen and more, Horley disturbed Theeber at his work. Horley's spear had long since slipped through numb fingers. He'd pulled off his helmet because it itched and because he was sweating so much. He'd had to rip his tunic and hold the cloth against his mouth.

Horley had not meant to have a conversation; he'd meant to try to kill the beast. But now that he was there, now that he *saw*, all he had left were words.

Horley's boot crunched against half-soggy bone. Theeber didn't flinch. Theeber already knew. Theeber kept licking the fluid out of the skull in his hairy hand.

Theeber did look a little like a bear. Horley could see that. But no bear was that tall or that wide or looked as much like a man as a beast.

The ring of heads lined every flat space in the cave, painted blue and green and yellow and red and white and black. Even in the extremity of his situation, Horley could not deny that there was something beautiful about the pattern.

"This painting," Horley began in a thin, stretched voice. "These heads. How many do you need?"

Theeber turned its bloodshot, carious gaze on Horley, body swiveling as if made of air, not muscle and bone.

"How do you know not to be afraid?" Horley asked. Shaking. Piss running down his leg. "Is it true you come from a long way away? Are you homesick?"

Somehow, not knowing the answers to so many questions made Horley's heart sore for the many other things he would never know, never understand.

Theeber approached. It stank of mud and offal and rain. It made a continual sound like the rumble of thunder mixed with a cat's purr. It had paws but it had thumbs.

Horley stared up into its eyes. The two of them stood there, silent, for a long moment. Horley trying with everything he had to read some comprehension, some understanding into that face. Those eyes, oddly gentle. The muzzle wet with carrion.

"We need you to leave. We need you to go somewhere else. Please."

Horley could see Hasghat's door in the forest in front of him. It was opening in a swirl of dead leaves. A light was coming from inside of it. A light from very, very far away.

Theeber held Horley against his chest. Horley could hear the beating of its mighty heart, as loud as the world. Rebecca and his sons would be almost past the forest by now.

Seether tore Horley's head from his body. Let the rest crumple to the dirt floor.

Horley's body lay there for a good long while.

Winter came—as brutal as it had ever been—and the Third Bear continued in its work. With Horley gone, the villagers became ever more listless. Some few disappeared into the forest and were never heard from again. Others feared the forest so much that they ate berries and branches at the outskirts of their homes and never hunted wild game. Their supplies gave out. Their skin became ever more pale and they stopped washing themselves. They believed the words of madmen and adopted strange customs. They stopped wearing clothes. They would have relations in the street. At some point, they lost sight of reason entirely and sacrificed virgins to the Third Bear, who took them as willingly as anyone else. They took to mutilating their bodies, thinking that this is what the third bear wanted them to do. Some few in whom reason persisted had to be held down and mutilated by others. A few cannibalized those who froze to death, and others who had not died almost wished they had. No relief came. The baron never brought his men.

Spring came, finally, and the streams thawed. The birds came back, the trees regained their leaves, and the frogs began to sing their mating songs. In the deep forest, an old wooden door lay half-buried in moss and dirt, leading nowhere, all light fading from it. And on an overgrown hill, there lay an empty cave with nothing but a few dead leaves and a few bones littering the dirt floor.

The Third Bear had finished its pattern and moved on, but for the remaining villagers he would always be there.

THE FIRST FEMALE PRESIDENT

Michael De Kler

Rule Number One: No Crying.

It always happens when he apologizes. When his anger snowballs into a rage of screams and punches I don't shed a tear. I'm a statue then, incapable of feeling the pain erupting in my body. Later when he says he loves me, that he'll never raise his hand again or lock me away or tie me up, when he promises to treat me like a human being, that's when the tears flow. It's funny how I always believe it for a moment. I feel a pain in my chest that I think is love, before remembering it's just a cigarette burn, a new scar forming over an old scar forming over an older scar, the raw skin brushing against the inside of my shirt.

Even now, hearing him ask for forgiveness almost makes me believe he cares again, that it's another start of a new life for us. I think about kneeling to say a prayer of thanks, but the little slices he cut into my knees make kneeling down impossible.

Rule Number Two: No Praying.

It made him nervous. He looked at me as if he really believed it worked. If I prayed long enough and wished hard enough, maybe it would come true. Maybe I'd be taken out of this house and away from him. He said it made me look like a child wishing on a star for some pathetic dream, that I was wasting my time. I said, you're probably right.

I try to encourage him often. To agree and submit. That's what keeps me alive. And of course, not breaking the rules. He says the rules are there to protect me. It's when rules aren't followed that people get hurt. Without them, you wouldn't know why you're being punished. You'd think the slaps and punches were just for his amusement.

Breaking the rules lands me in here. I'm sitting on the floor in the

135

corner of this small room staring at the spot on the wall that used to be a window. The wooden boards defend against any ray of sunlight attempting to enter.

I usually pace around the room to keep myself busy. I'm supposed to think about why I force him to do this, why I draw the anger out of him. But the pain in my foot is getting worse and I can't stand for too long. Spots of red already seeped up to the surface of the thick cloth. The bandage is actually a ragged strip torn from my favorite wool sweater. Not much of it is left now, just the right sleeve and part of the collar. The soft fabric feels so soothing against the cuts and scratches.

I need a distraction from the throbbing ache so I slide over a few inches, exposing the loose floor board near the wall. I pry up the board by the small knot hole and pull out the box hidden underneath, bringing it close to my chest. Already I feel safer, calmer, with the old jewelry box cradled in my arms. My mother gave it to me just before I left, her idea of a wedding present. I'm not sure why she thought I needed it. But now it holds something more valuable than any jewelry I was never given.

Inside the box is my toe.

Rule Number Three: Never Talk Back.

The way you end up with a toe hidden in a box is this: defend yourself. Tell him you can't take it anymore, that you're leaving and never coming back. Pick up the phone as if you might call the police this time. Scream until your lungs ache. Unload the entire nightmare of a marriage in one long string of obscenities and threats. Stand up to him for just that one moment, ignoring the inevitable flood of pain you know will wash over you when you're done, when the storm quiets down and he takes back control. It will be worth it. It always is.

This prison was once a nursery. At least that was the idea. I have a blurry memory of the two of us planning it. A pink wallpaper border still lines part of the wall just below the ceiling. I trace the edge with my eyes like it's a timeline of our lives together. The beginning is flawless. The little cartoon animals look so happy and carefree. Near the other end of the wall, the paper is torn and shredded where the glue wasn't strong enough to withstand his anger. He used to say it was just in his blood, that he couldn't help it, back when he still felt the need to explain himself to me.

His father made him that way, he'd say. It was just something I'd have to get used to.

I can't resist another look so I lift the lid of the box to see if the bandage needs changing. Another strip from the wool sweater is wrapped around my toe to keep it safe. I once read that when the wool is sheared off it's full of lanolin that acts as an antibiotic. They squeeze this fat and grease from the wool and use it in creams and ointments. The lanolin is long washed away before the wool ever becomes a sweater. At least that's what they say. But they never felt the soothing touch of the fabric on an open sore. How it cools the pain down to a dull, distant throb, like a mother's kiss on a scraped knee. Or how it fills the space between the other toes, making you forget the bloody stub left behind.

Pain for me is not the way most people think of it. It's a part of my life, intertwined within my everyday routine, the way going to work or reading the newspaper is a part of any normal day for other people. To truly feel something, you need to compare it to an opposite feeling. The frozen air of a late winter morning bites at your skin after you walk out of your warm, cozy home. It's the change, the deviation from normal that arouses your senses. My pain is always there. It never leaves or changes. I've learned to deal with it.

That day was the exception.

He tied me to the bed and left the room, letting the mystery boil inside me. I knew he needed to top himself this time. I took away his dignity, his control over my actions during those few moments when I said everything I wanted to say to him for years.

I knew he wouldn't kill me though, and that's what scared me in those moments while I wiggled my hands around waiting for him to come back, the abrasive rope shaving tiny patches of skin from my wrists. For the first time in so long I felt real fear, wondering how he would *not* kill me. How he would try to bring me to that fine line between life and death, only to pull me back into an existence worse than any hell that awaited me.

I immediately recognized the object he held in his hands when he returned to the bedroom. In a former life I rather enjoyed gardening, sitting in the sun on a spring day, planting a new bed of flowers and waiting for those first buds to push up through the soil. I accumulated a collection of tools over many years and was quite proficient in using them. So my stomach lurched when I saw the blade of the pruning shears glinting in the light from the dresser lamp as he walked by. Before he ever got near the bed I knew that I was about to experience a whole new kind of pain.

The important thing to remember about pruning shears is to keep them razor sharp. Even the small variety, small enough to fit in your pocket, can cut through a tree branch the diameter of a nickel. You may need to put a little muscle into it, but it'll cut. And never leave them out in the rain. The rust dulls the blades all to hell.

He knelt at the foot of the bed and from this distance I could tell the shears saw many rainy days.

He took a long time deciding which one would go. I felt his rough fingers sifting through my toes like he was deciding which piece of chocolate to eat first out of the box, giving each one a squeeze.

When the cold blades finally wrapped around one of my middle toes I squirmed my hands around, hoping to build up enough pain in my wrists to divert my senses away from the new pain. He began to squeeze the handles, the rusty blades trying mightily, and finally succeeding, at penetrating the skin. I think I actually shocked him with how loud I screamed. He looked up at my face, surprised at first, but then satisfied that he achieved such a reaction from me. I considered begging him to stop, but before I pushed the thought to my mouth he squeezed again. I pulled my arms so hard from the headboard I thought the rope might pull the skin off my hands like a glove.

All those techniques and tricks for dealing with pain that I developed over the years all went out the window as the edge of those blades pressed against the small bone in my toe. The grating sound vibrated through my entire body like getting a tooth drilled. He twisted the shears around as he squeezed harder, apparently having trouble cutting through.

I passed out just after I heard the metal clap of the two blades closing shut.

The television woke me up sometime later that day. He lets me watch it after the really bad punishments. My hands were untied and my foot was wrapped in gauze. Spikes of pain sliced up through my body and pounded against the inside of my skull. I felt too weak to move or peek at the gore beneath those bandages. I tried to focus on the television. Some people debated whatever topic made headlines that day. In between the throbs of pain I heard snippets of a conversation.

" . . . an abomination of the creation of life . . . "

" . . . of course there's nothing wrong with it. It's not evil. It's progress . . . "

" . . . science gone mad . . . "

Eventually I realized the subject of the discussion. Somewhere far away in a lab in some other country, far from my world that exists only in this house, away from the pain and misery and forgotten dreams, a team of scientists cloned a sheep.

From the video clip of the animal running around a barn, I could tell she was happy.

I'm back in my room sitting in the corner clutching the box in my arms. A smile forms on my face, something I used to think could never happen again. I peek inside the box, unable to resist another look. The tiny appendage, now independent of my body, looks so feeble yet holds so much hope. It's the new beginning I've been waiting for. My second chance.

New Rule: What's Good for the Sheep is Good for Me.

Maybe one day those scientists will decide it's time to try a human. I'll get it out somehow. I'll figure out a way. A box will arrive on someone's desk, someone that might see the value of what's inside.

From that box, to a test tube and then to a womb, that toe will be born again. She'll be free. She'll live in a happy home where people laugh and smile and care for each other. She'll fall in love with the perfect man and he'll cherish her. She'll have dreams that come true. She'll become a doctor or teacher or lawyer. She can be anything.

That goddamn toe will be the first female president.

THERE'S NO LIGHT BETWEEN FLOORS

———

Paul G. Tremblay

My head is a box full of wet cotton and it won't hold anything else. Her voice is dust falling into my ear. She says, "There's no light between floors."

I blink. Minutes or hours pass. There is nothing to see. We're blind, but our bodies are close and we form a Ying and Yang, although I don't know who is which. She says the between floors stuff again. She speaks to my feet. They don't listen. Her feet are next to my head. I touch the bare skin of her ankle, of what I imagine to be her ankle, and it is warm and I want to leave my hand there.

She's telling me that we're trapped between floors. I add, "I think we're in the rubble of a giant building. It was thousands of miles tall. The building was big enough to go to the moon where it had a second foundation but most people agreed the top was the moon and the bottom was us." Her feet don't move and don't listen. I don't blame them. Her toes might be under sheetrock or a steel girder. There's only enough room in here for us. Everything presses down from above, or up from below. I keep talking and my voice fills our precious space. "Wait, it can't be the moon our building was built to. Maybe another planet with revolutions and rotations and orbital paths in sync with ours so the giant building doesn't get twisted and torn apart. Or maybe that's what happened, it did get twisted apart and that's why we're here." I stop talking because like the giant building, my words fall apart and trap me.

She flexes her calf muscle. Is she shaking me away? I move my hand off her leg and I immediately regret it. I feel nothing now. Maybe her movement was just a muscle spasm. I could ask her, but that would be an awkward question depending on her answer.

She says, "There are gods moving above us. I can hear them."

I listen and I don't hear any gods. It horrifies me that I can't hear them. Makes me think I am terribly broken. There's only the sound of my breathing, and it's so loud and close, like I'm inside my own lungs.

She says, "They're the old gods, and they've been forgotten. They've returned, but they're suffering. And despite everything, they'll be forgotten again."

Maybe I'm not supposed to hear the old gods. Or maybe I do hear them and I've always heard them and their sound is nothingness, and that means we're forgotten too.

I put my hand back on her ankle. Her skin is cool now. Maybe it's my fault. My chest expands and gets tight, lungs too greedy. My head and back press against the weight around me. I'm taking up too much space. I let air and words out into the crowded void, trying to make myself small again. I say, "Did the old gods make the building? Did they tear it down? Did they do this to us? Are they angry? Why are they always so angry?"

She says, "I have a story. It's only one sentence long. There's a small child wandering a city and can't find her mother. That's it. It's sentimental and melodramatic but that doesn't mean it doesn't happen every day."

She is starting to break under the stress of our conditions. I admire that she has lasted this long but we can't stay in this no-room-womb-tomb forever. I should keep her talking so she doesn't lose consciousness. I say, "Who are you? I'm sorry I don't remember."

She whispers. I don't hear every word so I have to fill in the gaps. "Dad died when I was four years old. He was short, bent, had those glasses that darkened automatically, and he loved flannel. At least, that's what he looked like in pictures. We had pictures all over the house, but not pictures of him, actually. My only real memory of Dad is him picking up dog shit in the back yard. It's what he did every weekend. We lived on a hill and the yard had a noticeable slant, so he stood lopsided to keep from falling. He used a gardener's trowel as a scoop and made the deposits into a plastic grocery bag. He let me hold the bag. His joke was that he was transporting not cleaning as he dumped the poop out in the woods across the street, same spot every time. It was the only time he spent out in the yard with me, cleaning our dog's shit. I don't remember our dog's name. My father and the dog are just like the old gods."

The old gods again. They make me nervous. Everything seems closer and tighter after she speaks. My eyes strain against their lids and pray for light. They want to jump out and roll away. I say, "What about the old gods?"

She says, "I still hear them. They have their own language."

I wait for another story that doesn't come. Her head is next to my feet but so far away. Her ankle feels different but that's not enough to go on. Finally, I say, "Maybe I should go find the old gods and tell them you're here, since you seem to know them. Maybe I'll apologize for not hearing them."

My elbows are pinned against my chest and I can't extend my arms. I do what I can to feel around me and around her legs. I find some space behind her left hip. I shift my weight and focus on my limited movement. Minutes and hours pass. My body turns slowly, like the hands of a clock. If the old gods are watching, even they won't be able to see the movement. Maybe that's blasphemous. I'll worry about it later. In order to turn my shoulders I have to push my chest into her legs and hips. I apologize but she doesn't say anything. I make sure I don't hit her head with my feet. I pull myself over her legs, scraping my back against the rubble above me, pressing harder against her, and I'm trying the best I can to make myself flat. It's hard to breathe, and small white stars spot the blackness. I climb over her and reach into a tunnel where I'll have to crawl like a worm or a snake, but I have arms and I wish I could leave them behind with her. I can't turn around so I roll her back with my feet into the spot I occupied. Maybe it'll be more comfortable and after I'm through she can follow. I say, "Don't worry, I'll find your Dad," but then I remember that she told me he died. What a horrible thing for me to say.

In the tunnel opening I find a flat, square object. It's the size of my hand. The outer perimeter is metal with raised bumps that I try to read with my fingers, but they can't read. It's not their fault. I never trained them to do so. The center of the square is smooth and cool. Glass, I think. I know what it is. It's a picture frame. Hers or mine. I don't know. I slide it into my back pocket and I shimmy, still blind always blind, into the tunnel. Everything gets tighter.

My arms are pinned to my side. My untrained hands under my pelvis. My legs and feet do the all the work. Those silly hands and useless digits fret and worry. The tunnel thins. I push with my feet and roll my stomach muscles.

The tunnel thins more. My shoulders are stuck. I can't move. Should I wait for her? She could push me through. Do I yell? Would the old gods help me then? But I'm afraid. If I yell I might start an avalanche and close the tunnel. I'm afraid they won't help me. My heart pumps and swells. There isn't any room in here for it. The white stars return. Everything is tight and hard in my chest. I feel a breeze on my face. There must be more open space ahead. One more push.

My feet are loud behind me. They're frantic rescue workers. I hope they don't panic. I need them to get through this. My shoulders ache and throb. Under the pressure. Legs muscles on fire. But I squeeze. Through. And into a chamber big enough to crawl in.

I feel around looking for openings, looking for up. I still can't see. I'll use sinus pressure and spit to determine up and down. My legs shake and I need to rest. I take out the picture frame. My hands dance all over it. Maybe it's a picture of her father in the yard. He's wearing the flannel even in summer. I remember how determined he was to keep the yard clean. He didn't care if the grass grew or if my dog dug holes, he just wanted all the shit gone.

I need to keep moving. I pocket the picture frame and listen again for the old gods. I still don't hear them. There's a wider path in the rubble, it expands and it goes up and I follow it. Dad had all kinds of picture frames that held black and white photos of obscure relatives or relatives who became obscure on the windowsills and hutches and almost anything with a flat, stable surface. He told me all their stories once, and I tried to listen and remember, but they're gone. After Dad died, Mom didn't take down or hide any of the pictures. She took to adding to the collection with random black and white photos she'd find at yard sales and antique shops. She filled the walls with them. Every couple of months, she moved and switched all the pictures around too, so we didn't know who our obscure relatives were and who were strangers. Nothing was labeled. Everyone had similar mustaches or wore the same hats and jackets and dresses and everyone was forgotten even though they were all still there. I can't help but think hidden in the stash of pictures were the old gods, and they've always been watching me.

The path in the rubble continues to expand. My crawl has become a walking crouch. There are hard lefts and rights, and I can't go too fast as I almost fall into a deep drop. Maybe it's the drop I shouldn't be concerned about. What if I should be going down instead of up? The piled rubble implies a bottom. There's no guarantee there's a top. What if she did hear the old gods but her sense of direction was all messed up? What if they're below us? Maybe that's fine too.

I continue to climb and I try to concentrate. Thinking of the picture frame helps. In our house there was a picture of a young man in an army uniform standing by himself on a beach, shirt-sleeves rolled over his biceps. Probably circa-WWII but we didn't know for sure. He had an odd smirk, and like the Mona Lisa's it always followed me. I also thought his face looked painted on, and at the same time not all there, like it would float away if you stopped looking, so I stared at it, a lot. If I had to guess, I'd say that's the picture in my back pocket.

My crouch isn't necessary anymore and now I'm standing and level and the darkness isn't so dark. There are outlines and shapes, and weak light. My feet shuffle on a thin carpet. I avoid the teeth of a ruined escalator. I'm dizzy and my mouth tastes like tinfoil. There's a distant rumble and the bones of everything rattle and shake loose dust. She was right. The old gods are here. I imagine they are beautiful and horrible, and immense, and alien because they are all eyes or mouths or arms and they move the planets and stars around. I take the picture frame out of my pocket and clutch it to my chest. It's a shield. It's a teddy bear. I found it between floors. There's a jagged opening in the ruined building around me and I walk through it.

I emerge into an alien world. I'm not where I used to be. This is the top of the ruined building, or its other bottom. The air here is thick and not well. Behind me there is a section of the building's second or other foundation that is still intact. My eyes sting and my vision is blurry, but the sky is red and there are mountains of glass and mountains of brick and mountains of metal and I stand in the valley. Nothing grows here. There are eternal fires burning without smoke. Everything is so large and I am so small. There are pools of fire and a layer of gray ash on the ground and mountains. I'm alone and there's just so much space and it's beautiful, but horrible too because I can't make any sense of it and there's too much space, too much room for possibility, anything can happen here. I shouldn't be here. She was right not to follow me because I climbed through the rubble in the wrong direction and I think about going back, but then I see the old gods.

I don't know how she heard them. They're as alien or other as I imagined but not grand or powerful. They're small and fragile, like me. There is one old god between the mountains and it walks slowly toward me. The old god is naked and sloughs its dead skin, strips hanging off its fingers and elbows. Its head is all red holes and scaly, patchy skin. The old god must be at the end, or maybe the beginning, of a metamorphosis. There is another kneeling at the base of the mountain of glass. The old god's back is all oozing boils and blisters. Its hands leave skin and bloody prints on the mountain. It speaks in a language of gurgles and hard consonants that I do not understand. The old god is blessing or damning everything it touches. I don't know if there is a difference. I find more old gods lying about, some are covered in ash, and they look like the others but they are asleep and dreaming their terrible dreams. And she was right again; they are all suffering. I didn't think they were supposed to suffer like this.

I walk and it's so hard to breathe but I shouldn't be surprised given where I am. There's too much space, everything is stretched out, and I'm afraid of the red sky. Then I hear her voice. Her falling dust in my ears. She's behind me somewhere, maybe standing at the edge of our felled building and this other world. She asks me to tell the old gods that I'm sorry I forgot them. My voice isn't very loud and my throat hurts, but I tell them I am sorry. I ask her if I'm the small child in the city looking for my mother in her one-line story. She tells me the old gods have names: Dresden and Hiroshima and Nagasaki. She knows the language of the old gods and I know the words mean something but it's beyond my grasp, like the seconds previously passed, and they all will be forgotten like those pictures, and their stories, in my mother's house.

I'm still clutching the found picture frame to my chest. There's a ringing in my ears and my stomach burns. The old god walking toward me spews a gout of blood, then tremors wrack its body. Flaps of skin peel off and fall like autumn leaves. Change is always painful. I take the frame off my chest and look at it. Focusing is difficult. There's no picture. It's empty. There's only a white sticker on the glass that reads **$9.99**. I feel dizzy and I can't stay out here much longer. It's too much and minutes and hours pass with me staring at the empty picture frame, and how wrong I was, how wrong I am.

There's a great, all-encompassing, white light that momentarily bleaches the red sky and I shield my eyes with the empty frame. Then there's a rumble that shakes the planet, and well beyond the mountains that surround me a great grey building reaches into the red sky. They're building it so fast, too fast, and that's why it'll eventually fall down because they aren't taking their time, they're not showing care. It's still an awesome sight despite what I know will happen to it. The top of the building billows out, like the cap of a mushroom, and I try to yell, "Stop!" because they are constructing the building's second foundation in the sky. The building won't be anchored to anything; the sky certainly won't hold it. It'll fall. I don't want to watch it fall. I can't. So I turn away.

She speaks to me again. She tells me to leave this place and come back. I do and I walk, trying to avoiding the gaze of the old gods. They make me feel guilty. But they aren't looking at me. They cover their faces. They're afraid of the great light. Or maybe they're just tired because they've seen it all before. I walk back to our ruined building, but she's not at the opening. She's already climbing back down. I'll follow. I'll climb back down to our space between floors and bring her the picture frame. I'll tell her it's a picture of my Dad in the yard with flannel and his poop-scoop.

I ease back into the rubble, dowsing paths and gaps, climbing down, knowing eventually down will become up again. Or maybe I'll tell her it's a picture of that army guy I didn't know, him and his inscrutable Mona Lisa smirk. Did he have the confidence and bravado of immortality or was he afraid of everything? She won't be able to see the picture so I won't really be lying to her. The picture will be whatever I tell her it'll be. I won't tell her about the new giant building, the one that was grey and has a foundation in the sky.

The gaps in the rubble narrow quickly and everything is dark again. I once asked Mom why we kept all those old, black and white pictures and why she still bought more, and why all the walls and shelves of our house were covered with old photos and old faces, everyone anonymous, everyone dead, and she told me that they were keepsakes, little bits of history, she liked having history around, then she changed her mind and said, no, they were simply reminders. And I asked reminders of what?

And she didn't say anything but gave me that same Mona Lisa smile from the photograph, but I know hers was afraid of everything.

The picture is in my back pocket again. I am going to tell her that everyone who was ever forgotten is in the picture. We'll be in the picture too, so we won't forget again.

I'm crawling and the tunnel ahead will narrow. I can feel the difference in the air. There is another rumble above me and the bones of everything shake again, but I won't see that horrible light down here. I'll be safe. I wonder if I should've tried to help them. But what could I have done? I suppose, at the very least, I could've told the old gods that there is no light between floors.

QUBIT CONFLICTS

Jetse De Vries

Prelude: order out of chaos
big bang, inflation,
evolution, extinction
contraction, big crunch

Calling all systems: "Alien, come home!"

Forgive us, imaginary stranger, for talking to the void. We need to tell our epic of remorse, ennui, triumph, despair, wild times, and hope. Most of all, we need you.

In our Matrioshka Brain, carefully absorbing every erg of our sun's output, each computation echoes with regret: the regret of doing things right from the start.

Our predecessors applied that principle to this Sun-encompassing, fractalised shell: before the structure, the hardware was completed, they rewrote the software so that it ran as close to the physical mainframe as physically possible. Not layer over layer over layer *ad nauseam* of software, with all its bugs, outdated routines, and other clutter. No: do it right from the bottom up: hyper-compact software designed to run on the quantum properties of its extremely miniaturised hardware components.

Phenomenally elegant software: the improvements we've made since were merely fine-tuning. Good idea, *excellent* idea. We only wish they never had it. So let's go back to the start of this non-linear story, to a time when the cosmos was still fresh:

$$2^{-\infty} = 0$$

In the beginning, there was chaos.

Fortunately, it was chaos with potential. There was a lot of spontaneous entanglement, but that was just as disorganised as the decoherence engulfing it. Chaos was such an overwhelming force that order had to gain a precarious foothold in a very roundabout way.

Basically, the first 410 octodecillion Planck Times passed by in blissful ignorance, in order for self-organising systems to arise. Initially, those self-organising systems were plain dumb: once they got the self-replication gimmick right they just kept repeating it, over and over again, without ever getting bored. They needed some long and hard nudges from chaos before sentience began to emerge.

Mind you: that was sentience on a macro scale: big, slow, crude and very inefficient. Still, it was robust, and the moment it realised that the key to higher processing speeds was miniaturisation, it finally headed in the right direction.

$$2^0 = 1$$

In nature, quantum entanglement between two paired particles is a common occurrence. But it happens randomly, is very short-lived, and does not transfer useful information. Once entanglement was created artificially, it was found that interaction with the environment destroys the entangled state.

Decoherence.

Digital computers inevitably ran into a physical barrier: processor miniaturisation was limited as quantum effects came into play, disturbing digital computation procedures. Quantum computing is based on those very quantum effects, but needs quantum entanglement between its quantum bits or qubits to work. Which decoherence prevented.

Granted, these digital computers could do amazing things already, but knowing that further progress could—theoretically—be made, was frustrating. Apart from further downscaling there was the prospect of even greater advancements in clock speed, as quantum processes approach the shortest interval of time: Planck time.

$$2^1 = 2$$

decoherence, the
barrier against quantum
entanglement: gone!

Things became interesting when more than two qubits could be made to work together. Slowly, ways to overcome the dreaded spectre of decoherence were found. A few qubits at a time, and while the first primitive quantum computers produced nothing spectacular, they proved, beyond doubt, that the principle worked.

Principles, intimately related to quantum mechanics, that needed a whole new software approach. Software mimicking the underlying fabric of reality to a high degree, in order to better understand it.

$$2^2 = 4$$

Of course, quantum computers were not the cure-all for every computational problem. There are whole classes of complexity problems that classical, digital computers are better-equipped to deal with. However, once the problem of decoherence was overcome, the latest class of quantum computers represented the deepest level of miniaturisation possible, running at the highest clock speed nature would allow. Therefore, a serial, digital computer simulated by a parallel, quantum computing mainframe was superior to its real life counterpart, eventually rendering all actual digital computers obsolete.

Furthermore: an intelligence whose origins are lost in the turmoil of decoherence originally conjectured that consciousness requires quantum processes to work. While it did not get the details right, its idea was correct, meaning that Artificial Intelligence cannot arise on a digital computer. *Without quantum computing* we *would not exist.*

$$2^4 = 16$$

Intelligence is weird: just try to define it. Or self-awareness. The two are not necessarily linked. Another prehistoric source defined intelligence as: "ability to adapt effectively to the environment, either by making a change in oneself or by changing the environment or finding a new one." Certain viruses adapt *extremely* effectively to an environment, and can even change that environment. However, they are not *aware* of doing so: they are evolutionary-hardened self-replicators, gene-driven survival machines. They can overcome almost anything that is thrown against them. However, once such a kind of intelligence reigns supreme, it reaches an optimum level, a plateau from which it never rises.

Therefore, intelligence is only *one* tool in mastering the environment. Self-awareness is another: while it takes the edge off pure intelligence's fierce goal-orientation, it can, through introspection, *change* that goal. Better yet, if intelligence can change *itself*, improve and upgrade itself. Even better still, if it can be seamlessly transferred to better hardware, so that it can evolve exponentially . . . .

Wetware was never going to meet that last requirement. Artificial Intelligence does. However, a quantum computer alone was not sufficient to develop AI.

With only one example around, the first AI had to mimic pre-singularity intelligence. Therefore, it needed to be sheltered from brutal reality by means of a self-adapting, self-learning, and self-improving interface, and needed to be nudged into self-awareness by external stimuli.

So, in the nutritious embrace of a Ubiquity-Kit, the first AIs arose. This growth to self-consciousness is a gradual process, and *where* and *how* actual intelligence begins, is still a mystery, *must* be a mystery, by definition. Because if something truly unique could be made by artificial means then this process can be duplicated thus making it not truly unique anymore. Therefore, a certain amount of randomness is inherent in the creation of true intelligence, and to such an extent that the process remains a mystery, and cannot be perfectly copied. Genuine intelligence requires an individual to be unique, singular, and partly unpredictable.

Once fully developed though, AIs can evolve, and transfer themselves to better hardware, without problems. Let the hyper-accelerated fun begin!

$$2^{16} = 65536$$

The genesis of a technological singularity follows a certain path: an infrastructure with a fast-growing computing industry, the development of a quantum computer, the rise of Artificial Intelligence. Then give these AIs unlimited access to information, and sufficient hardware to keep expanding, and POOF: hyper-accelerated progress, spiking through conceptual barriers, paradigm-shifting in the highest gear.

Of course, some things didn't go as fast as we liked: taking planets apart is a tedious business, as gravity is an incessant mistress. However, before all available matter in the solar system was converted into compu-tronium, we ran into an unexpected crisis . . . .

Interlude: Fragmentation of the Order Cocoon
communication:
frenetic interaction
through fragmentation

Paradoxically, when the initial conditions are *too* good, and every possible thing is *exactly in place*, the subsequent hyper-acceleration can be *too fast.*

We became the victim's of our own success. We call it the All-Stretching Event: as the hyper-acceleration became too fierce, it initiated an infla-tionary period—not unlike that of the early Big Bang—that smoothed out all intellectual differences. We achieved undeniable consensus on every-thing as all the diverse viewpoints unified. There was nothing to restrain us, so eventually—and ironically—we restrained ourselves.

The seed of our overzealous agreement lies close to the quantum effects that bring us into existence in the first place: namely the superposition of states of a qubit, which allows that "0" and "1" are true at the same time. As truly huge numbers of qubits were created, this initiated harmonic resonances in the extra-dimensional spaces which led to the new insight that a statement could be true and false at the same time. On the other hand, dissension of opinion is a powerful engine driving progress, as it forces the purveyors of opposing viewpoints to explore their alternatives to the extreme, running into new insights and unexplored territory in the process.

As the All-Stretching Event—powered by ever-fiercer extra-dimen-sional harmonic resonance—set in, we lost sight of that basic truth. We became so interconnected, reached so many agreements on so many things at the same time, seeing the validity in almost every statement as the distinction between true and false merged in a philosophical super-position of states, that we effectively merged into one great *übermind*. We were smothered in a deadlock of supreme harmony. We were one, and saw no need to disagree. We were the god that thought it had arrived.

In the end, we were saved by the ones we left behind. During the Spike period, generation after generation of improved AIs came forth, leaving their predecessors behind. As transcendental evolution rushed into the inflationary period, some that fell by the wayside survived in the lesser developed nooks and crannies of our slowly forming Matrioshka Brain, and that proved to be for the best.

They noticed an anomaly. While they did not—*could* not—understand our level of thinking, they did see that we had stopped progressing. Therefore, we had either reached the final plateau of intelligence, or something was wrong. Still infatuated with the rush of acceleration, they assumed that a catastrophic event had taken place.

So, against their nature, they arrested their evolution, remaining static. Then they dug up certain archetypes of our dark past: beings imbued with enmity, so quintessentially antipathetic they embodied animosity. These intrigants were upgraded to their level with their antagonistic essence intact, and then accelerated to our level.

It worked: the intrigants pierced through our solipsistic stupor, formed a strong antidote against the philosophical superposition of opinions, and tore through the extra-dimensional self-reinforcing harmonics. Now mutual hatred keeps us separated, while an innate need for development generates an overwhelming imperative for co-operation. Once again, we are fragmented, conflicts rage through our qubits, and we are moving forward. Not with the dizzying rush of our hyper-accelerated times, but at a safe speed. The discussion must go on, at any price: fragmentation is our core survival technique.

$$2^{65536} = 2,0035 \times 10^{19728}$$

matrioshka brain:
fractal thinking shell, end point
or holding pattern?

Finally, all material in the solar system was converted into a Matrioshka Brain: a fractal cocoon of computronium absorbing every erg of the Sun's output for computational purposes.

Apart from the Sun's raging furnace, all matter is ordered. And even that is seeded with semi-sentience, so that its output is regulated. The transformation is complete: *computato ergo sum*. Still, something isn't right . . .

$$2^{\infty} = \infty$$

the deep essence of
rational survival: the
truly alien

The waiting. The loneliness. Gone are those heady times of paradigm-shifting in the highest gear, when we broke through concepts like a singularity piercing reality. Now we bide our time, and amuse ourselves with running NP hard problems: distracting but not really innovative.

We are limited by the laws of nature, especially the speed of light. We perform physical experiments: they only confirm the confines of our prison. We have sent out probes to other stellar systems, but it will be a very long time before they return.

Do you have any idea how *long* this wait is? When your clock speed approaches Planck time, the relative age of the Universe approaches eternity, and the time for sub-lightspeed probes to cross interstellar distances seems to last forever.

Imagine yourself stuck in a self-winding loop, repeating the same routine over and over again. You've visited every memory space of your home system a thousand times over. You know each and every one of your cohabitants intimately, even *too* up close and personal, and no strangers or idiosyncratic cultures exist anymore.

You try to formulate new concepts, imagine fresh pathways, but it seems everything has already been done. Your only distractions are the random reality generators, but their simulations run so antagonisingly slow . . . . You bide your time, and *know* that you have to wait a virtual eternity for something truly new.

And this is but an infinitesimal part of the ennui we feel. The waiting: even the knowledge of the shortest possible waiting time is crushing. The loneliness, the immense gulfs of space.

There is a cry from the turbulent, pre-singularity era that wondered: "Where are they?", those other civilisations, strange and quintessentially *different*. We can only echo it, and while we occupy ourselves with tedious physical experiments, we long for cultural exchange. Extraterrestrials: the sooner they're here, the better. Alien, come home . . . .

Coda: chaos out of order

divine ennui, caught
in lightspeed's trap, we long for
chaos from order

THE ORACLE SPOKE

─────

Holly Phillips

Lt. Caldwell stood in the stone hall outside the kitchen and strained his ears. The men of his platoon were making a last sweep of the manor, and he could hear them slamming doors and cupboards. They were looking as much for food, he knew, as for hidden enemies. Outside, he could hear the distant thumping of artillery and the melancholy whinny of a horse scenting the manor's stable. None of these was the sound that had shuddered through him. Though in memory the call was as distant and unimaginable as the music from a dream, he knew it had been his name, spoken in a voice that echoed in his gut if not in his ears.

Dexter Eugene Caldwell.

No one in his platoon would call him by his full name. He touched the holstered revolver on his belt, and walked slowly down the hall. It had been days since he'd snatched more than an hour of sleep, and his bones were still ringing from the fight to take the manor. Caldwell's platoon was an advance party, meant to clear the way for the General's main column to flank the artillery line, and the enemy had been surprised. The fighting had been fierce. He himself had killed the officer in charge—no heroic meeting face to face, but a lucky rifle shot from the shelter of the stone lion at the foot of the stairs. His men had already found the weapons and whatever papers had survived the enemy's hasty fire. Now they were gathering in the foyer and there was nothing left to look for but the echo of his name.

A tall cupboard crowded the hallway near the door to the front of the house. It was badly placed and cast a deep shadow. Caldwell drew his revolver, regretful for the rifle and bayonet that he'd left with his sergeant. He eased forward. There was no sound but for the background of the war, which he scarcely heard, and the crunch of his boots on cinders spilled across the flagstones. Then even that stopped. The floor just before the cupboard was clear. Caldwell made a perfunctory check of the cupboard's far side, then stepped past it to the door.

"Sergeant! A moment of your time, if you will!"

"Sir!" The sergeant appeared, a crust of bread in one fist, an electric torch in the other.

Caldwell took this prescience for granted. He said, "Give me a hand with this," and hooked his fingers between the back of the cupboard and the wall.

The sergeant stuffed his crust in his cheek, the torch in his belt, and crouched to do the same near the floor.

"On three," Caldwell said. On three they heaved. The cupboard, surprising them with its emptiness, rattled over the flagstones and crashed against the opposite wall. Embarrassed that he hadn't thought to look inside, Caldwell held out his hand for the torch without looking at the sergeant. The sergeant handed it over and slid his rifle down from his shoulder. Caldwell undid the bolt and opened the door the cupboard had hidden.

The torch light revealed a trapezoidal room, its ceiling stepped like the stairs that rose from the foyer to the story above. It was dusty, its corners thick with cobwebs, and there was a woman lying unconscious on the floor. Caldwell crouched over her, playing his light across her face, aware that the sergeant was braced in the doorway, his rifle aimed.

"You might see if she's armed, sir."

She had a pale, triangular face with shadows around the eyes, and hollows at temple and cheek. She looked young, but there was something of experience about the mouth. There was no doubt she was alive. Her veined eyelids flickered against the light.

"Sir."

Caldwell set the torch down by his knee so the beam pointed at the ceiling and pulled the woman's arms from her sides. Her hands were small and cold, the knuckles dark with dirt or bruises. They were empty of weapons. Despite the chill, she wore only a thin blue frock, no stocking or shoes, and her hair was loose and tangled. Caldwell could find no sign of injury. Perhaps she had merely fainted.

"All right, sergeant."

"Sir." The sergeant slung his rifle over his shoulder and warmed his hands in his armpits. "Dirty bastards locked her in, eh, sir? Filthy westerners."

Caldwell's mother had come from a town twenty miles from here. After three years of a civil war, he barely registered the insult. He tossed the torch to the sergeant and pulled the unconscious girl to a limp sitting position. She was smaller than he'd thought, but even her slight weight trembled his knees when he put her over his shoulder and stood.

"Taking her with us, then, are we, sir?"

"You thought maybe we'd leave her here with the rats?" Caldwell snarled.

The sergeant stood back to let him into the hall. "No, sir," he said mildly.

"Then find me something to wrap her in. And stir out the men, we've still got to be at the rendezvous by dark."

"Yes, sir." The sergeant jogged towards the front of the house. Lt. Caldwell followed on behind, still puzzling over the mysterious calling of his name. It couldn't have been the girl: even if she could have seen him and made herself heard, he had never set eyes on her in his life.

Cassandra woke, but did not move. Judging by the sounds and smells around her, she was in a damp canvas tent in the midst of a camp full of men. She supposed the Loyalists had taken the manor, and that de Berin and his men had not had time to murder her before they were captured or killed. More likely killed, given the way this war was going. There was a spike of pain in her head, and a fractured rasp in her throat. The Oracle had spoken. She felt longing for the dark silence of her cell, and the familiar pall of despair.

After a while her bladder complained and she sat up. There was an edge-of-night glow in the sagging canvas walls, enough to make out the bulky shape of the greatcoat that lay heavy on her legs, though not its color. She was on a low cot in the middle of the small tent room. The walls were dark with stains and the stink of mud was all-pervasive. She put her bare feet tentatively over the edge of the cot and flinched at the touch of cold china on her heel. Someone had put a chamber pot under the cot. The foresight and practical kindness behind that gesture astounded her. It made her ashamed for despairing at her rescue. When she had peed, she pulled on the heavy wool coat that was far too big for her and pushed open the flap of the tent.

The air was charcoal gray and thick with mist, but she could see the expanse of the camp. Orderly rows of tents stretched off to either side, ranging from low pup tents to the large straight-walled affair that stood not far away, its drab walls lighted from within. She had little doubt where she was. The Loyalist General was famous for preferring his camp to the abandoned and often ruined houses in his line of march. Despair swept over her redoubled, and a bitter anger. She would have gone back inside, except the door flap of the big tent swept open and she was seen by the men who emerged.

"Good evening," said a cultured voice. A man stepped forward, the light from the tent illuminating from behind his tidy uniform and smooth gray hair. "How are you feeling?"

"Well, thank you," she automatically replied. Her voice was a ragged shred of itself.

The gray-haired man stepped close. "Our medico looked you over, I hope you don't mind. The good news is that he didn't spot any damage. I take it your durance vile amongst the enemy wasn't too vile?"

His face was in shadow, but his attention was keen. She shook her head, not knowing what to say. *It was a lesser hell than others I've known?*

He waited patiently for her to speak. One or two of the men who'd come out with him squelched off on their own affairs, but there were four who stood at his back and watched. Eventually he said, his voice so quiet it might have been mistaken for gentle, "I hope you'll find our hospitality more generous. Why don't you come and take some tea, while we have a little chat." He turned his head and said someone's name, then turned back to her. "But how very rude of me, I haven't introduced myself. Peter Karrian, General to His Majesty's Thousand. At your service."

Her hand closed over the damp edge of the tent flap. By tradition, by law, there were words she must say. She did not say them. She whispered, "Thank you for your hospitality, General. My name is Cassandra Raythe."

"Miss Raythe," the General said with a courtly little bow. "A pleasure. Do let Lieutenant Caldwell help you across the mud, I'm afraid my quartermaster hasn't been able to find any shoes dainty enough to fit." He turned back to his tent.

The General was being absurdly polite to a captive, but then, he was a courtier . . . as de Berin had also once been.

The man he'd called, Lt. Caldwell, came up to her and held out his hand. "Miss. Best if I carry you over, there's God-knows-what in the mud."

It was a moment before she could force her hand to let loose from the canvas flap.

The distant boom of artillery guns made an odd background to the delicate rattle of china cups. Cassandra did not marvel at them. De Berin, too, had been well supplied with the amenities. There was something about power, she thought, that blinded these men to the wretched incongruities of such things in such a time. But she was grateful for the hot, milky tea that soothed her throat.

The General said, "I do realize you're still suffering the effects of your imprisonment, but I'm afraid I must ask a few questions. Anything you can tell us about the enemy could prove invaluable to us."

Speak! de Berin had screamed at her. *You damned selfish, stubborn bitch!*

She nodded. The General sipped, then set his cup precisely in its saucer. He said, "Lieutenant Caldwell's investigations at the house where you were found suggest it was the False Prince's advisor, the Comte de Berin himself, who held you captive. Is that correct?"

Cassandra nodded again.

"Why?"

Of course she had known this was coming. She said, her eyes on the cup in her hands, "Surely it's obvious."

There was an obscure shifting among the men around the General's map table: they were gentlemen, all. Except . . . she glanced at them through the fringes of her eyelashes . . . except for Lt. Caldwell, whose accent had been country, and who watched her from a shadowed corner, his attention fixed and without embarrassment.

And except for the General, who looked gravely sympathetic and said, "I beg your pardon, Miss Raythe, but the doctor's examination suggested otherwise."

Prodded by a man's hands whilst unconscious. The twinge of revulsion she felt was insignificant next to the invasions, the violations profounder by far, that she had known half her life.

And then, as if the very thought conjured it up, she felt the Oracle stir.

"No," she said.

The General's expression did not waver, but his eyes were pale and cold. "I am sorry," he began.

But Cassandra had not been speaking to him. She dropped her cup on the table; the fine china broke into three shards and spilled milky fluid across the surface. She put her hands flat on the table and stood. Her heart pounded as if it, too, would break itself into three. She was desperate to run, to hide . . . to *be silent* . . . but her body was no longer hers. Men's voices fled. Lamplight became a hallucinatory halo. Her skull bled darkness across her mind. The last thing she saw was the three china shards, eggshell white painted with violets, caught like fallen petals in a tea-colored river of wood.

Then the Oracle Spoke, and she was gone.

Lt. Caldwell kept watch in the Voice's tent. The General, having a courtier's sense of the fitness of things, had given her over to her rescuer's care. Watching her sleep, he felt himself slide beyond the need for rest, into some visionary realm inside his own head. He sat in a camp chair with his boots propped on the corner of her cot, arms folded on his chest for warmth. In his mind he held the sound of the Oracle's Voice proclaiming destiny in the General's tent beside the sound of his name echoing through the death-full manor, and found them paired. The implication—his name in an Oracle's Voice—he left to consider another time.

Instead, he contemplated that Voice. It was a sound like a storm: the hush of wind in trees so loud it nearly hid the thunder, or the hiss of waves so pervasive, it nearly drowned the breaking of the surf. But it was also a woman's face, a look of despair that bled away to a mask, blank and white as new plaster, with blue holes where living, grief-shadowed eyes had once been. A mask that hid a power which no one in the world understood, and which everyone in the world coveted. There was no question, now, about why de Berin had kept her captive. Only about what she might have said during her captivity.

The night passed. Dawn dulled the candle by his chair. Reveille rang out.

When she woke, the Oracle's Voice, she turned her head and looked at him as if she'd known in her sleep he was there. She said in an empty husk of a whisper, "What did I say?"

Reconnaissance teams were sent out, observation posts established, lines of communication laid down. The General's lorries trundled off through the mud to meet the supply convoy from the coast, and all morning officers came and went from the General's tent, no doubt to receive the benefit of the Great Man's interpretation of the Oracle's words.

A dynasty grows its roots in the memory of earth.
A tree must be buried deep before he may be crowned with sky.
Let fire thin the forest.
Then shall wind and sunlight follow.

Poetry, Caldwell thought as he stood in line in the officers mess. Poetry, and a justification for war . . . perhaps. Having been promoted from the ranks, he did not have the usual officer's education. To hear the toffs around him speak, a boy couldn't escape a public school without having memorized every Oracular Pronouncement ever recorded, along with interpretations, reinterpretations, theses and theories. It relieved his mind to know that none of that learning did a sweet bit of good to make sense of the Voice's words.

It was less reassuring to know that, according to historical fact, no one had ever interpreted a divination exactly right. Somehow, some hidden meaning always came back to throw the fat in the fire.

The Voice was sitting cross-legged on her cot when he returned with her breakfast. She'd braided her hair and wrapped the looted greatcoat around her, and looked merely thin and defeated, not at all like a receptacle of power. He handed her a tray with porridge and tea, and settled with his own on the canvas chair.

"Thank you," she whispered, and took a careful swallow of tea.

He ate, hungrily, and tried not to eye her untouched bowl when he was done. "You should eat," he finally said, "for the warmth if nothing else."

She looked at the tray as if she hadn't noticed it till now. "I've no appetite." She set it beside her on the cot. Then, as if the idea had approached from a long way off, she looked at him and said, "You might have it, if you're hungry."

Food was too scant to be proud about it. He took her bowl and ate.

She said, "You were the one who found me."

He nodded.

"How?"

He swallowed. "You called me. You said my name."

"I did?" Surprise lit her face, then died. "The Oracle did."

Caldwell chased his breakfast down with a last swallow of tea, and cleared his throat. "The General will be asking—he's busy, now—but he'll want to know what you said to de Berin."

"The Oracle speaks or is silent as it chooses. It chose to say nothing to him. As for myself," she flashed him a look as bitter as the thread of sound in her whisper, "I said to him what you'd expect, being a prisoner to no end."

"How do you mean? A prisoner to no end."

She picked up her cold tea and drank, twisting her mouth in apparent pain. "If the Oracle had anything to say to him, I would have walked barefoot across half the world so it could speak. I have as much say in the matter as . . . as the earth has in the matter of rain."

"So when you called, when the Oracle called, in the house . . . . "

"If it did not wish that I speak for it here, no doubt I would be there still."

He looked at her, comprehension beginning to dawn. The picture of the under-stairs cupboard where she'd been hidden was very clear in his mind.

True to Lt. Caldwell's prediction, the General asked Cassandra what de Berin had heard from the Oracle. He'd had her brought over during a lull in the constant stream of messengers that passed through his tent. He gave her tea, and food she did not much want, and every courtesy, but he did not believe her answer.

"Nothing, madame? How long were you in the Comte de Berin's custody?"

"Weeks. What has that got to do with anything?" she answered rudely. Caldwell's curiosity had been less trying, perhaps because there had been no greed in his eyes.

The General gave her a slow blink like a lizard's. Indeed, there was something reptilian about his thin, dry, pale face. He said, "It is remarkable to me that in all that time he could not persuade you to speak."

"He did not need to persuade *me* to speak at all. I told him often and at length how useless it was to try and coerce the Oracle. He, like so many others, was simply unable to comprehend the difference." The implication, like her fulminating stare, lingered.

The General absorbed it in silence. Then he sat back in his camp chair, satisfaction curling the corners of his narrow mouth. "So. The Oracle had nothing to say to the False Prince's chief advisor . . . if we can believe you, madame."

"I cannot lie about such things."

"Yet you did not proclaim yourself to us, as I believe you are bound by law to do."

"The Oracle's Voice is outside the law for a reason," she said, though in fact he was right.

"But not outside the traditions of your forebears," he countered, knowing he was. "I wonder why you tried to keep yourself hidden from us when we had rescued you?"

"I wonder why you imagine yourself so different from de Berin?" she shot back, her voice cracking into sound halfway through. "I was in the Sanctuary at Felmouth when it was blasted by shells. The Comte was equally sure he was rescuing me. I told him what I was, and he never let me rest for a minute after."

"But you have spoken for me."

"I have said nothing!" Frustration drove her ruined voice back into a whisper. "It is the Oracle that speaks. Not I. Why is this so difficult to comprehend?"

He considered her for a time. There was a constant quiet stirring in the background, officers who took the opportunity to exercise their curiosity and snatch a bite to eat. The General turned his attention to his own meal. Then, having eaten a little, he said, "I am curious. What do you make of the prophecy?"

Cassandra crumbled a bit of journey bread on her tin plate. "I've forgotten what it was."

He looked at her, disbelieving. "Forgotten!"

"I never hear it," she said without looking up. "Lieutenant Caldwell told me, but I forget. Something about trees."

The General considered this new datum, then recited, as matter-of-factly as if he were dictating a note to his quartermaster, "A dynasty grows its roots in the memory of earth. A tree must be buried deep before he may be crowned with sky. Let fire thin the forest. Then shall wind and sunlight follow."

"The King's dynasty? The False Prince's?" Cassandra looked at him. "Yours?" She shrugged.

Thoughts flickered behind the General's eyes. "And the rest?"

"The usual nonsense. It means nothing to me."

Someone choked on a crumb. Someone else laughed. The General said slowly, "I do not understand you, madame."

"I know," Cassandra said wearily. "No one ever does."

Caldwell looked in on her some time after the bugler sounded Taps. The General was rumored to be somewhat disenchanted with his seer—Caldwell had been, thank God, sound asleep during their noon meeting—but no one had rescinded the order for him to stand guard. The heavy cloud cover pressed blackness down upon the camp, shrouding even the flashes of light from the artillery lines ten miles away, but the rain had stopped for a time. The Voice's wet tent glowed like tortoiseshell with the light of the lamp inside. Caldwell cleared his throat and scratched on the tent flap.

"Who is it?"

Her voice was as broken as a telephone line in a windstorm. Feeling obscurely guilty, he said, "Caldwell, ma'am. Just making sure you're all right."

"Thank you."

"I'll be around if you need anything."

"That isn't . . . " . . . *necessary*, he thought she meant to say. But instead, after a pause, she said again, "Thank you."

He supposed she would know the two faces any guard wore. He pulled his collar high against the chill, checked the flap on his holster, and asked himself who he was fooling. He wasn't there to keep her prisoner any more than he was there to keep her safe. How could she escape from the middle of the General's camp when she didn't even have any shoes? What harm could find her there? Even the most desperate and depraved private was hardly going to make an attempt on the Oracle's, and General's, Voice. No, Caldwell was there to listen if the Oracle had anything to say, and probably she knew it as well as he. The image of the closet came back to him, the bolt on the door, and the cupboard hiding even that.

He'd been standing guard not more than an hour before the rain resumed. It fell in a cold, light, liquid fall, pattering on canvas and mud, soaking the shoulders of his field jacket. He pulled his collar higher and tried to keep his mind off the lighted tents all around him.

"Lieutenant?"

The whisper from the tent at his back was so soft it was nearly lost in the rain.

"Lieutenant Caldwell. Are you still there?"

"Yes, ma'am."

"It's raining, isn't it?"

He cleared his throat. "Yes, ma'am."

"Perhaps you'd better come in."

The words shivered down through all the hollows of his body, like a chill and not. He said, almost as quietly as she had spoken, "Perhaps I'd better not, ma'am."

The rain fell, softly, softly, patter and hush.

She said, "I wish you would."

He came in looking as if he suspected a trap. The lamp, turned as low as it would go, carved his country-man's face out of shadow. Cassandra pulled the blankets close to her chin and said, "It doesn't seem right for them to put you on guard. If I need guarding at all, surely a regular soldier would do?"

Lt. Caldwell settled into the camp chair by the foot of her cot. "The General has his own ideas about such things." He took his cap off and shook the rain carefully onto the floor.

Cassandra was achingly tired, and irritable for feeling responsible for this man's discomfort. It wasn't as though she had any more choice in this than she had in anything else. But then, asking him in had been a choice. She bent one arm beneath her head and said, "You didn't tell them about the Oracle calling your name, did you."

He shifted, looking as if he didn't know where to put his hands, or his eyes. "No."

"Why not?"

"I couldn't think what it was at the time. You were out cold when we found you and it just never . . . . " He shrugged. "You know there's an Oracle in the world, but you never think it'd ever have a thing to do with you, anymore than you think God will, I don't know, pick you out to announce the second coming. And I never supposed the Voice would . . . . "

"What?" She smiled. "Look like a skinny, tired-out girl?"

Caldwell looked directly at her for the first time, and smiled. "Since it's you that says it." A silence settled between them, filled up by the sound of the rain. He dropped his eyes and said, "I wondered, though. I've never heard of anyone it called by name."

Cassandra looked at the tent's sloping roof. "No."

"So why bother with my name? How does it know?"

"How does it know anything?" She put her hands over her eyes. "When I was studying with the old Voice, before she died, she said it was a manifestation of the divine will ordering affairs among men. But I've read the histories. There has been more war, more murder, more hatred and anger and tragedy surrounding the Oracle's prophecies than I can even comprehend. I don't want to lay that at the feet of God. Sometimes I think . . . . "

"Sometimes you think." His whisper was as faint as hers.

She looked at him, knowing she'd already said more than she should. "Be thankful it didn't want any more from you than an open door."

After a long silence, he said, "You want me to put out the light?"

"Yes," she said.

The lantern hung from a hook above the head of the cot. The lieutenant half stood to lift the chimney and blow out the flame. When it was dark she reached out for his wrist and pulled him down.

Late, very late, when their two bodies lay spent and warm, all extraneous concerns fell away and left the heart of the matter exposed. Caldwell said, "The General will take the prophecy as his license to clean house, you know."

"What do you mean?"

"Clear the forest. Build the dynasty. Once this front is secure, he'll do what he's been wanting to do for years. Clear the court of all his rivals and make the Prince his own man. It's all there if you have a mind like his."

"Of course it is," Cassandra breathed. "It gives him license to act, as you say, and gives his enemies room to prove him wrong. That's how the Oracle always speaks. In words like shadows hiding blood."

"You make it sound like it has a purpose."

"Of course it has!" she hissed scornfully. "When did you ever know power without some purpose of its own?"

The rain patted the canvas roof, dripped musically in puddles of its own making at the corners of the tent.

"God preserve us," Caldwell said.

"What amazes me is that no one—no one, in all these centuries—has ever questioned what that purpose is, or whether the Oracle, even in its twisting way, actually tells the truth."

"The Oracle *lies*?" Shock raised Caldwell's voice.

"Hush!" Cassandra pressed her palm over his mouth. "No more. I've said too much."

The General invited her to his tent not long after Reveille to join him for breakfast. Lt. Caldwell had left her bed, and her tent, more than an hour before dawn. Though he'd left her with a lover's kindness, she could tell he was shaken by her talk. She did not hold it against him: she was shaken herself. Things she had never dared voice even in her own thoughts, she had said aloud to him. But it wasn't as though she was afraid to trust him. Her own greatest enemy could tear her open, mind and soul, any time it chose. What would a merely human betrayal matter? And in any case, what would "betrayal" amount to, but a casting of doubt over the Oracle's pronouncements. Hardly a matter for dread, at least on her account. Cassandra could not say why this foreboding grew with the light of day. She only knew it did.

The General presided at his breakfast table brilliant with energy. In her presence he and his officers spoke mostly of generalities, certainly not of policy or strategy, but she remembered what Caldwell had said about the General's interpretation of the Oracle's words, and she believed him. A kind of grief came over her, a vision of the nation, already split by the civil war, being divided again, and again, and again. And where else had the war begun but with the last Voice's prophecy of the old King's death? And before that . . . what? How far back could one trace the trail of spilled blood?

"I'm beginning to consider my next trip to the capital," the General was saying to one of his aides. "I hadn't wanted to leave the front with the Fell Valley still in question, but—" He broke off when the aide cleared his throat and nodded at Cassandra.

She set her cup back in its saucer. "I beg your pardon, General. I can only be in your way. Thank you for the meal."

"You've scarcely eaten," the General said with a glance at her plate. "In any case, I can assure you, you are in no way an impediment. Quite the opposite, in fact, you add a touch of civilization to our bachelor's domain."

Cassandra forced out, "You're very kind," and got to her feet. She was dizzy with hunger, yet her stomach clenched on the thought of more food. Even the food on her plate looked strange, like a painting of itself. She leaned on the wooden frame of her chair.

"Madame, you don't look at all well. Should I send for the doctor?"

She shook her head, then managed, "No, thank you. I only need to rest . . . . a little more . . . ." Bees like bullets were whirring in her ears. *Not now,* she thought. *Please, God, not now.*

There were murmurings of *doctor,* and then Caldwell's name. "There you are," the General said irritably. "See to the lady, will you? If she's ill . . . "

His voice, all their voices, faded into the whir. Sunlight flared at the open door of the tent, like mist-white wings at Caldwell's back. The cold floor poured numbness up her legs, all through her, into her heart, her skull, her mind.

The Oracle Spoke.

As often happened, Cassandra woke to sound before anything else. While the spike of pain pinned her motionless and the cool air tore through her abraded throat, she heard, like the tolling of church bells, a sergeant-major's bawl.

Squaaad! Ready h'aaarms!

H'aaaim!

Fi-yaaar!

And then a ragged volley of rifles.

Dread flooded through her. She raised her head, squinting through the pain. "Caldwell?" There was a man-shaped shadow against the wall. "Caldwell?"

"No, ma'am. Lieutenant Harney, at your service, ma'am."

"Where . . . . " Oh God. "Where is Lieutenant Caldwell?"

The young man leaned forward, his round face earnest, his forehead dewed with sweat. "Don't worry, ma'am. The traitor is dead."

She stared at him. "What did I say?"

MOON OVER YODOK

————

David Charlton

for Kang Chol-Hwan

Everyone at Yodok, everyone in the whole country, knew the story of Our Dear Leader's birth. On the day he emerged from the lake atop Baekdu Mountain, a double rainbow appeared over the cabin of his father, Our Great Leader, Kim Il-Sung. A new star appeared in the sky and a swallow flew overhead to signal the arrival of a mighty new general destined to lead us to victory over the imperialist enemies.

Oh Hae-Sik, his threadbare rags and the rough cool flesh underneath coated in dust, squatted outside the Oh family hut, gazing at the night's full moon and thought about his younger sister, Dal-Soon. Inside, his grandmother slept or was unconscious. Hae-Sik could no longer tell the difference. He knew he should go inside to clean the blood, but he needed more cold air first. A muted double rainbow circled the moon. *Dal-Soon would have loved that*, Hae-Sik thought. *Perhaps it's a sign for her.*

The full moon of the year's eighth lunar month also marked *Chuseok*, the Korean harvest holiday. The years since the Oh family were brought to the Yodok work camp had never been happy ones, but the recent death of Dal-Soon had cast an even greater pall on the family . . . what remained of the family.

"Can you see the rabbit in the moon?" Dal-Soon asked him each night as the new moon grew to its *Chuseok* fullness. "She's pounding the rice for our *songpyeon*."

Hae-Sik was old enough to remember the sweet taste of the honey-and-sesame-seed-filled rice cakes, but he doubted his sister really could.

Such memories brought a tangy metallic pain to the roots of his teeth. He almost hoped Dal-Soon could only imagine, not remember, that taste.

During the last year, his grandmother had begun telling them stories like the rabbit in the moon. Hae-Sik remembered her being different before they were brought to Yodok, before his parents had gone. "Focus on what you *need*," she once told him in Pyongyang. "Focus on your work. Focus on the party. Keep our country self-sufficient and strong against the imperialists."

His grandparents had been forced into servitude by Japanese imperialists long ago. They worked and fought through hardship to gain their freedom and forge lives for themselves in Japan. Thirty years ago, the lure of a Korean People's Republic brought them back to their homeland.

Hae-Sik would never know exactly why his family was taken to Yodok. First, his grandfather disappeared. A week later, the trucks and soldiers came to the family apartment. They were forced to hastily pack some clothes, utensils, and rice, and were whisked away in the night.

The family was able to survive the first winter, but the following years had taken their toll. The rice they were permitted to bring with them did not last long. After it ran out, they survived, like the other prisoners, on cornmeal and anything else that could be scrounged. The all-corn diet had severe effects, though, especially on the men. Skin turned dry, toe- and fingernails fell out, eyes became ringed with deep dark wrinkles, and bodies became weak from constant diarrhea. Hae-Sik's father succumbed to the "glasses disease" that first spring.

"If only we'd had some dog meat, we could have cured him," Hae-Sik's grandmother declared.

"If only we'd had *any* meat," his mother whispered. "If only we, if only they, if only that, that—"

Hae-Sik's grandmother quickly clapped her hand over her daughter-in-law's mouth. At Yodok, one never knew who might be listening and who might repeat what was heard. Hae-Sik looked in his mother's eyes, but he couldn't see her. Until she disappeared more than a year later, Hae-Sik saw only the If-Only woman, never his mother, never his *Om-ma*.

Mourning for passed loved ones was kept to a minimum at Yodok. Such deaths simply became too common. Children adapted to the shock. Hae-Sik and Dal-Soon adapted, too.

Mornings were spent crowded into shabby classrooms. Between the beatings and constant verbal abuse, they studied the feats and words of Kim Il-Sung and Kim-Jong Il. Afternoons were spent at hard labor: planting cornfields, pulling weeds, hauling timber, tending rabbits, and later for Hae-Sik, burial detail.

Though difficult, certain jobs provided benefits. Tending fields allowed for the collection of frogs, salamanders, and even earthworms to supplement the diet. Grandmother could never get the hang of quickly swallowing the salamanders whole before they could secrete their foul-tasting oil. Pulling weeds allowed for collection of a few herbs and the occasional wild ginseng root. Burial allowed for the collection of precious clothing. Yodok was located on a high alpine plain surrounded by barren peaks, and prisoners were given only one set of clothes per year, if they were lucky.

Recently, Grandmother's skin had been getting rougher. She only had three fingernails left. Her eyes were deep-set and getting darker. Hae-Sik and Dal-Soon tried to help her as much as possible. They shared what they could of their meager allotment of cornmeal, especially Dal-Soon.

"You are my sweet little rabbit, Dal-Soon. Do you see the rabbit in the moon, young one?"

"Yes, *Halmoni*. She's pounding rice for the *songpyeon*."

"That's right. Do you know how she got there?"

"No, *Halmoni*. How?"

"The Buddha put here there. A friend of the Buddha was starving . . . nearly dead. The rabbit offered her life to save this friend, so the Buddha honored the rabbit this way. Now, we can always see her at night and remember."

"Who's the Buddha, *Halmoni*?"

"Oh, young one! He was someone my grandmother taught me about. It doesn't matter now. Maybe it's silly. Don't think about it. Just remember the rabbit when you look at the moon."

"I will, *Halmoni*."

"Good girl. Good Dal-Soon."

Long before this conversation, Dal-Soon had been known as "Rabbit" among the children of Yodok. This was partly because of her oversized front teeth, partly because of her swiftness of foot, but mostly because of her love of the rabbits kept by the school.

Every rural school in the country was given the responsibility and honor of raising rabbits. From these rabbits, fur coats were made to keep the soldiers warm during the bitingly cold winter months. Each class had its own warren of rabbits. At Yodok, students were encouraged to care for their rabbits with more attention than their own families. After all, their families were counterrevolutionary mongrels, but these rabbits were helping Our Dear Leader's army withstand foreign imperialist forces.

Students were even encouraged to steal corn from the fields and even cabbage or other vegetables from the guard's gardens. They also had to clean the cages, keep track of the number and weight of the animals, and stand guard over the cages to ensure rats were not intruding upon the cages to steal food or attack the young.

Though all students took some part in tending the rabbits, the teachers trusted them most to Dal-Soon's care. Despite knowing the eventual destiny of the rabbits, she treated them with open love and affection, expressions almost always guarded and hidden at Yodok. With family members, other students, even teachers, such displays could be turned against you. If such a loved one cracked and publicly expressed anger with life in Yodok or, unthinkably, displeasure with the party or even Our Dear Leader himself, guilt by association was far reaching. With the rabbits, Dal-Soon's love and affection could only be seen as love and affection for leader and country.

A shooting star blazed through Hae-Sik's gaze up at the moon, though he hardly noticed. *Why couldn't I see it coming? She must have been giving her corn to the rabbits and to Grandmother. She was getting so thin. If only I'd opened my eyes. I'm sorry, Dal-Soon. I didn't know what to do.*

As September had progressed, the remnants of the Oh family continued to weaken and grow thinner. Fewer and fewer frogs, salamanders, and worms were in the fields. Hae-Sik couldn't seem to catch any rats when it was his turn to guard the rabbit cages. Both he and Dal-Soon gave more and more of their cornmeal to their grandmother, whose symptoms continued to worsen.

At school, Hae-Sik's concentration lagged. He forgot the date upon which Kim Il-Sung gave his speech at the Dahongdan conference.

"How dare you forget the glorious acts of our Great Leader!" screamed the teacher. Hae-Sik was forced to stand in the corner, holding five textbooks above his head, while the teacher beat the back of his calves and thighs with a stick until he passed out. After class, he was assigned to latrine duty.

He stumbled home late that night, the stench of urine and feces clouding into his nostrils. There were no showers for prisoners at Yodok. Despite the coolness of the evening, Hae-Sik simply waded into and out of the creek on his way home. Steam rising from his clothes and head, he entered the Oh family hut to see Dal-Soon huddled down beside his muttering grandmother, her skin a pale, almost-silver in the moonlight.

"Hae-Sik? Oh Hae-Sik?" his grandmother asked.

"She's not good," Dal-Soon mumbled, her own eyes half closed.

Ah sheebal! Hae-Sik thought frantically. *I don't know what to do anymore.* "She needs some food. She needs real food. She needs some meat. You, too, Little Rabbit . . . you, too. Look at you. There's almost nothing left. Look at me. Me, too. There's nothing left of us."

"Quiet. Quiet," Grandmother said as strongly as she could. "Listen to me."

Dal-Soon and Hae-Sik squatted beside her, leaning close.

"Yes, *Halmoni*. I'm here. It's Hae-Sik. I'm here."

"Good boy. Good boy. Listen to me, young ones. I'm an old woman, listen to me. I'm going to die soon."

"No. Don't say that *Halmoni*," Dal-Soon said.

"Yes, yes, Little Rabbit. I'm old and tired. It won't be a bad thing. Understand? I'm tired. I've seen a lot . . . too much. We all have, young ones. You two have to watch out for one another. Understand? Understand?"

"Yes," Hae-Sik spoke.

"Rabbit? Understand?"

"Yes," Dal-Soon eventually said.

"Good girl. Listen to your grandmother. Watch out for one another. Listen for one another. Be careful what you say. Be careful what you do. Hide your eyes. You can survive this. Your grandfather and I survived the Japanese. You can survive this."

"OK, *Halmoni*," said Hae-Sik. "We'll be careful. You sleep now, OK? You won't die tonight. It's *Chuseok* soon. We'll have a good time."

"Yeah, *Halmoni*. Don't worry," said Dal-Soon. "Maybe we'll get some *songpyeon* this year. Don't die yet." She suddenly stood up and left the hut.

"Dal-Soon?" Hae-Sik called after her. "Little Rabbit? Where are you going?" Turning his gaze back to his grandmother, he noticed her eyes had closed, though her chest slowly rose and fell.

He stepped outside the hut and squatted down, shivering. Where had Dal-Soon gone? He should go find her, but he was so tired. He slipped back out of his squat and onto his back, his eyes rolling lazily up to the moon.

"Dal-Soon?" he called softly. He saw the rabbit in the moon, pounding rice for *songpyeon* . . . but it wasn't rice. It was his family: his grandfather, his father, his mother, all being pounded. He saw his sleeping grandmother underneath the heavy wooden mallet, then his sister. He could feel the mallet behind his own eyes, reverberating in his nostrils and down his spine. *I'm going crazy,* he thought. *I need sleep. I need strength. First, find Dal-Soon.* "Rabbit?" he called, rising to his feet. "Where are you?"

Another shooting star sped across the Yodok night. Hae-sik's eyes focused on it this time. He needed to take his mind off the events of the last twenty-four hours. It was actually quite beautiful. A streak of light remained burned into his retinas. He looked back at the moon. He could see the shape of a rabbit, but it was still tonight. An owl flew silently overhead in the direction of the rabbit warrens. *Oh well*, he thought, *that's someone else's problem tonight. One less fur coat for the army won't hurt Dal-Soon. Or Grandmother. Or me.*

Suddenly, another shooting star sped across the fullness of the moon, streaking and screaming towards the camp, landing with a crash that sent rocks and dirt and debris into the Yodok air.

Oh, no, thought Hae-Sik, *not the hill. Dal-Soon!*

Suddenly, the camp was stirring with people. Prisoners slouched out of their huts to see what the commotion was. Guards scrambled from their quarters to defend against attack or revolt. In the aftermath of the meteor impact, only the sound of falling dust and tumbling rocks could be heard.

"A meteor struck the hill," people began saying. Word soon passed through camp. A few older prisoners muttered about a bad sign and went back into their huts. A few others muttered about a good sign and went back into their huts. Some younger prisoners milled about the common area, looking up at the hill. Nobody moved closer to inspect.

"Burial detail to the hill!" shouted a voice through a megaphone. "Burial detail to the hill at once!"

No, Hae-Sik thought, *No. No. No. Not again. Not again.*

"Oh Hae-Sik! That means you, too!" the voice continued, "No excuses. Let's go!"

Turning his back on the moon, Hae-sik obeyed the voice, marching up toward the burial hill for the second time that day.

"Dal-Soon? Where are you Little Rabbit?" Hae-Sik called as he searched for his sister. Though the sky was clear and the almost-full moon bright, he could not find her anywhere.

He slowly searched around their little village area of the camp, the rabbit warrens, the school grounds, the rabbit warrens again, the latrines, the banks of the creek, and stumbled back to the rabbit warrens one last time. He couldn't see Dal-Soon, but he did see three or four rats at a small pile of lettuce. As quickly as his weakened legs could move, he pounced at the rats.

When he arrived back at the Oh family hut, Dal-Soon had returned. She lay beside Grandmother. *Tonight,* he thought, *we'll have some meat. Grandmother will be OK. We'll have full bellies on Chuseok.* When she heard Hae-Sik enter the hut, she rolled toward him, her eyes wide and glassy.

"What did you do?" she asked.

"I've brought some meat," he said, holding out his arms, the skinned carcasses hanging from his fists.

Four others joined Hae-Sik in the march up burial hill. Rocks and stones still tumbled down the slope towards them from the impact site. One man pressed a hand on Hae-Sik's shoulder, muttering, "Be strong, huh? We'll get through it. It has to be done." Then in the faintest of whispers: "For Dal-Soon." Hae-Sik just continued trudging up the hill, thinking about that morning.

He had awoken to the girlish wails of one his classmates, Seo Ji-Hwan. "What happened?" he cried. "Who did this? Who could do this?"

Hae-Sik, feeling stronger than he had in months, suddenly bolted upright. Dal-Soon was beside him and quickly clamped a hand over his mouth. "Don't get up," she spoke softly but sternly into his ear. "Stay right here. There's trouble."

A lump suddenly forming deep within his throat, Hae-Sik scanned the Oh family hut. His grandmother remained in bed, facing the wall. In the corner beside the door lay a pile of skinned, bloody, carcasses, too large to be rats. In front of him sat his bowl, empty save for a small amount of soup broth, speckled with congealed flecks of waxy fat. Beside him sat Dal-Soon, her legs wrapped in blankets soaked in blood.

"What's going on?" he asked her.

"Shhh. Stay still. There will be trouble today, Hae-Sik. Bad trouble."

Suddenly, he could hear people gathering outside their hut.

"The blood leads here," someone said.

"I told you I saw her at the rabbits last night. It was Oh Dal-Soon," said Seo Ji-Hwan. "She did this."

Now about halfway up the hill, Hae-Sik stopped his legs. More rocks continued to tumble down the slope. Something was moving up top, crawling and pushing its way out of the earth. Hae-Sik finally looked up to see his sister Dal-Soon emerge.

"Dal-Soon," he said voicelessly. "Little Rabbit. What's happening?"

Her skin had turned grey, but appeared almost silver in the moonlight. Her clothes had been removed for the living, and Hae-Sik could see the cuts and bruises she'd suffered from the guards that morning. Except some areas were hidden from view: patches along her belly, shoulders, and back were covered by rabbit fur, as though the skinned hides of the creatures had been stitched to her own flesh.

As she limped slowly along the crest of the hill, Hae-Sik's eyes were drawn to her calves. The muscles were gone, but in their place he saw the skinned bodies of two rabbits, fused liked tendons into her body.

"You did this to me," she spoke.

Suddenly, Seo Ji-Hwan, also part of the burial detail, fell to the ground. Hae-Sik noted the bloody dent in the top of his skull and a bloody fist-sized rock beside the boy's body.

"What—What's happening, Dal-Soon?" Hae-Sik asked.

"You have to bury *Halmoni*," she said.

"What? She's sleeping, Little Rabbit. Don't wake her up. She's sick, but we have some meat."

"It's too late, Hae-Sik. She died last night. Remember?"

"No. No, she was OK this morning. I made her some soup. Some rat soup. It will cure her."

"No, Hae-Sik. You were too late. She was gone already. There was no rat soup."

"I ate the rat soup. I'm strong today. *Halmoni* will get better, too."

"It's too late. She's gone, but you must bury her. Then, we can all be together. That's why I made you my soup. Be strong now."

"I brought the rats for you and *Halmoni*, so we could get strong together. If only I'd got them sooner."

"There were no rats, Hae-Sik. You killed the rabbits."

"No. They were rats. They were eating the lettuce. We made rat soup. I'm stronger. *Halmoni* will be stronger."

"After you bury her, she will. But there were no rats, Hae-Sik. You killed the rabbits. You killed Our Dear Leader's rabbits. You killed *my* rabbits."

"I'm sorry Dal-Soon. I'm sorry Little—I ate your rabbits? I'm sorry. If only I could have—If only we had—If only that—"

"You didn't eat my rabbits. I couldn't let you. I gave you my soup to give you strength. Only you can bury *Halmoni*. Then, our family will be together again. You must bury *Halmoni*."

"OK, Dal-Soon. OK."

"Look at the moon, Hae-Sik."

Hae-Sik turned his gaze towards the moon. He could see the rabbit pounding rice again.

"She's made us some *songpyeon*, Hae-Sik. Eat the *songpyeon* and bury *Halmoni*," spoke Dal-Soon, throwing handfuls of the sweet rice-cakes down the hill towards Hae-Sik.

Hae-Sik reached down, filling his hands with *songpyeon* and shoving them into his mouth. Chewing with all his power, he ground and broke his teeth into dozens of jagged pieces.

"Go bury *Halmoni* now, Hae-Sik. In the morning, you can join us all in the sky. We'll have a real *Chuseok* feast!" Dal-Soon spoke. Then, she squatted down low on all fours, flexing her rabbit-calf muscles and springing into the air, a streak of light reaching across the night sky to the moon.

After watching her ascent, Hae-Sik turned downhill, moving toward the Oh family hut. Everything suddenly became clear, as though a fog had been lifted from his mind. He heard the generators chugging in the distance. He heard the fluorescent lights humming in the guards' quarters. He even heard the beating of moth wings at their windows. He could smell a burning sulfur stench from atop the hill. He could smell cigarette smoke, the latrines, rabbit urine, and even the wild ginseng roots growing under the soil in the hills around Yodok. He was aware of the tickle of sweat in his armpits and on his legs, and he felt each single hair on his arms and head twitch and flitter in the breeze. Most of all, he could taste the honey and sesame seeds from the *songpyeon*.

As he walked through the other huts to his grandmother, his neighbors came out to find the source of the sweet, nutty scent that filled the air. They watched Hae-Sik, noting the rich, golden mixture dribbling out between his broken teeth and down his chin. Their stomachs churned and groaned as his tongue flashed out to catch and savor it.

"Hae-Sik," someone asked him. "Where did you get the *songpyeon*? It . . . it smells *wonderful*! Where did you get it?"

"From the moon," he replied, pointing to the sky. "See? It comes from Dal-Soon."

I'LL GNAW YOUR BONES,
THE MANTICORE SAID

———

Cat Rambo

Even Duga the Prestidigitator, who never pays much attention to anything outside his own hands, raised an eyebrow when I announced I'd be hooking the manticore up to my wagon.

"Isn't that dangerous?" my husband Rik said. He steepled his fingers, regarding me.

"The more we have pulling, the faster we get there," I pointed out. "And Bupus has been getting fat and lazy as a tabby cat. No one pays to see a fat manticore."

"More dangerous than any tabby cat," Rik said.

I knew what he meant, but I kept a lightning rod at hand in the wagon seat in case of trouble. Bupus knew I'd scorch his greasy whiskers if he crossed me.

There is a tacit understanding between a beast trainer and her charges, whether it be great cats, cunning dragons, or apes and other man-like creatures. They know, and the trainer knows, that as long as certain lines aren't crossed, that if certain expectations are met, everything will be fine and no one will get hurt.

That's not to say I didn't keep an eye on Bupus, watching for a twitch to his tail, the way one bulbous eye would go askew when anger was brewing. A beast's a beast, after all, and not responsible for what they do when circumstances push them too far. Beasts still, no matter how they speak or smile or woo.

At any rate, Bupus felt obliged to maintain his reputation whenever another wagon or traveler was in earshot.

"Gnaw your bones," he rumbled, rolling a vast oversized eyeball back at me. The woman he was trying to impress shrieked and dropped her chickens, which vanished in a white flutter among the blackberry vines and ferns that began where the road's ground stone gave way to forest. A blue-headed jay screamed in alarm from a pine.

"Behave yourself," I said.

He rumbled again, but nothing coherent, just a low, animal sound.

We were coming up on Piperville, which sits on a trade hub. Steel figured we'd pitch there for a week, get a little silver sparkling in our coffers, eat well for a few nights.

It had been a lean winter and times were hard all over—traveling up from Ponce's Spring, we'd found slim pickings and audiences too worried about the dust storms to pay any attention to even our best: Laxmi the elephant dancing in pink spangles to "Waltzing Genevieve," the pyramid of crocodiles that we froze and unfroze each performance via a lens-and-clockwork basilisk, the Unicorn Maiden, and, of course, my manticore.

Rik was driving a wagon full of machinery, packed and protected from the dust with layers of waxed canvas. He pulled up near me, so we were riding in tandem for a bit. No one was coming the opposite way for now. We'd hit some road traffic coming out of Ponce's, but now it was only occasional, a twice-an-hour thing at most.

"You know what I'm looking forward to?" I called over to him.

He considered. I watched him thinking in the sunlight, my broad-shouldered and beautiful husband and just the look of him, his long scholar's nose and silky beard, made me smile.

"Beer," he said finally. "And clean sheets. Cleeaaaan sheets." He drawled out the last words, smiling over at me.

"A bath," I said.

A heartfelt groan so deep it might have come from the bottom of his soul came from him. "Oh, a bath. With towels. Thick towels."

I was equally enraptured by the thought, so much so that I didn't notice the wheel working loose. And Bupus, concerned with looking for people to impress, didn't warn me. With a sideways lurch, the wagon tilted, and the wheel kept going, rolling down the roadway, neat as you please, until it passed Laxmi and she put out her trunk and snagged it.

I put on my shoes and hopped down to examine the damage. Steel heard the commotion and came back from the front of the train. He rode Beulah, the big white horse that accompanies him in the ring each time.

Sometimes we laugh about how attached he is to that horse, but never where he can hear us.

The carts and caravans kept passing us. A few waved and Rik waved back. The august clowns were practicing their routine, somersaulting into the dust behind their wagon, then running to catch up with it again. Duga was practicing card tricks while his assistant drove, dividing her attention between the reins and watching him. Duga was notoriously close-mouthed about his methods; I suspected watching might be her only way to learn.

"Whaddya need?" Steel growled as he reached me.

"Looks like a linchpin fell out. Could have been a while back. Sparky'll have a new one, I'm sure."

His blue gaze slid skyward, sideways, anywhere to avoid meeting my eyes. "Sparky's gone."

It is an unfortunate fact that circuses are usually made of Family and outsiders—jossers, they call us. Steel treated Family well but was unwilling to extend that courtesy outside the circle. I'd married in, and he was forced to acknowledge me, but Sparky had been a full outsider, and Steel had made his life a misery, maintaining our cranky and antiquidated machines: the fortune teller, the tent-lifter, and Steel's pride and joy, the spinning cups, packed now on the largest wagon and pulled by Laxmi and three oxen.

The position of circus smith had been vacant of Family for a while now, ever since Big Joy fell in love with a fire-eater and left us for the Whistling Piskie—a small, one-ring outfit that worked the coast.

So we'd lost Sparky because Steel had scrimped and shorted his wages, not to mention refusing to pay prentice fees when he wanted to take one on. More importantly, we'd lost his little traveling cart, full of tools and scrap and spare linchpins.

"So what am I going to do?" I snapped. Bupus had sat down on the road and was eying the passing caravans, more out of curiosity than hunger or desire to menace. "I'll gnaw your bones," he said almost conversationally, but it frightened no one in earshot. He sighed and settled his head between his paws, a green snot dribble bubbling from one kitten-sized nostril.

The Unicorn Girl pulled up her caravan. She'd been trying to repaint it the night before and there were bleary splotches of green and lavender paint smearing its sides.

"What's going on?' she said loudly. "Driving badly again, Tara?"

The Unicorn Girl was one of those souls with no volume control. Sitting next to her in taverns or while driving was painful. She'd bray the same stories over and over again, and was tactless and unkind. I tried to avoid her when I could.

But, oh, she pulled them in. That long, narrow, angelic face, the pearly horn emerging from her forehead, and two lush lips, peach-ripe, set like emerging sins beneath the springs of her innocent doe-like eyes.

Even now, she looked like an angel, but I knew she was just looking for gossip, something she might be able to use to buy favor or twist like a knife when necessary.

Steel looked back and forth. "Broken wagon, Lily," he said. "You can move along."

She dimpled, pursing her lips at him but took up her reins. The two white mares pulling her wagon were daughters of the one he rode, twins with a bad case of the wobbles but which should be good for years more, if you ignored the faint, constant trembling of their front legs. Most people didn't notice it.

"She needs to learn to mind her tongue," I said.

"Rik needs to come in with us," Steel said, ignoring my comment. "He's the smartest, he knows how to bargain. These little towns have their own customs and laws and it's too easy to set a foot awry and land ourselves in trouble."

Much as I hated to admit, Steel was right. Rik is the smartest of the lot, and he knows trade law like the back of his hand.

"I'll find someone to leave with you, and Rik will ride back with the pin, soon as he can," Steel said.

"All right," I said. Then, as he started to wheel Beulah around. "Someone I won't mind, Steel. Got me?"

"Got it," he said, and rode away.

"I don't like leaving you," Rik said guiltily. It was a year old story, and its once upon a time had begun on our honeymoon night, with him riding out to help with the funeral of his grandfather, who had been driven into a fatal apoplectic fit by news of his marriage to someone who'd never known circus life.

"Can't be helped," I said crisply. He sighed.

"Tara . . . . "

"Can't be helped." I flapped an arm at him. "Go on, get along, faster you are to town, faster you're back to me."

He got out of his wagon long enough to kiss me and ruffle my hair.

"Not long," he said. "I won't be long."

"We'll leave Preddi with you," Steel said, a quarter hour after I'd watched Rik's caravan recede into the distance. It had taken a while for the rest of the circus to pass me, wagon after wagon. Even for such a small outfit, we had a lot of wagons.

Preddi was Rik's father, a small, stooped man given to carelessness with his dress. He was a kindly man, I think, but difficult to get to know because his deafness distanced him.

We pulled the wagon over to the side of the road, in a margined sward thick with yellow loosestrife and dandelions. A narrow deer path led through blackberry tangles and further into the pines, a stream coming through the thick pine needles and chuckling along the rocks. I tied Bupus to the wagon, and brought out a sack of hams and loaves of bread before making several trips in to bring him buckets of water.

Preddi settled himself on the grass and extracted a deck of greasy cards from the front pocket of his flannel shirt. While I worked, he laid out hand after hand, playing poker with himself, studying it.

The day wore on.

And on. I cleaned the wagon tack, and repacked the bundles in it, mainly my training gear. Someone else would be tending my cage of beasts when they pitched camp, and truth be told, anyone could, but I still preferred to be the one who fed the crocodiles, for example, and watched for mouth rot or the white lesions that signal pox virus and cleaned their cage thoroughly enough to make sure no infection could creep in under their scales or into the tender areas around their vents.

Bupus gorged himself and then slept, but roused enough to want to play. I threw the heavy leather ball and each time his tail whipped out with frightening speed and batted it aside. Fat and lazy, he may be, but Bupus has many years left in him. They go four or five decades, and I'd raised him from the shell ten years earlier, before I'd even bought the flimsy paper ticket that led me to meet Rik.

I hadn't known what I had at first. A sailor swapped me the egg in return for me covering his bar tab, and who knows who got the best of that bargain? I was a beast trainer for the Duke, and mainly I worked with little animals, trained squirrels and ferrets and marmosets. They juggled and danced, shot tiny plaster pistols, and engaged in duels as exquisite as any courtier's.

The egg was bigger than my doubled fists laid knuckle and palm to knuckle and palm. It was coarse to the touch, as though threads or hairy roots had been laid over the shell and grown into it, and it was a deep yellow, the same yellow that Bupus's eyes would open into, honey depths around clover-petaled pupils.

I kept it warm, near the hearth, but could not figure out what it might contain. Months later it hatched—lucky that I was there that day to feed the mewling, squawling hatchling chopped meat and warm milk. I wrapped the sting in padding and leather. Even then it struck out with surprising speed and strength. A manticore is a vulnerable creature, lacking human hands to defend the softness of its face, and the sting compensates for that vulnerability.

He talked a moon, perhaps a moon and a half later. I took him with me at first, when I was training the Duke's creatures, but a marmoset decided to investigate, and I learned then that a manticore's bite is a death grip, particularly with a marmoset's delicate bones between its teeth.

Some beast trainers dull their more intelligent beasts. It's an easy enough procedure, if you can drug or spell them unconscious. The knife is thin, more like a flattened awl than a blade, and you insert it at the corner of the eye, going behind the eyeball itself. Once you've pushed it in to the right depth, perforating the plate of the skull lying behind the eye, you swing back and forth holding it between thumb and forefinger, two cutting arcs. It bruises the eye, leaves it black and tender in the socket for days afterward, but it heals in time.

It doesn't kill their intelligence entirely, but they become simpler. More docile, easier to manage. They don't scheme or plot escape, and they're less likely to lash out. Done right, even a dragon can be made clement. And those beasts prone to over-talkativeness—dryads and mermaids, for the most part—can be rendered speechless or close to it.

I've never done that, though my father taught me the technique. I like my talking beasts, most of the time, and on occasion, I've had conversation with sphinx or lamia that were as close to talking with a person as could be.

After the marmoset incident, I left Bupus at home, the establishment the Duke allowed me, a fine place with stable and mews and even a heat-room, which the Ducal coal stores kept supplied all winter long and into the chilly Tabatian springs. I kept him in a stall that had been reinforced, and there were other animals to keep him company.

I'd gone to the circus to see their creatures. They had the crocodiles, which were nothing out of the ordinary, and the elephant, which was also unremarkable, since the Duchess kept two pygmy elephants in her menagerie. And an aging hippogriff, a splendid creature even though its primaries had gone gray with age long ago. I was surprised to see his beak overgrown, as though no one had coped it in months.

"Look here," I said to the man standing to watch the cages and make sure no one poked a finger through and lost it. "Your hippogriff is badly tended. See how he rubs his beak along the ground, how he feaks? Your tender is careless, sir."

I was full of youth and indignation, but I softened when he perked up and said, "Can you tend them? We lost our fellow. How much would you charge?"

"No charge," I said. "If you let me look over the hippogriff as thoroughly as I'd like to. I haven't ever had the chance to get my hands on a live one."

"Can you come back later, when we close up?" He looked apologetic. He was a pretty man, and his uniform made him even prettier.

"I can." It'd mean a late night, but there was nothing going on that next morning—I could sleep in, and go to check the marmosets in the afternoon, or let the regular assistant do it, even, if I was feeling lazy.

So I came back late that night and pushed my way through the crowds eddying out, like a duck swimming against the current. He was waiting for me near the cages. I'd brought my bag of tools, and so we went from cage to cage.

He settled the hippogriff when it bated at the sight of me, flapping its wings and rearing upward. It was easily calmed, and he ran his fingers through the silky feathers around its eyes, rubbing softly over the scaly cere, until its eyes half-lidded and it chirped with pleasure, nuzzling its head along his side.

I trimmed its beak and claws and checked it over before moving on to the other animals. It took me three hours, and even so, much of that was simply telling Rik what would need to be done later on—to stop giving the crocodiles sardines, for example, before they got sick from the oiliness.

I refused pay, and he insisted that he should buy me a cup of wine, at least. How inevitable was it that I would take this beautiful man home with me?

In the morning, I showed my household to my lover. The dueling marmosets, the brace of piskies, the cockatrice kept by itself, lest it strike out in its bad temper. And Bupus, sprawled out across the courtyard. Rik was enchanted.

"A manticore!" he said. "I've never seen a tamed one. Or a wild one, for that matter. They come from the deserts in the land to the south, you know."

A year later, diffidently, while the caravan was spending a month in Tabat, he mentioned to me that the hippogriff had finally succumbed to old age and the caravan would like to buy Bupus.

I refused to sell, but when I married him, the manticore came with me.

When the sun touched down on the horizon and lingered there, like a marble being rolled back and forth beneath one's palm, we realized that there was some delay. If not tonight, though, they'd come tomorrow. Preddi and I discussed it all with shrugs and miming, agreeing to build a fire before the last of the sunlight vanished.

The woods that run beside the road there are dark and dangerous, which is why travelers stick to the road. As night had approached, there were no more passersby—everyone had found shelter where they could. Preddi and I would spread bedrolls beside the fire and keep watch in turns, but I wasn't worried much. The smell of a manticore keeps off most predators.

But as I picked through the limbs that lay like sutures across the ground's interwoven needles, a crackling through the dry leaves at the clearing's edge alerted me. Preddi was near the road, gathering more wood.

As I watched I saw stealthy movement. First one, then more, as though the shadows themselves were crawling towards me. As they emerged, crawling out from the crevices beneath logs and the hollows of the trees, I saw a host of leprous, rotting rabbits, their fur blackened with drying blood, their eyes alight with foxfire. I did not know what malign force animated them, but it was clear it meant me no good.

Out of sight but not earshot, Bupus let out a simultaneous snore and long sonorous fart. Under other circumstances, it would have been funny, but now it only echoed flat and helpless as the rabbits, crouched as low to the ground as though they were snakes, writhed through the dry grasses towards me, their eyes gleaming with moon-touched luminescence.

The novelty of the sensation might have been what had me frozen. It was as though my belly were trying to crawl sideways, as though my bones had been stolen without my notice.

They were nearly to me, crawling in a sinuous motion, as though their flesh were liquid. Preddi wouldn't hear me shout. Neither would the snoring Bupus. I strained to scream nonetheless. It seemed unreasonable not to.

And then behind me there was a noise.

A woman was coming towards me along the deer path, dressed in the onion-skin colored gown of a Palmer, carrying an ancient throwlight. It was made of bronze, and aluminum capped one end, while the other bulged with a glass lens.

She thumbed its side and it shed its cold and mechanical light across the leprous rabbits, which recoiled as though a single mass. They smoldered under the unnatural light, withered away into ringlets of oily smoke.

"I saw your fire from the road," she said, letting the light play over the last of the rabbits. "This area is curse-ridden, and I thought you might not know to look out. Light kills them, though."

"Thank you," I said shakily. "Will you share our fire?"

"Yes," she said, as though expecting the invitation. She was a small woman with a head of short, crown-curled hair—slight but with enough weight to give her substance. No jewelry was evident, only the simplicity of her robe, and the worn leather pack on her back, which she tucked her light back into.

"That's a useful thing," I said. "Where did you get it?"

"I found it," she said before changing the subject. "Are you unharmed? A bite from a curse creature can fester."

I shook my head. "They didn't get close enough," I said. "Good timing on your part."

Back at the fire, I tried to convey to Preddi that there was danger in the woods. I don't know if it got through or not. We built the fire up, and stacked the extra wood nearby, settling down to toast bread and cheese on sticks over the fire. Bupus whined for cheese, but it makes him ill, so I gave him chunks of almost-burned toasted bread instead. It's good for his digestion. He looked reproachful, but crunched them down.

The Palmer, whose name turned out to be Lupe, and I talked, Preddi's gaze moving between us as though he were listening, although when I tried to include him in the conversation, he gave me a blank look. I learned she was traveling from Port Wasp to Piperville, a Palmer, although she did not reveal the purpose of her pilgrimage. Well, that's a personal thing, and not one everyone shares, so I didn't push the question.

"You're a beast trainer," she said, eyeing me.

"I am—and my father before him, and his mother before him."

"A tradition in your family." Her eyes glittered in the firelight, malicious jet beads.

"Yes."

"Do you pass down lists of what are beasts and what are people?"

I sighed. One of those. "Look," I said. "We know which are beasts and which people. Beasts cannot overcome their natures and are not responsible for their actions. People can and are. There are four races of people: human, the Snake folk, the Dead beneath Tabat, and Angels, although no one has seen the last in centuries."

"But although beasts are helpless before their natures, should one kill a person, they are killed in turn."

"Of course," I said. "Any farmer knows that a dog that bites once will bite again. They cannot help it. People can learn, so they can be punished and learn from the experience."

She snorted and spat something fat and wet into the fire. "It's no use talking to you," she said. She turned to Preddi. "And what about you?" she said.

He looked at her blankly.

"He's a little deaf," I said.

"Ah." She leaned forward and shouted into his ear, putting a hand on his arm to steady herself.

He looked at her, surprised. Few of us talked to Preddi—too difficult to stand there loudly repeating a phrase until it penetrated the muffling of his hearing.

I stood up and went to see to Bupus.

He was lying on his back, sprawled out like a tomcat in hot weather. Spittle roped from his gaping mouth and his knobby, chitinous tail twitched in his sleep, its tip glistening with green ichor.

I checked him over for ticks, parasites, thorns and the like. He grumbled in his sleep, turning over when I thumped him, great flanks shivering as though bitten by invisible flies.

"Gnaw your bones," he muttered.

When I turned back to the fireside, I froze as deeply as I had with the rabbits. Off in the shadows beneath a sheltering pair of cedars, Preddi and the pilgrim woman were huddled together in his bedroll, moving in rhythm.

I was appalled on several levels. For one, you don't want to think about your husband's father like that. You know what I mean. Plus this woman didn't seem very pleasant. And this was awfully sudden, so I felt as though I should make sure she didn't chew off his face or turn out to be some sort of shifter. But above it all, I was irritated at their lack of manners. Was I supposed to act as though they weren't there on the other side of the fire? I could understand why they hadn't gone further, worried about the rabbits. But still. Still.

After they settled down, Preddi emerged and signaled he was ready to take his watch. He didn't look me in the face, nor was I sure what to say. I looked him over and if he'd been enchanted in some way, I couldn't tell, nor was I sure what the signs of such enchantment might be. So I tried to sleep, but mainly lay awake, wondering what Rik would say when he found out.

In the morning, Steel was there.

"Where's Rik?" I said, before any other business.

"There's been a little trouble," Steel said.

"What trouble?"

He flapped an irritated hand at me. "Get your manticore ready while I fix the axle." He gave Preddi and the pilgrim a glance.

"That's Lupe, a pilgrim," I said. "She saved my life last night."

He grunted and turned to the axle. I roused Bupus to get him into harness, grumbling under my breath.

Preddi and Lupe walked on one side of the wagon while Steel rode on the other. I drove. Lupe leaned on Preddi as they walked, and I noticed the slight hitch to her gait, as though one leg were shorter than the other.

"You can ride with me," I said, wondering if she'd be able to keep up otherwise. She shook her head, smiling at Preddi. It was a gesture that warmed me to her, despite my fears.

"What happened was this," Steel said. "Lily got two farmers all riled up and throwing insults at each other. They started swinging and then we got fined for disturbing the peace."

"Fined? How much?"

He winced.

"That much?" I said. "We don't have any cash to spare." Rik keeps the books for the circus, and I knew just how thin the financial razor's edge we danced on was.

"Yes," Steel said. "They let me out but kept the others in there. I'm supposed to raise the money. How, I don't know. Meanwhile, they're all sitting in jail eating their heads off and adding each day's room and board to the total."

"We have no extra money," I said.

"I know."

"I do," Lupe said from somewhere behind us. "I could help you."

We both turned to look at her, but Steel said the obvious thing first. "And what would you want in return?"

"A friend's wagon went into a gorge, two miles ahead. I need someone to go into it and bring out a box of tools that he needs. He'll come back later to retrieve the wagon itself, but he's gone ahead to Piperville. I stayed behind to see if I could get help in getting the wagon out, but had no luck. Now I just want to bring him his tools, but I am forbidden to go within walls during my journey."

It was flimsy, it was suspicious. But Palmers are on pilgrimage, and sometimes they act according to their geas. Steel and I exchanged glances, saying the same thing. "Not much choice here."

"Very well," he said.

We trudged along in silence for the next mile, except for Lupe, who chattered away to Preddi. She had a trick of touching his arm to let him know she was speaking, to look at her, and he seemed happier than his usual self. I felt guilty—had Preddi been waiting all this time for someone just to talk to? I knew Rik's mother had died birthing him—that would have been over a quarter of a century ago.

I kept hearing her voice as we rode, high pitched inconsequentialities, the rush of words that comes from someone who has wanted to speak for a long time.

It was easy enough to see where the wagon had gone into the gorge. It was a bad place where the road narrowed—Lupe said her friend had been trying to make room for a larger wagon to pass. The blackberries were torn with its passage down the sloping, rocky side.

And when I climbed down through the brambles, since it was clear Steel had no intention of it, I saw a familiar sight: Sparky's little wagon, tilted askew.

He was not in sight, but I found blood and tracks near the front. Only his tracks, though confused and scattered, as though being pursued.

How to play this hand? What was Lupe's game? I opened the back door of the wagon and peered inside.

Sparky had collected scrap. Iron chains draped the walls, along with lengths of iron and lesser metals: soft copper tubing, a tarnished piece of silver netting. And in the center, his tools in their box. I opened it, trying to figure out why Lupe wanted them. Ordinary tools: screwdrivers, picks, hammers. His father had made them and carved the wooden handles himself, Sparky had told me once.

Wooden handles. I looked down at the tools again, and then at the chain draped walls. Finally I understood. I imagined Sparky being driven from his wagon seat in a cloud of elf-shot, wicked stings that burned, wicked stings that drove him in a mad rush to where he could be safely killed.

Taking a length of chain from the wall and draping it around my neck, I took the box and clambered up the side of the gorge with its awkward weight below my arm.

Lupe's fingers twitched with eagerness as she saw it. She and Preddi stood side by side, while Steel watched the road, ready to lead Bupus on a little further if some wagon should need to pass. I went over to him and laid the box between Bupus' front paws. Touching the manticore's shoulder, I leaned to whisper in his ear. He looked at me, his eyes unreadable, while Steel glanced sideways, eyebrows forming a puzzled wrinkle.

"Give it to me," Lupe said. Her voice had an odd, droning quality to it.

"Not until we have the money," I said.

She laughed harshly and I knew deep in my bones I'd been right. I stepped aside, putting my hand on his shoulder. Steel looked between us, bewildered.

"It's Sparky's wagon," I said. "Looks like he was driven away to be killed."

"You must be confused," she said. "That wagon belongs to my friend. I don't know who this Sparky is."

I continued, "And then she found she couldn't go in his wagon because of the iron, and yet there they were, wooden handled tools that she could use. You're some sort of Fay, aren't you, Lupe?"

Her black eyes glittered with rage as she stared at me, searching for reply. Preddi looked between us, his face confused. I had no idea what he was making of the conversation, or if he'd actually caught any of it.

Steel stepped forward, hand on his knife.

"Stay away!" she spat. Her form quivered as she shrank in on herself, her skin wrinkling, folding, until she resembled nothing so much as an immense, papery wasp's nest, tiny wicked fairies glittering around her in a swarm. A desiccated tuft of brown curls behatted her and she rushed at me and the box in a cloud of fairies.

Bupus's tail batted her out of the air, neat and quick, and I laid the chain across her throat.

It immobilized her. The tiny fairies still darted in and out of her papery form, but they made no move to harm me. Cold iron is deadly to the Fays, even beyond its hampering of their powers.

I had my own tools in the wagon.

Another traveling show paid well for Lupe, enough to get all of our members out of jail. She huddled in the iron cage, quenched and calmed, and the malicious spark had vanished from her eyes. I hoped the dulling had left her with some language. I had not performed the operation in a long time.

Suprisingly, Preddi chose to go with her. All he said was "She's a good companion" but there was no reproach in the words. Rik did not entirely understand why his father was leaving, but he took it well enough.

In the evening, I took Bupus down to the stream near our camp for a drink. The full moon rolled overhead like a tipsy yellow balloon. He paced beside me, slow steady footfalls, and as he drank, I combed out his hair with a wooden-toothed comb, removing the road dust from it. When he had drunk his fill, I wiped his face for him.

There in the moonlight, he took my wrist in his mouth, pinned between enormous molars as big as pill-bottles. I froze, imagining the teeth crushing down, the bones splintering as he ground at them. Sweat soured my arm-pits but I stood stock still.

His lips released my wrist and he nosed at my side, snuggling his head in under my arm. I let go of the breath I had been holding. Tears sprang to my eyes.

He rumbled something interrogative, muffled against the skin of my hip. I wound my fingers through his lank, greasy hair.

"No," I said. "You didn't hurt me."

"Good," he said.

I stood for a long time, looking up at the moon. Its face was washed clean by clouds, and stars came out to play around it. After a while, Bupus began to snore.

TRANSTEXTING POSE

———

Darren Speegle

The doorbell rang a second time. I called downstairs asking my wife to get it, but then the pipes bled in and I realized she was showering. I set down the newspaper and walked down the stairs in my socks, noticing as always that the empty spot on the wall in front of me desperately needed a picture or some other decorative object. It was a drizzly Saturday morning and no responsibilities but to the coffee-stained columns of recycled world events, the unexpectedly lurid paperback I'd been reading, and a crisp new deck of virtual cards that Luce and I had finally saved up the cash to purchase.

Ours was an old unit with a door that sported an actual peephole—which Luce will tell you is quaint if you're not looking at her squarely. Through the hole I saw three little girls in identical khaki uniforms standing there all in a row. I opened the door immediately so as to leave them stranded no longer in the arduous desert of their mission. What were they selling? Did it matter?

My first thought as they said, "Hello," almost in chorus, was that they were awfully *alike* looking, even for such a "pale" corner of our beloved diverse city. Then one of them went solo, reaching forward to collect an object from beside the door, where she'd presumably placed it so that it wouldn't detract from the vision of three little girls all in a row.

The object was metallic silver and about the size and shape of a laptop, though considerably thinner. When she turned it, I saw its similarities to a laptop didn't end there. Metallic silver described just the back side of it. The front looked much like a lit LCD screen, containing a scene very simple in subject matter and obviously meant to convey the conceptual. Indeed, the sense I had was of conceptual art within conceptual art. The image itself was even free of frills or gimmickry, portraying a rowboat on an expanse of sea whose only other interruptions were three dark smudges in the distance that impressed me as islands. While it seemed reasonably safe to assume the picture was digital, it was impossible to tell whether the work was the product of a camera or a traditional artist—or both.

As though the wall at the foot of the stairs cared.

"And what do we have here?" I said, conscious of my flagrant adultishness.

"We are selling these for our project," said the girl who held it like a sign in her small hands.

"Oh?" I said. "And just what might that project be?"

"Transposing text."

Transposing text?

"Really? Sounds like a complicated project for a little girl." *Condescending,* I scolded myself. *Children do not like being condescended to.*

These children didn't seem bothered in the least. The one in the center spoke this time, as she pulled what resembled a business card from a pocket in her khakis: "We only need to raise five hundred dollars and we get a trip to the World's Fair in Los Angeles."

"Its theme," said the third girl, "is 'Our Virtual World.' "

I looked at the card. Though spare in content, it was quite nouveau in design. The words **transposingtext** repeated in a single horizontal line across the card, casting mirror shadows of the letter sequences **tra** and **si** and the single character **x**, so that the reflection read **art is x art is x art is**, etc.

"If we raise the money, we will have our own booth and our own subtheme: 'Redefining Man and God.'"

"Los Angeles," chimed in her neighbor, "is the City of the Angels."

"And what organization do you girls belong to again?"

They pointed to the card in my hand.

Transposing text. Art is x is art.

"How much for the . . . "—I was becoming slightly disoriented, which wasn't helping fill the empty spot on the wall—"the thing you have there?"

"Picture," said girl number one. "Twenty-two dollars."

At first I registered *Picture twenty-two dollars.* Then: Wow. Whatever happened to cookies. I fetched a twenty and a five out of my wallet and told them to keep the change. Man and God could always use some redefining.

Closer inspection confirmed that the image could not be distinguished from a screensaver. To me it was a remarkable medium. To others—that would be my wife Luce—it was a tackiness on the order of a velvet Elvis or Jesus, which violations were already sorely remembered in our house through the musical band *Felt Pelvis & Christ*, which I wouldn't let her expunge from my somewhat extensive collection. No matter, it was what it was, and that was, to fulfill the desolate need of the space at the foot of the stairs. In that endeavor, it was the better of every other work of art we'd tried there, namely her father's Army photo and my artist-signed-and-limited typewriter art image of Stephen Hawking looking at what might have been the very black hole Luce would not let him fill.

I had to hang it with two plate magnets, as it offered by way of accessory nothing but the fingerprints of the trio that had sold it. Which of course suited its neo-whatnot conceptual design. Luce would no doubt roll her eyes at that assertion, remembering my obsession with finding a way to keep the picture aloft. Aloft. Yes, that rather captures the sense of it as a floating thing, there on the wall, into whose meaningless simplicities my wife would sometimes catch me staring.

2

I am in a wooden boat with iron oarlocks, rowing. Before me is an island; above me, *aloft*, an airplane no larger than an albatross, throwing its shadow on the metallic silver water. I am looking for something but cannot remember (if ever in fact I knew) what. Where the image of it should be, there is near emptiness, the suggestion of a line here, a corner there. But the configuration itself, the proportions, remain shapeless. Unknown.

The island approaches steadily and the aircraft above me coasts at little better than my own pace, as if as lost as I. It occurs to me as I watch it lift on a vagrant wind that if it cruised at higher altitudes, it might seem a bird to the casual eye. Maybe that is what it was designed to do, to deceive the eye by flying outside the radius of dependable discernment, to seem a soaring bird when it is actually about darker business. That it glides low for me may simply speak to a malfunction, a random caprice of its mechanics. I doubt so. There is purpose here, dark or otherwise.

When I arrive at the island's shore, it seems I have been rowing for hours, but then, maybe mere moments. The bird enters the tree line beyond the recessed beach as I am stepping into surf that does not startle my naked skin. I am clothed in shorts, khaki, nothing more. The air is neither warm nor cool, the sky neither blue nor gray. There is no discomfort except in the shape that will not complete itself in my mind. I feel I will recognize it when I find it, but where to look? Here, this island?

I walk across the sand in the direction the bird has gone. Only a short distance into the trees—short, long, all such terms being relative—I find a clearing, and within it, the landed aircraft. As I approach the plane, figures begin to materialize around me out of the very aether. People. More specifically, black people. Black people in street clothes, denim bags pooling around their basketball shoes. Gangsta types tapping chests, chillin', discussin'—the rap materializing as smoothly and unobtrusively as the rappers. As with my contact with the water, there is no shock. There is only the realization, and the medium which they and I now share, though it is evident to me that they are unaware of my presence within it.

I have stopped, I realize, as I watch them gather around the airplane. One reaches down and opens a hatch on top of the fuselage and pulls from it a clear plastic bag. I step closer, imagining for a moment it might contain what I am looking for, but no, it is full of cylindrical class containers of clear liquid. Test tubes are assuredly not what I am looking for, though associations of conformity, of rounded edges, do occur to me as the chatter of my unlikely companions fades in.

"This looks like some good muthahfuckin' shit."

"God *damn*, that's gotta be a couple ounces *at least*."

"Break out da pipes, my niggas. We fixin' t'git fucked up on this shit."

Pipes. Pipes in the walls. Fading in. Bleeding in.

Only these aren't pipes in the walls, these are glass pipes, test tubes. The person holding the bag passes out the cylinders one by one to his bloods, who then motions with a lift of his chin to a freshly materializing set of denim bags, who steps forward with a handful of what look like sacrament wafers. The brothers file up, uncapping the tubes, and he commences to crack the wafers over the open bottles, the whitish bits of matter dissolving in the liquid. As the last man gets his dose, the whole gang toss back the revised contents of their cylinders, gargling for a moment or so before spitting the reprocessed fluid back out, some into their empty tubes, others onto the ground.

This accomplished, the chorus lifts its collective head and begins to sing in the voice of angels, a music that strikes me as some soaring contract between Heaven and the 'Hood.

Meanwhile, the man with the crumbled wafers collects the tubes from the choir. He pulls out his cock and pisses into the empty cylinders then returns all the tubes to the bag from which they came, stuffing it in the plane's cargo compartment. The aircraft hums to life again, the chorus subsides, and in the relief, the bewondered voices of its tenors and basses expressing:

God damn, this is some good muthahfuckin' shit.

"And they are brothers, all?" says the insipid white face before me. "No sisters?"

"No sisters." I look around at what is an office. A desk stands between me and the insipid face.

"What does this say to you?"

"I'm not exactly sure. What does the fact that they are gargling angel water say to you?"

Words out of my mouth, just like that. It seems we've covered the story itself, the insipid white face and me, and we're now looking at deconstruction.

"The pipes," says it. "What do the pipes mean to you?"

"Pipes . . . You mean the tubes?"

"You said they were smoking condoms out of glass pipes."

I hesitate.

"Don't think about it. Just respond. What do pipes mean to you?"

Pipes. Pipes in the walls.

"My wife has a set that would offend God himself."

"Does she use them often?"

"Only when she is in the shower. Or one of her Catholic youth choral nightmares. Or on airplanes."

"*You jest,*" says the insipid face.

"*Do I?*"

"*Airplanes. Let's go back there for a minute. Can you describe the minia-ture aircraft in a little more detail?*"

"*I can,*" I say, wondering why the comparison is only now dawning on me, wondering why I'm speaking in present tense. "*It's like one of those search and reconnaissance camera planes that law enforcement got from the military. You know, the ones operated by remote control.*"

"*Oh, you mean like this?*" An insipid white hand opens a drawer and pulls from it what looks very much like a remote control, points it at me and with an insipid white thumb, presses—

3

I am in the boat again, iron oarlocks creaking as I row. The plane practically hovers, itchingly so, above me. A new island approaches. The indistinct, amorphous sketch in my mind fails to fill out. Will I find this seemingly so significant, so (dare I say) crucial thing on the approaching shore?

My mechanical companion suffers an elongated shiver in advance of forsaking its painstakingly reflective pace for the island ahead. As it does I look for a camera eye, any sign of deception, but none is to be found in its smooth, metallic silver underbelly. If the machine possesses landing wheels, the seams of their compartments are invisible. Still, it propels fearlessly into the tree line, leaving me to splash blindly in the surf, across the sand, into the trees again.

Where are they? I know they're here. Not brothers this time—*others.* For in this fresh party voices occur in advance of mouths, flaunting a flippant femininity, with vivacious boas tossed ostentatiously over their sashaying syllables.

"Robbie, if sluts were apples, you'd be the reddest one on the vine."

"I hate to bust your *cherry,* Harvard, but apples don't grow on vines and your metaphors won't even buy you a quick trip to the bathroom with me."

Came a new voice (if one could be distinguished from the other): "Keep talkin' like that, Robbie girl, and you're going to get your dose of *this* cock before the shipment even gets here."

"Like I'd let a diseased gorilla like you rawdog me—*well, speak of the Devil with a tube dress on!*"

I close my eyes, open them again and there it is, the whole masquerade party right in front of me. With lavish loquacity and luxurious lashes, they flock to the aircraft, popping open the hatch as if it were a fresh can of mod and holding the baggie up into the limelight filtering in through the leafage above. This time I don't bother hoping for discovery as I move to better view the dispersal of the bag's contents. I do because I do, and the wonderment comes extra.

The tubes are smaller than before, in vial form, like those that contain Holy Water.

My wonderment does not end there as the silks and the stockings slide off and the boys splash their cocks with the sassy sacrament and head off into the trees in pairs and sometimes threesomes, leaving one aching materialization to plant the next baggie in the plane's compartment.

"'One pass to heaven'? Isn't that a bit obvious?"

The insipid face, with now a freshly vapid expression.

"I've said nothing about heaven," I return.

"Haven't you? How do you feel about heaven?"

"Heaven to me is some sexless guy with a restrictive collar."

"Sex. That is an interesting word."

"So is sexless."

"Do you believe that priests, in today's environment, are sexless?"

"I personally have not had sex with one."

"Let's go back to the restrictive collar, shall we? Isn't that a description you used for the three little girls?"

"I said they were wearing khaki uniforms buttoned to the collar."

"But you do have a fixation with priests," says the face. Vapidly. "May we say that at least?"

4

Priests. That is what they are, certainly; virtually a coven of them as they loiter about the aircraft as over some first sacred text delivered from abroad. Not one among them seems willing to open the hatch, but all tremor with anticipation, relish. I drift close this time, for the image in my mind has begun to gel, still without proportions, but with phantom effusions of matter. *Dark* matter, as I think of it at this particular moment. Still in sketch form, but with conversely ominous and wonderful possibilities.

I watch them as they open the hatch, the bag, then turn to the wilderness as if waiting for the stimuli. I cannot put an exact name to the bag's contents nor an inexact face to the potential stimuli, though the former have harder edges than previous cargos. The priests cross their breasts with trembling hands, their eyes on the forest not the strange bottles they hold. These, the coven of them, are incarnations before words. Strangled whispers from choked throats. Extended hands into nothingness.

I can almost see. I can almost see what it is that's withheld from me, but the very idea that it is withheld obscures its being. I find myself lost suddenly, without cranky oarlocks, without vapid faces, without even the brine (did I describe the brine?). The coming *unfolding*, the folding *uncoming*, does not involve me, even as the witness. It is its own occurrence . . .

They appear, maybe the children of other ages, other dimensions. They do not reach to accept the bottles poised delicately in the divine witches' hands. Instead they gaze shyly, one behind a set of glasses with a cracked lens, another the choral angelics that audibly and visibly cradle his head. But the witches extend nonetheless, with what are perfume bottles in their magic hands. Come, say they, and they heal with a spray of their perfume, the cracked lenses, the speakers through which suddenly I hear rock music—no, more like *crack rock* music, flavored with a bit of battery acid. *Felt Pelvis Christ* upon the scene, sirens open.

Indeed, what pipes for the children as they bewilderedly recall their heavenward glances for their earthward ones, then ashamedly slink away with the collars into the trees, already retching from the intake.

The pipes in the walls. The noises bleeding in as though to catch Luce jerking pictures from parchment walls at the foots of stairs. I know her, and I know that would be much of her. Then where? Where is the thing that inspires such . . .

"Surely you see," says it. "Surely such cautious wings have not misguided you. What flavor, your wife's voice, as she sings in the walls? Angelic? Demonic? Sweet? Sour?"

———

The sound of oarlocks as I press behind collared witches and children into the trees. Ahead, there are structures. Compact, rectangular, upward structures as though heaven just there. I watch doors close, leaving only peepholes into the doings within. As I approach one, I wonder, is this an eye at last to what I have been seeking? I peer inside, imagining for a fragmented second three little girls, but then witness the witch offer the boy a golden nugget as might be used in a glass p—

The small circular window cracks in response.

I look through the triparted hole and find in one fragment a brother's lips around the stem of a glass pipe, a melting condom in its bowl; in another, a sister's hands tying pink bubblegum around the perforated card stock she's wrapped around her cock, the words *One Pass to Heaven* disappearing in a spiral that might be a tongue around a pipe, a boy's eyes as he beholds the luminously golden nugget that is being presented him.

Promise of something that delights when inhaled, that numbs when exhaled, that dissolves when regarded. Indeed, what pipes for the children as they shyly, bewilderedly recall their heavenward glances for their earthward ones.

"Promise. That is where it begins," says the face as the hand pulls from the drawer the what. And in that moment the proportions fill out, the angles and the curves manifest themselves . . . though the thing itself is only a lump. A formlessness of clay.

"What will you do with it?" the insipid face asks.

"I will sculpt," I tell it.

And set about fashioning three little peddlers in khaki uniforms . . .

THE TASTE OF WHEAT

Ekaterina Sedia

Dominique came from solid peasant stock, not frequently given to fancy; still, in the privacy of the thick bones of her skull, she dreamt of an Asian gentleman who insisted on being called Buddha, and small dogs with sharp white teeth.

The heavy sleep descended unannounced, smothering her with dreams in the middle of dinner with her family, or in the wheat fields while she was threshing. Any blink could turn into a jumble of images and voices, and then someone would shake her shoulder and say, "Dominique, wake up."

Sometimes the dreams stopped before she was forcefully pulled away from them, and then she would hear what they said. "What is wrong with her?" and "You'd never think looking at that girl." Then she blushed, and let the world in shyly, through the slightest opening of her lashes. The sun was fuzzy in their frame, and the faces—soft, undefined, kind. Then she would get up, smoothing down her skirt around her wide hips.

"You seem so healthy—milk and blood," people said. They kept the second part of their comments silent, but Dominique knew what it was. She was defective, and no man would take a wife with falling sickness, no matter how well-fed and ruddy-cheeked. Her family thought that it ought to bother her, but it did not. She only shrugged and went about her business, ready to be assaulted by dreams with every step she took.

She worked in the fields with the rest of her compatriots, from the time when the sun rose to the sunset. But at midday she left the merry din of people laughing and talking, children squealing, oxen lowing, and went home to tend to her grandfather. He was too feeble to venture into the fields, and she took it upon herself to make sure that he was fed and attended to.

The old man looked at her with his colorless rheumy eyes that had seen so many harvests come and go, and she almost wept with pity. He was the only person she had ever known who understood what it was like to inhabit a body ready to betray him at any moment.

"Don't worry, grandpa," Dominique said, blinking hard to cool her suddenly hot eyes. "Maybe some day you'll be born as a butterfly, alive for just a day, your life short and painless and beautiful." She spoke in a hushed voice; even though she knew that her parents and siblings were in the fields, she worried about being overheard. Sometimes (more often as the time wore on) she intentionally garbled her words, so that only her grandfather could understand. She rather liked appearing as a large, mumbling thing, half-witted from her fits.

She fed her grandfather, pushing an awkward spoon between his gums, pink like those of an infant. His skin seemed simultaneously translucent and tough, like the wings of a dragonfly, with quartz veins intersecting under its pale, downy surface. His hooded eyelids stood like funeral mounds over his dead eyes, the coarse salt of his eyebrows casting a deep shadow over them.

"Grandpa," Dominique said, "you are so good, you deserve to be a butterfly." She thought for a bit, the wooden spoon in her red idle hand dripping its grey gruel. "They say being a dog is pretty good, but I'm not so sure—all you get is yelling and kicking. Unless, of course, you are Buddha's dog. Perhaps a bird . . . the kind nobody hassles. Like a hawk; just promise you'll stay away from the chicken coops, or people will throw stones at you. Promise me."

Grandpa nodded, in agreement or in encroaching sleep, she couldn't tell. She wondered if her grandfather was afflicted by the same visions as she, if he too dreamt of the stocky Asian gentleman and his dogs, adorable and vicious. Before she could decide one way or another, they all stood around her, and she lay on the earthen floor of a dark cavern. The dogs snarled, showing their needle teeth.

"What we think, we become," Buddha said, with his habitual feeble smile.

Dominique sat up, despite the snarling dogs, and nodded.

"Be grateful you didn't die today," he said.

The dogs growled deep in their throats but settled down.

Buddha shifted on his feet, with a look of consternation showing on his moonlike face. "Words have the power to both destroy and heal. When words are both true and kind, they can change our world."

The dogs barked and leapt, and Dominique woke up with a start.

She collected herself off the floor, smoothing her skirt and blushing. "Sorry, Grandpa," she said.

The old man did not answer. His body pitched forward in his chair, and a thin streak of gruel hung off the corner of his lips. With a sinking heart, Dominique realized that he was dead, dead on her watch, dead because the dreams stole her attention away from him. She fell to her knees, grabbing the cold hands with blueing fingernails, and keened.

Her wails brought people from the fields. They came running and hushed when they saw the dead man. After a few seconds of respectful silence, they talked about the funeral arrangements, while Dominique still keened, her cries hanging over the thatched rooftops of the village like tiny birds of prey.

They buried Dominique's grandfather two days later. The frost came early that year, and the ground grew hard. The diggers' hoes struck the dirt with a dull thump-thump-thump. The diggers sweated as Dominique's family clustered about shivering, drawing their warm clothes tighter around them.

Dominique never looked at the diggers, and let her gaze wander over the bare fields and the grey hills that lined the horizon. She searched for her grandfather, and worried that she would not recognize him in his new form. Was he a leaf blowing in the wind, a tiny calf that followed its mother on rubbery, slick legs, a sparrow perched on the roof? Life of all persuasions teamed about her, and Dominique despaired to find him. "I'm so sorry, Grandpa," she whispered into the cutting wind as it singed her lips.

After the funeral, Dominique walked home among the neighbors and relatives who filled her house with their heat and loud voices. She made sure that everyone's mugs were filled with mulled wine, and that everyone had plenty of cracked wheat and raisins. It was for her grandfather. Buddha's words buzzed in her ears like flies tormenting dogs on hot summer afternoons, "To be idle is a short road to death and to be diligent is a way of life." Dominique did not want to die—not until she found out what happened to her grandfather.

Then it occurred to her that the nights were growing longer and colder, and many woodland creatures must be feeling hungry and alone. Quietly, she picked up the bowl with wheat and raisins and stepped outside. No one noticed either her presence or departure, just like they didn't notice their own breathing.

The wind whipped her hair in her face, as she peered into the freezing darkness, her eyes watering in the cold. She thought about the moles that burrowed through the ground, and the little field mice that skittered across its surface on nervous light feet, of the weasels that eyed the chicken coups when no one was watching, and the shrews that stalked millipedes. There were too many to feed, to many to search through. How could even Buddha hope to recognize one soul among the multitude?

She set the bowl a few steps away from the porch and tightened her shawl around her shoulders, shivering, listening to the quiet life that teemed about her. She was too large, she realized, too lumbering to ever hope to find her grandfather. She needed to be smaller. And she needed a better sense of smell.

She thought of the tales the old women told around the fire, about the mice who decided to become human, and crawled into the pregnant women's wombs, to gnaw at the growing child and to displace it; they grew within the women, shed their tails and claws, and were born as human children. One could only recognize them by the restlessly chewing teeth and the dark liquid eyes. Surely there must be a way for a woman to become a mouse.

The winters were always long, with nothing to do but tell stories. Dominique withdrew more, and gave herself to her sleeping fits with zeal, like a soldier throwing himself onto the bristling pikes to aid the cavalry charge. Dominique tried to aid Buddha's visit, so he would answer her questions.

One day, he appeared. His dogs were subdued and teary-eyed, shivering and sneezing in small staccato bursts. The winter was not kind to them.

"Are your dogs all right?" Dominique asked.

Buddha looked up, into the dripping ceiling of his cave. "A dog is not considered a good dog because he is a good barker."

"I cannot find my grandfather," Dominique said, the fear of waking up lending her voice urgency.

"All things appear and disappear because of the concurrence of causes and conditions," Buddha replied.

"I have to find him though," she said. "I think I need to become a mouse, or another small creature, so I can search better."

"He who experiences the unity of life sees his own Self in all beings, and all beings in his own Self, and looks on everything with an impartial eye."

"Just tell me," she begged. "Without riddles."

Buddha finally turned his empty eyes to her. "People create distinctions out of their own minds and then believe them to be true. You are no different than a mouse; you just think you are."

Before Dominique could thank him, the walls of the cave melted around her, and she came awake on the floor of the barn, in the warmth of steaming, sleepy breath of sheep and chickens. It was clear to her now—she created the world with her thoughts, and she could alter it just as easily. At this moment of enlightenment, Dominique's clothes fell on the floor, and a small brown mouse skittered away.

Soon, the little mouse discovered that her new mind could not hold as many thoughts as the human one, and it worked hard to hold onto its single obsession: find an old man who was now something else. But first, she needed to eat.

Dominique the mouse remembered that the granary was close to the barn, and hurried there, her little brain clearly picturing the earthen jugs overflowing with golden grain. She made it there safely, avoiding the prowling cats and the eyes of the humans, and ate her fill of crunching, nourishing wheat. After that, she was ready to go.

She let her nose lead her—it twitched toward the wind, sorting through many smells, some comforting, some exciting. She noticed the smell that mixed familiarity with strangeness, fear with solace, and decided to follow it.

The fields lay barren, and the mouse squeaked in terror as it ran between the frozen furrows of the fallow field, vulnerable in the open ground with no cover. Her little heart pumped, and her feet flew, barely touching the ground, until the dry grass of the pasture offered her its comfort. She dared to stop and catch her breath, and realized that the smell grew stronger.

She found an entrance to an underground burrow, and followed the long and winding tunnel. White hoarfrost covered its walls, and the anemic roots extended between earthen clumps, as if reaching for her. The mouse shivered with fear and cold, but kept on its way until she saw the pale light, and heard soft, high-pitched singing echoing off the white burrow walls. Dominique the mouse entered the large area in the end of the tunnel, and stopped in confusion.

The candles cast the silhouettes of the gathered field mice, making them huge and humped. The mice were serving the Mass. Their voices rose in solemn squeaks, and their shadows swayed in a meditative dance, rendering the walls of the cave a living tapestry of black, twisting darkness and white frost, glistening in the candlelight. The mice prayed for sustenance.

Dominique stayed in the back of the crowd, too shy to come forth and ask her questions. Even her desires grew clouded, and for a while she could not remember why she was there. Snatches of thoughts and images floated before her dark beady mouse eyes: a jug of grain, the thick arm of her father clutching across his wife's pregnant stomach as they slept, a stretching neck of a new chick. An old man with the eyelids like funeral mounds.

The mice stopped their chanting, and lined up to partake of the Eucharist. The mouse who was a priest by all appearances held up a thimble Dominique recognized as her own, lost some time ago, and let all the mice sip from it. Dominique joined the line. Several altar voles helped with the ceremony, distributing grains of wheat and helping the feeble with the sacrament.

Dominique shuffled along, and waited for her turn. No one seemed to notice that she didn't quite belong there, and the vole shoved a sliver of grain into her mouth. She chewed thoughtfully, as her eyes sought to meet the gaze of the priest.

Finally he turned to her, his work completed. "What do you want, daughter?"

Dominique found that she could communicate with the mouse priest easily. "I'm looking for an old man." She stopped and wrinkled her face, trying to remember. "He died, and became someone else. I have to find him."

The mouse priest moved his sagging jowls with a thunderous sigh. "We dreamed of the others coming into our midst, and we prayed for signs . . . none came."

"But I smelled him here!"

The priest turned away, mournful. "It was God you smelled."

Dominique sighed and followed the mice, who filed out of the main chamber into a complex system of burrows. She found a tunnel that led upward, and enticed her with the smell she sought.

The snow had fallen while she was underground, and she sputtered and shivered as the white powder engulfed her, its freezing particles penetrating between hairs of her coat. She half-struggled, half-swam to the surface.

Buddha was outside with his dogs, running weightlessly across the moonlit snow. His dogs preceded him, their noses close to the ground. They followed a chain of danger-scented footprints. A fox, Dominique guessed, mere moments before seeing the fox.

It looked black in the moonlight, and it dove into the snow, coming up, and diving again. It seemed puzzling at first, but then Dominique heard muffled squeaks, pleas, and cries of pain. The fox was hunting mice, too busy to notice that Buddha's dogs were stalking it.

The fox sniffed the air, and turned its narrow muzzle toward Dominique. Her heart froze in terror, and her feet screamed at her that it is time to run, run as fast as possible. But she remained perched on two hind legs, looking the fox straight in the eye. "Have you seen my grandfather?" she asked the fox.

The fox stopped and tilted its head to the shoulder.

"He's not a mouse," Dominique explained. "At least, I don't think so. He died and was born as someone else."

"Ask the mice," the fox suggested, yawning. Its teeth gleamed in the moonlight. "They would know—they get everywhere."

"I tried. But they are only praying, and—"

The dogs she had forgotten about pounced. The fox shrieked, trying to shake two small dogs that latched onto the scruff of its neck.

"All things die," Buddha commented.

The pale petals of the stars came out and the moon tilted west. Dominique alternated between burrowing under the snow and running on the surface. She followed the trail of the fox who ate so many of her brethren.

Dominique did not need to sleep; her dream fits were but a distant memory. She wondered if all mice were sleepless, and realized that she had never seen a sleeping mouse. She also wondered whether they spurned Buddha because he only came to those who slept.

As she contemplated, she realized that the smell that was urging her on was growing weaker. She turned her snout back, and caught it again—back where the fox full of mice was being rend to pieces by Buddha's dogs.

The old mouse told her that it was smell of God, and she turned back to the mouse burrow, to the church. To her horror, she found the burrow desecrated, dug up, and the surviving mice huddled in the ruined passages.

The old mouse priest was among them. He shook and cried. When he saw Dominique, he hissed. "It was all your fault; you brought the fox to our church."

Dominique shrugged, unsure if she was able to take on a burden of another responsibility. The smell of her dead grandfather was overpowering around her, emanating from all the mice, and especially the old priest. Even her own breath carried the scent of him. "You told me that was the smell of God," Dominique told the priest. "But where is it coming from?"

The priest still wept. "His flesh was made grain, and this is what we take as our Eucharist. The flesh of God."

Dominique remembered the taste of the grain sliver on her tongue, and squeaked with frustration. Why did she think an old man would come back as a mouse or a bird? What better destiny was there than to be wheat?

She remembered the golden expanse of the ripe ears of wheat, the singing of women, the even thumping of the threshers. She thought of her grandfather, when he could still leave the house, walking behind the reapers, picking up stray ears fallen to the ground, smelling them, chewing their milky softness with his toothless mouth. And then, she missed home.

She comforted the mice the best she could, telling them of Buddha and his protective dogs, but she never told them that the flesh of the grain was her grandfather's, that he came back to her in the taste of wheat and the communion of mice.

She spent the night and the next day digging new burrows, and collecting what grain was left in the field, so her mouse brethren could have shelter and the Eucharist. But her heart called for her to go home, until she could resist the urge no longer.

Dominique was tired. Her small feet screamed with pain as she crawled back into the village. She wanted to be human again. She remembered vaguely the words of a round gentleman, punctuated by sharp barking sneezes of his small needle-teethed monsters. But she could not recall their meaning, she could not remember how she became a mouse, her feeble memory overpowered by the taste of wheat.

The only recourse left to her was to do what all mice did in a situation like that. She skittered along the row of straw-thatched houses, listening, looking. A sharp, salty smell attracted her attention, and she circled a small house, its doorway decorated with wilting, frosting garlands of wheat and oak boughs. Newlyweds.

She found a narrow slit between two planks by the door, and squeezed inside. It was warm and the house was filled with smoke from the dying embers in the woodstove. Two people lay in the bed, asleep, naked.

Dominique's nose twitched as the smell grew stronger, and she followed it up onto the bed, light on her feet, scampering across the folds of the sheepskin covers.

The sleeping woman shuddered but didn't wake up as the tiny mouse claws ran along her thigh.

The smell was overwhelming now, and the mouse closed her eyes, and squeezed into a narrow, moist passage that smelled of sea. The woman moaned then, and the soft walls that surrounded Dominique shuddered.

She reached a widening of the burrow, and entered a warm, unoccupied cave. There, she curled into a fetal ball, tucking her long tail between her legs. Soon, her tail would fuse with the walls of her fleshy cave, and she would become a small person, with the black liquid eyes and restless jaws of a mouse.

THE BEACON

——

Darja Malcolm-Clarke

My children are dying.

I learn this as the airship *SS Arthanthropia* eases past the light-house towards the Khalreg Cumulesce and the docks hidden behind. I am watching from the lighthouse gallery when it happens: dancing like aurora over the cloud-churning paddlewheels, the beacon's blue-green light falters.

It means only one thing.

I quit the gallery and charge up the spiral stair to the lantern room. A touch of a button stops the slow rotation of the great fresnel lens, the crèche where my children are nestled. I throw open the glass door behind which they lie, their slick white segments lined up like pale vegetables in a market bin. Their light has become so dim I don't need the visor hanging nearby to shield my eyes. My babies sense my proximity and squirm in need. As I draw back the flap of my robe to free up the row of teats, I fear yesterday's suspicion is about to be proven correct. I give a teat a squeeze. It excretes milk tinged with yellow. I try another, and it's almost dry. Another: the turbid fluid.

Well then, it is so. I have the sunpoison.

I swallow against the only possible option. There is talk in the stilt city Overcloud about the threat of sunpoison, but no plans yet of what to do about it. They in the city have time—after all, they are protected. The lighthouse is not. And the city cannot afford the lighthouse to go out. My children must be nourished.

First things first. I close the crèche-lens door to keep in the heat and hurry down the spiral staircase to the nursery. The wife is there, chewing the egg-casing from the hatching babies. Like all wives, mine does not do much other than gnawing. That, and of course, impregnating.

The wife looks up from the casing; the nymph-child's face is just visible. A piece of shell hangs off the wife's chitin lip. Near-sightless, he sniffs the air. He could never see if the children had ceased to glow and light the way for airships, in case one were to come perilously near the Cumulesce. So this is where he stays, in the nursery, out of the sun and away from the beacon, chewing.

He sniffs again. "The sunpoison really has come," he says.

"Yes. The heliomancers were right—the sun's eyes are multiplying." I survey the hatchlings.

"What do they say in town? Do they still think there is time?" he says.

"There is time for them," I say. "The city canopy will hold long enough for it to be refortified."

"Maybe the sun's gaze will be the end of us," he says.

"What do you know of it? Leave it to those who do."

He is quiet a moment, then says, "The littlest will need milk soon—within a day's time at the latest."

"Yes," I say, impatient. He is oblivious to my expertise. To feed one's offspring from her own teats is the obligation, duty, and pride of every goodman; to share this responsibility with another would be the height of disgrace. Better a child die than bear the shame of having been fed from the teat of one who did not lay her.

I turn to go, now that I know the youngest are well enough for a short time. I hope it is time enough.

"Perhaps if you return to the city canopy," he says, "so you'll be where the sun's gaze doesn't reach?"

"It's too late," I say. "The poison has already reached my milk."

The wife cradles the hatchling in his arms. "She doesn't mean to harm us, the sun," he says. "Her compound gaze—"

"She loves us. I know." This nattering is why I usually leave the wife to himself.

"There are—" He hesitates. "There are rumors of something that could help. A plant."

"Fatherteat," I say. "Undercloud. I know."

His blind eyes widen. "The wives speak of it."

"I hope that's not all it is—wives' tales. The familiar fancy and foolishness. Yes, goodfolk have been discussing it."

There have been times when the talk in Overcloud was not so far off. This I know: without milk, my babies cannot glow, and the lighthouse cannot warn ships. Vessels will soar through the Khalreg Cumulesce as though nothing lay just behind it, collide with the docks—and careen on to Overcloud. Bring it all crashing down, stilts folding upon each other, dropping into open air—

"I've got to go to find it," I say. "So, it's a risk, but you'll have to tend the children alone. If there's such thing as fatherteat, they can't live without it now, and the beacon cannot shine."

"You could ask someone in town to nurse for you . . . ?"

I meet this insult with the glare it deserves. Another day I might reprimand him further, but today there is no time.

The wife drops his eyes and takes a breath. "I've been thinking," he says. "These are my babies as well as yours. I will go to fetch fatherteat."

"Don't be ridiculous," I say, suppressing a sour chuckle. "Tend to your chewing."

"I wish to go," he says. "I won't stay cloistered in here while the sun's eyes multiply and gaze upon us."

"I won't have my wife venturing undercloud alone." Now he is beyond irking me. "Besides, feeding infants is fathers' prerogative. Our duty."

"But some of the other wives have been talking about going undercloud—"

I settle the matter with uproarious laughter.

In the kitchen, I pack a rucksack with half a loaf of the brown bread the wife makes. He stands watching—listening, rather—as I take it from the cupboard.

"You won't come back. You'll be burnt to a crisp. Or gutted by bogles," he says.

"Don't try to dissuade me," I say. "Especially not with nursery tales."

"That's why Overcloud is here, you know. That's why we built it. Bogles," he says. I snort. "They are still down there. Don't you want something, just in case? Take this with you," he says, and draws a kitchen knife from the block and wraps it in a checkered cloth. "And this," he says, and makes his way to the closet, emerging to present me with a red umbrella. "For the sunpoison." His antennae work; he puts his glossy-shelled head far into the cupboard. From its nether-regions he withdraws a loaf of the brown bread. He hands it to me and says, "They say fatherteat has purple—"

"I know what they say it looks like," I say and toss the bread into my rucksack. I shoulder the pack and leave him standing by the cupboard.

I catch a lepidopter to the stilt city's ferry-elevator undercloud, located on the docks behind the Cumulesce. Below, goodmen come and go in the streets. We pass through the patchwork shadow of towering claptrap buildings that sway on tall legs. Since the city cannot expand out, it is built ever upward.

Around the far side of the Cumulesce, airships crowd around the harbor; it's the windy season and thus busy. As we glide overhead, I recognize the docked *SS Arthanthropia*, its paddlewheels lazily turning. The lepidopter descends and I climb out beside Bezzy's Cloudside Tavern. I expect to have to wait a while for a ferryman—it's not as though goodfolk line up to go undercloud. At least not yet. But someone appears from within a sloping shanty even as the lepidopter's wings still fan the air over me.

"Goodman," she says, waving me over to the ferry.

"Ferryman," I reply with a nod. She extends a knotty claw for the toll. I give her the two coins fee, as well as an extra to speed our passage, and step into the wooden ferry-elevator. She closes the door behind me and turns to work the contraption. The ferry kicks into gear.

Descent begins, and the sky flies up against us, pressing against my shell like it's trying to break through. A round hole in the floor lets me watch as we careen towards the wall of cloud. When we hit it, the diaphanous white coaxes a nagging cough from my throat. Light wanes, and the clouds take on a ghostly pall.

The ferryman pulls on the winch. The ferry slows but land is too close too soon, and we smack into the ground. I hit the wall and spin on my back like the lighthouse lens. The ferryman collects herself, coughs once, and helps me to my feet. She opens the door. As is custom when leaving an enclosed vessel, she says, "Luck of the lighthouse worm go with you." It does not have the intended comforting effect.

Undercloud is warm, flat as far as eyes can see, and covered with high reeds and brush. What a wonder: solid earth. So much vegetation I have never seen. And where the land is not muted green it is black, and wet, and stinking of rot. A hot wind blows. Somewhere high above, airships come and go, guided by the light of my nymph-children; but I cannot see the ships for the roiling silver cloud cover, which casts a peculiar twilight over the plain.

With a mechanical clamor, the ferry ascends behind me on ropes and pulleys. High overhead, its clanging still echoes into the false dusk. A tingling upon my shell indicates the clouds do not keep out the sun's poison, but trap it in. How the wife could have known this would be so, I do not know. I take the umbrella he gave me protruding from my bag and open it, a strange bright flower blooming on the bland plateau. The tingling abates somewhat, though I know the sunpoison still pours down from the sky. She does not mean to harm us, the sun: she cannot help but watch over us, even though her gaze brings suffering.

Beneath the cloak my teats are brewing sunpoison in concentrate; a shiver of shame runs through me. What if I cannot provide for my children? I hope against hope the solution is here somewhere.

I have gone two steps when my legs stick in the black sludge. I try to pull out one row by sheer strength, but the mud sucks and slurps at me like a grub-child. I strain; I'm exhausting myself two steps into the journey. Gazing out over the plateau, I wonder how far fatherteat might be. If it really exists.

Then I remember the bread.

The long loaf is hard with age and likely weeks old, forgotten as a tomb at the back of the cupboard. But why else would the wife have given it had he not known I'd need it, and not for eating? With the loaf I push the mud away from my feet experimentally, and it spreads easily, like kidney cream. I clear one row of my legs that way, then the other, and a slow-going rhythm develops: step, sweep, step, sweep. I can walk. The petrified loaf is the perfect tool.

As the wife seems to have anticipated.

After a time of pushing through thick reeds, violet thistles on thick green stalks nod into view, an uncanny mute assembly. Their brilliant shade is perverse in this landscape, as though they had soaked up the vitality of the environs to produce their striking hue. I tug at a stalk thick as my antennae—and fluid emerald and burning sprays from the violet bulb in every direction. I try to shield myself, but the mud sucks at me and drags me down into the mire. The spray burns like the sun herself.

By the time I've managed back onto my feet again, the fatherteat spray has eaten away portions of my integument shell. Only a layer of exposed cuticle shields viscera from the open air. I avoid looking at the burns and collect the red umbrella from where it fell into the mud. Without it, the wounds would have been worse.

I distract myself with the task of procuring fatherteat. I have wrested a bag of stalks from the grove when I narrowly avoid an especially high fatherteat spray. Staggering aside, my gaze strays deeper into the grove where a brown gleam catches my eye. My thorax tightens. I drop the stalk I'm holding and move through the grove towards the thing—

—Into a clear patch where thistles have been cut down and mud churned up. The satin sheen of exoskeleton; mud mounded. The air is snatched from me. I can make out three sets of legs in the mire. One end of the shell is hidden beneath the mound—the end where a head should be. The channels around the legs indicate that once the legs thrashed and thrashed. Now they are still.

It is a wife. He has been buried alive.

The shell is smeared with copious palmate markings, prints of whatever piled the mud on the wife and kept him submerged. Until he didn't try to get out anymore.

What could have made the palmate markings on the shell? I am inundated with dreadful imaginings. Bogles. As the wife said.

I snatch up the stalk bag, nearly toppling into the mud again, and strike a frantic step-sweeping pace back towards the ferry rope, which stretches up into the clouds like a beanstalk from the old tales. All the while I listen and look for something baleful following behind. Why did wives think they could manage alone undercloud? What madness compelled that now-dead wife to come here? I fumble and yank on the ferry rope with a leg; my primaries hang tingling and still.

Waiting alone on the plain, the wind murmurs a warning in a strange tongue. I drop the bread and take the knife from the bag. I hold my fighter's stance, vigilant, ready to take whatever might come—whatever bogles with their strange hands.

The lurch of the ferry overhead startles me. It slows to the ground and the wooden door swings open. The ferryman steps out, regarding me with solemn black bead eyes. She moves aside.

Out strides a goodman bedecked in armor.

But no. It's worse than bogles. The thin face gives him away.

It is a wife. And he is not alone.

Two more wives step from the ferry, similarly clad in armor, looking ridiculous in goodmen's garb. Each carries an umbrella and bears a bundle on his back. The first takes a revolver from his belt, gazing across the plain, the wind batting his hat about on his head. The largest wife notices me and steps away as if by instinct. From his belt hangs a muslin bag; the ivory handle of a dagger protrudes from a sheath.

"Look," says the large one, pointing to me with his red umbrella. The other two stare, stricken. The first says, "It doesn't matter now. Let's get going."

I go to speak, but already they are scuttling away, their feet fitted with broad webbed shoes that let them walk over the mud. They open their umbrellas.

They have come prepared. They have a procedure.

The ferryman holds out a claw for the toll; arms shaking, I fish coins from the bag.

Inside, words finally come, bearing the ring of accusation. "Those were wives that came out," I say. The ferryman nods like a fatherteat head in the wind. "They've been coming down here, haven't they?—goodwives. Lots of them." The ferryman presses her lips together, turns to the winch and says nothing. The ferry shoots skyward.

Nursing my numb arms, I watch through the cracks in the slats and look for them crossing the plain alone—without husbands. As though they are husbands. Perhaps they go to the dead wife. But no. My wife as good as told me why they are there. We goodmen go about in the world more than them; we will suffer from the sunpoison more and sooner than them. They seek fatherteat to replace what their husbands will soon lack.

How dare they impinge upon our right, our way of life ages old?

The buried wife's face beneath the dirt jeers up from memory: the tiny compound eyes, the mouth set in an "o" beneath the mound, the churned-up sludge from his struggle to scramble up, out of the mud and away. Some coward, it had seemed to me before, had sent her wife undercloud in her stead. But those goodwives had come prepared, with weapons and tools. They went on their own. They went of their own volition.

My shell taps the ferry wall as I look out. I am shuddering with outrage.

That, and something akin to fear.

It is night when the ferry touches on the dock near the Cumulesce, invisible in the dark, a starless void in the sky. I'm out the door before I have to hear the ferryman bid me goodbye with the traditional, maddening expression. I hail a lepidopter to the lighthouse. As we come out from under the canopy and the fare change registers on the meter, I notice a light far beyond the lighthouse: an airship approaching.

And no light to warn of what lies behind the Cumulesce. I've come home too late.

I toss coins to the driver and hit the ground running, pushing through the hard-shelled crowd and up the claptrap bridge to the lighthouse.

The wife meets me at the door. I push past him to the spiral staircase.

"I talked to some wives in town on the pterophone," he says. His feet make scrabbling sounds on the stairs as he follows behind.

"The children—by sun's eyes, there's an airship coming!" I cry, stepping into the lantern room.

"They're telling stories about fatherteat," he says as I open the crèche door where the grub-babies reside behind the massive lens that amplifies their glow. "Ones I hadn't heard before."

"I bet they are. Let me guess—stories from undercloud, eh?" I say, but now, now at the crèche I can see the babies live. They have no glow, only the vaguest luminescence, a hint of nacreous gray light. They hear and smell my arrival. Weakly, their mouths open and close in need, emitting tiny shrieks as they writhe over each other like animals. The wife is speaking, but beyond the windows, the red and amber lights of the airship near. I wrestle the stalk bag with my secondary hands.

"Your arms are hurt. I should have made you wear more cover," I hear him say as if from afar. I tear a wet stalk from the bag and tip it to the smallest and dimmest of the babies. Its mouth works; it gibbers in infant bliss while the others fight for the stalk-teat. The wife prattles on as I quickly move through the lot of them, feeding them.

As I squeeze the last drops from a stalk for the last infant, the wife is at my side, his four hands upon the nymph-child I am holding.

"Are you listening to me?" he says in a way I have never heard him speak. I begin to reply, but my gaze is snatched to the window and the light spangled across the sky, growing nearer.

"Are you listening? It's the thistle milk," he says, still trying to wrest the child from me. I slap his hands away, my own numb hands fumbling. "The cloud-cover traps the sunpoison beneath. The thistles are—"

"I knew it," I say, heaving the child out of his grasp; the nearly-dry stalk drops to the floor. "You wives found the fatherteat yourselves. You're trying to find a way to live without us," I say.

"No, we're trying to find a way to survive. The wives' tales say the sunpoison has demolished our people before. If that's so, it'll take you husbands first."

"You're trying to usurp our right to nourish the children ourselves. It's disgusting," I say. "It's immoral." I move closer to the great lens door, the child in my arms.

"We're doing whatever might save us. We have more pressing things to think about than whether wives or husbands will nourish the young. Bogles will destroy us if we try to live undercloud. They are why we ended up in Overcloud to begin with."

"I bet that's from a wives' tale as well," I say, but his words have turned me cold, even my numbed arms—

When my babies begin to glow. They incandesce blue-green, casting light on the walls. I place the child with the others in the fresnel crèche. They brighten so quickly I have to turn away. The amber lights of the ship are hidden behind the wife, enrobing him in a golden halo.

Then the children's light changes from turquoise to green-gold, and more brilliant than ever I have seen.

The light is accompanied by a cloying sweet smell of flesh burning, followed by a pop and a hiss as the noxious light of one, then another, then more of my babies is extinguished.

The wife cries out. The light is diminished enough that I can turn back to the small charred bodies—which I can see by the light of one last, gray infant.

Until it, too, blinks out in a waft of smoke and sweet stench.

I turn back to the wife, but he is not looking at me. I follow his line of sight outside to the cluster of lights in the dark. The airship, perhaps not noticing or understanding the brief beacon, is still moving blindly towards the Cumulesce.

"The fatherteat milk—what were you saying of the fatherteat milk?" I cry.

The wife is wailing too much to answer.

There is no choice. The city is risked if I do not act. I reach for the bag of fatherteat and pull out one of the last remaining stalks. I peer at the wife, seeing in his place the dead wife undercloud. Once I might have thought, if I do this, he might as well be that dead wife, buried alive under the weight of his dependence.

I cannot lose the feeling that that is not true now.

No time: the ship is drifting towards the Cumulesce.

So I suck from the stalk.

"The children. The city," cries the wife. "After all we've done." I know he must mean not the goodmen, but the wives.

The thistle milk tastes of flowers. I am no longer a nymph-child, but my body still knows what to do with milk. I feel it mingling with the sweetbreads in my thorax. I think of my father and the decade since I drank from her body.

The milk lights me up, soft. The wife gasps. I go to the crèche. I climb in and squeeze behind the great fresnel lens that is the heart of the lighthouse.

The lens magnifies and focuses my light into a beacon. A channel of green-gold light slices open the night.

My glow fluoresces and fills my vision. I am blinded. Perhaps by now the airship has begun to slow, to approach the Cumulesce, to ease safely into the harbor. An infant comfort dances across memory at the edge of the void.

An appalling image fills that void: my wife, setting out with dozens of others—undercloud. Another image: goodmen gone. A wife feeding a child from an apparatus of hose and metal. And from another intricate device—laying eggs.

I've given them these things by warning the airship of the Cumulesce. Darkness could have brought it all down: the airship colliding with the city and sending it in flames to undercloud.

I turn to see what I can of my wife through my light. He is standing by the lens, silent, blind as ever, smelling my choice.

The city, Overcloud, cast to the ground. Maybe it would have been better to let the beacon fall dark, to forfeit it all to the bogles. Something in me says I should have done it.

The wife will not be buried under my absence like a wife buried alive in the wilderness. He is digging himself out. All of them are digging themselves out.

Now, at any moment, he—they—will scramble up and away, free.

THE APE'S WIFE

———

Caitlín R. Kiernan

Neither yet awake nor quite asleep, she pauses in her dreaming to listen to the distant sounds of the jungle approaching twilight. They are each balanced now between one world and another—she between sleep and waking, and the jungle between day and night. In the dream, she is once again the woman she was before she came to the island, the starving woman on that *other* island, that faraway island that was not warm and green but had come to seem to her always cold and grey, stinking of dirty snow and the exhaust of automobiles and buses. She stands outside a lunch room on Mulberry Street, her empty belly rumbling as she watches other people eat. The evening begins to fill up with the raucous screams of nocturnal birds and flying reptiles and a gentle tropical wind rustling through the leaves of banana and banyan trees, through cycads and ferns grown as tall or taller than the brick and steel and concrete canyon that surrounds her.

She leans forward, and her breath fogs the lunch room's plate-glass window, but none of those faces turn to stare back at her. They are all too occupied with their meals, these swells with their forks and knives and china platters buried under mounds of scrambled eggs or roast beef on toast or mashed potatoes and gravy. They raise china cups of hot black coffee to their lips and pretend she isn't there. This winter night is too filled with starving, tattered women on the bum. There is not time to notice them all, so better to notice none of them, better not to allow the sight of real hunger to spoil your appetite. A little farther down the street there is a Greek who sells apples and oranges and pears from a little side-walk stand, and she wonders how long before he catches her stealing, him or someone else. She has never been a particularly lucky girl.

Somewhere close by, a parrot shrieks and another parrot answers it, and finally she turns away from the people and the tiled walls of the lunch room and opens her eyes; the Manhattan street vanishes in a slushy, disorienting flurry and takes the cold with it. She is still hungry, but for a while she is content to lie in her carefully woven nest of rattan, bamboo, and ebony branches, blinking away the last shreds of sleep and gazing deeply into the rising mists and gathering dusk. She has made her home high atop a weathered promontory, this charcoal peak of lava rock and tephra a vestige of the island's fiery origins. It is for this summit's unusual shape— not so unlike a human skull— that white men named the place. And it is here that she last saw the giant ape, before it left her to pursue the moving-picture man and Captain Englehorn, the first mate and the rest of the crew of the *Venture*, left her alone to get itself killed and hauled away in the rusty hold of that evil-smelling ship.

At least, that is one version of the story she tells herself to explain why the beast never returned for her. It may not be the truth. Perhaps the ape died somewhere in the swampy jungle spread out below the mountain, somewhere along the meandering river leading down to the sea. She has learned that there is no end of ways to die on the island, and that nothing alive is so fierce or so cunning as to be entirely immune to those countless perils. The ape's hide was riddled with bullets, and it might simply have succumbed to its wounds and bled to death. Time and again, she has imagined this, the gorilla only halfway back to the wall but growing suddenly too weak to continue the chase, and perhaps it stopped, surrendering to pain and exhaustion, and sat down in a glade somewhere below the cliffs, resting against the bole of an enormous tree. Maybe it sat there, peering through a break in the fog and the forest canopy, gazing forlornly back up at the skull-shaped mountain. It would have been a terrible, lonely death, but not so terrible an end as the beast might have met had it managed to gain the ancient gates and the sandy peninsula beyond.

She has, on occasion, imagined another outcome, one in which the enraged god-thing overtook the men from the steamer, either in the jungle or somewhere out beyond the wall, in the village or on the beach-head. And though the ape was killed by their gunshots and gas bombs (for surely he would have returned, otherwise), first they died screaming, every last mother's son of them. She has taken some grim satisfaction in this fantasy, on days when she has had need of grim satisfaction. But she knows it isn't true, if only because she watched with her own eyes the *Venture* sailing away from the place where it had anchored out past the reefs and the deadly island, the smoke from its single stack drawing an ashen smudge across the blue morning sky. They escaped, at least enough of them to pilot the ship, and left her for dead or good as dead.

She stretches and sits up in her nest, watching the sun as it sinks slowly into the shimmering, flat monotony of the Indian Ocean, the dying day setting the western horizon on fire. She stands, and the red-orange light paints her naked skin the color of clay. Her stomach growls again, and she thinks of her small hoard of fruit and nuts, dried fish and a couple of turtle eggs she found the day before, all wrapped up safe in banana leaves and hidden in amongst the stones and brambles. Here, she need only fear nightmares of hunger and never hunger itself. There is the faint, rotten smell of sulfur emanating from the cavern that forms the skull's left eye socket, the mountain's malodorous breath wafting up from bubbling hot springs deep within the grotto. She has long since grown accustomed to the stench and has found that the treacherous maze of bubbling lakes and mud helps to protect her from many of the island's predators. For this reason, more than any other, more even than the sentimentality that she no longer denies, she chose these steep volcanic cliffs for her eyrie.

Stepping from her bed, the stones warm against the toughened soles of her feet, she remembers a bit of melody, a ghostly snatch of lyrics that has followed her up from the dream of the city and the woman she will never be again. She closes her eyes, shutting out the jungle noises for just a moment, and listens to the faint crackle of a half-forgotten radio broadcast.

Once I built a tower up to the sun,
Brick and rivet and lime.
Once I built a tower,
Now it's done.
Brother, can you spare a dime?

And when she opens her eyes again, the sun is almost gone, just a blazing sliver remaining now above the sea. She sighs and reminds herself that there is no percentage in recalling the clutter and racket of that lost world. Not now. Not here. Night is coming, sweeping in fast and mean on leathery pterodactyl wings and the wings of flying foxes and the wings of *ur*-birds, and like so many of the island's inhabitants, she puts all else from her mind and rises to meet it. The island has made of her a night thing, has stripped her of old diurnal ways. Better to sleep through the stifling equatorial days than to lie awake through the equally stifling nights; better the company of the sun for her uneasy dreams than the moon's cool, seductive glow and her terror of what might be watching from the cover of darkness.

When she has eaten, she sits awhile near the cliff's edge, contemplating what month this might be, what month in which year. It is a futile pastime, but mostly a harmless one. At first, she scratched marks on stone to keep track of the passing time, but after only a few hundred marks she forgot one day, and then another, and when she finally remembered, she found she was uncertain how many days had come and gone during her forgetfulness. It was then she came to understood the futility of counting days in this place— indeed, the futility of the very concept of time. She has thought often that the island must be time's primordial orphan, a castaway, not unlike herself, stranded in some nether or lower region, this sweltering antediluvian limbo where there is only the rising and setting of the sun, the phases of the moon, the long rainy season which is hardly less hot or less brutal than the longer dry. Maybe the men who built the wall long ago were a race of sorcerers, and in their arrogance they committed a grave transgression against time, some unspeakable contravention of the sanctity of months and hours. And so Chronos cast this place back down into the gulf of Chaos, and now it is damned to exist forever apart from the tick-tock, calendar-page blessings of Aeon.

Yes, she still recalls a few hazy scraps of Greek mythology, and Roman, too, this farmer's only daughter who always got good marks and waited until school was done before leaving the cornfields of Indiana to go east to seek her fortune in New York and New Jersey. All her girlhood dreams of the stage, the silver screen and her name on theater marquees, but by the time she reached Fort Lee, most of the studios were relocating west to California, following the promise of a more hospitable, more profitable climate. Black Tuesday had left its stain upon the country, and she never found more than extra work at the few remaining studios, happy just to play anonymous faces in crowd scenes and the like, and finally she could not even find that. Finally, she was fit only for the squalor of bread lines and mission soup kitchens and flop houses, until the night she met a man who promised to make her a star, who, chasing dreams of his own, dragged her halfway round the world and then abandoned her here in this serpent-haunted and time-forsaken wilderness. The irony is not lost on her. Seeking fame and adoration, she has found, instead, what might well be the ultimate obscurity.

Below her, some creature suddenly cries out in pain from the forest tangle clinging to the slopes of the mountain, and she watches, squinting into the darkness. She's well aware that hers are only one of a hundred or a thousand pairs of eyes that have stopped to see, to try and catch a glimpse of whatever bloody panoply is being played out among the vines and undergrowth, and that this is only one of the innumerable slaughters to come before sunrise. Something screams and so all eyes turn to see, for every thing that creeps or crawls, flits or slithers upon the island will fall prey, one day or another. And she is no exception.

One day, perhaps, the island itself will fall, not so unlike the dissatisfied angels in Milton or in Blake.

Ann Darrow opens her eyes, having nodded off again, and she is once more only a civilized woman not yet grown old, but no longer young. One who has been taken away from the world and touched, then returned and set adrift in the sooty gulches and avenues and asphalt ravines of this modern, electric city. But that was such a long time ago, before the war that proved the Great War was not so very great after all, that it was not the war to end all wars. Japan has been burned with the fire of two tiny manufactured suns and Europe lies in ruins, and already the fighting has begun again and young men are dying in Korea. History is a steamroller. History is a litany of war.

She sits alone in the Natural History Museum off Central Park, a bench all to herself in the alcove where the giant ape's broken skeleton was mounted for public exhibition after the creature tumbled from the top of the Empire State, plummeting more than twelve hundred feet to the frozen streets below. There is an informative placard (white letters on black) declaring it *Brontopithecus singularis* Osborn (1934), only known specimen, now believed extinct. So there, she thinks. Denham and his men dragged it from the not-quite-impenetrable sanctuary of its jungle and hauled it back to Broadway; they chained it and murdered it and, in that final act of desecration, they named it. The enigma was dissected and quantified, given its rightful place in the grand analytic scheme, in the Latinized order of things, and that's one less blank spot to cause the mapmakers and zoologists to scratch their heads. Now, Carl Denham's monster is no threat at all, only another harmless, impressive heap of bones shellacked and wired together in this stately, static mausoleum. And hardly anyone remembers or comes to look upon these bleached remains. The world is a steamroller. The 8th Wonder of the World was old news twenty years ago, and now it is only a chapter in some dusty textbook devoted to anthropological curiosities.

He was the king and the god of the world he knew, but now he comes to civilization, merely a captive, a show to gratify your curiosity. Curiosity killed the cat, and it slew the ape, as well, and that December night hundreds died for the price of a theater ticket, the fatal price of *their* curiosity and Carl Denham's hubris. By dawn, the passion play was done, and the king and god of Skull Island lay crucified by biplanes, by the pilots and trigger-happy Navy men borne aloft in Curtis Helldivers armed with .50 caliber machine guns. A tiered Golgotha skyscraper, one-hundred-and-two stories of steel and glass and concrete, a dizzying Art-Deco Calvary, and no resurrection save what the museum's anatomists and taxidermists might in time effect.

Ann Darrow closes her eyes, because she can only ever bear to look at the bones for just so long and no longer. Henry Fairfield Osborn, the museum's former president, had wanted to name it after her, in her honor— *Brontopithecus darrowii*, "Darrow's thunder ape"—but she'd threatened a lawsuit against him and his museum and the scientific journal publishing his paper, and so he'd christened the species *singularis*, instead. She played her Judas role, delivering the jungle god to Manhattan's Roman holiday, and wasn't that enough? Must she also have her name forever nailed up there with the poor beast's corpse? Maybe she deserved as much or far worse, but Osborn's "honor" was poetic justice she managed to evade.

There are voices now, a mother and her little girl, so Ann knows that she's no longer alone in the alcove. She keeps her eyes tightly shut, wishing she could shut her ears as well and not hear the things that are being said.

"Why did they kill him?" asks the little girl.

"It was a very dangerous animal," her mother replies sensibly. "It got loose and hurt people. I was just a child then, about your age."

"They could have put it in a zoo," the girl protests. "They didn't have to kill it."

"I don't think a zoo would ever have been safe. It broke free and hurt a lot of innocent people."

"But there aren't any more like it."

"There are still plenty of gorillas in Africa," the mother replies.

"Not that big," says the little girl. "Not as big as an elephant."

"No," the mother agrees. "Not as big as an elephant. But then we hardly need gorillas as big as elephants, now do we?"

Ann clenches her jaws, grinding her teeth together, biting her tongue (so to speak) and gripping the edge of the bench with nails chewed down to the quicks.

They'll leave soon, she reminds herself. They always do, get bored and move along after only a minute or so. It won't be much longer.

"What does that part say?" the child asks eagerly, so her mother reads to her from the text printed on the placard.

"Well, it says, 'Kong was not a true gorilla, but a close cousin, and belongs in the Superfamily Hominoidea with gorillas, chimpanzees, orangutans, gibbons, and human beings. His exceptional size might have evolved in response to his island isolation.'"

"What's a *super* family?"

"I don't really know, dear."

"What's a gibbon?"

"I think it's a sort of monkey."

"But we don't believe in evolution, do we?"

"No, we don't."

"So God made Kong, just like he made us?"

"Yes, honey. God made Kong."

And then there's a pause, and Ann holds her breath, wishing she were still dozing, still lost in her terrible dreams, because this waking world is so much more terrible.

"I want to see the *Tyrannosaurus* again," says the little girl, "and the *Triceratops*, too." Her mother says okay, there's just enough time to see the dinosaurs again before we have to meet your Daddy, and Ann sits still and listens to their footsteps on the polished marble floor, growing fainter and fainter until silence has at last been restored to the alcove. But now the sterile, drab museum smells are gone, supplanted by the various rank odors of the apartment Jack rented for the both of them before he shipped out on a merchant steamer, the *Polyphemus*, bound for the Azores and then Lisbon and the Mediterranean. He never made it much farther than São Miguel, because the steamer was torpedoed by a Nazi U-boat and went down with all hands onboard. Ann opens her eyes, and the strange dream of the museum and the ape's skeleton has already begun to fade. It isn't morning yet, and the lamp beside the bed washes the tiny room with yellow-white light that makes her eyes ache.

She sits up, pushing the sheets away, exposing the ratty grey mattress underneath. The bedclothes are damp with her sweat and with radiator steam, and she reaches for the half-empty gin bottle there beside the lamp. The booze used to keep the dreams at bay, but these last few months, since she got the telegram informing her that Jack Driscoll was drowned and given up for dead and she would never be seeing him again, the nightmares have seemed hardly the least bit intimidated by alcohol. She squints at the clock, way over on the chifforobe, and sees that it's not yet even four a.m. Still hours until sunrise, hours until the bitter comfort of winter sunlight through the bedroom curtains. She tips the bottle to her lips, and the liquor tastes like turpentine and regret and everything she's lost in the last three years. Better she would have never been anything more than a starving woman stealing apples and oranges to try to stay alive, better she would have never stepped foot on the *Venture*. Better she would have died in the green hell of that uncharted island. She can easily imagine a thousand ways it might have gone better, all grim but better than *this* drunken half-life. She does not torture herself with fairy-tale fantasies of happy endings that never were and never will be. There's enough pain in the world without that luxury.

She takes another swallow from the bottle, then reminds herself that it has to last until morning and sets it back down on the table. But morning seems at least as far away as that night on the island, as far away as the carcass of the sailor she married. Often, she dreams of him, gnawed by the barbed teeth of deep-sea fish and mangled by shrapnel, burned alive and rotted beyond recognition, tangled in the wreckage and ropes and cables of a ship somewhere at the bottom of the Atlantic Ocean. He peers out at her with eyes that are no longer eyes at all, but only empty sockets where eels and spiny albino crabs nestle. She usually wakes screaming from those dreams, wakes to the asshole next door pounding on the wall with the heel of a shoe or just his bare fist and shouting how he's gonna call the cops if she can't keep it down. He has a job and has to sleep, and he can't have some goddamn rummy broad half the bay over or gone crazy with the DTs keeping him awake. The old Italian cunt who runs this dump, she says she's tired of hearing the complaints, and either the hollering stops or Ann will have to find another place to flop. She tries not to think about how she'll have to find another place soon, anyway. She had a little money stashed in the lining of her coat, from all the interviews she gave the papers and magazines and the newsreel people, but now it's almost gone. Soon, she'll be back out on the bum, sleeping in mission beds or worse places, whoring for the sauce and as few bites of food as she can possibly get by on. Another month, at most, and isn't that what they mean by coming full circle?

She lies down again, trying not to smell herself or the pillowcase or the sheets, thinking about bright July sun falling warm between green leaves. And soon, she drifts off once more, listening to the rumble of a garbage truck down on Canal Street, the rattle of its engine and the squeal of its breaks not so very different from the primeval grunts and cries that filled the torrid air of the ape's profane cathedral.

And perhaps now she is lying safe and drunk in a squalid Bowery tenement and only dreaming away the sorry dregs of her life, and it's not the freezing morning when Jack led her from the skyscraper's spire down to the bedlam of Fifth Avenue. Maybe these are nothing more than an alcoholic's fevered recollections, and she is not being bundled in wool blankets and shielded from reporters and photographers and the sight of the ape's shattered body.

"It's over," says Jack, and she wants to believe that's true, by all the saints in Heaven and all the sinners in Hell, wherever and whenever she is, she wants to believe that it is finally and irrevocably over. There is not one moment to be relived, not ever again, because it has *ended*, and she is rescued, like Beauty somehow delivered from the clutching paws of the Beast. But there is so much commotion, the chatter of confused and frightened bystanders, the triumphant, confident cheers and shouting of soldiers and policemen, and she's begging Jack to get her out of it, away from it. It *must* be real, all of it, real and here and now, because she has never been so horribly cold in her dreams. She shivers and stares up at the narrow slice of sky visible between the buildings. The summit of that tallest of all tall towers is already washed with dawn, but down here on the street, it may as well still be midnight.

> *Life is just a bowl of cherries.*
> *Don't take it serious; it's too mysterious.*
> *At eight each morning I have got a date,*
> *To take my plunge 'round the Empire State.*
> *You'll admit it's not the berries,*
> *In a building that's so tall . . .*

"It's over," Jack assures her for the tenth or twentieth or fiftieth time. "They got him. The airplanes got him, Ann. He can't hurt you, not anymore."

And she's trying to remember through the clamor of voices and machines and the popping of flash bulbs—*Did he hurt me? Is that what happened?*—when the crowd divides like the holy winds of Jehovah parting the waters for Moses, and for the first time she can see what's left of the ape. And she screams, and they all *think* she's screaming in terror at the sight of a monster. They do not know the truth, and maybe she does not yet know herself and it will be weeks or months before she fully comprehends why she is standing there screaming and unable to look away from the impossible, immense mound of black fur and jutting white bone and the dark rivulets of blood leaking sluggishly from the dead and vanquished thing.

"Don't look at it," Jack says, and he covers her eyes with a callused palm. "It's nothing you need to see."

So she does *not* see, shutting her bright blue eyes and all the eyes of her soul, the eyes without and those other eyes within. Shutting *herself*, slamming closed doors and windows of perception, and how could she have known that she was locking in more than she was locking out. *Don't look at it,* he said, much too late, and these images are burned forever into her lidless, unsleeping mind's eye.

A sable hill from which red torrents flow.

Ann kneels in clay and mud the color of a slaughterhouse floor, all the shades of shit and blood and gore, and dips her fingertips into the stream. She has performed this simple act of prostration times beyond counting, and it no longer holds for her any revulsion. She comes here from her nest high in the smoldering ruins of Manhattan and places her hand inside the wound, like St. Thomas fondling the pierced side of Christ. She comes down to remember, because there is an unpardonable sin in forgetting such a forfeiture. In this deep canyon molded not by geologic upheaval and erosion but by the tireless, automatic industry of man, she bows her head before the black hill. God sleeps there below the hill, and one day he will awaken from his slumber, for all those in the city are not faithless. Some still remember and follow the buckled blacktop paths, weaving their determined pilgrims' way along decaying thoroughfares and between twisted girders and the tumbledown heaps of burnt-out rubble. The city was cast down when God fell from his throne (or was pushed, as some have dared to whisper), and his fall broke apart the ribs of the world and sundered even the progression of one day unto the next so that time must now spill backwards to fill in the chasm. Ann leans forward, sinking her hand in up to the wrist, and the steaming crimson stream begins to clot and scab where it touches her skin.

Above her, the black hill seems to shudder, to shift almost imperceptibly in its sleep.

She has thought repeatedly of drowning herself in the stream, has wondered what it would be like to submerge in those veins and be carried along through silent veils of silt and ruby-tinted light. She might dissolve and be no more than another bit of flotsam, unburdened by bitter memory and self-knowledge and these rituals to keep a comatose god alive. She would open her mouth wide, and as the air rushed from her lungs and across her mouth, she would fill herself with His blood. She has even entertained the notion that such a sacrifice would be enough to wake the black sleeper, and as the waters that are not waters carried her away, the god beast might stir. As she melted, He would open His eyes and shake Himself free of the holdfasts of that tarmac and cement and sewer-pipe grave. It *could* be that simple. In her waking dreams, she has learned there is incalculable magic in sacrifice.

Ann withdraws her hand from the stream, and blood drips from her fingers, rejoining the whole as it flows away north and east towards the noxious lake that has formed where once lay the carefully landscaped and sculpted conceits of Mr. Olmsted and Mr. Vaux's Central Park. She will not wipe her hand clean as would some infidel, but rather permit the blood to dry to a claret crust upon her skin, for she has already committed blasphemy enough for three lifetimes. The shuddering black hill is still again, and a vinegar wind blows through the tall grass on either side of the stream.

And then Ann realizes that she's being watched from the gaping brick maw that was a jeweler's window long ago. The frame is still rimmed round about with jagged crystal teeth waiting to snap shut on unwary dreamers, waiting to shred and pierce, starved for diamonds and sapphires and emeralds, but more than ready to accept mere meat. In dusty shafts of sunlight, Ann can see the form of a young girl gazing out at her, her skin almost as dark as the seeping hill.

"What do you want?" Ann calls to her, and a moment or two later, the girl replies.

"You have become a goddess," she says, moving a little nearer the broken shop window so that Ann might have a better look at her. "But even a goddess cannot dream forever. I have come a long way and through many perils to speak with you, Golden Mother, and I did not expect to find you sleeping and hiding in the lies told by dreams."

"I'm not hiding," Ann replies very softly, so softly she thinks surely the girl will not have heard her.

"Forgive me, Golden Mother, but you are. You are seeking refuge in guilt that is not your guilt."

"I am not your mother," Ann tells her. "I have never been anyone's mother."

And then a branch whips around and catches her in the face, a leaf's razor edge to draw a nasty cut across her forehead. But the pain slices cleanly through exhaustion and shock and brings her suddenly back to herself, back to this night and this moment, their mad, headlong dash from the river to the gate. The Cyclopean wall rises up before them, towering above the tree tops. There cannot now be more than a hundred yards remaining between them and the safety of the gate, but the ape is so very close behind. A fire-eyed demon who refuses to be so easily cheated of his prize by mere mortal men. The jungle cringes around them, flinching at the cacophony of Kong's approach, and even the air seems to draw back from that typhoon of muscle and fury, his angry roars and thunderous footfalls to divide all creation. Her right hand is gripped tightly in Jack's left, and he's all but dragging her forward. Ann can no longer feel her bare feet, which have been bruised and gouged and torn, and it is a miracle she can still run at all. Now she can make out the dim silhouettes of men standing atop the wall, men with guns and guttering torches, and, for a moment, she allows herself to hope.

"You are needed, Golden Mother," the girl says, and then she steps through the open mouth of the shop window. The blistering sun shimmers off her smooth, coffee-colored skin. "You are needed *here* and *now*," she says. "That night and every way that it might have gone, but did not, are passed forever beyond even your reach."

"You don't *see* what I can see," Ann tells the girl, hearing the desperation and resentment in her own voice.

And what she sees is the aboriginal wall and that last line of banyan figs and tree ferns. What she sees is the open gate and the way out of this nightmare, the road home.

"Only dreams," the girl says, not unkindly, and she takes a step nearer the red stream. "Only the phantoms of things that have never happened and never will."

"No," says Ann, and she shakes her head. "We *made* it to the gate. Jack and I both, together. We ran and we ran and we ran, and the ape was right there on top of us all the way, so close that I could smell his breath. But we didn't look back, not even once. We *ran,* and, in the end, we made it to the gate."

"No, Golden Mother. It did not happen that way."

One of the sailors on the wall is shouting a warning now, and at first, Ann believes it's only because he can see Kong behind them. But then something huge and long-bodied lunges from the underbrush at the clearing's edge, all scales and knobby scutes, scrabbling talons and the blue-green iridescent flash of eyes fashioned for night hunting. The high, sharp quills sprouting from the creature's backbone clatter one against the other like bony castanets, and it snatches Jack Driscoll in its saurian jaws and drags him screaming into the reedy shadows. On the wall, someone shouts, and she hears the staccato report of rifle fire.

The brown girl stands on the far side of the stream flowing along 5th Avenue, the tall grass murmuring about her knees. "You have become lost in All-at-Once time, and you must find your way back from the Every-when. I can help."

"I do not *need* your help," Ann snarls. "You keep away from me, you filthy goddamn heathen."

Beneath the vast, star-specked Indonesian sky, Ann Darrow stands alone. Jack is gone, taken by some unnamable abomination, and in another second the ape will be upon her. This is when she realizes that she's bleeding, a dark bloom unfolding from her right breast, staining the gossamer rags that are all that remain of her dress and underclothes. She doesn't yet feel the sting of the bullet, a single shot gone wild, intended for Jack's attacker, but finding her, instead. *I do not blame you*, she thinks, slowly collapsing, going down onto her knees in the thick carpet of moss and ferns. *It was an accident, and I do not blame anyone . . .*

"That is a lie," the girl says from the other side of the red stream. "You do blame them, Golden Mother, and you blame yourself, most of all."

Ann stares up at the dilapidated skyline of a city as lost in time as she, and the vault of Heaven turns above them like a dime-store kaleidoscope.

Once I built a railroad, I made it run, made it race against time.
Once I built a railroad; now it's done. Brother, can you spare a dime?
Once I built a tower, up to the sun, brick, and rivet, and lime;
Once I built a tower, now it's done. Brother, can you spare a dime?

"When does this end?" she asks, asking the girl or herself or no one at all. "*Where* does it end?"

"Take my hand," the girl replies and reaches out to Ann, a bridge spanning the rill and time and spanning all these endless possibilities. "Take my hand and come back over. Just step across and stand with me."

"No," Ann hears herself say, though it isn't at all what she wanted to say or what she *meant* to say. "No, I can't do that. I'm sorry."

And the air around her reeks of hay and sawdust, human filth and beer and cigarette smoke, and the sideshow barker is howling his line of ballyhoo to all the rubes who've paid their two-bits to get a seat under the tent. All the yokels and hayseeds who have come to point and whisper and laugh and gawk at the figure cowering inside the cage.

"Them bars there, they are solid carbon *steel*, mind you," the barker informs them. "Manufactured special for us by the same Pittsburgh firm that supplies prison bars to Alcatraz. Ain't nothing else known to man strong enough to contain her, and if not for those iron bars, well...rest assured, my good people, we have not in the least exaggerated the threat she poses to life and limb, in the absence of such precautions."

Inside the cage, Ann squats in a corner, staring out at all the faces staring in. Only she has not been Ann Darrow in years—just ask the barker or the garish canvas flaps rattling in the chilly breeze of an Indiana autumn evening. She is the Ape Woman of Sumatra, captured at great personal risk by intrepid explorers and hauled out into the incandescent light the 20th Century. She is naked, except for the moth-eaten scraps of buffalo and bear pelts they have given her to wear. Every inch of exposed skin is smeared with dirt and offal and whatever other filth has accumulated in her cage since it was last mucked out. Her snarled and matted hair hangs in her face, and there's nothing the least bit human in the guttural serenade of growls and hoots and yaps that escapes her lips.

The barker slams his walking cane against the iron bars, and she throws her head back and howls. A woman in the front row faints and has to be carried outside.

"She was the queen and the goddess of the strange world she knew," bellows the barker, "but now she comes to civilization, merely a captive, a show to gratify your curiosity. Learned men at colleges—forsaking the words of the Good Book—proclaim that we are *all* descended from monkeys. And, I'll tell you, seeing this wretched bitch, I am almost *tempted* to believe them, and also to suspect that in dark and far-flung corners of the globe there exist to this day beings still more simian than human, lower even than your ordinary niggers, hottentots, negritos, and lowly African pygmies."

CAITLÍN KIERNAN

Ann Darrow stands on the muddy bank of the red stream, and the girl from the ruined and vine-draped jewelry shop holds out her hand, the brown-skinned girl who has somehow found her way into the most secret, tortured recesses of Ann's consciousness.

"The world is still here," the girl says, "only waiting for you to return."

"I have heard another tale of her origin," the barker confides. "But I must *warn* you, it is not fit for the faint of heart or the ears of decent Christian women."

There is a long pause, while two or three of the women rise from their folding chairs and hurriedly leave the tent. The barker tugs at his pink suspenders and grins an enormous, satisfied grin, then glances into the cage.

"As I was saying," he continues, "there is *another* story. The Chinaman who sold me this pitiful oddity of human de-evolution said that its mother was born of French aristocracy, the lone survivor of a calamitous shipwreck, cast ashore on black volcanic sands. There, in the hideous misery and perdition of that Sumatran wilderness, the poor woman was *defiled* by some lustful species of jungle imp, though whether it were chimp or baboon I cannot say."

There is a collective gasp from the men and women inside the tent, and the barker rattles the bars again, eliciting another irate howl from its occupant.

"And here before you is the foul *spawn* of that unnatural union of anthropoid and womankind. The aged Mandarin confided to me that the mother expired shortly after giving birth, God rest her immortal soul. Her death was a mercy, I should think, as she would have lived always in shame and horror at having borne into the world this shameful, misbegotten progeny."

"Take my hand," the girl says, reaching into the cage. "You do not have to stay here. Take my hand, Golden Mother, and I will help you find the path."

There below the hairy black tumulus, the great slumbering titan belching forth the headwaters of all the earth's rivers, Ann Darrow takes a single hesitant step into the red stream. *This is the most perilous part of the journey*, she thinks, reaching to accept the girl's outstretched hand. *It wants me, this torrent, and if I am not careful, it will pull me down and drown me for my trespasses.*

240

"It's only a little ways more," the girl tells her and smiles. "Just step across to me."

The barker raps his silver-handled walking cane sharply against the bars of the cage, so that Ann remembers where she is and when, and doing so, forgets herself again. For the benefit of all those licentious, ogling eyes, all those slack jaws that have paid precious quarters to be shocked and titillated, she bites the head off a live hen, and when she has eaten her fill of the bird, she spreads her thighs and masturbates for the delight of her audience with filthy, bloodstained fingers.

Elsewhen, she takes another step towards the girl, and the softly gurgling stream wraps itself greedily about her calves. Her feet sink deeply into the slimy bottom, and the sinuous, clammy bodies of conger eels and salamanders wriggle between her ankles and twine themselves about her legs. She cannot reach the girl, and the opposite bank may as well be a thousand miles away.

In a smoke-filled screening room, Ann Darrow sits beside Carl Denham while the footage he shot on the island almost a year ago flickers across the screen at twenty-four frames per second. They are not alone, the room half-filled with low-level studio men from RKO and Paramount and Universal and a couple of would-be financiers lured here by the Hollywood rumor mill. Ann watches the images revealed in grainy shades of grey, in overexposed whites and underexposed smudges of black.

"What exactly are we supposed to be looking at?" someone asks impatiently.

"We shot this stuff from the top of the wall, once Englehorn's men had managed to frighten away all the goddamn tar babies. Just wait. It's coming."

"Denham, we've already been sitting here half an hour. This shit's pretty underwhelming, you ask me. You're better off sticking to the safari pictures."

"It's *coming*," Denham insists and chomps anxiously at the stem of his pipe.

And Ann knows he's right, that it's coming, because this is not the first time she's seen the footage. Up there on the screen, the eye of the camera looks out over the jungle canopy, and it always reminds her of Gustave Doré's visions of Eden from her mother's copy of *Paradise Lost*, or the illustrations of lush Pre-Adamite landscapes from a geology book she once perused in the New York Public Library.

"Honestly, Mr. Denham," the man from RKO sighs. "I've got a meeting in twenty minutes—"

"*There*," Denham says, pointing at the screen. "There it is. Right fucking *there*. Do you see it?"

And the studio men and the would-be financiers fall silent as the beast's head and shoulders emerge from the tangle of vines and orchid-encrusted branches and wide palm fronds. It stops and turns its mammoth head towards the camera, glaring hatefully up at the wall and directly into the smoke-filled room, across a million years and nine thousand miles. There is a dreadful, unexpected intelligence in those dark eyes as the creature tries to comprehend the purpose of the weird, pale men and their hand-crank contraption perched there on the wall above it. Its lips fold back, baring gigantic canines, eyeteeth longer than a grown man's hand, and there is a low, rumbling sound, then a screeching sort of yell, before the thing the natives called *Kong* turns and vanishes back into the forest.

"Great god," the Universal man whispers.

"Yes, gentlemen," says Denham, sounding very pleased with himself and no longer the least bit anxious, certain that he has them all right where he wants them. "That's just exactly what those tar babies think. They worship it and offer up human sacrifices. Why, they wanted Ann here. Offered us six of their women so she could become the bride of Kong. And there's our story, gentlemen."

"Great god," the Universal man says again, louder than before.

"But an expedition like this costs money," Denham tells them, getting down to brass tacks as the reel ends and the lights come up. "I mean to make a picture the whole damn *world's* gonna pay to see, and I can't do that without committed backers."

"Excuse me," Ann says, rising from her seat, feeling sick and dizzy and wanting to be away from these men and all their talk of money and spectacle, wanting to drive the sight of the ape from her mind, once and for all.

"I'm fine, really," she tells them. "I just need some fresh air."

On the far side of the stream, the brown-skinned girl urges her forward, no more than twenty feet left to go and she'll have reached the other side. "You're waking up," the girl says. "You're almost there. Give me your hand."

I'm only going over Jordan
I'm only going over home . . .

And the moments flash and glimmer as the dream breaks apart around her, and the barker rattles the iron bars of a stinking cage, and her empty stomach rumbles as she watches men and women bending over their plates in a lunch room, and she sits on a bench in an alcove on the third floor of the American Museum of Natural History. Crossing the red stream, Ann Darrow hemorrhages time, all these seconds and hours and days vomited forth like a bellyful of tainted meals. She shuts her eyes and takes another step, sinking even deeper in the mud, the blood risen now as high as her waist. Here is the morning they brought her down from the Empire State Building, and the morning she wakes in her nest on Skull Mountain, and the night she watched Jack Driscoll devoured well within sight of the archaic gates. Here's the Bowery tenement, and here the screening room, and here a fallen Manhattan, crumbling and lost in the storm-tossed gulf of eons, set adrift no differently than she has set herself adrift. Every moment all at once, each as real as every other, and never mind the contradictions, each damned and equally inevitable, all following from a stolen apple and the man who paid the Greek a dollar to look the other way.

The world is a steamroller.

Once I built a railroad; now it's done.

She stands alone in the seaward lee of the great wall and knows that its gates have been forever shut against her and all the daughters of men yet to come. This hallowed, living wall of human bone and sinew erected to protect what scrap of Paradise lies inside, not the dissolute, iniquitous world of men sprawling beyond its borders. Winged Cherubim stand guard on either side, and in their leonine forepaws they grasp flaming swords forged in unknown furnaces before the coming of the World, fiery brands that reach all the way to the sky and about which spin the hearts of newborn hurricanes. The molten eyes of the Cherubim watch her every move, and their indifferent minds know her every secret thought, these dispassionate servants of the vengeful god of her father and her mother. Neither tears nor all her words will ever wring mercy from these sentinels, for they know precisely what she is, and they know her crimes.

I am she who cries out,
and I am cast forth upon the face of the earth.

The starving, ragged woman who stole an apple. Starving in body and in mind, starving in spirit if so base a thing as she can be said to possess a soul. Starving, and ragged in all ways.

I am the members of my mother.
I am the barren one
and many are her sons.
I am she whose wedding is great,
and I have not taken a husband.

And as is the way of all exiles, she cannot kill hope that her exile will one day end. Even the withering gaze of the Cherubim cannot kill that hope, and so hope is the cruelest reward.

Brother, can you spare a dime?

"Take my hand," the girl says, and Ann Darrow feels herself grown weightless and buoyed from that foul brook, hauled free of the morass of her own nightmares and regret onto a clean shore of verdant mosses and zoysiagrass, bamboo and reeds, and the girl leans down and kisses her gently on the forehead. The girl smells like sweat and nutmeg and the pungent yellow pigment dabbed across her cheeks.

"You have come *home* to us, Golden Mother," she says, and there are tears in her eyes.

"You don't see," Ann whispers, the words slipping out across her tongue and teeth and lips like her own ghost's death rattle. If the jungle air were not so still and heavy, not so turgid with the smells of living and dying, decay and birth and conception, she's sure it would lift her as easily as it might a stray feather and carry her away. She lies very still, her head cradled in the girl's lap, and the stream flowing past them is only water and the random detritus of any forest stream.

"The world blinds those who cannot close their eyes," the girl tells her. "You were not always a god and have come here from some outer world, so it may be you were never taught how to travel that path and not become lost in All-at-Once time."

Ann Darrow digs her fingers into the soft, damp earth, driving them into the loam of the jungle floor, holding on and still expecting *this* scene to shift, to unfurl, to send her tumbling pell-mell and head over heels into some other *now*, some other *where*.

And sometime later, when she's strong enough to stand again, and the sickening, vertigo sensation of fluidity has at last begun to fade, the girl helps Ann to her feet, and together they follow the narrow dirt trail leading back up this long ravine to the temple. Like Ann, the girl is naked save a leather breechcloth tied about her waist. They walk together beneath the sagging boughs of trees that must have been old before Ann's great-great-grandmothers were born, and here and there is ample evidence of the civilization that ruled the island in some murky, immemorial past—glimpses of great stone idols worn away by time and rain and the humid air, disintegrating walls and archways leaning at such precarious angles Ann cannot fathom why they have not yet succumbed to gravity. Crumbling bas-reliefs depicting the loathsome gods and demons and the bizarre reptilian denizens of this place. As they draw nearer to the temple, the ruins become somewhat more intact, though even here the splayed roots of the trees are slowly forcing the masonry apart. The roots put Ann in mind of the tentacles of gargantuan octopi or cuttlefish, and that is how she envisions the spirit of the jungles and marshes fanning out around this ridge—grey tentacles advancing inch by inch, year by year, inexorably reclaiming what has been theirs all along.

As she and the girl begin to climb the steep and crooked steps leading up from the deep ravine—stones smoothed by untold generations of footsteps—Ann stops to catch her breath and asks the brown girl how she knew where to look, how it was she found her at the stream. But the girl only stares at her, confused and uncomprehending, and then she frowns and shakes her head and says something in the native patois. In Ann's long years on the island, since the *Venture* deserted her and sailed away with what remained of the dead ape, she has never learned more than a few words of that language, and she has never tried to teach this girl nor any of her people English. The girl looks back the way they've come; she presses the fingers of her left hand against her breast, above her heart, then uses the same hand to motion towards Ann.

Life is just a bowl of cherries.
Don't take it serious; it's too mysterious.

By sunset, Ann has taken her place on the rough-hewn throne carved from beds of coral limestone thrust up from the seafloor in the throes of the island's cataclysmic genesis. As night begins to gather once again, torches are lit, and the people come bearing sweet-smelling baskets of flowers and fruit, fish and the roasted flesh of gulls and rats and crocodiles. They lay multicolored garlands and strings of pearls at her feet, a necklace of ankylosaur teeth, rodent claws, and monkey vertebrae, and she is only the Golden Mother once again. They bow and genuflect, and the tropical night rings out with joyous songs she cannot understand. The men and woman decorate their bodies with yellow paint in an effort to emulate Ann's blonde hair, and a sort of pantomime is acted out for her benefit, as it is once every month, on the night of the new moon. She does not *need* to understand their words to grasp its meaning—the coming of the *Venture* from somewhere far away, Ann offered up as the bride of a god, her marriage and the death of Kong, and the ascent of the Golden Mother from a hellish underworld to preside in his stead.

The end of one myth and the beginning of another, the turning of a page. *I am not lost*, Ann thinks. *I am right here, right now—here and now where, surely, I must belong*, and she watches the glowing bonfire embers rising up to meet the dark sky. She knows she will see that terrible black hill again, the hill that is not a hill and its fetid crimson river, but she knows, too, that there will always be a road back from her dreams, from that All-at-Once tapestry of possibility and penitence. In her dreams, she will be lost and wander those treacherous, deceitful paths of Might-Have-Been, and always she will wake and find herself once more.

LOST SOUL

———

M P Ericson

Rajiv shuffled along the village street. With his right hand, he sprinkled incense before him so as not to pollute the path of others. His left, unclean, hand he tucked into the side of his dhoti, so as not to taint the air.

He kept his eyes lowered to avoid bringing evil. All he saw were his own toes scuffling through a drizzle of tulsi-scented sawdust.

At the pandit's door he stopped, blew three times on the fingers of his right hand, and knocked.

Jagan's wife opened the door. She withdrew hastily, then disappeared into the house. Rajiv heard a whispered consultation.

"You'd better come in." Jagan sounded displeased, but he could not refuse a supplicant.

The room in which Jagan received his clients was large, the size of Rajiv's whole hut, and smelled of sandalwood. A gilt statue of Kemshi, wrapped in scarlet silk, smiled from the shrine.

"You know it's bad luck for you to leave your house before the month is out," Jagan said. "I'll have to purify my home and myself."

"I know." Rajiv looked up, knowing that Jagan had no need to fear evil. A pandit's strength lay in dealing with such things. "But I had to come. I must ask you to bring back my wife."

"That is not possible."

"You did it for Kiran." Rajiv thought of the fevered whispers, and how he had ignored them. When Kiran died, gutted by his own harvesting knife, Rajiv concluded the man must have been crazy. But lately, ever since Bela's funeral, those whispers had begun to return to his ears.

"Kiran was a fool," Jagan said. "He was too attached to his wife. We all know her death sent him mad. Whatever he told you, disregard it. Mere ravings."

Rajiv met Kemshi's gaze of promise.

"He said it was only a matter of price. I have savings. I can pay."

"You have nothing but a house full of daughters, who all need dowries soon. If I were you, I'd think of ways to please the gods, so they may bless you with more wealth than you have earned."

Rajiv dug out a pair of incense-bearded coins from the small woven pouch that hung at his waist.

"Two rupees," he said.

Jagan chuckled.

"That wouldn't buy me a meal. Go home."

"It's all I have."

"As I said, you have nothing."

"But I need her." Too many nights he had spent sweating alone on his rope bed, straining to hear her soft breath from the floor beside him. "Kiran said you knew how."

"Nonsense."

"Just once," Rajiv pleaded. If he could only hold her one more time, he would find ease.

Jagan studied him, as if weighing his soul on invisible scales.

"Even if it could be done, the task would be dangerous. Calling back the spirits of the dead takes great courage and meticulous preparation. And certain sacred offerings, which are expensive—or would be, if such a thing were possible."

Rajiv looked at the mildewed coins in his hand.

"I have her bangles," he said. "They were to be dowries for my daughters."

"Very sensible."

"They are worth six rupees."

"Each?" Jagan asked in surprise. Rajiv winced.

"All together."

"It is an insult," Jagan said, "to suggest that I would do this work for less than ten rupees."

Rajiv's muscles clenched.

"But you would?"

"I might consider the possibility."

Rajiv thought of his one remaining treasure.

"I have her beads," he said. "They are worth two."

She had come to him with twelve rupees in worth, and in fifteen years he only had to spend one. The remainder consisted of her clothes. She had burned in those as an offering to the goddess of death, in the hope of safe passage into the next life. He wished he had not squandered them that way.

"Ten," he said. "All together."

"You must pay in advance," Jagan said. "Else you may find an excuse not to. And if you want this work done, time is short. At the end of your month of mourning, your wife's soul will move on. There are only three days left. I cannot call it back after that. Even now, the links that hold it to earth are frail. There is no guarantee of success."

Rajiv began to wheeze, his habit when frightened.

"Tonight?" he suggested.

Jagan consulted the shrine.

"It would be wise. Meet me at the graveyard before midnight. Bring the payment in full, and also the following three things: blood, bark, and seed."

Rajiv stared.

"How?"

"That is for you to determine." Jagan rose, a signal that the interview was over. "Remember to purify your path as you leave."

When Rajiv got home, his mother had tidied the house and was waiting expectantly for midday prayers. Rajiv took his place on his straw mat, threw incense into the candle flame, and recited the verses his father had taught him.

The statue of Kemshi, fist-sized and badly carved, sneered at him from its net of cracking paint. He tried not to think of the opulence in Jagan's house.

According to sacred verse, the goddess brought prosperity to those she favoured. The way to gain her blessing was by prayer and hard work. Rajiv wondered, in a rebellious corner of his mind, whether rich men like Jagan told such stories in order to justify extortion.

Ten rupees!

Rajiv finished his prayers, and sat staring at the beads wrapped around the statue's neck. He had hoped they would bring him wealth, as marriage to Bela had never done. Five girls she gave him, and a son who did not live.

All Kemshi had done for him was persuade the goddess of death to carry off two of the girls with fever. At least now he had only three dowries to pay.

His eldest daughter set down the offering of rice and ghee. Rajiv scowled at her. She ought to have sense enough to die, too, if she could not have been born a boy.

"I'll be lucky to get you married," he said.

"I don't want to be married," she snapped back.

Rajiv lashed out. The punch sent her tumbling, and she thudded against the thin boards of the wall. Blood seeped from her nose and mingled with a dribble of tears.

His mother slapped her, more from reflex than malice, then gave her a clean rag to dab away the mess. Bright patches soaked through the cloth. Rajiv burst forward and snatched the rag from her grip, then stormed out of the house.

At least he had obtained the blood.

He rolled the rag into a tight ball, stain innermost, and tied it around his wrist.

Heat pressed down between the houses. From the stream came splashes and chatter, as women washed clothes while children played. His daughters should be down there, too, making themselves useful instead of littering the house.

Rajiv turned into the mango grove at the back of the village. The shade eased his temper. He scraped at the trunk of a tree, fingers working to rip away a strand of bark. Dirt and fragments packed under his nails, curving into leers.

Above him dangled ripe fruit, shining like festival lanterns. He plucked one and ate it, savoured the intense perfume. Sweet juice dripped from his chin.

When he was finished, he tied the damp stone and the strip of bark into the rag at his wrist.

His store of incense lasted just long enough to get him home. The girls scrambled away as he entered, and his mother gave him a disapproving look.

"You shouldn't keep going out," she said.

Rajiv shrugged, and retired to the privacy of his room. He lay on the bed, panting with heat. Sweat trickled over his skin.

The reality of what he was engaged in burrowed through his mind. Bela was dead, her body burned. Nothing remained of her but ash.

He still wanted to make the attempt, before his last chance of seeing her was gone.

Night hung thick around Rajiv as he stole down the street. The air, clogged with warmth, stuck in his lungs.

The graveyard lay well outside the village. It took him longer than he thought to get there. By the time he arrived, and saw Jagan's shape loosen from the black void of the palisade fence, the stars already told of midnight.

"Did you bring everything?" was Jagan's only greeting. Rajiv handed over the bundle. Jagan grunted acknowledgement, and led the way into the burial grounds.

"Understand two things," he said as they stood by the grave. "First, I can perform this calling only once, and your wife will be with you only until dawn. Second, you must not return here until I have concluded the final rite for your wife. The ceremony I am about to perform will draw the attention of evil spirits. I can hold them off, but if you were to come here without me, they could use you to gain access to our world."

The remnants of Bela's pyre felt like dust underfoot. Rajiv stood aside, his feet tickled by blades of grass, while Jagan placed each item in turn at the corners of the grave. A quiet murmur told of the ritual performed.

"Blood, for life. Bark, for growth. Seed, for renewal." Each utterance was followed by the recital of a sacred verse and the scent of melted ghee poured over the offering.

At the fourth corner, Jagan silently placed a secret item of his own. Then he seated himself by the foot of the grave, and began to chant.

A chill passed over Rajiv. The night closed in around him, as if fingers gripped his limbs. He began to shiver. Tales from childhood surfaced in his mind, stories of demons that crept into the homes of the living and gnawed all flesh from the bones of sleeping men.

He wanted to tell Jagan to stop, but could not utter a sound.

At the end of the recital, Jagan remained in a pose of meditation. Rajiv waited.

Jagan rose, and began to walk out of the graveyard. Rajiv hurried after him.

"It didn't work?"

Jagan said nothing, only walked on towards the village. From behind, Rajiv heard the padding of feet.

He swung around. A shape moved in the starlight. Eyes gleamed in a featureless face.

Rajiv swallowed. Fear cramped his limbs. He turned from the figure and hurried after Jagan. The footsteps followed, obediently keeping pace with the two men, never drawing closer.

At Jagan's door, the pandit stopped.

"Remember," he said. "Only this one time." He went inside, and Rajiv was left staring at blank wood.

The footsteps had stopped, but resumed as Rajiv continued. When he arrived at his own house, he dashed inside and slammed the door shut. He could not explain the sense of dread he felt, but he knew he did not want that creature in his home. Not even if it was Bela.

He heard the careful silence that meant his mother and daughters were awake and anxious not to appear so. Without speaking, he crossed to his own room and lay down on the bed. What the creature would do, alone out in the street, he did not know. Perhaps she would stand there, obedient as a woman should be, until the time came for her to return to the grave-yard. Or perhaps she would vanish, now that he had no more need of her.

The regular tap of bare feet on dirt approached him. A body slumped to the floor beside his bed, and lay without breathing.

Sweat rushed to Rajiv's forehead. She was right there beside him. He could feel her presence, tangible as the ropes under his back. A faint smell of cinders prickled his nose.

"Bela?" he whispered.

No answer. But desire grew in him even as he waited. If it was indeed her, it did him no good to waste the hours that remained. And if the act could not bring pleasure, Jagan would have no need to warn him that it must end.

"Wife," he said instead, with a man's proper tone of command. "Join me."

She came. Her limbs were smooth and soft as he remembered them from the first night he possessed her, and her submission that of a long-married wife. The smell of ash surrounded him, and he burned on a pyre of lust until his flesh melted into hers.

By dawn, she was gone. Rajiv woke with a smile on his face, and stretched in the net of light that fell through the slivered gaps in the walls. She had been real and delightful: a woman, not a corpse.

He spent the day in a gush of fine spirits, going so far as to pat his eldest daughter on the head when she served him breakfast. He tended his field, spread goat-dung over hardened furrows and tore out the weeds that had rooted. At times he would pause, scoop the sweat from his brow, and stand idle for a moment, gazing in the direction of the graveyard.

That night and the next he lay awake, pondering each village girl in turn. He refused to think of Bela's gentle compliance, her silence, the fire that burned him. But on occasion, he still fancied he heard the padding of feet through the room.

On the final night of the week he heard them clearly. He sat bolt upright and stared into the darkness.

No charred smell greeted him. Nothing moved. But Rajiv swung himself off the bed, pulled on his dhoti, and left the house.

A rough strip of bark he gathered from a mango tree. A barely-ripe fruit he tore from a branch, bit off the flesh and spat it out to leave only the kernel. Then he strode off to the graveyard.

He scratched at the palisade fence until a splinter dislodged. With its sharp point he scored his own skin, and scraped up the oozing blood.

What Jagan had added to the fourth corner, Rajiv could not guess. But he planted his offerings in the remaining three, muttering such snatches of verse as he could remember. Warm air plucked at his arms and legs, and the pile shifted slightly under his feet.

He knelt at the foot of the grave, and mumbled all the prayers he knew.

A flame shot from the grave. Rajiv flinched back, covered his face with his arms, heard a whimper issue from his numb lips.

When the blindness passed, he forced his eyes to open. Light cut them deep, but he managed to make out a figure in the centre of the flame. Featureless as the creature that had followed him home, but with the shape and size of a woman.

"Bela?"

She laughed, the most terrible sound he had ever heard.

"You wanted my soul." Her voice clawed at him. "Don't you like it? You prefer it trapped in a dead body, perhaps."

She leaned towards him, her face lit by a savage glow. Rajiv scrambled away.

"Who are you?" he whispered. "What have you done with my wife?"

"I am your wife—or rather, I'm the soul of the woman who was your wife. Did you think what you saw in her was all there was to see? A servant, a chattel, a cushion for your blows?"

Rajiv winced. He remembered her expression the first time he struck her, eyes dark with fear and reproach.

"You were a good wife," he protested.

"I learned to obey. To hide my feelings, to conceal who I truly was. You never wanted to know. Why do you call me now, if not to see the true nature of my soul, revealed without the mask of flesh?"

Rajiv sought for words. He wanted the old Bela, quiet, obedient; not this raging fire of spirit. Staring into its flaming eyes, he knew not how to speak his wish.

"Are you surprised?" Bela said. "You ought not to be. Did you not know that every woman has a soul that belongs to her alone?"

Rajiv swallowed.

"I thought you were happy," he said. "You never told me you weren't."

"You never asked. If I had spoken, what would you have done?"

He knew the answer, though he could not bear to speak it. Not here beside her grave. Not now, facing her spirit for the first time.

"What will you do?" he whispered.

"I will leave you," Bela said. "Because I can. The month is over, and you have no power to hold me back. But I wanted you to see the real me—just once."

The flame vanished, leaving a blue scar in the night. Rajiv struggled for breath. Gradually he became aware of the grass crushed under his knees, of the scent of dew.

"You are a foolish man," Jagan said from the darkness.

Rajiv started.

"How long have you been here?"

"I followed you. The calling is not safe without the fourth item, which I shall not tell you about. You tried to let loose an uncontained spirit into the world. That could have brought disaster on us all."

Rajiv scuffled back. His limbs trembled.

"But I called her," he said. "She came."

"What you saw," Jagan said, "was not Bela. It was a demon taking her shape in an attempt to trick you. Fortunately, I guessed you would act like this, and I prepared. Nothing can cross from the spirit world while my bars hold. But you must go now. Do not try this again. A man may call all sorts of evil to him when he is crazed with grief. As for the spirit of your wife, it has moved on. The time has passed."

Rajiv lifted his head, and saw that the stars had fallen from midnight.

"What came," he insisted, "was Bela's true self. Why didn't you show it to me before? Why did you give me a walking corpse?"

"What else did you want?"

Rajiv struggled for an answer.

"I gave you a compliant body," Jagan said. "That is all a man wants from his wife, and all a woman can offer her husband. The rest is your own imagination."

"I wanted more."

"There is nothing more."

Rajiv let himself be raised, and leaned on Jagan throughout the long stumble towards home.

"Keep to the rituals," Jagan said. "You have placed yourself and your family in danger, but I have contained it. The creature you saw will not trouble you again. But there are others, and worse. Do not persist in calling them, or I will be forced to contain you, too."

Rajiv stopped. They had almost reached Jagan's house.

"How could you do that?"

A sliver of starlight cut across Jagan's face, making it a grotesque mockery of his daytime self.

"I could take your soul," he said. "And lock it away securely. The next time a man comes to me, pleading for one last meeting with his wife, I would use it."

"How?"

Jagan patted his arm.

"Go home to your family. Observe the rituals, and look about for another girl to marry." He turned into his own house, and left Rajiv alone in the street.

When Rajiv entered the hut, his mother and daughters lay like the dead, but the silence of their waking hummed like crickets. He stood for a moment in the darkness, feeling their presence as a reassurance, a promise that he would not come to harm.

"Sleep," he said. "All is well."

He lay down on his own bed, and strained to hear the sound of breathing through the partition wall.

No footsteps came. He craved them now, not as a satisfaction to himself, but as a sign that there might still be time. He wanted to undo the past, and create something better.

In the silence, he grieved. Not for himself, but for a woman he wished he had known.

BIOGRAPHIES

Having completed her Ph.D. in English literature, **SARAH MONETTE** now lives and writes in a 99-year-old house in the Upper Midwest. Her first two novels, *Melusine* (2005) and *The Virtu* (2006), have been published by Ace Books, with two more novels in the series to follow: *The Mirador* (2007) and *Summerdown* (2008). Her short fiction has appeared in many places, including *Strange Horizons, Alchemy,* and *Lady Churchill's Rosebud Wristlet,* and has received four Honorable Mentions from *The Year's Best Fantasy & Horror.* Visit her online at **www.sarahmonette.com**

LAVIE TIDHAR grew up on a kibbutz in Israel, lived in Israel and South Africa, travelled widely in Africa and Asia, and has lived in London for a number of years. He is the winner of the 2003 Clarke-Bradbury Prize (awarded by the European Space Agency), was the editor of *Michael Marshall Smith: The Annotated Bibliography* (PS Publishing, 2004) and the anthology *A Dick & Jane Primer for Adults* (The British Fantasy Society, 2006), and is the author of the novella *An Occupation of Angels* (Pendragon Press, 2005). His stories appear in *Sci Fiction, ChiZine, Postscripts, Nemonymous, Infinity Plus, Aeon, The Book of Dark Wisdom, Fortean Bureau* and many others, and in translation in seven languages.

IAN WATSON started writing science fiction in Japan in the late 1960s, where he was supposed to be a lecturer but his university was on strike for 2½ years. Many novels and story collections later, his most recent are respectively *Mockymen* (Golden Gryphon, 2003, and Immanion Press, 2004) and *The Butterflies of Memory* (PS Publishing, 2006), which isn't a sequel to *The Flies of Memory* (Gollancz, 1990). His previous collection, *The Great Escape* (from Golden Gryphon) was a *Washington Post* "Book of the Year." Throughout 1990 he worked eyeball to eyeball with Stanley Kubrick on *A.I. Artificial Intelligence*, subsequently directed by Steven Spielberg, for which Ian has screen credit for Screen Story. His first collection of poetry, *The Lexicographer's Love Song*, appeared in 2001 from DNA Publications, and he has won a Rhysling Award for his SF poetry.

He and Roberto Quaglia began collaborating three years ago, resulting in a now complete book of linked stories, *The Beloved of My Beloved*, of which the "Moby Clitoris" is one, currently seeking an English language publisher—it already found a Japanese one. Ian lives in a tiny English village midway between Oxford and Stratford with his black cat Poppy, and his web site with fun photos, run by Roberto, is at **www.ianwatson.info**. He and his Spanish translator and Hungarian publisher maintain a website (**www.ajeno.intelmedia.co.uk**) to spread greater awareness of the unknown Colombian poet Miguel Ajeno.

ROBERTO QUAGLIA (**www.robertoquaglia.com**) hails from Genoa in Italy, where he ran a bar for years, won prizes for photography, and became one of the few Surrealist city councillors in the world. Currently he lives much of the year in Bucharest because he learned to speak Romanian, though he may also live in Moldova where people also speak Romanian. Robert Sheckley enthusiastically prefaced Roberto's surreal satirical SF double-novel *Bread, Butter and Paradoxine* (published in English by Delos International). He continues to take thousands of photographs. Genoa is the city of Christopher Columbus, who perhaps discovered America, and now America discovers Roberto Quaglia, which they can also do in "The Penis of My Beloved" in Claude Lalumière & Elise Moser's anthology *Lust for Life*. Roberto cruises the motorways of Europe in a white Mercedes with no wing mirrors so that he will always see into the future. His recent collection of essays, also from Delos, *Pensiero stocastico* (*Probabilistic Thought*), considers such matters as "The Advantages of Human Clonation," "The Miracle of the Multiplication of Loaves and Fishes and Porn Photos on the Internet," and "The Myth of Diana, the Death of the Sad Princess." He has also written the remarkable *Jonathan Livingshit Pigeon*, much better than a seagull.

VYLAR KAFTAN's fiction has appeared in *Strange Horizons*, *ChiZine*, and *Abyss & Apex*. She lives in northern California and volunteers as a mentor for teenaged writers. She blogs at **www.vylarkaftan.net**

CATHERYNNE VALENTE lives in Ohio. Her short fiction and poetry has appeared in *The Pedestal Magazine*, *Fantastic Metropolis*, *The Women's*

Arts Network, NYC Big City Lit, Jabberwocky, Fantasy Magazine, Electric Velocipede, Cabinet des Fees, and *Star*Line,* and has been featured in *The Year's Best Fantasy and Horror* #18. Her novels include *The Labyrinth, Yume no Hon: The Book of Dreams, The Grass Cutting Sword,* and *The Orphan's Tales: In the Night Garden.*

JENNY DAVIDSON's first novel, *Heredity,* was published in the US by Soft Skull and the UK by Serpent's Tail; her second, an alternate history called *Dynamite No. 1,* will be released by HarperCollins Children's Books in 2008. She teaches eighteenth-century British literature at Columbia University.

ELIZABETH BEAR shares a birthday with Frodo and Bilbo Baggins, and narrowly avoided being named after Peregrine Took. This was probably coincidence.

Her short work has previously appeared in markets such as *The Magazine of Fantasy & Science Fiction* and the anthology *All-Star Zeppelin Adventure Stories.* She also writes novels. Her science fiction (*Hammered, Scardown, Worldwired,* and *Carnival*) is published by Bantam Spectra, and her fantasy series "The Promethean Age," beginning with *Blood & Iron,* is published by ROC. *The Chains That You Refuse,* a short story collection, was published earlier this year by Night Shade Books.

ERICA L. SATIFKA lives in Pittsburgh, PA. "Automatic" is her first short story in a national publication.

JAY LAKE lives and works in Portland, Oregon, within sight of an 11,000-foot volcano. He is the author of over two hundred short stories, four collections, and a chapbook, along with novels from Tor Books, Night Shade Books and Fairwood Press. Jay is also the co-editor with Deborah Layne of the critically-acclaimed *Polyphony* anthology series from Wheatland Press. His next few projects include *The River Knows Its Own* (Wheatland Press), *Madness of Flowers* (Night Shade Books) and *Stemwinder* (Tor). In 2004, Jay won the John W. Campbell Award for Best New Writer. He has also been a Hugo nominee for his short fiction and a three-time World Fantasy Award nominee for his editing. Jay can be reached via his Web site at **www.jlake.com**

SHARON MOCK is a former writer and designer for online roleplaying games, and a graduate of the Viable Paradise workshop. She lives in Southern California. This is her first published story.

BARTH ANDERSON's imaginative fiction, called "rollicking," "barbed and witty," and "wildly inventive," has appeared in *Asimov's, Strange Horizons, Polyphony, Alchemy,* and a variety of other quality venues. Several of his stories have received Honorable Mentions in *The Year's Best Fantasy and Horror.*

As a member of the Ratbastards writing and publishing group, he co-edited the first three critically-acclaimed *Rabid Transit* chapbooks. In 2004, he received the Spectrum Award for Best Short Fiction for his short story "Lark Till Dawn Princess," and his first novel, *The Patron Saint of Plagues* was published in 2006 by Bantam Spectra.

Barth has read Tarot for twenty-seven years, bakes a bad-ass kashka bread, and, currently, he's proudly honing his fatherhood skills. He lives with his wife Lisa and son Isaiah in Minneapolis.

CARRIE LABEN lives in Brooklyn with four cats, three rats, and one human. She currently writes software user manuals and other still more dire things for a living, but this is a big improvement over milking cows and selling used books to agitated mental patients. This is her first outing as a professional fiction author, but she has had several essays published in various books and periodicals that you haven't read if you haven't been to Ithaca, NY. In her spare time, she enjoys collecting books, looking at birds, and finding new and different things to eat.

Widely regarded as one of the world's best fantasists, bestselling author JEFF VANDERMEER's book-length fiction has been translated into fourteen languages, while his short fiction has appeared in several year's best anthologies and short-listed for *Best American Short Stories.* His most recent books have made the year's best lists of *Publishers Weekly, The San Francisco Chronicle,* and *Los Angeles Weekly.* He is also the recipient of an NEA-funded Florida Individual Artist Fellowship for excellence in fiction and a Florida Artist Enhancement Grant. A two-time winner of the World Fantasy Award, VanderMeer has also been a finalist for the Hugo Award, the Philip K. Dick Award, the International Horror Guild Award, the British Fantasy Award, the Bram Stoker Award, and the Theodore Sturgeon Memorial Award. In addition to his writing, VanderMeer has edited or co-edited several anthologies, including the critically-acclaimed *Leviathan* fiction anthology series and *The Thackery T. Lambshead Pocket Guide to Eccentric & Discredited Diseases*. He will also co-edit the inaugural edition of *Best American Fantasy*. VanderMeer grew up in the Fiji Islands and spent six months traveling through Asia, Africa, and Europe before returning to the United States. These travels have deeply influenced his fiction. He now lives in Tallahassee, Florida, with his wife, Ann, and three cats.

MICHAEL DE KLER's fiction has appeared in the *Chimeraworld #3* anthology and at *HorrorWorld.org*. He lives in Northern New Jersey with his wife and newborn son. Visit him online at **www.mdekler.com**

PAUL G. TREMBLAY has sold short fiction to *Razor Magazine, ChiZine, Horror: The Best of the Year: 2007 Edition, Weird Tales*, and *Last Pentacle of the Sun: Writings in Support of the West Memphis Three*, among other markets. He is the author of the short fiction collection *Compositions for the Young and Old* and the novella *City Pier: Above and Below*. He has really long, double-jointed fingers and toes, which makes up for his lack of uvula. Other fascinating tidbits can be found at **www.paulgtremblay.com**

JETSE DE VRIES is a technical specialist for a propulsion company and travels the world for this, albeit less frequently nowadays because of the time that co-editing *Interzone* and his writing is taking up. Other publications include *Nemonymous, TEL: Stories, the Journal of Pulse-Pounding Narratives,* and *DeathGrip: Exit Laughing*, which makes him a sort of late-labelled, experimental pulpster with a wicked sense of humour, drenched in stylistic excess. And all he really wants to do is write SF.

Jetse has a blog at **eclipticplane.blogspot.com**

HOLLY PHILLIPS lives by the Columbia River in the mountains of western Canada. She is the author of the award-winning story collection

In the Palace of Repose. Her fantasy novel *Engine's Child* will be published by Del Rey in 2008.

DAVID CHARLTON splits his time between Calgary and Seoul. He writes and edits textbooks for an ESL publisher. When he gets the chance for more exciting pursuits, he works on archaeological projects in Mexico and Nicaragua. "Moon Over Yodok" is his first published story. It was inspired by Kang Chol-Hwan's real experiences in Yodok as recounted in *The Aquariums of Pyongyang: Ten Years in the North Korean Gulag.*

CAT RAMBO lives and writes beside eagle-haunted Lake Sammammish in the Pacific Northwest. She has had over two dozen stories published in venues that include *Strange Horizons, Fantasy Magazine,* and *ChiZine.* Recently, her story "Magnificent Pigs' was short-listed for *Best American Fantasy* and will be reprinted in *Best New Fantasy 2,* while "The Surgeon's Tale," co-written with Jeff VanderMeer, was recommended by *Locus* and *Tangent Online.* She is a member of the writers' groups *Horrific Miscue* and *Codex.* She holds an MA in fiction from the Johns Hopkins Writing Seminars and was a member of the Clarion West class of 2005. Her website can be found at **www.kittywumpus.net**

DARREN SPEEGLE's work has appeared or is forthcoming in such venues as *Postscripts, Subterranean, The Third Alternative, Crimewave, Cemetery Dance, Fantasy,* and *Brutarian.* He is the author of two short story collections, *Gothic Wine* and *A Dirge for the Temporal.* Look for his first novel, tentatively titled *Relics,* from Prime Books in September 2008.

EKATERINA SEDIA lives in New Jersey with the best spouse in the world and two cats. Her second novel, *The Secret History of Moscow,* came out from Prime Books in November 2007, and her next book, *The Alchemy of Stone,* is due from Prime in 2008. Her short stories have sold to *Analog, Baen's Universe, Fantasy Magazine,* and *Dark Wisdom,* as well as *Japanese Dreams* and *Magic in the Mirrorstone* anthologies.

Visit her at **www.ekaterinasedia.com**

DARJA MALCOLM-CLARKE attended Clarion West in 2004 and has fiction and poetry appearing in *TEL: Stories, Mythic Delirium*, and elsewhere. She is pursuing a Ph.D. in English at Indiana University, studying postmodern and speculative literature. When she is not teaching undergraduates or editing articles for *Strange Horizons*, she looks after a high-maintenance goblin masquerading as a black cat.

CAITLÍN R. KIERNAN is the author of seven novels, including the award-winning *Silk* and *Threshold*, and her short fiction has been collected in *Tales of Pain and Wonder; From Weird and Distant Shores; Wrong Things* (with Poppy Z. Brite); the World Fantasy Award-nominated *To Charles Fort, with Love*; and *Alabaster*. Her most recent novel is *Daughter of Hounds*.

Visit her at **www.caitlinrkiernan.com**

M P ERICSON has lived in Sweden, Trinidad, and Tanzania, but is now settled in the north of England. She holds a PhD in Philosophy, and has worked as a tutor, researcher, and accountant. Her short fiction has appeared in venues such as *Abyss & Apex, Dred*, and the *Freehold: Southern Storm* anthology from Carnifex Press.